T0284818

The Turtle
House

The Turtle House

A NOVEL

AMANDA CHURCHILL

HARPER

An Imprint of HarperCollinsPublishers

THE TURTLE HOUSE. Copyright © 2024 by Amanda Churchill. All rights reserved. Printed in the United States of America. No part of this book may be used or reproduced in any manner whatsoever without written permission except in the case of brief quotations embodied in critical articles and reviews. For information, address HarperCollins Publishers, 195 Broadway, New York, NY 10007.

HarperCollins books may be purchased for educational, business, or sales promotional use. For information, please email the Special Markets Department at SPsales@harpercollins.com.

FIRST EDITION

Designed by Michele Cameron

Library of Congress Cataloging-in-Publication Data has been applied for.

ISBN 978-0-06-329051-8

23 24 25 26 27 LBC 5 4 3 2 1

for Grandmommy:
you were right, they are good stories

Book 1

Chapter 1

Curtain, Texas
March 1, 1999

Paper hates water. It hates wind. And fire. Paper falls apart. There is no home safe enough for paper, did you know this?

Sometimes my grandmother speaks like an oracle. I mess with the tape recorder settings, make sure the microphone will pick up what she says next, feeling that she is about to tell me something I will need to know, sometime, somewhere.

"And that's why you'd rather me record you instead of writing everything down?"

"Yes, I like my voice. It's a good voice, even after all these cigarettes. The doctors say, don't smoke, Mrs. Minnie-ko Cope, and I say, I do what I want, you old man. Minnie-ko? A man who goes to so much school and who can't pronounce an easy Japanese name? Sheesh. Mean-echo. Not hard."

"You can't expect everyone to know how to pro—"

"You know why I smoke? I like smoking. Cigarettes, very small pleasure. Very small. Home is a place for small pleasures."

But this house we're now sitting in isn't my grandmother's home. Hers is a half-soggy heap of blackened plaster and ash. She burned it down last month. Accidentally, of course. So she's living with my parents. So am I. If I'm being honest, I burned down my architecture career. But, I didn't have a choice. We are both squatters on my parents' land; eaters of cereal and consumers of ham sandwiches, drifting along out of place. There are nearly fifty years between us: I'm twenty-five, my grandmother is now seventy-three. Today is her birthday. And now we share a bedroom, a tub, a toilet. We tell each other it's temporary.

My grandmother cracks my bedroom window and sparks a Salem Light, but the smoke comes back at us in a confused rush from a tricky breeze. In response, she hands me her cigarette, opens the window all the way, pops the screen like a cat burglar, and without any hesitation climbs onto the roof. She has already been scolded about this a few times, but scolding doesn't work on my grandmother.

After the fire, my dad and my aunt fear for her to be alone again, and don't know where she should live. They chat on the phone late at night. Find an apartment? *We'll just end up moving her again in a few years when she needs more care.* Let her live with one of them? *She'll drive us to drink.* Move her into a senior living community where they take Saturday trips to casinos up in Oklahoma? *She'd hate the people but love the casino.* Aunt Mae gently brought up the subject again tonight at Grandminnie's birthday dinner, and my grandmother shut it down, refusing to discuss any of these options.

"The roof is the most important part of the house, Lia, you know this?"

She is getting situated, carefully settling her rear on the rough shingles, her voice loud on our quiet road. It's been a rainy spring, and we can hear baby frogs chirping from the water-filled ditches that line Cope Street.

Curtain is small in population and spreads through Dennis County, uneven in shape. It has a downtown, which is just the main drag, the farm-to-market road that runs along the railroad tracks. That one, accurately called Main, has a few perpendicular streets jutting off it. On one side of the tracks, the names are pretty standard, and that's where the businesses and the churches are—Oak, Pecan, First, Second, and Church. Where they cross the railroad tracks the names change to the names of the people who started the town. Thomas, Whitebrew, *Whitehall* (don't dare get them confused, they hate each other), Morris, and Cope. We live off of Cope Street on land that has been in our family for generations. My parents' house is our "town place"—the "country place" is where Grandminnie lived and where my dad was raised. It was a working ranch until my grandfather died years before I was born.

"Nope. It's the foundation. That's the most important part of a house."

"Yah, little Miss Architect, that's important, too. But the roof—so much happens under a roof. These shingles are better to sit on than my roof in Japan. Tiles hurt my bottom."

I contemplate taking a puff off the cigarette before handing it back but don't, because I suppose I've become a woman who just *thinks* of things and then doesn't do them. I'm like a squirrel in the middle of a road, doing that back-and-forth thing, holding an acorn. I don't know what to do next in my life. It's complicated and shameful. A BA in architecture—the five-year program—from the University of Texas and a career-making job with Burkit, Taylor & Battelle on *the* team, the one reimagining the skylines of Texas cities. A few months until I had enough hours accumulated to take my Architect Registration Exam ahead of schedule. The apartment overlooking the Colorado River, right at the mouth of Lady Bird Lake, a kayak still hanging in the "ship shack" on the grassy bank just a few steps from my balcony.

Basically, I left my dream. I left live music and tacos and my sweet, goofy roommate, Stephie, who quotes teen movies like they're Shakespeare. I think of the Colorado, rolling slow and wide and green, my Day-Glo life vest strapped around me as I paddle out. Sometimes, I'd cut through water-skimming fog in my kayak, all those minuscule droplets of cloud against my face. I thought I had everything figured out.

The drag off the Salem burns like a snake of fire down my throat. I have asthma and really shouldn't be smoking.

I cough from the cigarette and my scalp hurts, which is funny, because no one ever complains of scalp pain, do they? At dinner, my mom ran her hand over my head and picked out a piece of flaky skin, the size and shape of a sequin.

"I'll buy you some Selsun Blue, baby girl."

But my grandmother, back in our room, had yanked my head toward her stomach pooch as I sat on the bed in front of her and, her hand on my jaw, her other hand parting my hair in sections, just whistled low and said, quietly, *I know this thing you do.*

Grandminnie is retired from the Dennis State Home for Mental Impairment. She was a nursing assistant for thirty years and retired last spring.

Her words comforted the dizzying bat-like anxieties swooping and swirling in my brain. Anxieties that make me pick my head until it bleeds.

I remember the way the bats used to fly out from beneath the Congress Avenue Bridge, a black cloud that separated into vibrating clumps like television static. Today, I got a cheery greeting card from Stephie asking me if I'd be coming back or if I wanted her to find a replacement on the lease.

"You are missing Mars! Stop being scarediddy-cat slowpoke-girl!" Grandminnie calls to me through the window. "Hand me my cigarette."

I thrust her cigarette out the open window toward her. My grandmother is talking to herself about how much has changed on Cope Street in the last forty years.

My window is nestled over the gently angled hip roof that covers the porch, but no fall from it would be gentle. My grandmother does not let this faze her. Her legs are clad in dark gray polyester slacks, and she's wearing her upstairs house shoes (she has a different pair for downstairs). She is still muscular, stocky. My aunt Mae, my dad's only sibling and Curtain's lone pharmacist, in charge of everyone's blood pressure and rosacea flare-ups, thinks Grandminnie is growing forgetful and going through a regression of sorts. My dad says it's like a midlife crisis, to which my mom will quietly mutter, *Well, hell's bells.*

I carefully perch beside her. The shingles are still warm from the sun, but the air is growing chilly. The pecan tree is budding with dangling yellow-green worms of pollen. It has grown crooked and is so close to the house, I can nearly reach out and touch it. I don't know many details about my grandfather, not much is said, favorable at least, about the man. But he was fond of his pecans and babied the trees planted by his own grandfather at the ranch. This one is a relative of those ancient trees, stuck in the ground the same year I was born.

"Your daddy needs to look at this roof. Some bad places here. That hailstorm last year! Needs to be replaced, maybe. Also, that tree, it needs to be trimmed. He's so busy with work, too busy!"

My grandmother isn't being rude. This is who she is. When I look sloppy, she tells me. If the food's too salty, she says something. Everything is noted. I used to take offense, but after living with her for twenty-eight days, reaching for the same coffee mug each morning, even sharing some of my clothes, I see now, perhaps for the first time, that she filters life this way. It's like I've slipped into Grandminnie's skin. This is how she loves, by taking note. Why, I don't know. My mother says it's *cultural*, and my father just usually leaves for work—*he's always working*—when Grandminnie gets this way. I think there's more to it.

I have the Sony microcassette recorder in my lap. I feel the tape turning through my sweatpants.

"Okay, back to what we were talking about. You never chose to write down your history before because you don't trust paper and you don't want me to do the same."

"And I don't write English. Only Japanese. And you don't read Japanese. So that's why I never write this down."

"You never *taught* me."

"I was busy. To learn Japanese, to really learn it, you have to be born there."

"Then I suppose colleges need to stop teaching it."

Her brown hand, all chiseled bones and sinew with perfectly shined nails, reaches out and slaps me on the leg. It smarts because my grandmother does not know softness.

"To learn Japanese the way you need to to understand my story, you need to be born there."

I suggest that I could watch some of her favorite shows, maybe that would help me pick up Japanese faster. She thinks about this. Grandminnie's shows, soap operas set in bygone eras sent on VHS from a friend in Tokyo, are what she misses most about her old house. In fact, my parents think—Grandminnie will not confirm their suspicions—the soap operas were the reason for the fire in the first place. She had just received the final season of her favorite the night of the fire, and so she stayed up all night watching it. Sometime in the early morning, they presume she fell asleep while smoking. Her hand dropped the cigarette on the floor, lighting the old shag carpet before spreading to the walls of the hundred-year-old wood-frame house. Up climbed the fire, gorging itself on the old place.

All that was saved is what she carried with her and what my dad raked through to find. Now, her stuff is packed in a few boxes in the garage, surrounded by Odor Eaters because a house doesn't burn clean like a campfire.

My grandmother stumbled out of the fire with her cat under her arm and a bowling ball bag clutched in her hand. Then the fire trucks raced down her long caliche drive. How she didn't even suffer a bit of smoke inhalation is a mystery to all. My mother says it's because her lungs are so used to carcinogens, they thought the smoke-filled room was just a normal Friday night.

My grandmother takes a long drag off her cigarette and points to the full moon.

"Mangetsu."

"Oh, *now* you plan to teach me some Japanese!"

"Fine. I will teach a few words. And I will tell you some stories since you're being so bossy. But you might not understand. Things are different now."

"Like what?"

"See, you won't understand."

She's shaking her head, and I'm worried she'll change her mind again.

Try me. I want to know. I'm bored at my job at Bags-N-Bows, an awful strip-mall store that sells, well, gift wrap bags and bows, along with greeting cards and those faceless angelic figurines that you buy for people whom you don't really know that well. My other job, the one I loved, perhaps my entire career as an architect even, now feels lost, and I can't help but think it's because of him, *Darren*. When his name drifts into my head, I feel my insides twist. I can't say I'm lost because that sounds so pathetic. Because I trusted him, because I am who I am, because I was in the right place at the wrong time, because, because, because . . . I'm stuck in a losing situation. I make a weird grunting sigh, just thinking about this, and Grandminnie raises her eyebrows, flips the lighter closed, and carefully stuffs it into the pocket of her slacks. Through the square of light from my bedroom window, I see her lipstick has bloodied the end of the cigarette. She blows out a thin cloud of smoke and closes her eyes.

For a moment I see her young, younger than me.

"I need to tell you about the beginning, way back. Back when I was a little girl. But you have to do something for me."

My grandmother is both a dealmaker *and* a dealbreaker. I know this because I've grown close to her now, as an adult, not as a kid. When I was younger, she was busy, she says. My mother complained to her friends on the phone that she wasn't *interested* in her granddaughter, in me. Daddy would say, "Just stop, Tam, you don't get it." But then he wouldn't explain either, because I don't think *he* knew.

Grandminnie's thinking. I watch her chewing on her words, her jaw grinding, her skin still taut over that jaw. What could she want me to do? Or help her do? I'm willing. I have nothing else going on. And I have this need. I can't even name it. I wonder if this is part of growing older, having needs without names.

And just before I can ask her again she says, "I want to go home."

Chapter 2

Kadoma, Osaka Prefecture
July 1936

The child was dressed in trousers with an ill-fitting sailor fuku on top, half tucked in. She had a red scarf tied on her head, was holding a slingshot, and was sneaking behind an azalea bush that had lost its blooms for the year, leaving crispy yellowed tufts nestled into the dark green leaves.

"Sagi-shi!" the child yelled, hands on hips. "You can't hide outside the garden! It's not fair!"

"I'm not!" came another little voice, this one softer and more gentle. And from beneath the bush a tiny girl crawled out. "I'm tired of being the good admiral. I want to be the pirate for a while, please, Mineko-chan?"

"You don't have it in you, Fumiko! Pirates need to be fearless, and you are like a little chicken, chittering all the time."

"And you're a loud monkey!"

Mineko dropped her slingshot and, placing her hands on the ground, her backside in the air, scampered and screamed like a monkey.

"Stop it! People will see you! Your mother—"

But it was too late, and Mineko's mother, Hana, was now outside, her hair still down but gleaming, her morning robe wrapped tightly around her thin frame. She had lost another child, another little brother, only a few months before and still looked washed-out and ghostly. She carried the fire poker and pointed it at Mineko, then at Fumiko, then at Mineko again.

"You're not mine, Fumiko, but I'll beat you like you are! Stop encouraging her!"

Hana paused by the open-wide morning glories, hanging heavy on the trellis that hid the outhouse from view, and even with her face crinkled in disgust, even though she appeared hollow-eyed, she was one of the most beautiful women in all of Kadoma.

"Rowdy girls! Into the shed with you! Stay there while Hisako has her dancing lesson! You'll mess her up with all your squawking." Hana hit the ground with the iron poker for emphasis, which spit up a little loose dirt, then pointed to the koyo. "Now!"

"It was me, Kaasan! Don't punish Fumiko!"

Hana swatted at Mineko's legs, and through the pants Mineko could tell that it had been a while since the fire had been stoked, thankfully, and the iron was only warm. The girls held hands and opened the door to the koyo and shut it firmly behind them.

"Ugly girl," Hana said, loud enough for both to hear.

"You're not," Fumiko said.

"I am," Mineko said.

Fumiko kneeled on the mossy earth that lined the floor of the shed. Mineko sat cross-legged.

"You're smart, though."

"She doesn't care. I look like a stump. It's okay. I'm used to it."

"But—"

"No, call me stump face. Really! Call me that!"

Mineko squeezed Fumiko's hand. They had been best friends for over a year, when Mineko's father had finally received a promotion to assistant stationmaster and help was hired for the house. Along with a housekeeper came the housekeeper's daughter. When Mineko was not in school and Fumiko was not helping her mother, the two spent time in the lush backyard of the Kamemoto home, playing until the sun set, leaving Kadoma in long gray shadows.

Fumiko whispered it. *Stump face.*

"Louder! Don't be scared!"

"Stump face!" Fumiko said with a giggle.

Mineko pulled her hair back from her forehead and made the most ghoulish face she could conjure. Her hair needed to be cut, and because she hated being still—her mother's hands on her shoulders, the glint of scissors and their icy touch across her forehead—she managed to escape this torture until before festival days. The bridge of her nose was low, her face wide, her skin the color of a walnut from being outdoors without a hat or parasol. She was thick and muscular. And to make things worse, she was, indeed, smart. The kind of cleverness lauded in firstborn sons, but Mineko was the firstborn *daughter* and thus this brain, her mother Hana often wailed, was wasted on her. What a firstborn daughter should have is a pretty face and a calm demeanor. *Our daughter*, Hana complained to her husband, Hiroshi, *is the exact opposite of what I wanted.* Her mother felt betrayed by the gods. And while her father rather enjoyed his daughter's pluck and precociousness, he kept this, like his other feelings, hidden.

Hana had four more babies after Mineko—two sickly boys who lasted only a week after birth—and, finally, a baby girl who resembled Hana in every way she had ever wished. Then the most recent loss. While Hana used to be occasionally tender—Mineko remembered holding her mother's legs and Hana's hand heavy on her head—the last death seemed to Mineko to push her mother further and further from her. Once, her father broke rank and told Mineko that her mother had never suffered before motherhood and that, sometimes, a beautiful bird used to perfect weather could be downed in its first storm.

But a bird was gentle. A bird didn't hit or curse. A bird didn't squeeze until a blue bruise bloomed. Her mother was no bird, and Mineko was tired of being caught too close to her.

Mineko pulled her knees toward her chest and buried her nose between the knobs.

"Kaachan wants a nanny for me. Someone to tame me, she said, so she can focus on little sister. But my father said that he doesn't make that kind of money and that she'll just have to wait for the next promotion, and my mother said that if the gods weren't watching, she'd run his boss off the cliff into the river just so Papa could get a promotion to stationmaster and so she wouldn't have to deal with me."

Fumiko breathed a long, surprised ohhhhh.

"'Oh, bah! She'll never be matched!'" Mineko said, in imitation of her mother's worrying, pinching the bridge of her nose, as Hana did to dull the headache that Mineko always brought about.

Fumiko tucked her hands into her sleeves, and Mineko knew it was because she feared the spiders in the koyo. Fumiko was half the size of Mineko, small from early-in-life malnourishment, and even though her mother's finances had improved since moving into the village, her arms and legs were iris-stalk thin. Fumiko had helped at many homes with her mother and had a mouthful of gossip, which Mineko delighted in. Fumiko scooted an inch closer to Mineko.

"You can live with me and my husband."

"Your marriage! That's a hundred years from now. I need a place to go now. Someplace I can be as wild as I'd like," Mineko said, staring up at the straw ceiling of the koyo. Hana had yelled at Mineko yesterday for tracking mud into the genkan, and the day before that for talking too loudly and interrupting young Hisako's afternoon nap.

"Mistress Kamemoto scares me."

Mineko nodded. She had been born during her mother's yakudoshi—her year of misfortune—and while her father had told her that any bad luck regarding her birth had long since blown away, Hana mentioned it often, and Mineko was split between believing her kind father or her difficult mother. More recently, she had decided that while she was pretty certain she was bad luck, she perhaps did not care.

Fumiko looked at her friend, who sat in thoughtful silence.

"Maybe you stay out of her way. Go find a good place to play during the day, then come back for dinner. An old auntie told me there's an abandoned house not far from here, but you'll have to look very hard to find it. It's haunted though."

"I'm not afraid of ghosts. Besides, I bet it's easier to talk a ghost into being kind than my mother."

The house, Fumiko had heard, was off the road toward the mountains. Instead of continuing left, as everyone usually did to get to the next village, one went right at the fork and found a bamboo stand, young, fresh, and thick. There, on the other side, was the path to the kominka of a wealthy banking family that had been built long ago. Back when the big banks in

Osaka went through hatan, this family lost everything, including their beloved country house. They had moved out in the middle of a feast weekend
in shame, selling most of their belongings and taking only what could fit in
a couple of carts.

"Well, I'll go see if this place even exists."

"Are you doubting me?" her friend asked.

Mineko twirled a chunk of her hair tight around her finger, then let it
unwind like a dervish. Fumiko was naive and could be easily led astray.
But she could be right this time. Even if there was no abandoned house,
she would at least have a good adventure to talk about later.

"No, I believe you, Fumi-chan. I'll always believe you."

The morning was pleasant, with a breeze picking its way between the
houses along Mineko's street. Mineko walked casually at first, pretend-
ing she was on the way to the market or to her father's train station. But
when she was a good enough distance away, her legs picked up speed. The
sun was attempting to gather its first strength, warming the tanada on
either side of the path. Finally, Mineko ran, a full satchel beating against
her hip, her straw hat in her hand. As the elevation increased slightly,
Mineko began to feel winded; she stopped only to walk for a moment,
then skip, then run some more. She passed by the bamboo cover the first
time, then had to double back to find it. After pushing aside a few stalks
she squeezed through. She counted her steps and at step forty-four, the
eerie green light from the bamboo was replaced with blue sky. There she
found a weedy stone path that led far into the distance and, to her right,
an overgrown cart-rut road.

The uneven path led to two monchu at the entrance, as large as those at
a provincial palace and covered in ivy. The granite plinths stood at least
five feet taller than Mineko. The wooden arch that connected them was
also laced with shoots. Mineko wiggled and kicked open the gate and
followed what had been a trail but now was even taller weeds. The house
stood two stories with a deep hip-and-gable roof. Granite stairs rose to
the engawa and the proud, tall front doors. Mineko felt a big rock under
her shoe and picked it up, to see what it looked like. It wasn't rock, but a

chunk of ceramic roof tile, mineral gray and heavy, broken into a sharp-edged square. Mineko nestled it in the pocket of her dress.

And to think, for all of her life, this had just been down the road from her!

The path wound around to the left of the grand house, through another gate, and down a slight hill. There, the weeds began to give way to tall, soft grass. The flowering bushes that had been trimmed into lovely shapes many years ago were now hulking versions of their previous form. The blooms were copious, and there was a buzz in the air from the bees.

Mineko didn't know if she should attempt to explore the house or the grounds first, but decided to get the most haunted part over. She took out an ofuda from the shrine that her parents kept in the genkan to protect their home, which Mineko had expertly pilfered that morning. Waving it in front of her, she approached the house, singing a little song to make herself brave.

At the granite steps, she looked up and saw a beautiful kawara staring back at her, a minogame turtle with its bushy seaweed tail sculpted behind it, as if floating through the water. It was a moody gray with glints of silica that had been baked into the ceramic. Unlike some she had seen before with menacing mouths, this one had a slight feminine smile, more mischievous than evil. Mineko felt her insides soften. Nothing to fear when such an auspicious creature was watching over her. The word *turtle* was in her surname, after all. This was destined.

"Hello, sister turtle," Mineko said in greeting.

She entered into a rather spacious genkan with dirty shelves for shoes and hooks where only cobwebs hung. Moving cautiously, barely breathing, Mineko circled around the house through the engawa, the interior walls on one side, the storm shutters on the other. The air was cold and stale, made worse by Mineko's silence.

Back at the entrance, Mineko slipped off her shoes and slid open the door that led into the front yoritsuki.

The ceiling reached to the top of the second story, creating a cavernous expanse. Dust motes drifted down and, with one wave of the ofuda, were propelled up again. An old-fashioned square irori was centered in the middle of the main room. A chain dangled from the ceiling with a beautifully wrought hook where a boiling pot had once hung over a fire. The beams were dark with years of smoke. She had never seen a place so magical.

"This *is* an old house," she breathed. She gently touched the fusuma. The painted scene was of cranes and turtles, a willow and a brook. More turtles, she said quietly. Mineko loved how they moved slowly but could swim and carried their home on their backs. This place wasn't haunted, surely, and even if it was, she felt the turtles' protection. Why, this might be the luckiest kominka in the entire empire. And it was all hers.

The tatami was still in good condition, despite years of small creatures finding their way into the house. A few mousetraps lined the room, along with the skeletal remains of their catches. She climbed the stairs and slowly opened doors to find smaller bedrooms. Very little furniture was left, save for a couple of framed drawings and other odds and ends.

She picked out a room that she would like to have if her family lived in this house, but then thought about this—she would allow her grand-parents and her father, but her sister and her mother, they could stay in town. She'd allow Fumiko—she'd get her very own room! And Fumiko's mother, of course. Mineko slid open the door to the room's balcony and there, below her, was a green pond, fed by a stream, dammed at the far side. An azumaya was perched at the very edge of the water, its wood gray with age.

Mineko raced down the stairs, grabbed her satchel, and burst outside, forgetting her shoes as she made her way to the water's edge. Algae floated on the sides, but the center of the pond was clearer due to the delicate current, just enough to keep the middle clean. She ran to the azumaya, feeling it wobble slightly as she bounced on the boards. Lying on her stomach, she let her head and shoulders fall over the side so she could peer beneath. Just as she suspected, the gazebo had been built into the water, and as she wiggled her body back and forth, she saw how the piers jiggled.

"Water rot," she said, and she liked how grown up she sounded.

Mineko bounced to her feet to explore where the stream went on the other side of the small rock dam. She followed it as it snaked along, growing faster as the property dipped down a small slope. She came upon a low rock wall, and there, just on the other side, the ground fell away and the water became a miniature waterfall. Mineko climbed over the wall and made her way to the edge, testing the soil with her feet. Closer and closer to the edge she went, a few pebbles loosening and tumbling off the side, soundlessly.

Below, the stream joined the river—her village's river—rushing toward Kadoma.

It was a long drop, but she felt no fear.

Mineko made her way back to the azumaya, spread out her jacket, and sat watching the water bugs land, creating a circular ripple, then taking off again. She opened her satchel, took out a small bag of arare, and popped a few into her mouth, pleased with her unladylike way of eating. She had a book, a canteen of water, and a handkerchief. She chided herself for not bringing a quilt. Stretching out her legs, she let her feet flex and point over the side of the decking. There, just over her big toe on her right foot, she saw movement in the water, something swimming toward her. Mineko again lay on her stomach and flopped over the edge, her fingers nearly touching the still pond.

There were turtles! A whole family of mossy-backed turtles swam near and, getting closer, pried their heads out of the water, their necks as long as possible, then, as if frightened, dove back under. She noticed that below them were fish, swimming over each other like clumsy children. Carp, Mineko thought, but not the pretty bright kind at the fancy park in Osaka. These were silver-white and lazy.

"Oh, you want food, do you?" Mineko took a few crackers and sucked off the spicy coating, spat them out into her hand, and tossed them into the water, where they floated for just a moment before being gobbled up by the first turtle.

"Naughty and greedy! You're not sharing!" She sucked and spat out more crackers, this time tossing them over the first turtle's head and toward the others. More cautiously appeared, including a baby, the size of a dolly's tea saucer.

Mineko couldn't help but giggle. She jumped up, ran through the grass, tugged at a flower, stuck it in her collar, skipped along the bank, and then, unable to control herself, slipped out of her dress. She waded in, the water warm at top and cool below, the ground squishing and sucking at her feet.

Mineko stuck out her tongue and scrunched up her nose, but still she moved in farther and farther, until the water reached her waist, her chest, her shoulders. Then, looking up at the sun, raising her arms and shouting banzai like she did at school, Mineko disappeared under the water, even daring to open her eyes like one of her new turtle companions that swam nearby.

This is my place. My house, my rules, my ghosts, my turtles.

Mineko played in the water and tramped all over the grounds that day, and when the sun began to slide toward the horizon and her stomach begged for dinner, she packed up her satchel and ran her fingers through her damp hair. She waved goodbye to the minogame before she slipped through the gate. *I'll see you tomorrow.*

When she arrived home, Hana said nothing about missing her, as she had not missed her, only realized the quiet of the house. Hana had spent the day leisurely with Hisako, and because Mineko was not missed, her absence was not mentioned to Hiroshi.

Before leaving that night, as she was lighting the lantern that would lead her and her mother home, Fumiko quickly asked if Mineko had seen the ghosts.

"Yes, many ghosts," Mineko said, watching Fumiko shudder. "But they said I could visit. In fact, they told me I was free to live there if I needed to."

Fumiko drew in a deep, admiring breath, but when Hana came around the corner, she pushed the girl toward the door.

Chapter 3

The night my grandmother's house burned down, we could see and smell the fire from the highway. It had burned like its shape. A collection of squares. A big square in the middle, two smaller squares, one at either side.

My dad parked, and we ran to where Grandminnie stood under the pecan tree that my great-great-grandfather had planted, its curvy arms reaching to the flames. The fire replicated in her oversized glasses, her face and silver hair reflecting the orange blaze. My great-aunt Dimple and great-uncle Calvin were already there. Dimple had seen the fire from her kitchen window, just a burning dot on her horizon, and had called 911, which had dispatched the volunteer fire department. *If my hip hadn't hurt tonight, I wouldn't have been up for my pain pills*, she had said. Dimple's arthritic hip was a constant source of consternation, caused originally by a fall from a hayloft when she was a teen. *Thank God for that accident so long ago or I would have lost my Minnie.*

This is a thing in our family—thanking the heavens for past pain. I don't know where this concept comes from, Grandminnie certainly doesn't ever say anything like this. She doesn't willingly say much about her past at all—and when she does, she doesn't cut it to pieces and hold it up to see how it was cooked. This, she has insisted many times, is an *American* thing, and she, she also insists, is *not* an American.

Oh yes, you are, my mother will always respond, I've seen the photos from the day you got your citizenship!

My grandmother will then give her *the stare*—the straight at your eyes, slightly ajar mouth, about to say something insanely hurtful, but stopping because the receiver is weak and will not be able to withstand judgment. I wish I could get away with such a death stare, a classic Grandminnie move.

She did it the night of the fire when the new sheriff's deputy questioned her about how the blaze began, how she escaped without a smudge of soot, and why she was carrying a bowling ball bag. To his questions, she was short and sharp, like a dagger.

My mother and father are now recalling this night over oatmeal in the kitchen. They are having a conversation in hushed tones about what is next. *Last night, getting a call from the neighbor that my mother-in-law is ON THE ROOF AGAIN*, my mother says, *is the straw that broke the camel's back*. My father says, *I know, I know. It's dangerous*. Yet I'm certain the break-your-neck aspect is not what broke my mother's camel's back. *But you don't*, she says, *you go to work and I'm stuck with her, unless Lia is home to entertain. And Lia—she's just so . . .* My mother emits a long, drawn-out sigh that ends in a little sneeze from her spring allergies.

It's not that Mom and Grandminnie openly argue, but it's a matter of boundaries. My mother likes to control hers. My grandmother does as well. My mother is from a good Fort Worth family with firm beliefs on how things are done. My grandmother, I see now, is from a good Kadoman family with equally firm ideals. They are alike because of this, but to ever mutter such a sentiment would be mutinous. And Daddy is in the center of these two quietly conflicting countries, both wanting him like he's a landlocked valley with considerable natural resources. It's their great love of this man that helps to keep our family so ridiculously close-knit. It also is why my grandmother has now overstayed her welcome.

She's still adjusting, my father says, *she'll come to her senses*.

Which one? Our daughter or your mother? Mom snaps.

Then there is silence. I listen to them, listening for me.

"Lia, honey, is that you?" Mom has righted her voice. "You're up late, baby. D'you sleep okay?"

"Good morning, sweetheart!" Dad says cheerfully.

Last night, my grandmother talked to me for a long while, then I plugged in my headphones and listened to what I had recorded. I rewound her description of the turtle house twice.

I tell my mom I'm fine, walk quickly into the kitchen, pour two cups of coffee, doctoring one with copious amounts of cream for me, one black for Grandminnie, and slip away before any further questions. I tap on my bedroom door with my foot, she opens it slowly.

I hand her the coffee, and she thanks me. She is dressed—my high school track sweatshirt, my sweatpants, my socks—and we make our way outside to the back deck together. There are birds everywhere in the trees, a few divebombing Grandminnie's little orange tabby, who looks confused. For a feral barn stray, Yoshi seems to have forgotten how to fend for herself.

I comment that I hope Yoshi doesn't find our yard turtle.

We have a box turtle that has lived in our yard forever, it seems. He (or she) comes around sometimes and enjoys nibbling Mom's plants. I leave out celery tops when I think of it. I named it Boxy when I was a kid for lack of a better name.

My grandmother's eyes widen, and she puts down her coffee and snatches up Yoshi as if that cat had been planning a murder. Then she reaches out and pats the kangaroo pocket of my hoodie, where I've been storing the tape recorder.

I pull it out. We both look over our shoulders to see if Mom and Dad are watching us. I think this is what it must be like to have a sister, a co-conspirator. Growing up, I would have liked to have someone else who shared my genetics, who *looked* like me, who understood the somewhat suffocating over-love of my folks' sharp-eyed parenting style. Where my mother focused on appropriate skirt length, shiny hair, good manners, my father's focus was interior. His was an intense appreciation for creative thought, hard work, resiliency, aptitude. The worst thing, to him, was to not try my hardest. Because, surely, if I did that, given all of my innate talent and gifts, I would do the very best, no? Had I a sibling to share this load, would I have been the same person going off to college? Had there been another Cope girl, someone else with suspiciously dark hair and whose eyes the Avon lady could never quite figure out how to apply eyeshadow to—*Well, the diagram has me putting this color in the crease but the crease isn't where it should be!*—I wonder if I would have approached life differently.

Sleeping in my childhood trundle bed has given me ample time to ponder these things.

I turn on the tape recorder. My grandmother clears her throat, lifts her chin, and sits up straighter, Yoshi now curled on her lap.

"Turtles are very good luck and mean a long life."

She says nothing else. I ponder if I should just turn off the recorder. We watch the birds, house wrens, splash in the birdbath then fluff their feathers with a shimmy, becoming puffier. Yoshi works her claws on Grandminnie's sweatpants. Finally I suggest we take a walk before I have to get ready for work. She puts Yoshi in her outside cat carrier so she doesn't follow, and we walk down the gravel driveway, holding our coffee. I have decided to keep recording, planning to rewind and tape over another time. My mind wanders. The wind whips my hair in front of my face, and it sticks to my ChapStick. There's a horse galloping through the pasture across the road from us, a pretty paint who is new since I've been home. She tosses her head and snorts as we go by. I used to ride horses through that field. I learned to trot and lope on a swaybacked old mare.

Our blacktop road has gaping ditches along either side that are still full of water from the rain. It has potholes, as big and deep as a pie pan, filled with sticky mud that captures bugs that land too long on it. Gnarly Bois d'Arc trees stand guard along the barbed-wire fence line, sometimes with the barbs actually growing through their trunks. The oldest houses in Curtain have Bois d'Arc foundations, stumps holding up floors, walls, and roofs. My grandmother comments on the few houses we pass. People who need to shape their shrubs, people who need to paint their trim. One place, the worst of the bunch, has the carport falling off, creating a triangular space where a few bikes are parked. Yard art—the painted plywood rear end of an old woman leaning over the flower beds, her polka-dot bloomers exposed—and weeds surround the place. Several old cars are parked in the pasture.

"Do they not like their houses? Sheesh. If I had a house that I loved, I would take such good care. I had a house I loved, and I tried to take good care of it. Me and my—"

She stops and I wonder what she was going to say. I think of the house with the turtles she told me about last night and her ranch house. I wonder which she's speaking of, which was the house she loved and tried to care for? Now that the ranch house has been declared a total loss by insurance, my dad has borrowed a bulldozer from the concrete company he works for and is going to take down the remains tomorrow morning. Flatten the place where he grew up. I offered to go out with him, but he said it would be more helpful if I took off work and stayed with Grandminnie. My aunt Mae is coming to help, he said. But what can she do, really, besides stand by and watch? I know it will be harder for Daddy. He's more sentimental.

Then, my grandmother does a very un-Grandminnie-like thing. She takes my hand and holds it as we walk. I try to remember a time, even when I was little, that she held my hand. I cannot. She squeezes it so that my fingers are pressed tightly together, my pinkie folding over the top of the stack. I can't tell if she's trying to hurt me or hold on to me.

"This old town. It was better looking when your daddy was a kid. Needs a good cleanup. A makeover, like on one of those morning shows, you know? Why did you ever come back to such a place, Lia-chan? Your cousins left. I know they're not coming back."

I don't answer her. Her curiosity is more direct than my own parents'. And the fact that it's combined with a comparison to my cousins, Sam and Sallie, both engaged and living in big non-Texas cities, is a bit hurtful.

Just her asking makes my anxiety chug to life again.

Darren Miles. Darren had started as a professor at the architecture school the spring of my third year and was put in charge of my Design IV Intermediate Group Discovery class. Even though he was new to the faculty, everyone knew who he was. He's the model "starchitect": the ones with the hot-shot degree, who become a principal after their very first major project and top that off with a Henry Adams Medal. Darren Miles had done all these things by thirty-five. He was married to the daughter of a wealthy oil family, a family that had named buildings all over the state, including UT. Rumor had it they had moved because his wife was homesick for Austin.

My head itches, so I reach into the thick black mop and pick, just a little bit, until Grandminnie slaps my hand away.

"Nah!" she bleats.

I shake the thoughts of Darren away—I don't want to hear it, I don't want her asking, so I point out a gutter that's dislodged itself from the roof of an otherwise pretty 1960s colonial. She grunts her disapproval.

"It's the angle and the flow of water from that roof that has made it unstable over the years," I say.

My grandmother beams. She loves to problem-solve.

"You know, Lia, you are a lot like me."

I don't recall the first time I saw Darren. Surely, it was the first day of class, but I don't remember his strolling into the room, putting down a stack of books, and writing his name on the whiteboard. Nothing like that. It wasn't until early February, when I was getting a drink of water at the fountain outside the Design IV lecture room, parched because I had mistakenly thought it would stay cool throughout the day and at 1:15 it had topped off at eighty-five degrees. My hair, longer then, knotted into a bun and skewered with a sharpened pencil, came loose and tumbled into the water fountain. I jerked up, splashing lukewarm water down the front of my fuzzy baby blue angora that was smelling increasingly like Lady Speed Stick.

Laughter, behind me. I turned and it was Darren, whom I was uncertain if I should refer to as Dr. Miles (he didn't have a doctorate) or Mr. Miles (which sounded cheesy).

"I've had a day like that, too," Darren said. He opened the men's bathroom door and leaned his long body in, retrieving a stack of paper towels. I noticed he was wearing a tennis racket strapped to his back. I could imagine him wearing those white shorts, running across a court. That's all I knew about tennis. Neon yellow ball, white shorts.

"Here, mop yourself off."

I thanked him and thought he would turn and leave, but he stayed, handing me one towel at a time.

He watched me wipe water off my face, squeeze it out of the tips of my hair. He handed another one to me and I took it and blotted my chest where wet angora was stuck to my bra.

"You missed a spot." Darren pointed at my shoulder. Then he reached over and gently held the last brown towel up on the damp circle. "All good."

Then, he was gone. "Have a better day," he said over his shoulder as he made his way to the hallway where the lecturers had their offices.

I thought about this moment for the rest of the afternoon, the stickiness of the heat, the splash of the water, my embarrassment at being seen, his eyes on me, his hand on my shoulder. In class at four, the last of a long day, he didn't even glance at me, and I was simultaneously relieved and—I've thought about this word for a long time, this feeling I had that was hiding like a child behind the other feelings—*irked*. I wanted some recognition of our previous moment in the hallway. Even when he was passing out a project schedule, even when he handed me the stack of papers, he looked past me, counting the bodies in my row. His lack of attention caught my attention. I now wonder if it was purposeful; I now wonder if that was the plan.

But the other me, the shadow me, the one who wears shame like a dog collar around her neck, thinks, C'mon, Lia. This stuff just happens. Get over yourself. But also, in the beginning, I wanted Darren Miles to *like* me. I am filled with regret.

I think Grandminnie can feel this, and she squeezes my hand even harder. I remember where I am.

"I'm not that sad about the old house being torn down. Everyone thinks I'm upset about it. Aunt Mae, your daddy, your mother. I have bigger memories, Lia. No, not my favorite place to live."

My grandmother continues to hold my hand, but I stay quiet. In an early studio, the instructor told us that clients will tell you what they want in their structure, be it a home or an office complex or a backyard cabana, in their small talk. So ask the question, What do you want, and then . . . wait. Humans hate lulls in conversation, so they'll fill it. *And if you have any sense*, my teacher said, *you'll let them fill it with their vision.*

Chapter 4

Kadoma
May 1943

The river was wider than Mineko had thought—from the bridge and shore, it had looked easy, swimming from one side to the other. It was cold mountain runoff, and it was barely summer. Village boys, those who still had not reached the age to join the fight in Manchukuo and in the islands, cheered her from the side, she could hear them when she flipped her head to breathe. Fumiko stood on the bridge, holding Mineko's robe. Mineko knew her beautiful younger sister Hisako had hurried home just before she dove in, gone to tell on her, to make the evening hard. Hana would tell Hiroshi, Mineko sitting quietly across from her, that their seventeen-year-old daughter was an ugly, rebellious disappointment. Hiroshi would just eat his dinner, sad eyes on her only when her mother turned to pour the tea. Years of war and life with Hana had worn him down.

Mineko was cutting through the water with precision, her legs and arms synchronized, lungs burning. The boy she was racing, two years younger, had stopped and turned around when the current picked up toward the middle. They had tossed reeds in from the bridge to see if the center waters were running faster, but it had appeared safe, or if not that, possible. Just a little faster. Nothing that young arms and legs couldn't tame.

But the current was pulling her. She knew if she could get through it, just another forty meters, the water would calm and it would be a re-markable finish. The first girl to swim across.

Mineko's arms tired before her legs, and like that she was suddenly disorganized, her breathing off, gasping. She tried to keep kicking, but Mineko began to sink. Her legs stopped thrashing on top and instead began to pedal below, her face still above water, her head back. She could see the sky, the brightest blue. A heron swooped and dipped overhead. Mineko's mind sharpened to the water around her. She watched the heron. *When it flies out of sight, I'll swim again.*

The heron disappeared, and Mineko's feet kicked in the numbing cold below. She grabbed the deepest breath she could and aimed her torso down, diving, and felt as if she were swimming through the icy water that cooled the soba noodles for summer dinners. Yet she pushed and broke free, cutting through the depths, and then swam up, bursting through to the sun, gulping fresh air. She had swum below the current.

Mineko heard the wind-carried cheers behind her. Floppy-armed and tired, she kept going until it was shallow enough to stand, her feet resting too heavily on the sharp rocks, the water a little lower than her waist. Mineko made her way to the bank and the pebbled sand of the edge. Then she climbed the steep slope, legs shaking, teeth set into a smile, chattering. There was sweet Kadoma, gardened homes and meandering paths. The big bathhouse with its majestic roof, the red-topped shrine where the old monks scattered kids like pigeons, the mochi man's cart smelling of burnt sugar and toasted rice. Somewhere, down below, was her mother, a woman made small by Mineko's vantage point, and she liked this idea, a miniature mother, her miserable voice just a squeaking mouse.

Mineko then focused her attention on the children on the other side. A few had wandered off, but most were there. She waved. A few whooped and cheered. Fumiko was making her way carefully down the bank with Mineko's robe, a wide smile on her face.

Mineko turned to the water again and across from her, toward Mount Ikoma, perched hidden on the cliff, was Mineko's favorite place in the world, the stately kominka that loomed like a loving mother, watching from afar. Mineko thought she might float.

Later, Mineko watched her sister talk to her mother, closely, quietly, through the open window.

"She's telling," Fumiko whispered. Although Mineko couldn't hear them, she could tell by the way her mother grimaced that it was about the race.

"I need to go in and help with the evening meal," Fumiko said. "Are you coming?"

"No, go on. I'll sneak in before we eat. What are we having?"

"All I could get from the lines was barley again. And some cabbage."

"Better than some." And Fumiko agreed, as Mineko's family fed her and her mother from their evening meal, a generous arrangement seen to by Hiroshi.

Mineko then ducked, trying to stay low in front of the windows, grabbed the burlap sack that she had hidden under the peonies earlier in the day, then sprinted off at the gate, back to town. She was wearing a loose dress over her bathing suit. The dress was wet at the breasts and her hair hung in thick, damp snakes around her neck. Neighborhood women glanced at her and then looked away quickly as she passed, so she slowed to a fast walk and, marginally embarrassed by her appearance, the glory of the swim faded, she looked down at her feet. Her mother called Mineko's feet "ogre feet," the feet of peasants, and Mineko pondered this, and wondered if her flat feet were the reason she was such a good swimmer—wide like paddles—and she couldn't help but smile.

Mineko had the distinct ability to push off mean-spirited comments, years of Hana's subtle and not-so-subtle disappointment had trained her. After all, Mineko had no illusions about her looks or her future. Where other girls her age had grown into waiflike beauties, Mineko had remained snub-nosed, plain. She wasn't small and she wasn't big, but somewhere in the middle, and her torso was built like a rectangle. Her breasts were almost muscular and, when she swam in her heavy black bathing suit, unrecognizable. The only part of herself that she found remotely attractive were her legs, which were well-turned with a strong calf, but even that was boyish and unseemly on a girl.

On the main road into Kadoma's shopping district, Mineko was still smiling to herself, caught in an elaborate daydream where she was competing in the Olympics, when she heard yelling. Out of the corner of her eye she saw a young man, dressed in gray pants covered in a film of grime, astride a bike and coming at her from the skinny alley between buildings. He was going too fast and was trying to pedal and turn to look behind him at the same time.

"Thief! My bike!" Another young man was running behind him.

Mineko stopped and, without thinking, stuck out her leg. The bike rammed into her shin, knocking her down, the bike falling to the side. The young man riding it toppled off in the opposite direction, rolling as he hit the ground.

"Kutabare!" the thief yelled. He hopped up and sprinted away, Mineko watching as she lay on the cobbled sidewalk.

"Are you okay?" the young man whose bike was on her leg asked from above her. Mineko, suddenly embarrassed, squirmed out from beneath the bike and made her way to her feet, trying to appear unhurt. Her left shin felt hollow and achy; she could feel something warm drip down her ankle and into her shoe.

"I can't believe you did that." He was more boy than man, but Mineko could see the shadow of someone important in his face.

"I— I don't know why. I just did." Mineko picked up the bike and as she stooped, she saw the gash in her leg, the blood thickening on the skin, congealing dark and oozy. She would have a scar. Still, she stood and held the bicycle's seat.

"These desperate times are making the dishonest dangerous."

This careful statement, like an old man, made Mineko smile. "Do you think the frame is bent?"

"I don't know—that's easier to fix than buying a new one." The young man relaxed his shoulders. "Let me walk you someplace. Where were you heading? I'm Sato Akio." He bowed.

"Kamemoto Mineko. I'm the stationmaster's daughter." Mineko knew his family name. The Satos were one of the more wealthy families in their part of the prefecture. "It's a great honor to meet you."

"Likewise—let me help you." Akio gently took his bike from Mineko and balanced it against his thigh. "You're brave. Thank you." Mineko stepped away and bowed.

Mineko couldn't imagine what her mother would say if she came home damp and bloody and bruised. There was a good chance that Mother already had been told about Mineko hurrying toward town in her bathing suit and cover dress. The neighborhood ladies gossiped and did so quickly. All this alone would have her eating dinner outside. Any more distress and she wouldn't be eating tonight at all.

"I better go. I'm in a bit of a hurry. I'm heading to feed the turtles, and I want to get home before dinner."

"At the park?"

"No." Mineko paused. She considered Akio for a moment, the way he nervously gripped and loosened his hand around one of the handlebars, the glistening of sweat on his upper lip. She lowered her voice. "At the abandoned house on the other side of the bridge, toward Daitō. In the pond there."

"The ghost house?"

"It's not haunted. Just unloved."

Akio's brow folded, and his lips twitched. He paused, and Mineko thought he was going to say goodbye and thank her, hurry off to his parents' home on the north side of town, a neighborhood where the gardens were so vast, one couldn't see who lived next door. But then he smiled, and Mineko couldn't help but smile back.

"And what's in the sack?" Akio asked, motioning to the parcel that Mineko gripped.

"Old noodles. For the turtles. They're stale, but turtles like anything. They're not spoiled."

Spoiled turtles, he repeated and laughed as if it were the funniest joke.

"This is crazy," Akio said, his breathing labored. He had been slowly riding his bike as Mineko walked, then switching out of courtesy. Mineko was used to the steep hill that led to the house. She had walked it for nearly ten years now and knew every jutting stone along the path.

"Not crazy. And not haunted. Just an old house with a beautiful pond. You'll see." Mineko let her hand graze the mosodake bamboo as they walked, their thick, hardy stalks a brilliant spring green. "Of course, you didn't have to come."

Akio did not reply.

At the monchu, Mineko handed Akio the bag of noodles and ducked down behind an overgrown yew, pulling out a hatchet.

"What's that for?" Akio seemed alarmed.

"Things are overgrown, it's a constant battle. I usually do a little hacking while I'm here, just to keep it up. Oh, and to scare off the demons, of course."

Akio whistled low and slow like a cinema comedian. Mineko smiled at his discomfort. There was a buzz in the air.

"There's a hive over there," Mineko said, glancing to the other side of the property. "That's where a vegetable garden was. The other side of the house was all productive, and this side is all beauty."

"This grass is shorter than I thought it would be," Akio said.

Mineko smiled and pointed to herself. "With a scythe I borrowed from a farmer down the hill. I need to save up and buy my own, perhaps, store it in the kura."

"Is this *allowed*?"

Mineko shrugged. "The turtles enjoy having a more manicured yard. I sit in the gazebo over there and feed them."

"How often do you visit?"

"A few times a week."

Akio lay his bike in the grass. He took a few steps and looked up at the house, to the beautiful roof. "A minogame," he said, pointing to the onigawara tile on the corner closest to where they stood. The turtle smiled down at them.

Mineko looked up, and there was her favorite bushy-tailed turtle, perched wise and proud on the roof.

"Usually they are so fierce-looking, look at his smile."

"*Her smile*. And that's my favorite part. And the tail—it looks like real seaweed. There's an entire turtle theme to this house. They're all over the inside, too. Whoever built this place wanted to live forever." Mineko stood next to Akio so her shadow fell onto his.

"You've been *inside*?"

Mineko couldn't tell if he was surprised by her rudeness or her bravery.

"Well, I have to—someone has to clean the mousetraps."

Akio laughed and shuddered at the same time. Mineko walked to the gazebo and sat on the edge of the deck. She took off her shoes and let her legs dangle over the side. With each movement the gazebo trembled. Over the years, Mineko had tried to steady it with extra wood nailed and roped to the original posts, but all she had accomplished was slowing its decay.

The turtles, no longer shy, splashed below, nearly swimming into one another. The bigger ones made it to the top of the heap and opened their mouths for food. Akio came and stood next to her, then, looking around, sat on his knees.

"You look like an old woman, squatting like that," Mineko said, but then caught herself. She sounded like her mother.

Akio moved closer and peered into the water. Again the gazebo swayed slightly.

"Is it deep, do you think?"

Mineko watched him. He seemed skittish.

"No, I bet it's only five feet here. Maybe six. Really depends on how much fish and turtle dung is at the bottom, I suppose." Akio scrunched up his nose at this comment, and Mineko laughed. "Why do you care? Can't you swim?"

"I never learned. I take it you can? Or were you fresh from a freak rainstorm earlier?"

"Yes, I love it. I'm the best swimmer, girl at least, in Kadoma."

"You don't say? But of course, how many competitive girl swimmers are there in Kadoma?"

Mineko accepted his slight, after all, she had just called him an old lady, but then she told him of her great feat earlier in the day, of the current in the middle of the river, of how the boy turned around and she kept on. She told of the heron that had waved her toward victory. She knew she sounded like a braggart. She knew, but somehow couldn't help herself.

"And then you came to save my bike."

Akio opened the bag of old noodles, some stiff as chopsticks. Mineko broke off a few and tossed them in. A graceful feeding frenzy began.

Akio finally sat and let his legs with his smart wool trousers and shiny shoes hang over the side as well. They took turns tossing small pinches of noodle over the edge, the turtles swimming and opening their ancient mouths, gulping them down and diving under again, only to come back for more. In the distance, a pair of curious ducks swam closer, then hid behind a willow growing close to the water, its branches like a curtain.

"That turtle, there, the big one with the thick moss on his shell"— Mineko tossed the turtle a noodle—"I think he's the oldest. He's definitely the ugliest. So he must be a god. I make sure to feed him well, since I know his secret."

Akio smiled. "A turtle god *is* a good reason to keep visiting. We have a lone turtle in our yard. My father thinks it's the soul of an old samurai warrior. My mother just thinks he eats all the peonies."

"Then they're wise and both correct," Mineko said, with a flourish of propriety.

Akio laughed. "Just ask them."

His comment made Mineko warm toward him.

"Are they difficult?"

"What a question! Are yours?"

"My father is wonderful." Mineko didn't mention her mother and hoped Akio wouldn't ask.

Mineko learned that Akio was the oldest, like herself, but as a son, the pride of his family. He was heading to college in the fall, to Kyoto Imperial University, where his father suggested that he study economics as the degree would be helpful when he eventually took over his father's company. Akio discussed these things while squinting at the sky, as if watching for rain.

"Oh," Mineko said. "I think people should be able to choose such things."

"Very modern thought," Akio said, tossing another noodle that landed squarely on the back of a turtle, causing the turtle to elongate his neck in an attempt to retrieve his prize. Mineko felt that there was more behind his comment, perhaps a recent unwelcome conversation, different expectations. Or, she reasoned, a little panicked, he felt her ideas were too modern, too forward. She was the girl, after all, who stopped his bike from being stolen with her own leg.

Mineko felt a cool breath of relief that Akio, as the firstborn son and a student, would not be leaving for war, and then she wondered why she thought such a thing. Mineko chided herself for even caring about what this rich college boy thought. Mineko was not the boy-crazy or marriage-focused type, unlike her sister, Hisako, and Mineko's lack of interest, her mother felt, contributed to the embarrassing state she was in. Despite Mineko's being from a good family and of appropriate age, her parents had failed to match her. They had many arranged meetings with friends and friends of friends. Each time, they'd return, quiet, Mother going right to bed, her father nodding silently at Mineko before he went out to smoke a cigarette in the garden. But this did not despair her, in fact, as time wore on, she was almost happy that her life was not set. Mineko hoped that she could somehow earn a living on her own, care for her father and, because she absolutely must, her mother.

"And you?" Akio asked, interrupting her thoughts.

"If I could study anything, I think it would be engineering. I like how things are put together."

"So, no ryōsai kenbo for you?"

Mineko didn't respond, as she didn't want to tell him outright that she hadn't been matched. It was hard to become a devoted wife and mother of the empire without that key piece. Each school morning, during calisthenics, the fierce teacher of the older girls had them all repeat as they jumped: I will bear sons—ichi, ni, san—for my nation—shi, go, roku—where the sun never sets—hichi, hachi, ku, juu! Mineko felt each shout was a lie.

Yet while she felt that the empire's binding of wife and motherhood was too tight, she was not a moga either. Mineko did not escape into the city to sit at the European cafés, springing up like mushrooms after rains. Theirs was a rebellion without thought. Tossing out old fish for someone else's old fish. Ridiculous.

"No, marriage and motherhood is my sister's role. She's my mother's favorite, and she's beautiful and very talented. If you knew her, you'd be asking me to introduce you."

Akio sighed. "I've already been matched."

"Of course you have," Mineko said, feeling foolish. "What I mean to say is that it would befit your situation to be matched to a lovely young woman."

"Well stated. And she is, what you say, lovely. I've met her a few times.

She's not from here. The daughter of a business associate of my father from Kobe. We'll marry after school. And you?"

Akio took the last noodle and handed it to Mineko, who wiggled it over the water, teasing the turtles. She lowered her eyes.

"Just as well. You'll be designing buildings and skyscrapers."

"And you will be married to a lovely wife, with lots of children who can't swim."

Akio said nothing.

Mineko turned to look at him, certain that he had been chiding her with the skyscraper comment, but saw that he was being perfectly sincere. She was unnerved by his kindness and felt a pang of regret, dropping the last noodle.

Why did she say such a thing? She looked away from Akio, who she figured was flummoxed by her comment. She felt they should leave, immediately. Her mouth always got her into trouble.

"Well, we're out of noodles. I should be getting back. I have a punishment awaiting me for the swim earlier. And, if anyone saw me after that—" Mineko stood, straightened the skirt of her dress. "Let's just say I should have saved some of the noodles for my dinner."

Akio stood and bowed. Mineko did the same.

"Thanks for . . ." but she couldn't verbalize what she was thanking him for. A nice walk? Helping her feed the turtles?

"I should thank you. The bike, the ghost garden visit, now all this luck . . ."

His voice was kind, not angry with her after all. Mineko looked down at her hands, her jagged nails, her forearms dark from spending time outdoors, away from home. She blushed against her will but looked again at Akio. He was oddly handsome. Skinny, yes, but with a good, broad forehead and shining eyes. There was a gentleness in his smile that reminded her of her father.

"I accept your appreciation. And good luck in school and in that swimming class."

Akio grimaced.

"Yes, but I've heard their way of teaching is rather severe: you must jump into deep water and find your way to the side. But"—he leaned forward a few degrees—"maybe you could teach me to swim. If I learn, I can take a test and then apply for another class."

Mineko laughed at first. She had taught many of the village children to swim, so she knew how to teach, but Akio was grown. She thought of him in a swimming suit in the water and then felt hot sweat beads quickly pushing themselves through her skin. *Would it be a scandal?* Scandal or no, her sister would be pale with jealousy for Mineko to be paired up, even in rumors, with someone from such a well-respected family.

Mineko stood a little straighter. "Meet me tomorrow morning at ten. I'll be at the gate. We can swim here." She took a step back. She felt that same prickly heat rise from her feet. The breeze had stopped. The turtles seemed to be watching them.

Akio eyed the green water suspiciously.

"It'll be fine. It really is safe," Mineko said. "You'll barely feel the water plants." Before he could protest, Mineko stepped away. "I need to go— I'll see you tomorrow?"

"Fine, here at your turtle house," Akio called after Mineko, who was walking quickly away, feeling his eyes on her back. *Your turtle house.* She turned to bow and then, just beyond the monchu, broke into a childish run.

Mineko arrived for Akio's first swim lesson early, with a knife that Fumiko had stolen for her from the Kamemoto kitchen. When Mineko had told Fumiko what she was doing, Fumiko vowed silence and, with great sincerity, promised to provide anything that these secret lessons required. *Anything*, she had said, a breath later, a twitch in her lips, and Mineko had stomped her foot in embarrassment.

Mineko changed into her swim clothes in the great home's genkan and waded into the water. She tucked a rogue piece of hair back into her swim cap and attached the chin strap. It was a size too small since rubber products had all but disappeared during the war. But to prevent her mother from knowing what she was up to, she felt it necessary to keep her hair as dry as possible. The turtles, seeing her, began to swim closer, but then, spying the bright glint of blade, turned around. The slimy bottom squished between her toes until it became too deep. Mineko had swum in the pond enough to remember where the tallest water plants liked to grow. She didn't know this Akio well, but she guessed he'd be hesitant to swim where the long, meaty leaves wrapped around ankles. She dove down as far as she could and began to saw at the stems. When she was done, she tossed the plants over the fence and met Akio at the gate, where he was glancing nervously from side to side.

"You could have just come in," Mineko said. Akio was fully dressed, but Mineko could make out the tank of his bathing costume beneath his shirt. She felt silly, standing there, dripping, and hurried back to the water.

"I was being courteous!" Akio said to her back as she rushed away.

"No need here!"

At the side of the pond Mineko explained to Akio that they would begin with floating and dog paddle. They waded in, Akio moved slowly, arms out like wings for balance. From the way he was walking, Mineko could tell that his feet were sinking into the muck.

"See, it's the pond's secret lesson in floating—your feet don't want to touch the ground, so you'll be more inclined to learn quickly."

When they were chest deep, Mineko showed Akio how to pull his legs into a tuck and move his arms for buoyancy. Then she asked him to ride a bicycle in the water, teasing him that at least this bike would never be stolen from him. When he groaned from her joke, Akio swallowed pond water. He coughed and spat it out, and Mineko tried to stifle a laugh.

"Now, we float." Mineko brought her legs up, arched her back, and put her arms out at her sides. She gracefully moved her arms and stared up at the sky.

"This is an important skill, when your body tires of swimming, you can always float; it uses less energy. Won't get anywhere, but you won't drown."

But Akio was rigid. His body folded and he went under, found his legs, and stood.

"Impossible."

"No, your body just isn't used to it. And your brain doesn't believe that it's possible. Try again."

This time, Mineko took a deep breath and placed her fingertips at the small of Akio's back, keeping him from sinking. He shuddered once. She felt the cobalt-blue wool from his bathing suit, which appeared to be brand-new, the cat-eye button on the shoulder of his tank still shiny.

"Move your arms a little and make sure your back is pushed up a bit. See? Not too difficult."

"But you're holding me up."

Mineko removed her pinkie, so now only four fingers kept Akio afloat.

As Akio adjusted to less assistance, Mineko smiled and nodded. She walked around, gently guiding Akio in a circle like she did for children.

"I feel silly."

She removed her thumb, and he found his way again.

"I feel like if I do anything, say anything, I'll sink."

"You're talking now. You're not sinking."

Mineko walked him slowly into where the hauchiwa kaede trees had begun to shade the edges of the pond. From their vantage, the old house loomed like a giant.

"Was your mother mad last night?" Akio asked.

Mineko nodded. "Yes, but she's often angry with me. I'm always doing the wrong things. She wants me to stay still and sew, arrange flowers in the parlor."

"Definitely not sit for engineering exams." Akio moved a little and then regained his balance in the water.

"Oh no. But I just like to study how things are built. Like that roof over there—how can it hold up the weight of all those tiles? And if you change the angle, does it make it stronger or weaker? I wasn't asking, of course. But these are the things I think about, and because of it, I'm not very good at—"

"Sewing and arranging flowers?"

Mineko removed another finger, now only her pointer and middle fingers were on Akio's back. He sank a little and the pond inched closer up the sides of his face.

"Oh no, I'm very good at sewing, and very fast. I'm not as interested in embroidery and that sort of work, the type of sewing my mother loves. She just likes to make things pretty. So does Hisako."

"Beauty is important," Akio said.

Mineko removed both fingers and Akio's eyes went large. He buckled and went under, but came back up sputtering and standing.

"You didn't let me finish."

"You were supposed to float."

"Beauty is important, but only if things are made well."

Mineko felt her entire body flush and disappeared under the water like a turtle and emerged near the edge again. She dried off as Akio slowly made his way through the thick sticky bottom of the pond. He dried himself quietly as Mineko slipped on her keta and made her way up the slight incline toward the house.

She paused, waiting for him, one hand on her hip, the other shielding her eyes from the sunlight. She tried not to be angry, but all she could envision was her enchanting younger sister, her beautiful mother, sitting in the garden and chatting as they had been that morning when she snuck away from the house. The shadow from the roof's onigawara lay on the path in front of her; she could make out its head and elaborate tail.

They walked into the genkan and through to the main floor of the home, Mineko watching Akio's response. She was holding her breath and she felt a little light-headed. She had shown only Fumiko this place before, no one else.

"It's beautiful. The light in this room—old houses usually seem so dark and dank."

Mineko nodded. "It's the direction the house is facing, and how far back the trees are from the perimeter."

He kneeled next to the irori, filled with sand and ash. "You would like to live here one day," Akio said.

Mineko shrugged. "I'll live with my parents unless I marry. But this place was built as Kadoma was, and so I think that one day it might be of use to the town. Everyone wants newer and more modern buildings, but there's something still beautiful here." Mineko paused. She made sure to look Akio in the eye. "It's made well."

Chapter 5

"She isn't smoking in there, is she?" My father is calling from Great-Aunt Dimple's gas station. "Your mother will spit nails if she's smoking inside."

Mom, meanwhile, is up at the church office where she volunteers with the Curtain United Methodist Women, photocopying Sunday bulletins and organizing pew Bibles and hymnals.

"Nope, not smoking." This is an out-and-out lie. My grandmother is in our (my) bathroom, in the tub, and I can smell the smoke mixed with her citrus bubble bath.

"Tell your mom and Grandminnie that I'll be late, need to return this equipment."

"How's it looking?" I ask. Today was the knockdown. Today what remained of the old Cope homeplace was scooped into a dump truck and carried away.

"Flat as a flitter. And a little sad." I try not to imagine it.

I hear another voice—Aunt Mae—and she takes the phone from Daddy.

"Hey, Lia Bird. Forgot to tell you! I'm getting rid of all of last month's magazines from the pharmacy. Saved you some back if you want them."

I love Aunt Mae's nickname for me. Once I asked why she called me that, and she said that it was because when I was a kid I sprinted around all the time, arms out, and because I never stopped whistling. My aunt Mae has encouraged my love of architecture from the beginning, ordering glossy home design magazines for years, although there isn't much of a market for them at the pharmacy. It kept me stocked up in *Architectural Digest* and *House Beautiful* during high school. I thank her and tell her I'll stop by tomorrow, because if I don't, she'll pitch them. Aunt Mae runs a tight ship; her employees would call her perfectionistic. And they would not be wrong. But with all of her efficiency, she's incredibly kind.

My dad tells me to call if the house catches fire, and they hang up.

Upstairs, I rap on the bathroom door. My grandmother tells me to come in. Yoshi sprints past me, happy for an escape.

Grandminnie's in the tub, and she does not have the shower curtain drawn. No more bubbles, just my grandmother's naked body submerged in filmy Vitabath and hot water. She's wearing my shower cap and is flipping ashes into a decorative teacup. The potpourri formerly contained in the cup, my mother's perfumed twigs and flowers, is piled onto a tissue on the counter.

I mention she's been in the bath for nearly two hours. She tells me to sit, and I do, on the fuzzy peach toilet seat cover. I look at the mirror, take in my face, which has the contours of my mother and the coloring of my father. My bangs are too long, and I look like a sheepdog with a dye job. I put my hand to my head to pick—the sores are healing, which makes it even more impossible not to touch the scabs—and my grandmother splashes me. I sneer at her.

I try not to stare at Grandminnie's breasts. They're oblong and wrinkled, and I think of the awful prunes that she made me eat when I was constipated as a kid.

Grandminnie laughs at me.

"I used to be flat-flat-flat like you, Lia-chan. Babies did this to me." Her laughter shakes the water, creating a pleasant splishing noise against the white porcelain tub.

Tell me, she asks, finally serious.

"Tell you what?"

She cups her hands together, fills them with bathwater, and squirts a perfect arc at me.

"Rude!" I squeegee bathwater off my face with my hands; my bangs are now extra-long because they're soaked.

"I'll trim," she says.

I think of photos of Aunt Mae as a little girl, her super-short-and-straight Japanese-girl bangs, and know that is her plan for me.

"No thank you."

She gives me the look, and I switch my gaze to the ceiling, to the buzzing fan that keeps the room from becoming a steam sauna. The bathroom begins to feel smaller and smaller, and I lay my head against the wall, the navy-blue with peach roses wallpaper soft against my cheek.

I've had a few more calls from my old UT architecture friends. Rumor has gotten around my graduating class, all of us sprinkled throughout the United States and abroad on design teams, all of us testing our mettle in the real world. *Lia Cope up and quit Burkit, Taylor & Battelle a couple months ago.* I can almost hear their speculation from here.

My third year in architecture school, I finally found my people in Design IV, which featured a last-chance weed-out project guaranteed to remove students who weren't going to finish their degree and funnel them somewhere else—graphic design, interior design, art history. The previous two years had been challenging, but the third year was the beginning of true hell. And we all had to suffer through Design IV in order to get assigned a studio space and start our individual projects. We all wanted those blank studio walls to decorate and access to the materials lab. We wanted to pop a NoDoz, chase it with too much coffee, and live at the Arch Building, shaving stubble or hiding our raccoon eyes with concealer in the fourth-floor bathrooms before critiques. This is the architecture equivalent of med school, except with AutoCAD instead of cadavers.

The groups were chosen at random, and each group was assigned a small conference room down a long hallway, the fluorescent lights buzzing barely green light against pristine whiteboards. Because we knew just enough to get into trouble when it came to using the materials lab, we were told that a TA would be assigned to serve as a babysitter, taking attendance and sitting at a desk in the hallway, grading papers and waiting for our problems. But when I got to the check-in desk for that first evening lab, no one was there. I made my way to Group 8's assigned room. Before long, the rest of my group showed up. First was Bradley, a guy with a head of hair so perfectly formed and gelled, it looked plastic. Then came Rochelle, who had a septum piercing that I couldn't help but stare at and think about the

Curtain Future Farmers of America bulls. She was from New Hampshire and the first person I had ever met from New Hampshire. Our fourth was Antares, a Chinese exchange student who had been lapping all of us in applied thermodynamics, a well-liked guy with an unending supply of Texas Longhorn T-shirts and football stats. He brought with him a plastic clamshell of pillow-soft sugar cookies thick with icing and sprinkles.

The project was to create separate designs of the same building, the crit team choosing the best plan from the group, then work together to build the model of the chosen design. All of the buildings were community structures, and the hope was to get very individualist students to agree and complete something as a team. Darren had had us pull the buildings out of an empty tissue box.

Our building was a women's shelter with family housing. Bradley sneered at the slip of paper as he took it out of his wallet.

"Residential design piece of shit," he muttered.

Bradley had asked Darren if he could perhaps choose again and was denied.

"I was hoping for something sexier, you know?" A piece of fluff had fallen from the heating duct and was stuck, shimmying, on his head. "Like a theater complex or even a fancy organic grocery store."

"Eh. It's a group project. Do our best so we can get into individuals in the fall. That's all that matters," Rochelle said.

"But I can do better work when *I'm* inspired. This is, like, one step off designing a fucking apartment building."

"Cookie?" Antares held out the cookies. I took one. He smiled warmly, encouraging me to put my two cents in. I felt my armpits prickle. I dislike having to choose sides but also didn't want my new group to think I was too vanilla.

We heard a knock and then the door opened. I looked up, thinking I'd see the TA, but it was Darren. I had to say something.

"At least we have a variety of spaces to think about within the shelter. There's room for creativity in the big common areas, right?"

"That's what I like to see in a student—adaptability." Darren held a coffee carrier with four identical cups, half and half and sugar balanced in the middle. "Brought the drink of vitality," he said. The tie he had been wearing in class was gone, the top two buttons of his shirt undone. He looked rumpled. "I remember my first big group project. All the late nights. Here, take."

We gripped the cardboard sleeves of coffee, each popping off lids and sprinkling sugar as needed.

My coffee sleeve fell to the floor as I dumped in cream and Sweet'n Low.

"That stuff will kill you," Darren said, pointing to my pink packet. "Know the name of these sleeves?"

"Zarfs," I answered.

"You're not supposed to know that! That's my patented trivia opener!"

"A zarf?" Bradley asked. "That sounds totally made up."

"She's right, though." He winked at me and grinned. "Keep an eye on Lia, she's the one to watch."

While everyone chuckled around me, I felt their low-grade envy. But inside I was like a fire, freshly stoked.

Lia! my grandmother yells. I am twisting and pulling the yarn shag of the toilet seat cover between my fingers, another nervous habit.

"You're not paying attention," she says. "You feel okay?"

"I'm fine."

"Maybe you're hungry?"

Grandminnie flicks water at me again and tells me that she has something important to say. Something that she hasn't told anyone in this country, something that no one knows except for those who knew her *before*.

"In Tokyo?" I ask.

Before, before is how she responds.

I ask if she wants me to record it, and she says no. Then, sighing, snubbing out her cigarette and poking a toe into the spout like I did when I was a kid, she changes her mind. I race to get the tape recorder, happy to take a break from my memories, make sure the cassette has enough room, and return to my post. I'm not sure what these tapes are for, really, but listening to Grandminnie's voice play back is helping me relax at night.

Grandminnie is out of the water, wrapped in a robe that my mom bought for her shortly after she moved in—white with happy yellow flowers. It looks too cheerful on her. She sits on the vanity stool and starts rubbing lotion into her feet.

Grandminnie motions to the folded clothes next to the sink. I pick them up.

"In the bra. Look there."

My grandmother has sliced the front of the right cup away from the pad and created a pouch. Inside, there's a very small manila-colored envelope with Japanese characters, maybe two inches by three inches, wrapped in a sandwich bag. I open it and slide out a photo. It is sepia and the corners are soft with wear. It's of a man, or a teenager, more accurately, wearing a uniform. He has a large sword in his hand. A fancy helmet sits on a stool next to him. He is wearing wire-rimmed glasses. His face is interesting, but he looks scared.

"That's my Akio."

"The guy you taught to swim?"

"Hai."

"Wait a sec—were you *married* before my grandfather?"

"Never married Akio."

I look down again at the boy and try to absorb whatever he is feeling in the image. I've seen photos of my grandfather before—not many—and he always looked like he had a rock in his shoe, slightly perturbed. And this was when he was attempting to smile. My dad has never had anything good to say about him, and Aunt Mae has always quipped that to complain about him now would just give him power beyond the grave. But just below the fear in Akio's face, there it was: a gentleness.

My grandmother switches feet, rubbing diligently, massaging her instep.

I wait for her to say more, letting the tape run, listening to the hiss of the mechanism and the gentle plunk of a drippy faucet hitting Grandminnie's cooling water.

"No, we never married. But I loved him so much."

I look closer at the photo. It seems to have been taken at some sort of studio. A banner hangs behind him.

"What does that say?" I ask.

"Honor for the Empire. And some other stuff."

"How long have you carried his photo with you?"

Grandminnie winces, like she has stepped on a tack.

"You're hungry," she announces, then moves to the door. "I'll make some soba. That sounds good."

She has left me holding the photo of Akio and the tape recorder, which I keep on, hoping to capture the recipe for Grandminnie's noodles. I follow her to the kitchen, where her well-moisturized feet have left marks on the tile. She is singing a little song, pulling out a pot from beneath the electric range and filling it with water.

"Rice vinegar, sesame seeds—the black ones and the white ones, get the sugar, get the oil . . . where are my noodles?"

Grandminnie refuses to keep her food in the pantry with my mother's, as she thinks the smells will mix and "poison" her rice. This irritates Mom to no end, and she is constantly moving my grandmother's small plastic storage bin of noodles, rice, and nori back into the pantry, which Grandminnie, in turn, moves again. She locates the container, this time on a low shelf, close to the onion basket. She mutters a curse under her breath.

"Give it a rest, Grandminnie," I say. She ignores me.

"You get the green onions. I want you to cut them, but cut them like this." My grandmother holds out her finger and with her other hand as a knife, slices at an angle. "More surface area."

I have put Akio in the back pocket of my jeans, and I am trying to keep up with Grandminnie's instructions. I clean the early-spring onions from my father's little patch out back. My dad will eat them raw at dinner, like a rabbit. Bite of onion, bite of cornbread on repeat. I start to cut as requested, but Grandminnie pulls the knife out of my hand, inspects it, then puts it in the sink. She finds a different one in the drawer, tests the blade with her finger, and hands it back to me.

"Not too thick, but not too thin."

"Like this?" I ask.

She scrunches up her nose and peers through her glasses. "Not too bad," she says, which, I know, is the closest thing I'll get to a compliment for my knife skills.

My grandmother whisks with her long wooden chopsticks and tastes, plops another drop of sesame oil in the bowl and whisks again. The water is boiling. And she dumps in the pretty brown soba and squints at the clock.

"Want tofu?"

"No thanks," I say.

Grandminnie shrugs. "Okay, Lia. But if you are hungry later, you'll know why."

She scrapes the green onion into the sauce and whisks it a few times again. *Bowls*, she commands, *chopsticks*.

As I do these things, she puts the noodles in a colander and rinses them with water, but not with ice water as she does in the summertime. It's a little cool outside today, the sun is behind a layer of clouds. Today the noodles will be lukewarm.

She makes a nest in the bottom of my mother's cereal bowls and sighs. I wonder if she's thinking of her porcelain bowls that had been lost in the fire. She pours in the sauce and hands me my serving.

"We eat outside. I need some fresh air."

The atmosphere is thick with pollen that gives everything a yellow tinge, like I'm looking through tinted sunglasses. The noodles are nutty and a little chewy, the onions a mix of sweet and pungent.

"I was hungrier than I thought," I say, and she nods.

"You've been worried a lot. That burns energy, makes you hungry. Get some more."

"You never answered me. About Akio." I remember that his photo is in my pocket, and I jump up to remove it, happy to see that it isn't bent inside its little paper envelope. I hand it back to her, and she puts it in her robe pocket.

"Lia, it was so long ago. So much has happened. And I don't think of him often."

"But you carry his photo."

"Habit. Like you and your picking." She points to my head.

I ignore the slight.

"Why carry a photo around of someone you don't love anymore?"

"I did not say that. I *did not* say that. Sometimes love is like a fire, you know, and sometimes it's like a heavy rock. This love is like that. I carry the photo because if I put it down it might—sugata o kesu—"

"Sugata o kesu?"

My grandmother takes the last slurp of her noodles. She squints up at the sky, at the trees that are budding out.

"Disappear."

Chapter 6

Kadoma
Mid-Summer 1943

As the summer continued, Mineko began to teach Akio the front crawl and then the backstroke in the deeper part of the pond. He was passable at going forward, not fast, but steady. He was clumsy at the backstroke, always veering off to the left when he tired. He was generally agreeable, yet mentioned several times how he disliked the plants that had regrown long and floppy just a few feet from the bank. He said that they felt like fish when they brushed his legs, and Mineko couldn't help but poke fun at him for this. Mineko had never met a boy who concerned himself with such trivial things and worried that perhaps he had changed his mind about lessons.

"Then where do you suggest we practice? What would befit Master Akio?" Mineko finally demanded during their fourth lesson.

"Nowhere else," he said. "I think this is the only place that's right. My, you have a temper."

Mineko splashed him.

"I'm fine with it, your temper suits you!"

To be certain Akio would continue to return, Mineko took her mother's gardening shears from her home and again dove under to cut the most offensive of the plants, the shears able to get down closer to the root.

Akio, in turn, brought sweets and snacks, difficult to make or find now that most food went to the soldiers fighting throughout the Pacific.

The Sato family chef, originally from Tokyo, worked with better ingredients than the rest of the prefecture, it seemed to Mineko. Shoyu senbai, crunchy and salty. Dorayaki, tender and golden on top and bottom and filled with the sweetest bean paste that Mineko hadn't tasted in years. And chewy fruit candies—Mineko's favorite—rolled in sparkly sugar. Mineko had not realized how hungry she was until Akio began bringing food. The supplies for her family had dwindled steadily over the past few years, each week bringing a shortage of something or the other, then the shortage becoming a disappearance altogether. Mineko tried to surreptitiously save food back for Fumiko, stating that she wasn't too terribly hungry, but Akio called her out on this lie and began to bring an extra portion to share.

Fumiko declared that Akio was wooing Mineko, which Mineko loudly denied. She would not give herself over to such fantasy, not when he was matched. And she disliked the wispiness of girls with a crush. Despite the teaching that women found utmost happiness within the favor of marriage, Mineko could see evidence of the opposite. Her mother was definitely not happy nor fulfilled. Just the same, each time Fumiko came into the room where Mineko was, she would hum a popular love song and dance a quick little foxtrot, blowing kisses at her friend as she left to tend to the fire.

After seven lessons, Mineko thought it was time to teach Akio to dive; this way he could enter from the gazebo and not be bothered wading through the muck to the deeper part of the pond. She started her lesson from a rock that jutted out into the water from the edge, where the water was about five feet deep.

"All you have to do starting out is hang your toes over the edge, bend your knees like so, arms out straight and hands like this, and then jump in with a little—" Mineko pushed her body forward gently, gliding into the water. But when her head hit the pond, her swimming cap, far too tight and already beginning to tear, ripped in two.

"Chikushō!"

"Language, young miss!" Akio said in mock horror.

"Look at me! I'm a mess!" She ran her hand over her wet hair. Her fingers became tangled in the ends. "I want to cut it so badly."

"Bob it? Short?"

Mineko nodded. "My mother said that I could cut it only if someone marries me!"

"I think short hair would suit you."

Mineko ducked under with this compliment, dove down, and stood on her hands, her toes pointed above the water. When she couldn't hold her breath any longer, she flipped back over with a grin.

"Show-off," Akio said. "And I mean it, you should cut your hair."

"I do so many things wrong according to her, I don't know if I can add one more. Not that I care what she thinks, but my father—"

Since the war, Papa had become quieter and quieter, slipping away into silence. Where he had used to chuckle at Mineko's comments, he now gave only a pained nod, perhaps a flicker of a tight-lipped smile. His stomach hurt many nights, and he often went to bed with a hot water bottle long before the evening meal. His clothes hung on his frame. When Mineko tried to talk about this with her mother, she would snap that they were all hungry. But it was more than hunger. Perhaps Papa was sick with worry. Or maybe he was just sick.

At the edge of the rock, Mineko pushed off and glided backward like a swan in reverse. The only place she felt truly graceful was in the water. Her hair, halfway down her back, floated around her like the plants that she had just trimmed earlier in the day.

"Let's get back to work. You need to learn to dive." But Akio was gone, and Mineko looked at the bank to see him near her satchel.

"We can cut your hair with these!"

Mineko clapped a hand over her mouth.

"I can't. My mother will slap me into the new year."

"Well, maybe the new year will be the end of the war and you'll be better off!"

They both paused and took a breath. They both hated to mention it, for when they were together, it felt so far away, a rumor, as distant as the moon or old age.

"Oh no, this is so silly. I'm not cutting my hair with garden shears. I'll cut it, but only with real scissors and only after you learn to swim like an adult and not a diapered baby."

Akio began to laugh so hard that he doubled over onto the grass. He lay on the bank, breathing heavily, and Mineko stood in the water, watching his chest move up and down. She felt it then, as if something were pushing her out of the pond and into the morning sunlight.

I might love him.

Akio propped himself up on his elbows and smiled.

"Okay, I'll grow into a better swimmer and you'll disappoint your mother."

"More than I already have."

"More than you already have, although your mother must be the most hard-hearted woman, because—"

And Mineko was standing on her hands again in the water, her hair wrapping around her face, feet in the air, the wind cooling her toes. She wiggled them, hoping Akio would notice.

By late June, Akio knew how to dive. They had increased their lessons to every other day, and when it rained, they'd eat lunch inside the grand house on a blanket that Fumiko had swiped for her, Fumiko giggling until Mineko pulled her hair. While they ate, Mineko talked about how she'd improve the house if it were hers, Akio in rapt attention, asking for more details. It had been a rainier summer than anticipated, and Mineko found herself praying for clouds so they could sit side by side and ponder an imaginary future.

Once he had touched her hand. Another time, she had leaned over him to grab a bottle of ramune, lost balance, and had steadied herself by holding his knee. He had helped tuck a strand of loose hair into another too-tight swim cap stolen from her sister. She had resewn a button onto the shoulder of his swimming suit.

Then, in mid-July, they met at the gates on an overcast morning, and when thunder rumbled, they decided to skip their lesson altogether and instead go to the Nippon Theater in Osaka.

The movie, *Poppy*, both had seen before, but no new movies had come out, good ones at least. All the newer shows were about war, and although the newspapers lauded them, most found them boring, including Mineko, who felt that living with nonstop fear of war was bad enough, why should one be forced to watch it as well? Akio agreed, and so they bought the tickets for *Poppy* and found their seats in the theater.

The movie wasn't set to begin for another fifteen minutes, so Akio left to buy orange slices and returned with a damp bag to share.

"It's pouring. I hope they aren't wet."

"Oh, these are the good ones. I haven't seen these in years!" Mineko grinned and held an orange slice up in the dim light. "And they're so bright—I wish I had a coat this color."

"Candy orange?" Akio thought about it for a moment. "That would be pretty on you."

Mineko was surprised to hear this, and she looked down at her lap. *He couldn't be teasing me, could he?* But when she looked back at him, he, too, was holding an orange slice to the light, smiling. For an instant, her mind played with the idea of future movies, future bags of candy, future smiles. These unborn bubbles of joy tickled in her chest.

"Then it's decided. After the movie, you can take me to the store to look for fabric. I do need a new coat—I gave my old one to Fumiko since she spent last winter traipsing all over town, standing in food lines. I doubt we'll find any good fabric, though."

"We'll try."

"Thank you."

"And you better get started on this coat. Fall will be here before you know it. I'll be back in school. And the end of the war, that's what my father is predicting."

Mineko slowed her chewing. She thought of the days that they had left. Three or four lessons a week, maybe only four weeks left, as surely he'd need time to pack and ready himself for the new semester. Twelve more lessons. Sixteen? And what if one of them caught a cold? Or her mother finally found out and told her father and he asked her to stop her nonsense and be a lady? She swallowed her orange slice, but didn't reach for another.

"I don't believe it," she finally whispered, although she didn't know why she said this exactly.

"The war ending?" Akio lowered his voice. "They go and go . . ." What he didn't say, couldn't say, was that the boys were not returning.

In the spring, only twenty village boys had gone to war, but over the summer, in just a month or so, that number had tripled. Papa counted more and more leaving on the trains. Conscription rules had been gently modified over the months, allowing more boys and men to be eligible. Mineko wondered after they spent these bodies, who would be next. College students? The next class of eldest, then the next? She couldn't imagine some of the eldest sons who had grown up on her street going to war.

"And you? What rumors have you heard? You're in the best position to avoid service . . ."

"I'm no soldier," he whispered back. "I'm not certain I even believe . . ."

Mineko knew what he meant. Many years ago, as so much more of a child, she had asked her father why the Japanese soldiers couldn't just return home. Why couldn't everyone simply return to their own countries? It seemed more fair that way. Her father had only said that was not the way these things work. And now, as she tried to picture Akio in a uniform, she couldn't think of a more unbefitting place for him.

"Think of being sent to a tiny island, surrounded by water." Mineko tried to joke, but it fell flat, and Akio looked at her, clearly the first time he had thought about this.

"We really should increase our practices. Just in case—"

"—they decide that eldest rich-boy sons who are also college students will finish the war," Mineko whispered.

"Rich-boy sons who can barely backstroke across a pond. And who are scared of fish."

"Then I suppose we *should* practice more," Mineko said, reaching into the bag for the last orange slice. "Maybe Saturdays, too."

"Agreed. Because if I'm ever a soldier, I'll be swimming away."

"In a current. Wrapped up in kelp."

Akio laughed and neatly folded up the paper bag. "You're funny."

A hand tapped Akio on the shoulder, a slender pale hand with oval fingernails. Mineko could smell gardenias. Akio turned around, and Mineko followed the hand to the wrist to the arm and up to its owner. A lovely face stared back at her.

"Miss Kaori. What are you doing here? I thought you were visiting your family in the north."

"I could ask you the same, Master Sato. I thought you were supposed to be working this entire summer in your father's patent office. And, here *you* are! Securing a patent somehow?"

The voice was melodic. She was in a well-cut silk dress, covered in pink roses. Her hair was held away from her face with two pearl-encrusted clips and curled down her back, like an American movie star. But she wasn't cheap-looking, like some girls when they tried to imitate Bette Davis. She looked refined, a teacup in a modern design.

Next to her, a friend, frumpier, with a frown implanted on her pudgy face.

"Mineko, this is Kaori and her friend—"

"Chiyo," Kaori said sweetly. Akio looked sheepish. And Mineko knew that this Kaori was the one to whom he was promised, the woman Akio was set to marry.

"I have been helping Akio with swimming," Mineko said flatly. She felt foolish, orange slice remnants coating her molars. She wondered if Kaori had overheard the talk of the coat. Stupid bright orange coat. Mineko stood, brushed the crystallized sugar from her skirt.

"I'll be back," she said, but she took her handbag. Akio opened his mouth to protest, but nothing came out, and Kaori was still chatting to him about a party, someone's home in the mountains, a lake with a dock and floating lanterns. As Mineko walked away, she could feel eyes on her, and she wondered if they were Kaori's or Akio's or maybe the friend's, who had remained quiet and who, without a doubt, would gossip with Kaori as to why her promised one was there with a plain, squat village girl.

The lobby smelled of sugar, and the carpet, a repeating design of pine needles stretching to the door, made her dizzy. She put on her rain cape and walked out into the humidity and traffic. Soldiers on leave splashed by on motorbikes, and a gaggle of old women in kimonos, umbrellas overhead, timidly crossed the thoroughfare. In the distance was the department store where Mineko had planned to buy the fabric with Akio. Just the sign, bright red and glaring, made her angry. For one tiny moment she had felt as if all was possible, but it was an entire fairy future, and looking in at it had made her blind. Happiness with Akio, someone to love, someone to sit with and talk. This was something she had never wanted before, something that she had grown to believe was nothing but a snare for women, caring for a man who, like her father, couldn't find his own shoes without assistance. Never doing anything but arranging dinners and flowers and eventually marriages.

Best not to dwell. She straightened her back and decided that she would send a note to Akio, canceling the rest of the lessons for the summer. He'd go back to school. The war would end, Japan the victor. School would start for her; she'd be forced to choose between sewing or shop work. She would choose sewing. She would care for her parents. And life would be lived, spent and used, back and forth, swimming beneath the pond water like an ordinary silver carp.

Chapter 7

Curtain, Texas
March 5, 1999

It's Grandminnie's idea to sneak out to the detached garage in the middle of the night. I tell her we could wait until both Mom and Dad were gone and I was home from work, and she swears at me in Japanese, the few words she has taught me, and then she squeezes my jaw and whispers, "Tonight!" like a rebel planning a coup. She has a flair for the dramatic.

I wake to her shaking me, her strong hands planted on my shoulders. In the moonlight, I can tell that her bed is barely mussed and figure she has stayed up while I slept. I wonder what she could have been doing, sitting there in the dark for so many hours, though, I have sat like that, curled up on a made bed, my thoughts a black hole.

"Come on!" she hisses, and her breath is in my face. I instinctively look for it and there it is—a Thermos of coffee. I know that tomorrow morning my mom will be muttering under her breath about spilled coffee grounds on the counter.

"Are you anti-sleep?" I complain, and Grandminnie pulls me up by my arm.

"No, are you lazy?" she asks.

A few weeks into the group project for Design IV, I wandered into the fourth-floor bathroom blurry-eyed during our evening studio session, knowing I had torn a contact. We had been working for hours, and I had that stale coffee breath scent about me that was the combination of my own exhalations and those of the other Group 8-ers. We had taken our individual pieces and compared them, using the critique methods taught in class, and then went in circles about minuscule aspects of each design. Unlike everyone else, it seemed, I actually enjoyed the safety net of the group. When I was designing on my own, I felt every bit of doubt creep in. I had wavered so much on my initial concept, I was at least a week behind my group. When I finally showed my first plans to the critique team, the very last in class to do so, they were not impressed, one was even harsh in his appraisal. I had decided that I would create a building that had a plain, almost austere exterior, which would open up inside to a space with a sunlit ceiling of skylights and a walled garden, leading to the individual family suites. I called the facade of the building *protective*, but one of the critics called it a mullet: business in the front, party in the back. There had been laughter when he said this, and I silently sobbed in the restroom following the critique. Just the same, I continued on with my concept, not because I was confident, but because I was so far behind that I didn't have time to rethink it.

My brain was spinning by the time I went to fix my contact.

Group 5 was still working in their conference room, light slanting from their door, so I wasn't surprised to run into Aimee, the tall, blond sorority girl, in the bathroom. Unlike the rest of us, who lived in long-sleeved T-shirts and leggings because the Architecture Building was consistently frigid, Aimee was able to work for long hours in a short denim skirt, a tight T-shirt, and a push-up bra. *She'll crack or she'll freeze,* Rochelle had commented that night, *it's just a matter of time until she shows up in sweatpants.* I had my doubts.

"How's it going in your group?" Aimee asked, applying a layer of slick lip gloss. "Darren's supposed to be back in about fifteen minutes for questions. Think you'll be ready to break by then?"

After the first studio night, we all thought that Darren was going to let the TA take over check-in duties, but he had surprised us by sharing the responsibility, showing up at least once a week. His visits were helpful, always generous with his compliments and his observations. The last time, he handed each one of us a beer as we left the building, a party favor for surviving another long night.

Aimee shimmied her skirt down so the top sat even with her hip bones, revealing a still-tan stomach, which meant that she undoubtedly fake-baked. Somewhere, I tried not to imagine where, she probably had one of those *Playboy* bunny sticker outlines used to check the status of one's roasting.

"Darren's sweet. I bombed the first part of this assignment, and he said that he'd help me figure out where I went wrong," she said. I wondered if Darren was the reason for this late-night primping. I felt drab and stale compared to Aimee, who looked as glossy and fresh as she did that morning. I quickly told myself that looks didn't matter and that Darren had said I was one to watch because of my intellect. I mean, did Aimee have an Outlandish Word of the Day calendar that she tore off every morning?

"Hey, Darren mentioned all of us going to Cain & Abel's. Thursday-night drink specials. He's buying the first round. Did he say anything to your group?"

Envious, I said that he hadn't, he was too busy discussing *our work*, to which she fluttered her long mascaraed lashes.

Back in our conference room, I told my group what Aimee had told me about Cain & Abel's.

"Fuckers! Getting in good, are they? I'm going," Bradley said, wadding up a piece of graph paper and tossing it toward the wastebasket next to the door.

"You're pathetic. Darren only said something to them because of Aimee," Rochelle said. "And you missed."

I looked down and my contact lens bubbled again out of my left eye. I picked it up and held it to the light, noticing that the tiny tear had grown down the middle.

"Whatever. I'm doing this for my grade—and yours," Bradley said.

"I have class at six a.m.," Antares said. "And that's not my scene."

"Drinks are free at home," Rochelle said.

I didn't say anything, but I knew I'd go, even if I could see only half of the campus clearly. I couldn't tell if I was starstruck, in the throes of a crush, or just desperate for someone to believe in me.

Grandminnie whispers something in Japanese while she hands me my hoodie and kicks my slippers toward my feet. Then she asks why I'm being a scarediddy cat. She grabs my wrist, her short fingernails digging into the flesh where my pulse beats fast, and pulls me up.

"I'm not scared, I'm exhausted," I groan. I follow her quietly down the stairs, but can't stop thinking about that night.

At Cain & Abel's, Darren was ordering Texas Teas for everyone.

"These things are strong, ladies," Bradley had said, gulping. "Watch yourselves."

Rochelle, who had said no but had walked over with us anyway, flipped him off.

Darren had commandeered a long indoor picnic table, the wood worn smooth and dark with beer stains. He sat on the bench at the end while the members of Group 5 clustered around him. Aimee sat on the table, her long legs stretched out below her. Every few minutes, someone would yell out, *Hey, Aim!*

"I'm here a lot," she said.

"Like, she has to be smart, right? Or she wouldn't be in the program?" Rochelle whispered to me.

"Tell us about Berkeley," Bradley said to Darren. "That's my dream school. My dad wants me on the East Coast, *of course* . . ."

"Which was your favorite internship?" a Group 5 guy asked.

I listened to Darren's careful answers and watched all of us vying for his attention. Aimee was pointing her body toward Darren, then Bradley, like a car careening out of control. The group was now talking about our first individual projects, about which studio areas they had already scoped out. We were going to inherit space from the graduating class before us, gone in May. Everything would be stripped bare and then we'd be released upon the floor to find our studio homes for the remainder of our time in school.

"How about it, Lia?"

"Pardon?"

Darren smiled at me. I felt my eyesight fluctuate, trying to focus. My lack of vision, combined with whatever combination of liquor that made up the Texas Tea, made me feel dizzy.

"Residential or commercial?"

I hadn't allowed myself to think about specialization. It felt silly even to contemplate it—I couldn't manage to come up with a design that didn't elicit jeers. As I dropped off into a shallow sleep each night, I wondered if I was cut out for this place. Everyone seemed to have something figured out, not just their life path, but who they were at their center. Had they built this awareness during their teen years while I was trying to find a group of friends to sit with at lunch? Was this some sort of inheritance, a gift from their super-confident parents? I had always felt a distance, a disturbance within my core. My mother claimed that it was normal because I was bright and serious. But it was my father who told me, one night during an asthma treatment, the hissing nebulizer strapped to my face, that it might be because I was *just Japanese enough* and people can sniff out anyone different. And once you're treated differently, you feel different, and that's just that.

There was a buzzing in my head—like a jigsaw had been plugged in and was splitting me in half. *Say commercial, because that's what makes the most money and makes you into a starchitect.*

"No idea. I don't even know if—"

But Bradley cut me off and started talking about some huge architecture scandal, and with relief, I pulled my body from the group, finding comfort in the edge of the conversation.

Another Texas Tea was shoved into my hand by a Group 5 girl who had the soft white face of a dollop of whipped cream.

I knew I shouldn't.

But Darren raised his glass to Groups 5 and 8, the most hard-core of the class, and so I sipped. The rest of the night is like a torn-up photo.

Bradley disappeared. Then Aimee is there, oddly serious, wearing someone's straw cowboy hat and talking about how she loves homes where the living area and kitchen interconnect—how she used to babysit her cousins and struggled to make them lunch *and* see what they were doing in the living room, so she had suggested to her uncle that he knock down the wall that wasn't load-bearing and create a great room. He had done just that.

"Can you believe I didn't even know what an architect was? Everyone in my town works in the oil fields or is a teacher or nurse or something. I asked the librarian at my school the name of the job that didn't build the houses, but made the plans for them." Aimee cackled, her head thrown back.

I understood. Our towns sounded similar.

"So, she's *clearly* going residential," I remember Rochelle saying as she walked away.

The girl with the whipped-cream face waved goodbye. Bradley showed up again. The lights went on hot and bright, and the music was turned down. Then Darren was leading us all out to his Jeep-looking thing.

"Whoa—is that a Defender?" Bradley asked. "Don't see those ever around here."

We all squished in: Aimee in front, Rochelle on Bradley's lap, me in the center, and some other guy on my right. The back bench seat was hard. I was now wearing the straw cowboy hat.

It felt like we were driving slow, and I had the sudden impression that we were kids in a carpool minivan, listening to Aerosmith, which made me giggle to myself. After many stops, it was just Darren and me. I was still in the dorms and on the west side of campus. It was part of my financial aid package, so it was a dorm or nothing for me. "Love in an Elevator" began to blare through the Defender.

"Want me to pull over so you're not stuck in the back?" he asked.

"I'm fine, really," I said, though I wondered how I was last when I actually lived the closest to Cain & Abel's.

"National Merit kid?" Darren asked.

"One of the semifinalist ones. I got a couple of other scholarships that fill in the holes."

"That's amazing."

"It makes my folks really happy. I mean, I don't think I would have ended up here without it."

"Me, too. The scholarship. At Columbia. And I was in the dorms, also. It was either that or a well-designed cardboard box. What the others don't get is how little they'll be seeing of their own apartments soon. And *you'll* have the easiest commute."

"Is it that much more chaotic?"

"Every bit. And amazing. I'd go back in a heartbeat. That's why I'm so stoked to be here."

We pulled into the U-shaped drive, and he parked as close as he could to my dorm. Then he hopped out, and I watched him with my one good eye go through the headlights at a mid-jog. *I'm important enough for him not to walk*, I thought. He opened the passenger door and popped the front seat forward, extending his hand to help me out.

He cleared his throat.

"So why are you winking at me?"

I felt myself redden as I stood in front of him. He didn't let go of my hand.

"No, it's not— I tore my contact earlier, and I've been trying to see out of one eye all night."

Darren grinned and I could tell that he was about to laugh.

"Hey." He squeezed my hand. "It seems like you're flailing a bit, let me help. Come by my office next week."

I let his words float between us.

"Like during your office hours?" I asked.

Darren looked over my shoulder at the sound of another car pulling up, rap spilling out of the open window. He let go of my hand, but then looked back to me and smiled.

"Sure. Or whenever. Consider me a friend."

Consider me a friend, I think, now. The squeak of the storm door brings me back. We're outside, and Grandminnie has produced a small flashlight from her pocket.

We locate the boxes behind Dad's lawn mower in the garage. My grandmother points the flashlight at the largest one. I pull open the flaps and there, beneath a couple of wrapped teacups and porcelain odds and ends rescued from the house, is the baby-blue bowling bag. I carefully shimmy it free.

JAC in gold letters shines on the top in the center, right below the teeth of the zipper.

"Grandfather's?" I ask, and Grandminnie nods. "Why a bowling ball? Why did you want this?"

The zipper is sticky and slow, louder than modern ones, and when the mouth of the bag is wide, I reach in and do not feel the cold smoothness of a ball, but something hard and bumpy. I wrestle it out, and my grandmother takes a deep breath and shines the light on it.

It looks like a sculpture in black stone. But it's so dark, the light is sucked into the— I don't know what to even call it. I squint. A turtle!

With a bushy tail and a yawning mouth on its face. I take the light from Grandminnie and try to make out more detail. I place it down carefully and fumble around Dad's workbench to find the camping lantern and fire it up. I realize that it's not black, but dark gray with tiny glints of crystals.

"Minogame. It's a minogame onigawara. Goes on the roof, on the corners."

"Like the—"

"Yes. Same one. It's as old as Japan because it's made of mountain soil. Soil that is baked."

I watch as my grandmother gently traces the long, variegated tail. To me, it looks like a wiglet stuck on the turtle's back. The turtle has ears the shape of a yappy chihuahua's. The eyes protrude; the mouth looks like it's asking for a treat.

"It's a little weird-looking," I finally say.

"Oh, maybe to you. Maybe to someone who doesn't know."

"Know what?"

"So much luck. Such a long life in turtles. They carry their homes on their backs! And this, this tail is moss because the turtle is old."

"And the ears?"

"Okay, that's what you called it—a little weird. Gods need big ears. But see this?" Grandminnie traces the mouth and at the very corners, it turns up a bit. The smallest smile possible on a mythic turtle god.

"He called it a happy turtle. He climbed onto the roof, and it took all his strength. But the wood it was bolted to was rotten and finally it came off. We called it a pet. He was so silly, so—oh, what do you call it—goofy. Just a happy boy."

"Y'all did this before he married that other girl?"

My grandmother laughed, her mouth as wide as the turtle's, and I can see the glint of a silver filling in a molar in the back. Her laugh calms me, takes away the buzz of worry from the back of my brain, away from Cain & Abel's, away from Darren's hot handshake that night. She squeezes my knee and then pats my leg. Then she leans over and kisses the turtle on its head. Nuzzles it with her nose. The Coleman lantern hisses a little, and we stay there for a while with the minogame, my grandmother animated by the heat of past love, cuddling with a cold statue.

Chapter 8

For three days, Mineko didn't answer the notes from Akio that he had delivered by bike messenger. They were not declarations of fault, but more friendly inquiries: When are we meeting for lessons? Are you ill? Finally, the phone, installed just in case the train station ever needed her father, rang. Mineko heard her father answer it, and heard him say, *my daughter Mineko?* and then he made a noise like a surprised laugh.

Hiroshi came into the backyard, where Mineko was perched moodily on the swing.

"A young man called to tell you the turtles are hungry and it will be feeding time in one hour." Her father looked confused, but handed her the little slip of paper.

Mineko felt the cartilage in her ears burn as she accepted the message. She didn't look at it, but held it between her knees as she swung slowly. Her father disappeared back into the house, called out to Hana, and asked her to take a walk with him. Mineko was happy he felt good enough to walk, but she caught him in the corner of her eye grimacing and rubbing his hollowed-out belly.

He called from the window, "We're taking a stroll. Hisako is coming with us. You may join or, maybe, go feed these turtles?"

Mineko's cheeks flashed hot. How dare Akio use her turtles at her house as bait for her. She looked away from her father as she said she'd stay at the house. When they were gone, she wandered the garden, checking on the progress of the late-blooming yellow roses that climbed the trellis outside her room.

Mineko pondered this note. It was a clever message, she had to give Akio credit. She hadn't been to the turtle house since the movie incident, afraid he'd show up and afraid just being there would make her ache for him. But staying away made her doubly angry. Not only had she allowed herself to feel something for him, something pleasant and tender, she had allowed him into her secret place of belonging.

I will go and tell him to leave and live his life. That the turtle house is mine and I'm done sharing it. Mineko found her shawl, gathered up a couple of radish tops from the kitchen, and took off across town and up the steep hill, her heart pounding as she traveled.

The sun was slowly beginning its descent, the shadows cast about were lovely, hiding the pockmarks in the road. So much was going undone now. The trees near the little Kadoma temple had been cut back too far, the grasses scalped, either by ill-equipped fill-in gardeners or because of an order to do so, a generous cut lasting longer. But the shadows, too, hid this, and things looked almost as they always had, enough so Mineko could pretend that the war didn't exist.

As she neared the turtle house, she felt a little jolt of cool air. What would he say to her? She had never even sent him word that they would no longer be meeting. She just failed to show. She suddenly saw how silly this was. How childish. What could he possibly think—a boy betrothed to that beautiful girl, a boy heading back to school where he would rise to the status of his father or beyond?

Doubt swarmed her, and she stopped just before the path that led to the gazebo. Usually, when she was afraid or worried or embarrassed, she would just imagine herself swimming or watching her turtles. She pictured herself breaststroking, cutting through water, facedown. But now even swimming reminded her of Akio. She had even given away her favorite pastime! And now, she had nothing. Anger swelled in her again. How stupid! How idiotic!

Before she could stop herself, she marched down the path to the gazebo, and when she saw Akio sitting there, feeding the turtles, and he looked up, shy, she didn't stop until she was peering over him.

"How dare you call me to *my* spot. These are *my* turtles," she spat, furiously.

Akio stood, leaving the bag of food he had brought—the cores of several cabbages—on the ground.

"Settle down, Mineko. These aren't really your turtles . . ." he began, but Mineko stomped her foot, the gazebo shuddered. Akio grasped the railing.

"But they are. You didn't even know they existed before me. You have other spots to go. With other people! You thought this house was haunted!"

"What is this about? I called because I was worried that I had said something wrong and that's why you skipped our lessons. Now, I'm certain that I—"

"Wrong? Wrong?" Mineko panted her words. The world burned hot. She realized that she was too close to Akio, that she could smell his breath, could see the not-yet freckles on his nose, hiding beneath a layer of skin. She stepped back and onto the radish tops that she had let drop from her hand. They squished beneath the heels of her shoes, and she stumbled a little bit. The gazebo shook again.

Akio was the first to laugh. "What is this? What are we doing?"

"I'm angry," Mineko sputtered. "I'm angry because sometimes I just don't understand things."

"What do you not understand?"

"You could take lessons from any instructor. You don't even need to learn, really. I bet your father could call the university and you'd be placed in a fencing class, just like that. And we are friends, but I don't know anything about *her*, and I'm certain that your parents don't know anything about *me*, which, of course, they shouldn't, because I'm just your swim teacher, a swimming teacher you don't even need anymore . . ."

And Akio nodded. "We are unlikely."

Mineko looked down at her feet, at the radish greens stuck to her heel. She took off her shoes and stepped to the edge and tapped them together, allowing the leafy top to fall into the water. Five turtles were there before it even hit, fighting one another for the bites. The word *unlikely* rattled in the air around her. So accurate, so hurtful.

"Unlikely, yet I have enjoyed our time so much. So much more than I—" Akio stepped close, took one of the sandals from her hands, and flicked off a chunk of soft browned radish that clung to the wood. It flew and landed, devoured immediately. "You see, I hated missing our lessons, and when I thought you were mad at me, I wondered if it was because of that day at the movie when you left so quickly and I . . . I didn't choose to be engaged to . . ."

Mineko sighed. Other girls, she thought, might cry right now. They would cry, and their boys would either pat them on the back or pull them into their arms and the truth would be there. But Mineko wasn't a crier. She turned to Akio.

"You didn't choose it. That's true. And I was angry about her. Because she's your future life and we, our friendship, are just temporary. I felt foolish."

They were quiet for a few moments, the turtles swimming silently below them, looking up with their ancient eyes to see if any food would be falling from heaven.

Akio said, "We don't have to be temporary."

"We could be friends for a long time, true," Mineko said quietly.

"We could be more than friends," Akio said.

She held his gentle gaze and hope surged within her. She grabbed his shoulders and the words rushed out of her.

"If you choose me, I would never let you down. I am strong and smart. I am not scared of anything. That other girl would take from you. But I'd only give. I'd give you all of me, and beauty fades, but I wouldn't. I don't depend on that and I know, I simply know, that if you could love me, I would be better, too."

It was the most honest thing she had ever said to anyone, and her voice trembled. It was then, with turtles swirling and the sun setting, giving shadows life everywhere, that Akio kissed her.

How simple it was to fall in love. How simple it was to fall in love with the right person! It was floating down a meandering stream in sunlight, not thrashing through a current. It was the view from a rooftop on a starry night, or the feeling of warm grass under one's body after a perfect meal. It was just the right level of close, Akio's hand on her shoulder or his foot next to hers at dinner. It thrilled her, a girl for whom life had never been easy, a girl who had always tripped through experiences outside of her own world.

Akio broke off the engagement with Kaori, which went remarkably well as she, too, admitted to having fallen in love with another. How could such luck happen, Mineko wondered, it felt too perfect, but there it was. Akio loved her. He loved her quick temper and her common sense. He loved her for her strong arms and her big laugh that shook the gazebo. All the attributes that her mother had scolded her for, Akio treated as gifts.

His parents were at first disappointed but then resigned to Akio's choice. Was Mineko as beautiful or as esteemed as Kaori? No. Not at all. But their beloved Akio was happy and at least a marriage to a local girl would encourage roots within their own town. If this progressed, they could grow Mineko into what they needed her to be, maybe? And a war was on, and any amount of happiness, even if unlikely and unusual, was palatable to his family.

Mineko's family, Hana in particular, was stunned into an admiring silence, as was Hisako. Over the next days and weeks, they watched gap-jawed as Akio tapped on the garden gate and bowed at them through the windows, visiting for dates. Even Fumiko earned a reprieve from Hana's domination, as Akio treated Fumiko with unparalleled respect when they met in the garden, asking her to use his first name and calling her *loyal Fumi*. Mineko's father just smiled at all of this and gently reminded his wife that he had once said that Mineko would surprise them all one day.

No longer needing the guise of swimming lessons, Akio and Mineko spent day after day together, from the earliest morning hours possible to as late as propriety would allow. The turtles were well fed. Akio, somehow, procured the candy-colored fabric, and Mineko sewed her bright orange coat and then wore it on the quietly cooling evenings like a blazing flag of happiness. They swam nearly every other afternoon in the turtle house pond, Akio not complaining once about the water plants.

Toward the end of summer, Akio suggested that they make a trip into Osaka to attend the late-summer matsuri, near the river, where there would be food stalls set up and a boat and lantern procession. While it would be smaller than in years previous, before the war's restrictions, it would be a good reason to stay out late together. Akio summoned his cousin and his new wife to meet them at the train station, a chaperoning that allowed Mineko to go at night.

When they met up with this couple, Mineko was surprised to see them hold hands briefly, when they thought no one was watching. Akio explained that the cousin had shocked his family when he had refused being matched and instead chose this girl whom he had met on the trolley car. Akio's father had said that it figured, as his wife's side had always flaunted the rules.

The two couples contemplated what they should eat, enjoying the discussion just as much as the ordering of the food. It was wondrous having options. Akio and Mineko wandered closely together, Akio emboldened by his cousin's displays of affection for his bride. The night was beautiful and, for a moment, it seemed like all of Osaka had forgotten about the war, instead lighting lamps with red and yellow rice paper shades and letting music pour from their homes and businesses. It was a gentle party, and Mineko let the feeling float her along. Between two large trees at the edge of the river, as the sky darkened, Akio and Mineko watched as the skinny lantern-lit rowboats began to glide down the river, drums and bells mixing together as they passed.

"Can you imagine being married like my cousin?" he whispered into her ear, his words tickling.

She waited, still as a rabbit spied in the garden. *Say more,* she pleaded inside, *please say more.* The dress she was wearing felt too tight suddenly, like her lungs were too full of air.

"And perfectly happy, Mineko. Not like our own parents. It makes one wonder why that system is still in place."

Mineko pondered this. Her parents were also matched, but it was a mix of match and madness on her father's part. Her mother had bragged how her father couldn't wait to marry only her, the most beautiful girl in Kadoma, and when it came up, her father had said nary a word. But yes, she could imagine being married and indeed had, a thousand times since the day of the bike.

Just then, a group of rowers in matching hatchimaki stood up on their boat, oars above their heads, and chanted. One man wavered, nearly falling, and the spectators burst into laughter. The boat teetered and then settled. Akio moved with his breath, just a centimeter away from her. Then they ducked into a space between trees, alone. Mineko felt a surge of energy and was speaking before she could stop herself.

"Of course you'll marry me, Akio. What else can you do? You can't live without me now." Mineko turned to him. She jutted out her chin in defiance. Akio stared at her. His smile was broad, the kind where eyes crinkled just a bit; he took both of her hands up to his chest.

"Thank you for saying it, I was losing my nerve."

"I could see that."

"Then I guess the question is when. I graduate in two years."

That felt like a lifetime, and she did not want to be on the Kaori timeline. The last month had felt like both an afternoon *and* four years. So strange how happiness worked with time—extending and shortening the minutes and hours like taffy. Maybe it was war. Maybe it was young men disappearing and food disappearing and maybe it was the combination of the two, one laid upon the other, heavy and stifling, messing with time.

Akio looked at her as she pondered these things and frowned, deep in thought. "Exactly—it's too long. So therefore, we need to marry when I come home for winter break. That will give my family time to secure us a little married student flat. There's so few of them. You could live with my parents, I know that would be expected, but I don't know if you'd like that. Mother said we could have the old settee after we marry, from the drawing room, to make it look more Western, as I think those apartments are arranged . . ."

Mineko flung her arms around his neck and squeezed. She dotted his cheeks with kisses and then began to leave, dragging Akio with her.

"Stop, where are we going? My cousin will be looking for us!"

Mineko, breathless, said, "I'm going to pack my sewing machine and clothes."

Akio's eyes widened. He shook his head. "I said over break—that's four months away. Are you planning to sleep on a suitcase for four months? We must give our families a little time. Our parents must meet! This is going to shock them anyhow . . ."

"You've already told your mother! She's giving us furniture!"

"I hinted at it, and she said in the future. My father is still not entirely accepting. She needs to work on him a bit more. But she will."

Mineko dropped his hand. In just a couple of weeks so much had changed in Kadoma. Flags draped on the little fence surrounding homes told of the deaths and mourning. And far away, London was getting bombed nightly. Germany was taking over more and more. Parts of Manchukuo were still Japan's, and the news said there was nothing to fear, but gossip said it had begun to slip from the Imperial Army's grasp in a few corners. Mineko wondered what it all meant. It felt dangerous to be alive and she said this, contemplating aloud if other boys, even firstborn sons, might soon be drafted to fight for the empire.

Akio scoffed at this, putting his finger to her lips to silence her talk. He picked up her hand again. "Never. Never, Mineko. I just can't see it," he whispered.

Mineko marveled at his confidence. Someone who was so prone to accepting Western ideas, but clung to those traditional ones that were as comfortable as old slippers. She wanted to say something but stopped herself. This will be something to contend with in marriage. Yet she hoped Akio was right, after all.

"Please, when can your parents talk to mine?"

"You know your mother will have a stroke. Your little sister might turn to dust."

"I'll have Fumiko sweep her up and toss her over the gate." Mineko laughed.

Akio took both of her hands. "I can't change your mind, can I? And really, I don't know if I want to. Let's go talk to my mother at least, let her know that we are serious and need her help to plan."

And they took off for the next train to Kadoma and for Akio's family home, glowing with hope on a late-summer night, ready to find a path to the next step, and the step after that, and all the steps that led to a long and joyful life.

• • •

Together, Fumiko and Mineko packed her belongings, keeping only a few necessities out. Mineko slept next to her suitcase. She knew it was ridiculous, but she was resolved. She'd roll her futon and fold her quilts as if she could be called away at any moment to marry. To irritate her, Hisako would take small things from her case and put them back in the wardrobe or even hide them. Once, she even dared to cut off each button from the orange coat, leaving long threads where the buttons had been. It was Fumiko who had discovered the crime and helped Mineko search all over the house, finally locating the buttons near the pit in the outhouse.

"I'm surprised she didn't throw them in with the nightshade."

"I'm going to kill her before I marry, I fear," Mineko said, wiping each button with a cloth.

Fumiko stroked the orange coat lovingly. Mineko had noticed her more sullen of late and had wondered if it was the engagement.

"What bothers you, hiyoko?"

"Your little chicken is worried. When you go to your new house, you won't forget me, will you?"

"Never. As soon as we get into a bigger place, you can come live with us in the city."

"I'll work for you."

"You'll just live there and get a job. Be a shopgirl!"

"Akio will balk! Men want a quiet space with their wives."

"Akio knows what I need."

Fumiko bowed, and when she stood again, Mineko saw the tears in her eyes.

In early September, on a cool night two weeks from Akio's planned departure, Mineko's family had just finished dinner when there was a knock at the door. Fumiko answered the door and gasped. The entire family adjourned from the meal and wandered outside. In the lane, their neighbors milled about, some ashen, some crying. They would bow to each other and say the words they were supposed to say, "I am pleased he will serve the nation," but the air vibrated with a sadness that Mineko could feel in her bones. After tiny edits to life, some so minute that they felt only like a gnat landing on one's arm, it came down from the emperor that all men over the age of nineteen—regardless of birth order—would be enlisted.

"In the new year, yes?" a neighbor pleaded, walking past their gate, following a friend, hoping the government was going by a new year's date. Her son would turn nineteen in a few weeks, but if the government was going by age in the new year, as was tradition, then he had a few months. A war could end in a few months. Anything could happen in a few months.

Fumiko caught up with her and squeezed her wrist, but Mineko shook her free.

Akio had just turned nineteen. Mineko had taken old material from the scrap bag and created a quilt that could be folded into a square and flipped inside out into a pocket to create a pillow. On the inside of the pillow, she had made a tag that said "for my husband." Not fiancé. In her heart, she was married, and had given him the quilt for his birthday. As the neighbor woman pleaded, Mineko hoped that this was the case—age by new year, not by the month, day, and year. Then, they'd have four more months together. Enough time to marry, perhaps.

"No, no, actual date of birth, the proclamation says. It's right here," another woman said as she walked past, pointing to a page in the evening's paper.

Mineko found herself clutching the garden gate to hold herself steady. She'd remember this, she knew, all her days. The entire neighborhood out on a beautiful night, like it was a national holiday, but different, as it was a mix of kitchen helpers and regal grandmothers, yelling children and stoic fathers, their hats left in the house, rubbing their bald heads with both hands.

"You should unpack," Hisako whispered to Mineko.

Mineko pulled her hand back before she could think, her palm flat and ready, meeting Hisako's face where her cheekbone met a pretty curl of hair. The sound was the pop of a firecracker, and Mineko's hand stung as if it had been burned. Hisako stumbled and then, clutching her face, began to shriek as she ran to their mother. Mineko opened the gate and sprinted to the turtle house, as fast as she could.

Mineko was yelling his name before she even opened the gate. On the steps of the house, Akio sat with a lantern. He was pale, dull-eyed; he stared up at Mineko.

"Have you started my thousand-stitch belt?"

Mineko shook her head, not willing to comment on his joke. She could not imagine herself near the shrine, holding out a senninbari, asking women passing by to make a dark red stitch to keep Akio safe from bullets. A stitch. A stitch couldn't even keep her buttons on her coat.

"If we weren't on an island, we could cross a border and escape," Mineko said.

Akio shook his head and then rubbed his temples.

"Headache?" Mineko asked, and she moved his hands and placed her own on his head and rubbed his temples and the top of his scalp and the long back of his neck, feeling a marble at the base of his skull, kneading it with her thumb and pointer. She kneeled on her knees and kissed his head.

"It will be okay, we will be okay."

"It won't last long and I'll return and I'll convince the government to sell me this house."

"And we'll live in it."

"Us and the turtles and—"

"Babies. I'll give you children, and I'll teach them to swim and sew."

"You can go to school! I'll support you."

"I'll do both."

"You'll do both. And we'll live in a new world, a different place."

"Let's go in, the turtles can wait," Mineko whispered into his ear. And Mineko jumped up, tugging him behind her, Akio's eyes big with something that resembled excitement or fear. Into the genkan, shoes kicked off, they didn't bother closing the doors behind them; no one but the carp and the turtles and the birds were there, the minogame looking down, laughing with knowledge.

Chapter 9

"Your mom isn't eating well," my mother whispers into the kitchen phone to Aunt Mae. I'm home from work, my feet tired, sucking on a paper cut from sorting anniversary cards. In the pantry, I search for a snack. It always smells like baked goods and roasted chicken in there from the hanging spice rack on the back of the door. All of my mother's little jars of Spice Islands are organized in order of use. Cinnamon, garlic, and seasoned salt are front and center. I unscrew the lid of the nutmeg and inhale as I listen to my mother's conversation. Grandminnie's right, I think, all these scents *would* contaminate her rice. I sniff the spice again and think how strange it would be to eat rice that tastes like pumpkin pie. I have a pang of guilt for not understanding sooner.

My grandmother has been in a funk for days. She is quieter today than she was yesterday or even the day before. Downright docile for Grandminnie. My parents think it's the ranch house. How her homelessness is real to her now. But I know it's because Aunt Mae has dropped off three different glossy brochures for retirement homes. I'm amazed there are so many in our area, but then I figure that the population is aging because no one comes back to Dennis County, no one but me. My mom has flipped through these brochures in front of Grandminnie, holding them up like it's story time at the library, pointing to photos. *Your own washer and dryer—well, that's nice, but just the same, you'd have to keep up with your laundry. Oh, look, a hot tub next to the pool! Fancy!*

I wish they'd stop it with the retirement places. I want to know more about Akio and because of Aunt Mae and Mom's badgering, Grandminnie hasn't said a word. I thought of him today as I sorted those anniversary cards—on our fifth, on our twentieth, on our golden anniversary. I adore their love and even though I know in my mind that somehow she got from *that* village to *this* town, and that war is awful and that Japan lost the war and that my country won the war, I tell myself a story that Akio, somehow, is alive.

I even found a book from the Dennis library about the Pacific front and read about the Japanese involvement in World War II. I had a long lunch break and thought I'd just duck in, read a little, then get back to work. Previously, I hadn't understood why the Japanese were even in Manchuria to begin with. Now that I do, I see even more why Grandminnie has never spoken of it. One chapter went into the forced labor of the locals, even little children. Then I read about how the Japanese Kempeitai tortured civilians, how family samurai swords were used to cut off heads and those were then put on spikes. By the time I reached the paragraph about how a secret group within the Japanese military focused on human experimentation, I was on the stained carpet of the stacks, legs pulled toward my chest, trying to get my nausea to pass. I called my manager from the circulation desk phone and said I was sick and going home. When I got there, I tried to ask Grandminnie about what I had read and all she could do was look at me, stricken, and nod. It's all true, she finally said.

I hear my mom say, in a worried whisper, "Oh, the same, quiet and standoffish."

I know that's about me.

My mom then says in her normal voice that she needs to get off the phone and put the good foot toward fixing supper, pork chops are thawing, and tells Aunt Mae she'll stop by soon.

"Where is Grandminnie, anyway?" I ask, settling on an apple cereal bar and grabbing another just in case. My mother purses her lips and hangs up the receiver.

"Up in her room. She acts like a child, she gets treated like one."

My mother says this like she has raised a pack of children, not just *me*.

Leaving my mother in the kitchen, I find Grandminnie deeply settled on the upstairs love seat. It's just a little plaid sofa on an oversize landing, but the windows high above filter down the best light for reading. Grandminnie is stroking Yoshi and looking at something, and when I get closer, I realize that it's an ad that ran in *Texas Monthly* featuring a double-spread photo of all BT&B architects in matching company button-downs, dark blue, logo on the pocket. My face is tiny and on the end, a thumb-width away from the edge of the page.

She thumps the magazine and points a finger at me.

"This advertisement. Very nice photo. You look happy."

I remember the day we were herded out of the building at nine, a bunch of too-busy architects, wiping glasses and fixing flyaway hairs. I stood close to my team. We knew that Birkit or Battelle had pushed for this—Mr. Taylor didn't care for publicity, just design—and that the company was forking over a huge amount for this ad. This gave us something to talk about at happy hour that night, but I think we were all rather excited to be featured under the words *Designing the Future of Texas*.

"Why are you going through my stuff?" I reach my hand out for the magazine. "Mom says you've been a pain in the rear today."

My grandmother ignores me. Then she pulls something out of her shirt pocket. It's a cardboard coaster, and I know it immediately. I should have tossed that coaster a long time ago. I just thought I might need it. On a visit home, I had stuffed it in the back of my desk drawer.

"Seriously, Grandminnie, stop going through my things!"

"Boyfriend's number?"

I start to pick at the crown of my head. She throws the coaster like a Frisbee, hitting my hand lightly.

"Still got good aim," she says about herself.

A few days after that ride home, I visited Darren. At his office door, a little after four p.m., I knocked once and Darren yelled for me to come in. He had the phone receiver tucked under his chin. His office was painfully bright, all the shades open, a room of sleek white furniture and black-and-chrome desk accessories. It was also sweltering, which I thought explained why Darren was sitting in his undershirt and dress pants.

"Listen, I can't do this right now," he said, wincing a bit as he said it. I thought he meant me, so I stepped back out into the hall, closed the door, and sat on the padded bench between offices. I heard him put the phone down, a little hard, then he swung the door open.

"Not you! Never you, Lia!" He laughed, cheerful again.

"Everything okay?" I asked.

"Family drama," he said. "I'm so glad you showed up. I've been meaning to ask you something," he said, a little breathless, maybe from the phone call. "I think you'd be great on the Architecture Student Advisory Board. I get to nominate someone from third or fourth year. Interested?"

There was a flutter in my chest cavity. That board was an honor, a way to get closer to the school leadership, the first to know about internships and jobs, an instant in for rec letters.

"Are you sure? I mean, I'm not knocking it out of the park right now."

"Sure I'm sure. And you will. Once we work on your concept a bit."

I should have said no, but in his luminous office, glancing at the underside of his chin in the reflection off the shiny desk, I told him I'd love to and thank you so much. It was an opportunity, an open door. My parents hadn't even finished college, but here I was, getting ahead.

Darren then grabbed a sheet of printer paper and drew a quick but nearly perfect version of my shelter's elevation from memory. He took the pencil eraser and rubbed his top lip with it as he thought, then started sketching again. Within a minute, he flipped the page and held it up to me.

"Great impulse. Intuitive, really. You are thinking about what these women need. A fortress and hope. But fortresses don't sell. Even Roman walls had some style."

He made his edits—high windows, a few awnings, wider doors. It looked totally different, softer.

"And I'll talk to the committee. They're nice guys, really. Put in a good word."

"I don't know what to say. Thank you."

I stood to leave, straightening my skirt. I had taken time to get ready that day for class, knowing I'd be stopping by his office. I questioned myself as I gave my reflection the once-over before leaving my dorm, feeling as if the skirt and high-heeled mules were too much. All day long, friends asked me what I was up to, all dressed up. Each time, I asked myself the same.

"Oh no you don't, you're not leaving just yet." Darren jumped up from his seat, patted his back pockets for something, then reached over to his credenza for his wallet. "You can't leave without me taking you to happy hour. I hate drinking alone." He put on a dress shirt that was hanging on the back of the door on a hook, buttoned it up as I intentionally looked through the blinds at the tops of trees.

As we walked, Darren pointed out interesting aspects of campus that I had never truly seen. It was as if he wore special architecture glasses that allowed him to understand and visualize structures in a deeper way.

"Hey, UT quiz question: Were you aware that there's a Himalayan cedar on campus that was planted *with* its original Himalayan soil? It's the only one of its kind in South Texas."

"I was not aware of this. Also, I have no idea what a Himalayan cedar *is*."

"Oh, well, it's a cedar tree from—"

"The Himalayan region of Tibet, yes, I got that much."

"I was walking through campus today and saw this huge tree next to the Littlefield Home, you know the one, and I was like, what the heck is that doing here? Had to research it. Was planted in 1893 by the builder of the house, Colonel Littlefield."

"Littlefield, big tree," I said.

"Good one. But I bet that soil is long gone."

"At least it had it while it was putting down roots," I said, and Darren smiled, a big toothy grin. His teeth were so straight, so white, like his desk.

We crossed another street or two until we reached a few restaurants.

"Dos Compadres? I've heard they have great queso. Is that true? Is it spicy? Remember that I don't have native taste buds."

"You'll be fine."

Inside, at a two-top, I ordered an iced tea, which Darren tsk-tsked, and he ordered a beer. A large bowl of queso, fresh hot chips.

"So where are you from?" Darren asked.

"Curtain. It's a small town about four hours north. My whole family is from there."

Really? he asked, and I knew by the way he phrased it he was trying to figure out my ethnicity. Some people point out my eyes, like that Avon lady. Others, my skin tone, my hair color. It makes me feel like a Mrs. Potato Head, all my parts strewn out on the table. And genetics are so strange. I look less Japanese than my cousin Sallie, but Sam is the spitting image of Hollis, copper-haired, blue-eyed, and built like a linebacker.

"My grandfather's side is from Curtain. My dad is half Japanese. My grandmother came to the States after World War Two."

Darren enthusiastically nodded. "That's it—I see it now. The Japanese are a beautiful people. I was thinking maybe Hispanic, with being in Texas . . ."

This was a common misconception and one that I often didn't try to fix. In fact, only two people had actually guessed my Japanese identity correctly in all my years in Austin—my Korean suitemate, who, in turn, dubbed me the "Almost Asian" for the rest of the semester. It got a lot of laughs from our dorm crew. I wanted her friendship, so I didn't tell her that it hurt. The other was Antares.

"What does he do—your American dad, I mean."

"Construction. Foundations."

"An engineer?"

"No, a foreman. He pours slabs. He's good with his hands and can do just about anything."

Another *really* from Darren. I couldn't tell if this one was because there aren't a lot of students from blue-collar families in the architecture program or if it was because there aren't a lot of Japanese American dudes directing trucks where to dump their concrete. Most people hear Japanese and think of computers or cars. I guess if one has to live with a stereotype, it's best that it be one with a higher socioeconomic career choice? I don't know.

"Many kids from your high school here in Austin?"

I shifted in my seat, uncomfortable in my skirt.

"Not too many—one guy got a track scholarship here, but I don't see him much, we weren't friends in school. Another couple of girls, but they pledged and we weren't that close either, really."

"Pledged?"

"Sororities. Not too many sorority girls end up in Architecture. Except for Aimee, that is."

"Do you know her very well?"

I said that I didn't. Darren was quiet for a moment, finishing the warm last sip of his beer. I wanted to talk more about my project, but didn't want to appear opportunistic. As if reading my mind, Darren took a napkin from the stack and began writing down names of books, a reading list to help sharpen my instincts. After he handed it to me, I dug through my JanSport for my burnt-orange wallet for some cash. I felt very young suddenly, listening to the Velcro rip open.

"Put that away, this is on me," Darren said. "And I need you to fill out an application for the board. You're totally on, just a formality."

"That's so kind of you. I promise I'll do my best."

"Just call me," Darren said and wrote his number on a coaster, the ballpoint carving into the cardboard. "I left the application at home, so we'll need to meet up or I can drop it at your dorm, even." He pushed the coaster across the table, and his fingers lingered on it a moment, tapping it gently, and just the gesture made me feel unmoored, floating in a place that I shouldn't be.

I trace the number on the coaster. Grandminnie eyes me suspiciously, then stretches her body long like a cat. I hand her the cereal bar. It has been a week since the night we spent in the garage. We had come in when the sky lightened and signaled that dawn was on its way. We had slipped into our twin beds, and when my father came upstairs a few hours later, asking if we'd like bacon and eggs, we gave simultaneous moans, and he muttered, quite loudly, that he wasn't certain which Cope female was being the bad influence, but it needed to stop.

"Eat it, Grandminnie. Mom has been on the phone with Mae, saying you're in the middle of a hunger strike. I know you're upset about all the brochures and the house being knocked down, but you just can't starve to death."

My grandmother sneers at me, but tears open the cereal bar and takes a bite. She sips her coffee, long gone cold. A cloud passes over the sun, which takes the cheerful light away from our nook. The stupid Dos Compadres coaster is in my hand—I make a note to throw it away in the trash can outside. I can feel my grandmother's bad mood pull at me and wonder if I've added to her sadness by asking too much of her. Have I opened up old wounds?

Well, no more than she has today.

My grandmother taps my knee.

"I need to get out of this house. Maybe go feed the turtles at the swimming hole? Fresh air is good for us."

The swimming hole is on the ranch. It takes five minutes on the drive-as-fast-as-you-can FM and then ten minutes of driving slow and cautious over the pasture to get there. The grass hasn't been cut, and this part of the land is resting for a year before it is leased out again to neighboring ranches for grazing. Years of Copes—cousins, second cousins, third cousins once removed—cutting across the same swatch of acreage has permanently trenched a road.

There is a little rise and then we see it, Curtain Creek, our own personal swell of it. It's not a fast-moving body of water, more like a slow, thoughtful ramble. It's a tributary of a larger river, and eventually, our thread of creek hits another thread of creek, and again and again this happens, all the way to the Gulf of Mexico.

"How does this compare to your river in Kadoma?"

My grandmother reaches over and pinches the skin above my ribs.

"You think you're so funny, Lia-chan! It's like the gift-wrap store compared to your fancy architecture firm."

I park my little blue Corolla under some trees, Grandminnie grabs the recorder, and we pick our way along, careful for snakes, through the few scrawny bluebonnets that are hanging on for dear life and the purple winecups that are starting to take over. A few of my grandmother's favorites, fiery Indian paintbrush, are growing, too. I have created many Mother's Day bouquets in this field and have had many chigger bites along the tops of my socks and the elastic of my underwear as a girl.

The metal porch furniture from the 1950s still sits on the banks. Heavy camo tarps cover it, tarps that we have to restake into the ground when we leave. It's a family tradition—any Cope relative can use the furniture, but you for damn sure better put the tarps back and don't go carrying off the sledgehammer.

"Now, this is much better. You asked about this creek and, you know, I remember your grandfather talked about Curtain Creek this, Curtain Creek that, and I thought it would be deep and cold like the Kadoma. Clear, all the way down. I thought, hey, not too bad to have a house with such a nice river that runs by it! But this, oh Lia! So many mosquitoes when it runs low. Muddy. Had to learn to shoot just to kill the water moccasins!"

"But you like it."

"I *learned* to like it. My favorite part of the ranch, now."

My grandmother has a Mrs. Baird's bag of white bread heels and stale rolls. She makes her way carefully down the bank and I follow her. Then, when we're close, we hear it, plop, plop, plop, and three small red-eared sliders fall into the water from their grassy sunning spots.

My grandmother tosses bread to them, but only one turns around to gulp it down, and the other chunks begin to sink into the green and then disappear just a few inches below.

"The sliders are always so jumpy. Those mud turtles, they're lazy and will come up to you for food. The lazier the animal, the more willing to get near a human. It thinks, I'm tired of finding my own food, but maybe that old lady has some bread for me to eat."

"Is that so?"

"Just a thought. Maybe I'm feeling lazy now."

"What do you mean?"

"Maybe I need to sign a lease. Go live in one of those places. That one that's named after the trees."

"They're all named after trees."

"So stupid. Why is that? Is it because old people like trees? I guess so. I mean, I do like trees, and I am old, so maybe I . . ."

I hate how she's giving in to my parents' and Aunt Mae's plans. I know they've been at her for weeks, but I'm hurt that she's caving. I start to pick at my scalp again without thinking, and Grandminnie slaps my hand down.

"No! You have such a bad nervous habit. I'm putting gloves on you tonight. I have the soft kind from the Japanese store."

"I'm just on edge. It's not a big deal."

"You have good hair, my hair! If you pick at your scalp, you'll damage the whatever-they're-called—"

"Follicles?"

"Yes, those things. And, then, *poof*, bad hair. Thin, stringy, not so good. Like people from here."

People from here is Grandminnie's euphemism for white.

"Mom would kill you if she heard you say that. And she has good hair."

Grandminnie raises her eyebrows.

"You don't need to leave, Grandminnie. I know you don't want to."

"And you need to go back to Austin. Back to your apartment and that roommate who is always calling. Stop worrying your parents. Life keeps going on, you know."

The night I got home, I had told my parents that I didn't know if I wanted to be an architect anymore. They didn't believe me. So I told them I was lonely and I hadn't made any good friends. They didn't believe that, either, because they had called a million times and gotten my answering machine, so they knew I was out. I told them I was going through a quarter-life crisis. I told them that I missed them, that I missed home. Finally, I told them that I had screwed up designs for a building. But you're so careful, they said. Finally I yelled at them, *You don't have to know everything about me!* Shocked, they gave up asking and I got a job at Bags-N-Bows a few days later.

"Tell me more about Akio."

"You can't fool an old lady like me. I know how life can be."

We're quiet for a moment. I grab a slice of bread and tear it into itty-bitty pieces for the littlest sliders, tiny things that get picked off by hawks when they are sunning themselves, end up just a shell somewhere in a field. Maybe, I think, as I toss bread, they'll eat this and grow just enough that they can't be carried off.

Chapter 10

November 7, 1943

My love,

I have completed the most basic of training and have settled in Hsinking. I am living with many other new soldiers in the guesthouse of a mansion. Our leaders have the big house, and we are all camped out in a few rooms. We had our bikes parked in the front, chained to the fence, but they were stolen in the night when the fence was cut apart. Now we keep our bikes next to us as we sleep. I am married to my ten-speed. I share a pillow with my handlebars.

During the day, my main duty is to deliver letters and such from person to person. The bicycle the army gave me has wooden tires. Madness! It is like swimming in a current, trying to pedal through town. I'd like rubber tubes, and since you are so good at everything, I was wondering, dear future wife, if you could conjure up a rubber plant, plant it among our mothers' peonies, and maybe make some tubes for me . . .

November 28, 1943

Thank you for the socks, dear Mineko. I do think their thickness will help with the blisters. My feet are unaccustomed to the amount of pedaling. Who has ever heard of infected feet due to bicycle overuse? It would be embarrassing if it weren't happening to the others. We're all university students, all learning how to make rice on our own. Which reminds me: yes, I'm eating well. When we fail to cook for ourselves, our superiors are kind enough to share food from their table. They have a full staff in their house! Maids, valets, cooks. The cooks are locals and have been taught Japanese recipes, and they are better than at home. I haven't confessed any of this to my mother. She would be appalled.

I am sorry to hear about how Hisako is being cruel. You should trick her—tell her that if she stares into the water at the turtle house she'll become a princess, then push her in. The turtles will eat her, since they eat everything you throw in there.

. . . Any luck on my inner tubes? How is the rubber plant faring?

December 11, 1943

I hate that in two weeks it would have been the end of the session and I would have been back with you, preparing to marry. I hate that I will be missing Shōgatsu. Light an extra-large and extra-hot bonfire for me to scare off the demons. It is increasingly ▉▉▉▉▉▉▉▉▉▉. ▉▉▉▉▉▉▉ ▉▉▉▉▉▉▉▉▉▉, ▉▉▉▉▉▉▉▉▉▉▉▉▉. What I thought were pranks, were just a prelude ▉▉▉▉▉▉▉▉. Trip lines for bikes, women ▉▉▉▉▉ ▉▉▉▉▉ in the marketplace, little ▉▉▉▉▉▉▉ here and there. No great ▉▉▉▉▉▉▉▉▉▉▉▉▉▉▉▉▉▉▉▉▉▉▉▉. But do not worry about me, as I have become quite close to my superiors and they only send me to the safest of places in town. They like my winsome personality. And did I mention that the big house has an in-ground, indoor pool? It's heated, Mineko, like a bathhouse. We bike boys can use it when the superiors

aren't bathing. I'm keeping up my strokes. You would be impressed.
Must be my newly strengthened leg muscles . . .

December 29, 1943

Yes, I fell off my bike due to a ███████████████████████████████
███
██████████████████████████████ *or I have good turtle luck.*
I landed on my pretty face, but my cheek will heal in time and the scar
shall be quite dramatic and mysterious. Nothing broken, just bruised.
I'll be back in action in less than a week, which will be good. I hope that
things will settle down as the new year approaches. ████████████████
███████████ *I've heard plans of a big feast at the mansion*
(this is the benefit of the infirmary: gossip). Many of us will be invited,
I think. Or, at least, we will be allowed to attend as the night wears on
███████████████ *I plan to fill up my plate and pockets with fish*
cakes and return to my cot to write you letter after letter to celebrate the
new year, which will surely bring the end of this war with an Imperial
victory. We are only hearing good news from the islands, ████████████
███
██████████████ *Of course I want to hear all the news of home: How*
is your sister? Your mother? Your father? ███████████████████████████
███
I hope for only the best for you and miss you greatly. Bundle up and say
hello to our turtles and our house, my love . . . .

Mineko waited for another letter from Akio. The last few, with their
blacked-out sentences, made her feel unsteady and shaky, like they were
holes Akio could fall through. She had known their letters were being
read, but evidence of it, the thick black ink painted with precision, dyeing
the paper and bleeding through to the other side, felt ominous. She wondered how much of her nearly daily letters were readable, how many had
been delivered. She was also convinced that Akio was trying to protect her
with his light and joking language. The letters themselves felt as polished

as the newspaper articles she read and the truth as slippery as a fish. So, Mineko tried to censor herself as she wrote, tried to channel a perfect loyal citizen and still have her thoughts come through. *I don't care about this war. I never have. I want you home.*

Letters from soldiers abroad came on Wednesdays, and a line formed at the mail outpost on the edge of Kadoma near the train station by six in the morning in fair weather and in the rains and snows that moved in upon them in the near-winter. Hunchbacked old women with tight white buns and thin, proud men, leaning on bamboo canes; young mothers with babies strapped to their backs, holding the hands of toddlers, rubbing their eyes; field-workers kept from active duty by a cleft palate or twisted limbs, wearing rough blue fabric, who once grew food for the populace, but now for only the military. Everyone in line was hungry, the audible rumbling of stomachs a wartime equalizer among classes.

Mineko grew friendly with this queue of waiters and hopers, remembering a tiny bit of candy from her stash for the little ones, playing peekaboo with the babies. Often she brought her sewing and because the wait was long and because she felt she should, she darned an elderly woman's shawl if there was a moth hole, patched a worker's woolen cap to keep out the rain. It was one of the oddities of war, she thought. Never had she spent so much time away from those her family associated with, the ones she had routinely passed on the sidewalks of her neighborhood, those of her station. Mineko enjoyed her line-compatriots and spoke of them at dinner, much to the chagrin of her mother.

"You and your downtrodden friends. This better not get back to the Satos."

"We're a nation at war, aren't we all downtrodden?" Mineko responded angrily one evening, her nostrils flaring. Her mother yelled for her to be quiet and darted to the window to see if anyone had been passing by of note to hear such insolence. But being promised gave Mineko newfound prominence in her family, even if her mother and Hisako refused to admit it, so she wasn't sent outside when she said this. Instead, she got to stay in her place at the table while her mother glared at her and Mineko's words lingered at the edges of the room.

The last Wednesday before the new year, the post officer climbed on top of his service-window desk and announced that due to the overwhelming amount of Shōgatsu letters and gifts from their country to all over the Pacific and Manchukuo, it would be well into the new year, months maybe, before any would receive letters from abroad. When a woman burst into tears, causing her baby and two young daughters to do so as well, the postman became flustered and jumped down from his perch.

An elderly woman clicked her tongue in dismay. Even when a CLOSED sign was hung outside the door and the window hatch rolled down, the line lingered. The farm help left first. Mineko stayed until all had gone away.

Through the fall, Akio's mother had been inviting Mineko to private weekly teas. Their meetings were awkward at first as Mineko struggled to sit still in her pine-green kimono, having worn mostly monpe as mandated by the state and learning that she much preferred the pants. But she brought with her Akio's letters, willing to read aloud some parts of the correspondence, especially those pertaining to Akio's health, food, and day-to-day life, and it became clear that he was protecting his mother from the less savory aspects of his experience. Mrs. Sato was impressed with Mineko's serious attention to the details in Akio's letters, how she was able to read between what Akio was saying and what he meant, as if translating a rare language. Mineko had researched his location as best she could, given the military's strict control of the post, and described the terrain and what she believed the buildings around him looked like.

"Akio told me that you have the remarkable ability to see how things are built and are very curious. That you have an innate sense of scrutiny."

Mineko did not know if this was meant as a compliment or as a statement of fact, and her face must have conveyed this confusion, because Mrs. Sato smiled gently.

"Mineko, it is like you study minutiae in order to treasure. You treasure him and you show honor to my Akio."

Mineko was so struck by this woman's understanding and immediately got to her knees and bowed before Mrs. Sato, something she did not foresee occurring. Mrs. Sato reached out her arm toward Mineko as she rose.

"Next time, we take our tea quickly and we walk together, yes? Maybe look at the foliage before winter falls?"

But that walk was never to happen. Before the new year, Mineko stopped receiving invitations. She had hoped that she could spend Shōgatsu with Akio's family; she had hoped that she was making headway into the lives of her future in-laws and secretly worried that, perhaps, it was something she had said or done.

"Your precious Akio's people have forgotten about you," her sister said one afternoon, coldly, while slowly embroidering an apron. She had been working on it for months. Mineko remarked that Hisako had the hand-eye coordination of a drunk sloth. Even a sober sloth would be done with that apron by now.

Mineko had noticed the mourning flags. She had kept count on her way to the house to feed the turtles. She knew when a flag was put up; she noticed the holes growing larger in the ones that had been hanging too long in the cold. But after counting, she folded them away in her mind and cleared the streets to a time of less chaos. This is where she wanted her love of Akio to live—among the calm, pretty lanes of Kadoma, on the mossy backs of turtles, and in the purifying cold of the green pond of the turtle house.

And it was there that she daydreamed of her family with Akio. She imagined their children, gave them names and quirks and personalities, little arguments and little passions. Mineko assigned them bedrooms, walking through the house and seeing mats and toy trucks and dolls spread out. She imagined a mama cat giving birth in the genkan and spaniels running through the yard. She imagined herself at a desk in the corner, designing a new gazebo for the pond or an arched bridge to span the stream after the rainy season, Akio rubbing her neck because she had spent too much time looking down. She imagined improvements to the home, could hear the hammering that would be needed as they replaced boards and updated the kitchen. And in all these dreams, so real that she could nearly disappear into them, Akio was there, by her side, smiling.

On February 15, a telegram was delivered to the Sato home. As was village tradition, Akio's mother and father came to the Kamemoto home, choosing to walk most of the distance in the cold. Mineko watched as they came through the gate, snow thick on Mrs. Sato's umbrella. The crocheting she had been working on much of the winter, an impressive length of lace that wound into a cobra-like pile at her feet, fluttered as her father opened the door and a cold draft came in. There was a quiet, wordless hello. Mineko dropped the hook, her stitches falling apart, unknotting themselves before they hit the ground.

From Mrs. Sato, Mineko received the small official photo of Akio in his uniform.

There was no funeral, no pyre lit, just a small gathering at the temple and a flag draped on the Satos' gate. Had they been an arranged match, a smaller flag would have been placed on the Kamemoto gate, but because they were a love match, there would be nothing.

Nothing, nothing, nothing. The words took root in Mineko's very soul. Akio was now nothing. He once had a body, but now they waited for bone fragments in a box to be returned at a later time. Then they'd be able to pick through them, arrange them in an urn, place him to sleep with his ancestors. But only if a body had been found. Or maybe there had been and it wasn't identifiable. Nothing had been specified. The telegram raised more questions than answers. The Imperial Army gave few details inside their frilly language about honor and glory.

What she knew and what she carried with her: Akio had indeed attended the Shōgatsu celebration at the officers' home. No one knew at what time, if they came to eat with the other men, or if they came after, if the meal was separate from the higher-ups, or if they filled their plates from the same table. What was known was that a member of a guerrilla group had become a cook, had planted himself within the ranks of servants and waited, months and months, until he took the poison provided by the Hans and used it in the feast. Which food, no one knew. How many died, no one knew. They were told simply that the garrison was quickly overrun with local men and women, waiting in the snow for a sign. Mineko imagined the raucous soldiers, drinking and eating and then suddenly growing ill, dying one by one until the mansion that Akio had described in his letters was quiet. Just lights on through windows, just a poisoned feast growing cold, a Buddha surrounded by orange slices and flowers overlooking the entire scene. Eventually, a fire was set, that night or the next day, or maybe it was the fire that had killed so many, not the poison. Who knew really?

Mineko's sleeping brain dreamed every night that she was outside the officers' garret, that she could see Akio leaving the party, walking along the path that led to the guesthouse. In his hands, he carried a bowl, he was singing a song. When he went inside, a light flicked on, gently, then the singing stopped. In the dream, Mineko screamed, but no one heard her, and she couldn't move, her body wet and dripping, stuck in a glass box. A pale, silent swan flew from the roof of the house where Akio lay dying, a swan with wide wings and no water in sight, flying into the moon, like a painting. It was a dream that would repeat for hours, night after night, for many years, a dream that she would awake from sweating, but to which she always wanted to return.

Six months passed slowly, painfully. Mineko carried Akio's photo with her at all times. To keep it from becoming too worn, she made a small canvas pouch for it, safety-pinning it onto her camisole. The family moved in a quiet dance around her. In between her duties, Fumiko would sit mournfully next to Mineko for a few minutes, her silence a vigil. Even Hisako took a break from pestering her sister, which Mineko did not fully appreciate. She wanted her younger sister to say something, anything. She wanted a reason to pounce, and yet she felt undone and open, as if her skin had been removed and she was all nerves and muscles out in the world. Nerves and muscles choking down breakfast. Nerves and muscles trudging to the turtle house. Nerves and muscles waiting, for what, she did not know.

Gossip spread that soon there would be Americans coming. Americans! Big men, dirty feet, and loud voices. And although the newspaper proclaimed victories each week, tiny islands that Mineko had to look up on a map to locate, the number of flags draped seemed to be too many. She came to feel that someone was lying, even mentioned it surreptitiously to her father, who shook his head and suggested that it was her severe sadness that caused such thoughts. But he, too, stopped sleeping, often out in the garden in the middle of the night. Mineko sometimes watched him, pacing, staring up at the moon. He lost so much more weight that the doctor visited twice in the spring.

It was her father who came to her one morning and suggested that the weather was now warm enough, and perhaps she'd like to go for a swim. Mineko had never imagined he found her swimming habit likable, although he had never confronted her on the subject. But the idea of being in the pond, of feeling the sloppy stones beneath her feet, made her queasy.

"I don't know if I'll ever swim again."

"You will, my daughter. I know this loss is great. I have lost people, too. But there will be an opening, a moment from the gods that will help you move on. It will be like a foothold when you're hiking—remember when we hiked when you were young?" Her father sipped some of the medicinal tea and tried not to grimace.

Mineko nodded. But it was difficult to remember scrambling over rocks with her father. Childhood felt so long ago.

Nearly another year passed. The days were slow-fast-slow-fast. Food was even more scarce, so Mineko was constantly hungry. She awoke, tried to find food for her family, slept, and repeated the pattern, which tightened the knot inside her gut. She joined up to dig ditches next to the main roads, in case of air raids, foxhole shelters for locals to hide in, and, ultimately, to fight from when needed. The Americans were coming, the rumors continued.

When timid Fumiko was ordered to visit the black market by Hana, Mineko went in her stead after a particularly harrowing visit. She wanted to deal with the rude men in ugly tunics, their rough language. Mineko wanted a fight. At first they teased her, but then, when she stabbed her knife into the desk, they saw her seriousness, muttering that she acted like someone who had nothing left to lose, and Mineko laughed hard and loud until the black-market men shooed her away, but not before she carried a small bag of potatoes and an even smaller bag of barley.

She dropped off her prizes in the kitchen to an amazed Fumiko.

"How did you do it?" Fumiko lowered her voice. "They only grabbed at my breasts until I ran away crying."

But Mineko didn't know how to explain the change that had come over her. Perhaps, she pondered, she had fermented with sadness. Her independent streak was now a ravine, her fearlessness was now, at times, almost suicidal. She patted the knife she kept tucked into the wrap that held up her pants.

"I'm different."

"You're the same, just *more* so."

A few evenings after the first black market visit, at the turtle house, Mineko changed into her swimming suit, slowly. She had been visiting, but only briefly, rarely wandering into the house. It now held too many memories. She undressed behind a yew as the sun set, not daring to enter. That time of day was yet too tender.

The air had a strange charge to it; she had felt it down her spine all day, ever since awaking. Maybe that was why she decided to swim—maybe icy water would dull this feeling. Maybe it was just her grief, playing tricks on her. But others might have felt it as well. Mineko's neighbors seemed corpse-like and slower-moving as she walked through the late-afternoon lanes to the turtle house. We are all dying inside, she had thought.

She waded in and shivered. A turtle dove in with a tiny splash, and for a moment she closed her eyes and felt Akio near. Mineko went deep and deeper still. Then she went below, eyes open in green water, swimming to the bottom, touching, touching. She could stay below, perhaps. The sun's last rays reached into the pond, but then got darker and darker until the farthest reaches of the pool were a green that was more black, the color of nori. Mineko's lungs burned, but she knew she could stay longer beneath.

It was then an odd shadow passed overhead, a large bird, a swan maybe, but then another and another, so many in fact that these swans were flying too close and too quickly, and there was a noise—a muffled roaring—and the bottom of the pond, where Mineko reached out one foot, tremored. Up she went, like a bullet, and above she spied the end of a line of planes. Foreign planes. A memory from a newsreel popped into her head, B-29s, American. She squinted at the tails, and yes, they looked like that, silver hateful things. But then they disappeared.

Looking for information, making maps, she thought, shaking away the strange sighting. Mineko swam to the edge and made her way, dripping, to the gazebo, where she had brought a few rotten carrots that had been snuck into the middle of the bundle she had stood in line for. Two hours for carrots that were limp and black, surrounded by a skinny cadre of fresher, yellowed ones, limp but not quite gone. She cut them with her knife and tossed them slowly. The turtles swam and emerged and gulped all she had. It was getting dark and her eyes had to adjust to the lack of light. She lay back and looked at the beams of the gazebo, where a female wolf spider had made an elaborate web and was ceremoniously wrapping a sad fly in a shroud of white.

"Good for you, madam spider," Mineko said. She must have dozed because when she awoke she was dry, her mouth parched, but her brain was shaking inside her skull. It was now night and the gazebo rattled. She opened her eyes and indeed the entire world was moving in shadow, and it was them, again, the planes, flying low, a vibration she could feel in her gut. Mineko sprinted to the edge of the property, where the river cascaded down the cliff, and there, all around, were falling bundles, silver white babies with a funny twist to the blanket that created a bow at the feet. Mineko squinted. She could hear them cry as they fell. Waaaaaaaaaah, waaaaaaaaaaaah. She felt buzzy as she watched the swaddled babies fall, all with the same speed, and she thought to herself, Why, those are heavy little ones, otherwise they wouldn't be able to—

A roar behind her flattened Mineko to the ground, her chin hitting the grass. Her mouth filled with blood. All was black in front of her, something wrong with her sight, but she belly-crawled to a tree, her hand feeling the bark, then to another tree, back to the pond, to the turtles.

Bombs not babies. Water around her ankles, water around her knees, she dove into the pond and made her way below, and somehow, maybe the cold shocking her brain, her eyes worked again, and just feeling the water plants swaying in the black water around her made Mineko feel alive and ready. She burst through the top of the water and saw a corner of the turtle house roof on fire, but she did not have time to retrieve the gift that Akio had left for her inside or gather the quilt that they had wrapped around themselves that night. She watched as the fire that crept across the roof grew, devouring the space above her future children's bedrooms. No, no time to stop it, she thought, and Mineko was running, barefoot and barelegged, down the hill to home, through fire and screams, back to her family.

The whole village was outside, every face frightened, mouths agape, fire everywhere. Mineko ran past a child, clutching a sweet potato, and she wanted to scoop up the little one, but another blast and that space was gone and Mineko was thrown again off balance, into something. Then she was up again, running. She found the bridge, the one she had tossed the reeds off so long ago, and below it, in the water, were people who had made a human chain from one edge to the other, thinking that the engineering marvel that was overhead would shield them. People were floating away. Mineko thought, *They will bomb these bridges soon*, so she ran over the top and yelled this, her voice disappearing, and then turned to race down the rocky hill toward home. She heard an explosion behind her and knew the bridge was gone, as the bomb babies kept falling from the sky, an unending birth of fire-bringers.

She was on her street, or she thought she was on her street, houses had disappeared in flames all around her. She counted where she felt the homes should be, moving through the acidic black clouds of smoke, ichi, ni, san, shi, go, roku, hichi, hachi, ku . . . At the ninth house from the corner, she yelled for her father. Fire was falling from the sky and leaping up from the ground, and Mineko wanted only the water then, the turtle house and the pond, so she imagined this as she pushed. A searing wind that was continuous drove against her, and Mineko thrust her body into it. Hands grabbed at her and squeezed her arm, a dark ghost put its face close to her and then wailed, burying its head into her neck.

Hisako.

"Where's Father?" Mineko screamed, but the roar had changed from the mechanical sound of gas engines to the thunderous roar of fire. Hisako began to skip away backward, the heat taking the gravity from her, and Mineko sprinted a few steps toward her and grabbed at her arms, worked her hands to her shoulders, then embraced her, dragged her.

"The ditches," Hisako screamed, and Mineko knew that's where the family was and so they made their way to the deep shelter and threw themselves in, landing on other wiggling bodies.

"We can't lose each other," Mineko yelled at Hisako, and they pushed through people, only whites of eyes showing. She squeezed Hisako's wrist and both walked and crawled. She heard her name on repeat, but the voices were scattered. Some sounded like neighbors, one sounded like Akio, one sounded like herself. A woman, the old midwife, usually so stoic, was just calling names, the names of all Kadoma, maybe all the names of those she had pulled into the light from darkness.

Still the fire fell in chunks.

Finally, she felt a tug on her thigh. Fingernails in the muscle, and it was Fumiko. Her hair was burnt to her left temple and across her cheek-bone. Beneath Fumiko was Mineko's mother and Fumiko's mother, both women pressed into the oil mud, wailing.

"Father? Where is he?"

"We saw him last running toward the abandoned house. Looking for you!" Fumiko said.

Hisako wedged her body between the older women. Fumiko lay her body on top of them, covering them again, and Mineko knew that her friend did this out of deference to her family, even in fire, remembering her position, and Mineko felt thankful for her, wanting to lie down and wait until this was all over.

But first, she must find her father. And so she scrambled out of the ditch, pulling up with her arms and legs, just a body running in the remains of a bathing suit. Running through sparks and debris back to the turtle house, and when she got close, she saw the flames flying high above the trees, where the beautiful roof had been, and she felt Akio behind her, pushing her. She made her way up the hill and through the plinths. The grass was on fire, and it was spreading across the yard, and there she saw her father, there next to the water's edge, staring up at the sky. Mineko ran to him, grabbed his arm, and walked him into the pond. Her father said nothing but continued to look up. They were waist-deep, then chest-deep, then neck-deep. Mineko held him close, safer in the water, but surrounded just the same.

Chapter 11

Autumn Leaves Senior Living Community is the last visit of the day. Aunt Mae set up the tours from least expensive to "somebody better sell our mineral rights to pay for this" with the hope that Grandminnie would settle somewhere in the middle and that by noon, we'd be tucking into chopped-beef sandwiches, decision made. Things have not gone that way.

My mother is holding flyers with different floor plans. Unlike the other two we visited, Autumn Leaves is brand-new, having opened just six months ago. It is a redbrick two-story building and U-shaped, with the base of the U for the cafeteria, dining room, living room—all the group-related spaces—and the arms of the U for the suites and mini-apartments. Each residence has an expanse of windows overlooking either the highway, parking area, adjacent field, or, if you really want to pay more, the well-manicured courtyard complete with water feature.

It's a well-designed building, and although I hate to say it, well worth the fortune it will cost to keep Grandminnie here for the rest of her natural life. My dad already has a list of things he will sell to help pay for her first year here.

"Where's the pool?" Grandminnie asks, grabbing a map.

"Not open yet," Dad says. "Next year."

"So soon!" Mom says, and then she beams at the front desk lady, a woman wearing a dark green button-down with an orange leaf embroidered on the pocket, tucked into brown pants.

She *looks* like a tree, Grandminnie whispers, a little too loudly, to me.

The furnishings at Autumn Leaves are all shades of fall. Sadie, the woman dressed as the tree, mentions they have just finished the interiors with utmost care. I hear Mom and Aunt Mae oooh and aaah. My dad clears his throat. We walk in a close gaggle through a grand sitting room with a wall of books and a sliding library ladder. Grandminnie pokes me in the ribs and looks at me. That looks risky, her glance says. There's a gas fire that doesn't appear to give off any heat, and the smell of vanilla candles and bleach hangs in the air. Mostly, older women sit around. One elderly man holds court at a wooden game table. It's difficult to tell the ages of the residents—a few appear to be around Grandminnie's age, the majority much older.

The dining room is equally fancy with white, starched tablecloths and small crystal salt and pepper shakers. Real carnations are arranged nicely in white vases. The rug beneath our feet is thick, maybe too thick for someone with a walker, but perfectly vacuumed with lines that run in neat rows.

"We have a regular menu and also theme nights on Thursdays and Fridays. Tex-Mex fiesta is coming up soon. We have Italian nights—those are really popular. And then"—the woman pauses and contemplates her words—"we have Oriental Night as well. Next one is in May sometime, I believe."

My grandmother's ears are pricked. I sense her muscles tightening.

"See, Minnie!" my mom says, touching Grandminnie's arm.

My aunt and dad remain quiet.

"Oh yes, sweet-and-sour chicken, eggrolls, moo goo gai pan, the works!"

Sadie has lost her audience. With the woman's menu recitation, even Mom knows what is going through Grandminnie's mind.

I wait for her to say something. Her jaw is set, she balls her hands into fists. Where is the speech that we have all internalized over the years? *I am from Japan. Very many different countries and many different people are Asian, but my country is Japan.*

Sadie, sensing her misstep, rushes through the next two rooms and into the Maple Suite, with its wide entrance, its bright, spotless (and large) bathroom, a tiny Formica countered area with a microwave, mini-fridge, and coffee maker, and a single bedroom and sitting room combination. There's a section of floor-to-ceiling windows overlooking the highway that runs between Dennis and Dallas. Thick curtains can be drawn to shut out all the light. A television sits inside a mahogany entertainment center, and it's on a loop of Autumn Leaves information: exercise classes, wine nights, Wal-Mart trips, excursions. There are photos of happy seniors drinking hot tea. Everyone, everywhere, is *people from here.*

Yet it's a really nice room and a very lovely place. It would be perfect for any other grandmother. I sit on the edge of the bed, watching my parents and Aunt Mae interact with Grandminnie, coming up with stories of how she'll live here, how she'll make more friends, how she'll dominate the sewing circles (true), how she'll love the heated pool and swim lanes (also true).

"Yoshi can live with us," Mom offers. "You can see her whenever you want."

"Yes, because we don't allow pets, I'm so sorry to say, Mrs. Cope." I can tell Sadie has said this exact phrase time and again. Little dogs and cats and parakeets, all relegated to new homes.

Grandminnie sighs.

She runs her hand over the beige Formica, brushing invisible crumbs to the floor. She looks up, where daisy-shaped sprinkler heads are embedded in the fissured drop-ceiling tiles. Then she waves her hand in the air, scattering imaginary chickens. She does it again, angrily. Between gritted teeth, she mutters the word *fine.*

We can't sleep. She'll be moving in two weeks, as soon as they get her studio apartment ready, and Mom says she needs that time to get Grandminnie's new place together—nice linens and coffee mugs and a few odds and ends for decorations. Mae is donating a beautiful painted screen that Grandminnie has always admired, small butterflies floating over shapely cedars, and my mother is using that screen as her color palette. Mom is sincerely trying to get this decor right, as if the correct Japanese-inspired stoneware would make her mother-in-law happy.

Stephie called after we got back from Autumn Leaves, wanting to chat about finding a new roommate again. *You have a job there now, so I was just wondering*, she said. She also mentioned that my former boss had been asking about me.

What? I asked, my voice louder and up an octave.

He seems genuinely concerned about you.

Listen, just stay out of it, I had said in a quiet rush. I took the phone and stretched the cord long and straight into my closet. *Please trust me on this.*

I don't know what you exactly have against him, but, anyway, he asked for your number at home, so I gave it to him. I hope this is okay.

What? When?

Today. Just a little while ago. He caught up with me in the parking garage.

I pick at a scab right above my ear in my hairline. After hanging up, I dry heave in the bathroom.

Tonight, I *69ed two phone calls back-to-back, and they both were from an unknown number with an Austin area code.

I think of that afternoon in late January, of how it felt like spring had snuck into town for a boozer down Sixth Street. I knew it was a joke from Mother Nature and that it would be sharp and cold again by midnight. Stephie and I made it to the BT&B rooftop deck just as the sun was turning everything soft pink. We grabbed beers from the coolers that were kept out there, rain or shine. We found our normal seats. We talked about our evening plans. I offered to bake a frozen pizza for us. She offered to make a salad to go with it.

Mr. Birkit picked up the mic to the portable sound system, and it squeaked.

"Oh, here we go," Stephie said. She hated Birkit, called him the Skeez in Spectacles. The Double S. It was an accurate description.

"I have some great news today. Just a few minutes ago, I got a very special signature on a very special contract."

No one seemed shocked, Birkit was always landing big deals.

"But this signature is one that is going to improve all our futures here at BT&B. Come on out here, son. Meet our new partner! Darren Miles."

I felt a flush of adrenaline. Birkit explained that Darren would be tasked with overseeing large-scale commercial projects. *My team.*

I hadn't seen Darren since graduation. I heard it through the grapevine that he had left UT and moved to Seattle, where there was a boom. But then, there he was that January evening, on the rooftop deck of BT&B, holding a Tecate, waving to the party as old man Birkit beamed. Around our office building, construction was springing up, some of our own designs growing out of freshly scraped dirt. The noise of progress was unavoidable.

My right hand is in my hair, my freshly cut fingernails digging in.

"Stop it, Lia. Put on your gloves." Grandminnie's hand is on my arm.

Darren had seen me, sitting there with Stephie, and he smiled. After his introduction and a few words—I didn't hear what he said, as the sound of my heartbeat and the crushing cacophony of an excavator breaking concrete next door took over my brain—he handed back the mic and started walking toward me. Without even a hello, he swept me up into a huge hug, lifting me a little off the ground. It was grandiose, too much, and when our bodies pulled apart, I felt the eyes of the gathering on *us.*

Dutifully, I find the polka-dot gloves on the bedside table and slip them on. My grandmother has on a pair, too, over a generous amount of hand cream. *I might be over seventy, but my hands look fifty,* she always says. *Maybe even forty-five.*

"Long time, no see," Darren had said, again slipping his right arm around me, shaking new coworkers' hands with his left. Stephie cocked her head and mouthed *What?* I maneuvered away to my seat, embarrassed, but before I could regain my composure, Darren yelled back to me that we were going out to dinner that night.

"Dos Compadres, for old times' sake—seven?"

Stephie jerked her head to look at me. "Looks like you have a hot new boyfriend, Cope," she said.

I hear my grandmother breathe in the dark.

"I can't sleep with all your picking and sighing, Lia-chan."

Finally, up she stands, moves to the dresser, and rummages around in her drawer. The click and flash of a lighter. She opens up the window, magics the screen off and settles it against the wall, spreads out the quilt with one big flap of her arms, and is outside again. I grab the recorder, follow her, my socks clinging to the asphalt shingles. I lie next to her.

"I'm sorry they're making you do this."

"*I'm* doing this."

"I'm sorry they are making you *feel* like you need to do this."

The sky is clear, and we are still far from ambient city lights—not for long, my dad warns, we will be all suburban one day. Dallas and Fort Worth are coming to gobble us up. But tonight, the stars multiply the longer we lie outside and look up.

"I am used to moving, Lia. This is what happens. After Kadoma, I moved to Tokyo, looking for Fumiko. After Tokyo, I moved to Curtain with James and kids. Now I am moving to Autumn Leaves."

"But you don't want to."

"I never wanted to move. Anywhere. That's what's so funny about it all."

"You said you went looking for Fumiko. What happened?"

"Oh, after the bombing, nothing left. Nothing. Just a few houses made it. Ours was mostly gone. Just one wall still there. My father and I made a tent. Hisako and me and Mother and Father, we stayed in that tent. But no food. Water from the stream, but we were worried about drinking it."

I wonder if this is why she's always pushed food on us grandkids, why she had previously prized her five-gallon bottled-water dispenser with a passion.

"I saw one of the women from the post office line. She said if I came to steal the leftovers in her husband's fields, he wouldn't stop me. Only radishes left. This is why I've never planted them in my garden. I love their taste, but I will never pull them up again. I went in the night and dug them out with my hands. Just puny ones. Tiny things. A man—her husband, I don't know, too dark—tried to get me to leave. He yelled at me with some bad names, but I kept digging. My fingernails fell off, I dug so hard."

"Why haven't you ever told this? Does Dad know? Aunt Mae?"

She doesn't answer but pauses, looking down at her fingernails.

"And acorns. Did you know you can eat acorns? And grasshoppers."

She takes a deep breath and closes her eyes. She has a few skin tags on her eyelids. I know tomorrow morning she'll pick at them in front of the mirror and curse as I brush my teeth. I try to take her hand, but she shakes mine away. The cigarette smoke curls a flimsy white snake from her other hand.

"You asked me to do something for you. You said you wanted something. Remember?"

"Nah."

"You want to go home, that's what you said."

"I bet all the food at this old-person place tastes like one of those slow-cooker meals your mother makes. All the same, those. Soft and salty."

"Did you mean home like in Japan or home as in here?"

"The swimming pool will be nice. I will have to look at all those old ladies. But I'll stay in good shape—better shape maybe."

"Grandminnie?"

She shushes me and tells me to go, make sure my parents aren't snooping, she says, and declares that the only thing she wants in the world is some Dutch chocolate ice cream from the freezer outside. I take the recorder, but catch the last of her words as I fold my body through the window.

"I want both."

Book 2

Chapter 12

Tachikawa Air Base, Tokyo
April 1947

The homes had been built in just over two months. The men called it
American Village, Phase I. The wives called it Box City. Each house was
a white rectangular prism with a simple roof. Each front door had three
steps leading to it and a small porch, the size of a steamer trunk. There
were matching windows, matching bushes, and everything was in neat
rows. After the houses are put up, they're gonna start on the theater and
the swimming pool, the men said. It'll be real nice, they said. There were
already clubs for both the officers and the NCOs. One was nicer than the
other.

Mineko opened the front door and was surprised at how easily it flew
open, how flimsy it was compared to how it looked. She left the pram
with her sleeping baby outside, sidled up next to a tiny maple tree that
had just been planted and that already looked sickly.

The house was empty, hollow, but full of light. In the square window-
panes, glass. Mineko opened the bathroom door and there was a tiny
toilet on which to sit and an enamel sink and a stand-up shower in need
of a curtain.

The hallway held two other doors. One room was slightly bigger than
the other and had a high window. The other room was small and still. The
floors were green linoleum throughout, and when Mineko squinted, she
pretended it was spring grass.

She had expected more ladies touring the homes, but back at the picnic grounds the American ladies stayed in one sticky group like nattō, the few new Japanese wives in another. The husbands were in several groups, according to rank, and they had already seen the homes being built, so it was old news to them.

Mineko still ached from laboring. She was healing, and her undergarments were lined with gauze. Mineko had wanted solitude with Mae that morning, just five days old, not to attend a picnic, but James refused. So she had wandered off as soon as she found an opportunity, and even though she heard James call her name, she kept walking as she pushed the pram, as if she couldn't hear him, as if the small military band was still playing and not on a break. Her baby needed to be fed. She wanted to see these houses.

Mineko sat on the porch steps, stretched and spread her legs, her chitsu aching and swollen. She lit a cigarette and blew the smoke away from Mae. She reached down with a gloved hand and touched her baby's bootied foot, then took off the glove so she could see if Mae was too warm or too cold. Gloves are stupid, she thought, created for women too scared to touch anything. Mae's pink socks swallowed her slender feet, a gift from across the sea from a woman named Dimple who had sent them over without a card. Simple little things. Probably took just an evening to make, but stitched with a knowledgeable hand. The lack of any greeting card or note gave Mineko the impression that this Dimple didn't approve of James's new life, but she perhaps had a softness inside her. The gift was more than Mineko's own mother had sent.

Mineko peered down the lane, ready to spring up like a squirrel if she saw anyone.

Tachikawa Air Base was formerly Tachikawa Air Field. It had been around for many years, originally the Imperial Guard's headquarters for protecting Tokyo, which was due east. Baby Mae had been born in Tachikawa town in a tiny apartment with a midwife, but as soon as James had heard his daughter had come and was not being seen by a doctor, he arrived and took the baby to the air base hospital to have her checked out, coming back a few hours later, the baby simpering for her mother.

Because of this visit, Mae's birth certificate said Tachikawa Air Base. It also said Mae Cope, typed in fuzzy black letters.

"You might be a Cope, but I'm still a Kamemoto," Mineko said as a beetle landed on the hand she was touching the baby with.

James was sly, but Mineko had surmised this the first night she had met him, at the little ramen restaurant, which was just an ordering window and two rickety wooden tables outside. He had slid onto the bench seat across from her, along with a buddy who had picked up a bit of halting, childish Japanese.

"My friend wants to buy you dinner," the interpreter said.

"Tell your friend that I'm clearly already eating my dinner."

"So he says he'll give you money for the dinner you already are eating." The buddy was grinning, a sloppy, youthful smile.

"Tell him that will not be necessary. Besides, I saw him at my work earlier. I don't accept meals from men who come to my work."

The buddy spoke quickly to James, who pursed his lips and then shook his head no.

"Not him."

But Mineko knew he was lying. She had seen him as she delivered the small glasses of beer to the soldiers, and had felt him stare at her back as she counted out change. Even plain girls in Tokyo could get a date with an American if they wanted. In the months since arriving in Tokyo, all sorts of soldiers had tried to buy her dinner. A tall one with buck teeth. A short one who shuffled when he walked. Even an older one who had followed her home calling her Tokyo Baby. But this one was almost handsome, with his hat cocked to the side over heavy black eyebrows. Everything about him looked serious—a hard chin, a strained smile, eyes that were small and dark. He was not a large man, only a half foot taller than her, and she looked at his hands, tan from labor, that sat folded on the table.

Mineko stood and returned her bowl to the counter, told the old woman to look out for herself, and then began to walk away.

"Stop! I'm sorry. My friend just wants to talk. He's not a bad man. His name is James. He's from Texas. You know of Texas? Place with the cows, the big hats?"

Then James, in a fine, clear tenor, sang, "Give me land, lots of land, under starry skies above . . ."

And Mineko, for the first time in many, many months, had smiled.

Mineko snubbed out her cigarette and picked up baby Mae, who had begun to cry with hunger. She unbuttoned her blouse and looked around again to make sure she was alone, as the American ladies didn't like to see other women's breasts.

"Not too much, we don't have time," she said, and she squeezed and plopped her nipple into Mae's open maw. Mae's latch was forceful and greedy, which made Mineko oddly happy, as if she had created something that wasn't scared to fight for what she needed.

Mineko traced the edge of Mae's hairline with her finger, going behind her baby's tiny ear, noticing a little cradle cap, rough skin beginning to flake off in yellow scales.

"Oh, my little baby dragon! That's why you have such a strong mouth!"

Somewhere nearby, she heard a bugle call.

James and Mineko didn't go out on dates as much as they met after work at the noodle place. They didn't meet at bars because Mineko was tired of the smell of beer. There wasn't much conversation, as James had only a few Japanese phrases and Mineko knew only how to count money in English. Mineko never knew when she'd see him; she couldn't plan on it and many nights, walking home, he wouldn't show up at all. But then, sooner than later, he would be there, out of the darkness, calling her name, guiding her to a café by the elbow, speaking English in that funny way of his, slower, steadier. At dinner, he'd draw her little pictures of what Mineko understood was his home in Texas. He was good at sketching, something that Mineko tried not to admire, but his house with the tree, the windmill, the barn, the bull with the horns so ridiculously large she thought surely his pen was fibbing, these images were delightful. He never asked her to draw her home, she noted, but a beat later, she thought she never could. After dinner, he'd walk her back.

The place she lived was less of an apartment and more of a forgotten cloakroom, ten Mineko-feet by nine Mineko-feet. A few girls from work lived in this same building, which was painted with smoke and had large holes in the roof where fiery bombing debris had gone through it like hail. Mineko straightened out cans, cutting along the tops and bottoms with tin snips, slicing down one side and pounding the cylinder flat to patch the damage. In her room was a mildew-stained futon and vegetable crate for a table, six cheap candles, and, of course, her minogame, which had traveled with her all this way, heavy against her back in a patched knapsack. Before leaving Kadoma, she had visited the turtle house one last time, surprised to see it damaged but still standing. The minogame was in the great room where she'd left it, dirty but whole.

She had tried to get Fumiko to live with her in the shabby room, but she had offered excuse after excuse, always saying she was fine where she was. Fumiko was not fine, and Mineko knew this. The burn on her face was well healed by then, leaf-shaped and puckered. No, none of them were truly fine. *Little chicken*, Mineko would prompt, trying to get her to change her mind. Fumiko would just shake her head. Fumiko never called her monkey anymore.

So if it weren't for her turtle, it would have been a hopelessly lonely room, but each night it was waiting for her by her bed. Sometimes she kissed its nose before closing her eyes. Sometimes she fell asleep with her hand draped upon its bushy tail. She hoped that touching it would color her dreams with orange and pink, that for a while she'd be back swimming with him, eating candy in the wobbly gazebo, sugar coating her tongue. Sometimes it worked. But most often, her sleep was dreamless and as black as the room at night. Upon reflection and considering her current situation, she felt that this was perhaps as good as it could be. Shikata ga ni. Besides, was she really here anyway? All of her countrymen and -women, walking about with dead eyes, just skin-draped ghosts.

So when James took her hand one evening after dinner, she let him. That was that.

When he lifted her chin, gently, to kiss her, she let him.

When, after such a kiss, her eyes drifted to the side in response to a rat scuttling by, and James took his thumb and the side of his pointer finger and pinched the thin skin over her hip as hard as he could, she let him.

"Pay attention to me," he said. "Act grateful." But Mineko didn't understand him until years later when her English was much better. So much went misunderstood in those years.

Without a mirror and with fading candlelight and at an impossible angle, Mineko stretching her head over her shoulder like a crane, she tried to see the bruise James had made on her.

"I can't see it, so it's not there," Mineko whispered to the minogame.

But she could feel it still, slightly, a pulsing ache. Maybe she deserved this pinch. She had eaten orange slices while others were killing innocents without any mercy in her name. Little snippets of these stories were passed around, whispered in shame, and Mineko was beginning to think that it was perhaps just that they had been defeated. And, if so, she was getting off lightly.

He cracked his knuckles after dinner.

He hated making mistakes in his drawings, wadding up the paper with one errant line.

He smirked at younger officers' comments on the street, but never truly smiled.

He had two lines between his eyebrows, two crevices, like the monchu that stood guard over the path to the turtle house. They deepened and took on shadows and made him look battleworn and tired.

He did not use the swearing words that she had heard other soldiers use.

He gave her his coat when it rained.

He once walked away without her when she let his hand drop.

Then, two months into their meetings, while on the market street looking at stalls, lanterns casting a reddish glow on all of the faces, James pulled a stack of photos from his billfold. *Home*, he said, and it was just as he had drawn: land, sky, crooked trees, and cattle. A barn, a wide place in a small creek, a gate with a big crescent-shaped marking on a sign above, along with other marks. Mineko looked at the nameplate on his chest and realized it was his name. COPE.

His home was marked with his name. This felt important to her, steady, unchanging. Something shifted inside her. But before she could nod and say "good," a dark-dressed man raced past, a purse in his hands, pushing Mineko to the ground. She landed hard and could feel a few sharp stones embedded in the side of her leg and in her palms. Mineko looked up, the crowd parted just so, just in time to see James now at the end of the street punching the man. Mineko bounded up and sprinted toward him. In the dancing lamplight, she could see that it wasn't a man whom James was beating, but a boy, one of the charinkos who lived in abandoned places. A boy with a soft baby face, now bloodied. A boy who squeezed his eyes shut. A boy who dropped the purse and who then vomited on the purse, a starving boy's vomit, nothing but rose-colored liquid gushing to the ground.

"Stop, stop!" Mineko said in English.

But he did not stop. And no one stopped him because James outranked the men around him.

Finally, Mineko managed to pull James away, and he stopped hitting the boy as if he had wanted to stop, dropping his fists as if he were doing nothing at all, turning and walking back to the stall where the onions had started to burn on the flat top, all the people still watching this scene.

The boy disappeared. He was so beaten, Mineko didn't know how. Maybe the sidewalk swallowed him. The purse stayed in its place. James ordered some dinner. Mineko, full of the heat of fear, ducked and disappeared into the crowd, walking at first and then running.

The American wives and the Japanese wives were folding up their separate quilts. The men were nearby, still talking. This picnic had been put on by one of the many organizations with funny names within the US military. Mineko could never keep them straight, as much as she tried. Each organization had a purpose, each gathering a reason. This one, she understood, was to let the women meet one another and to allow everyone to see the new American Village, Phase I. The American women were new to Japan, as the military had just deemed Japan "safe enough" for the more adventurous wives. The Japanese wives were new to the base because the military had just deemed them "safe enough" to marry the soldiers. *With so much in common*, Mineko thought, *we should be sitting together*, but it also made much sense that they were not.

Having men in common is never enough.

Even within the group of Japanese women, old divisions lay quiet and waiting. Some of these girls were country dwellers, raised among only their own family. Some were small-town girls, like Mineko, daughters of decent means at one time. And many were city girls, girls from Tokyo proper who had somehow survived the bombing, had come out of destroyed homes and into the arms of the soldiers.

And most importantly, the biggest difference: some were locally married by a well-meaning Presbyterian or Methodist missionary preacher, and a few, but not many, were in marriages permitted by the Japanese government.

Mineko was neither, but she did not let on.

"Hello again," a few of the Japanese girls said.

"Did you go to feed the little precious one?"

"Did you go back to look at our houses?"

"Did you have a chance to get the ice cream? It is still there, but just a little melted."

Mineko smiled and answered their questions but she still moved, slowly, away. She never felt like being still because being still meant engaging in conversation. She hadn't felt like talking much since becoming pregnant with Mae, after her falling-out with Fumiko. Since Mae's birth, Mineko only wanted to speak to Mae and to hear her odd baby gurgles in return.

On the edge of the group of men was James. He felt her presence, hearing the squeaky wheels of the pram, and he turned.

"And here is my baby," he said. James was proud of Mae in front of these men. He was distant most other times.

"She barely looks Japanese!"

"You gonna teach her to ride one day, hoss?"

"She's gonna be a looker."

The men were warm and friendly. Mineko tried to catch their comments, but only gleaned a few words.

"Where did you go?" James asked in Japanese. He was improving in his language. Mineko had to give him credit for his quick mind.

"Oh, to see the new house and feed the baby."

"We get a corner one. I already discussed it."

"Whatever you think is right."

"It will have a bigger yard."

"That will be good for Mae."

"Where did you go again?"

"I told you, to see the new house and feed Mae."

"Don't you have something you need to say?"

Mineko stared at him, blankly.

"Don't I get a thank-you?"

"Oh yes. Thank you."

James sneered slightly, imperceptible to anyone but Mineko. Mineko felt her insides heave.

"I have news. Tell you later."

After the boy and the purse incident, Mineko started taking the long way back to the apartment block after work. She already ended her day after ten p.m., so with her new walk, she wasn't arriving in her room until close to midnight. The places she now bought food weren't as good and were more expensive, so she didn't eat as much and went to bed with her stomach talking to her, moaning its displeasure. She would wind herself into a ball, squeezing her abdominal muscles into her spine, trying to quiet the noise.

Hunger wound around her grief to form a tight twist inside her. She took this twisted feeling to work, where she weakly tried to be bright and pleasing, but where she put the beer glasses down too hard, where she let the cabinets slam.

The women at work told her she needed to forget the past and live for the present. We have accepted this, they said, and look what we have to show! Gifts from the P/X: chocolates and tuna in cans and stockings and thick lotions for hands and feet. Lipstick in three shades of red. Hair ribbons. Hairpins. Stop being so drab, Good Girl Mineko!

After two weeks, James was outside her door when she arrived home. He held up a small brown paper sack that Mineko could tell, even in the low light, was transparent with grease.

"Ika geso karaage. Did I say that right?"

Mineko took a deep breath. She could smell the salty squid.

"Let's go inside," James said in that long, slow voice.

Mineko nodded and led him to her tiny room, shutting the door behind him.

• • •

When Mineko became pregnant with an American soldier's baby, the woman in charge of the building, hoping for better treatment, had given her a slightly larger yet still leaking room, this one with a window for light. Mineko had done the same trick with the tin cans. The room came with a newer futon and a cheaply made tatami. With money that James gave her, she bought a tiny cradle and an oil lamp, since electricity was still spotty. She bought a few pieces of clothing for Mae and enough diapers for a day's use, cleaning the soiled ones in the busy shared laundry at night. She bought slippers for her room and a small washbasin for Mae's baths. And even though James did not live there, as he had to be back in barracks by eleven p.m. each night, his presence was felt in every corner, by what his status could provide.

Mineko walked the pram to its owner, a woman who lent it for a couple sen for such use. Then she carried Mae back to her room and placed the sleeping baby in the crib, although she needed a good changing. The light clicked on easily in the room, which meant the electricity was working, so Mineko plugged in her Westinghouse hot plate, another gift from James, and began to boil water for a little bath. Mae was plagued with diaper rash and fighting it had become Mineko's small war.

Soon there was a knock and then James opened the door.

"Stinks," he said, looking into the cradle where Mae slept. He lit a cigarette. Mineko waited to be offered one, which he would do if he was in a good mood. He did not.

"We will be married on Tuesday," he said. "That's my news."

Mineko let these words sink in. Almost everyone thought they were already local-married. But this chance passed them by, neither partner taking advantage at the same time. When Mineko wanted a local marriage, soon after her monthly flow stopped, James was uncertain and stopped meeting her. When James had come around, Mineko was too morning sick. Then James was sent to another base up north, and he stayed there for four months. Mineko both worried he'd never return and then, once used to the idea that James was gone, was concerned he would come back.

When James arrived back at Tachikawa, she was out of the money he had left and had been laid off from her job. She mentioned the local marriage again, and he said nothing. Then finally, when he did decide he wanted to go to a preacher, Mineko's belly had popped out like a balloon. No, they couldn't go to a minister with a pregnant belly on display.

Rumors had circulated that the US government might be issuing American marriage certificates, albeit briefly, to those couples already locally married. Was this what he was offering to her?

"American marriage?" she asked.

"Not yet. Local. Over the summer, real certificate. So you two can live on base. Get Mae out of this dump." James motioned to the apartment, just to make sure Mineko understood.

Mineko looked around at the better-but-still-awful room.

"Two months. Then base house. Best place you've ever lived, I bet."

"Tuesday at the chapel?"

The chapel was on the edge of Tachikawa AB. It was cinder block and painted a glossy white. Soon after it was built, gifts from American churches arrived. There was a plaster Jesus holding a smiling lamb from the Catholics and a carved oak kneeler bench from the Presbyterians. The Methodists sent benches with backs and red cushions. Mineko didn't know that there were other Christian churches because they hadn't sent anything yet.

"No, someplace else. I'll tell you when I know."

"I'll wear kimono," Mineko said flatly.

"No, a dress."

"I have no correct dress. But I can borrow a fine—"

"This is an American wedding. Wear what you have on, that's good enough."

The fried-squid night, Mineko ate and ate, standing up inside her dark room, James not taking a bite.

"Good?" he had asked, and she nodded yes. He reached out and took the sack from her hands, wadded it up, and threw it in the corner of the room. Then, he put his mouth on hers, even though she knew she smelled like a fish market. James didn't ask, but reached up under her dress and pulled down her bloomers. He stuck his pointer finger inside her, as if testing the temperature outside or to see if a breeze was blowing. Deeming her weather acceptable, he pulled down his pants.

"Please lay down," he said in Japanese, and Mineko did. Out of instinct, she forced the minogame into the corner. James did not notice it.

Then he pushed himself inside her. Somewhere, during his pushing, he unbuttoned her blouse and wrenched down her camisole, but finding small breasts on her muscular chest, he made a frustrated face, like he had seen an oasis that had been a mirage.

She felt a strange surge of triumph at his moment of disappointment. Mineko divided herself. The woman Akio had loved was the best part of Mineko, this woman, lying here, was the leftovers.

So while he moved and worked, Mineko stayed still, enjoying only the salty taste of food lingering in her mouth. While she hated herself for it, she thought that this barter was not altogether awful. There is no purity after a war, she thought. This will be over soon.

For three more nights in a row, he arrived by her side after work, already with some sort of dinner in tow, and walked her to her apartment, his hand placed on the back of her neck, guiding her.

"Tsuyoi," he said one night near the apartment, and Mineko wondered if he was calling her strong or commenting on himself.

"Me?" she asked. And he nodded.

It was a strange compliment, a truth that she appreciated about herself, but didn't think others noticed.

The someplace else where they were to marry was an empty room behind a bar that was the least favorite of the soldiers because of the prices. Mae was in the borrowed pram, in the corner. It was her morning nap, so she stayed blissfully unaware of her parents' nuptials.

The minister was a soldier with dark skin. His uniform had a little cross on the chest. Mineko had seen these men only from afar. They had never come to her previous workplace, although she knew that they frequented another, and stayed in groups away from the white soldiers. Mineko thought of the groups of wives at the picnic, each in their own clump. No darker faces there, either.

"Negro Chaplain, different unit," James explained.

Mineko looked at her own arm and the face of the man in front of her. She was barely a shade lighter than this man.

"Go," James said. And he looked behind him at the doorway, the curtain closed. Mineko knew then that this chaplain was a way to keep the ruse going. That using a white chaplain would clue all the men in James's squadron that they were not married before Mae. And while this would not have been shocking—it was happening everywhere—James needed this to keep this lie going, to protect a reputation that was important to him.

Mineko was prompted throughout the short ceremony as to what to say and when. Within two minutes she was married to James.

"Omedetou," the chaplain said, and he extended his hand.

James did not take it and it lingered there, between them, so Mineko reached out and held it like she had seen soldiers shake hands before. She squeezed and the chaplain squeezed back. His hand was warm, and then he gave her a nervous smile.

"Good luck, y'all."

"Yes, good luck for you, too," Mineko said in English. She let go of his hand, and James, right hand firm on her hip, guided her nearly through the curtained door, until she reminded him: baby Mae.

She had gone to visit Fumiko a few weeks after she realized she was pregnant. James had gone missing after the first week of regular visits but had come back around a few weeks later. He had since helped her find a new office job, and so Mineko no longer saw Fumiko at work. Mineko met her at a little tea shack and told her of the baby, before either of them could take a first sip. Fumiko had begun to cry and Mineko, embarrassed, walked her friend around the corner of a building.

"Stop this. What is done is done."

"But I've shamed you!"

"You have done nothing of the sort."

"You wouldn't be here if it weren't for me. And you wouldn't have met the American, and you wouldn't have—"

That much was true. After the Osaka bombings, their paths had diverted sharply. With no home to care for, there was no need for a housekeeper nor the housekeeper's daughter. Mineko spent most waking hours trying to hunt down food for her family, and what was not spent looking was spent trying to build shelter where their home had stood. Fumiko, desperate, had run away from Kadoma, leaving her mother a note that she was going toward the city to find food and would send word to her when she was settled. Weeks later, word came by mouth from a cousin of a cousin of a neighbor that Fumiko was safe and she had a job, she had food and shelter. *What job?* Mineko had asked. The boy had shrugged. *A ramen stall girl, maybe*, he suggested. Mineko, tired of scraping the ground, decided that she would go to Fumiko and make a little money, too.

"It is what it is. I want this baby."

"You do?"

Mineko stood straight and closed her eyes. She couldn't speak of this to her friend with open eyes. Yes she did, no she did not.

"You love him?"

"Had I been matched, I would have married, even if I didn't love him. I would have had his children and tied our families together."

Fumiko began to cry harder. She pushed the heels of her hands into her eyes. "You've always been so strong. And because you are, those around you are allowed to be weak. But then you see this weakness and answer it with more strength. It's too much for you."

"Why do you say these silly things? I came to you out of my own free will. I came to make money and get food for my family."

"A family who will totally cut you off now. You know they will."

"A family who is alive because I followed you."

"I should have died. Look at my face! I wish I had died—"

"Hush! You're being stupid! I'm happy you're alive!"

"You followed me and you have shamed the memory of your Akio!"

Mineko felt suddenly nauseated, her belly too empty of food. All this talk of the past. All this regret. And Akio—how dare she mention him like this! She felt an anger fly through her that she hadn't felt toward her friend. Not ever. Fumiko had fallen to her knees, and Mineko pulled her to her feet and then she shook her, Mineko's hands on her shoulders, rattling her until she was quiet and her face a surprised orb, its pockmarks from the fire like the shadows on the moon.

• • •

James lay next to her and Mineko wondered about the time. Mae was asleep in her little crib. He would be leaving soon for base, and then Mineko could really sleep, spread herself out and drop away. But for now, they were all together, chaplain-married with child, a family.

Mineko wondered how she'd sleep when they lived in the same house, permanently.

"You know we'll all go home someday."

Mineko dissected his sentence. *Home* was all she surely understood. And then *someday*, which she always confused with yesterday or today. *Day*, she knew with certainty, had to do with the sun being up. It also had to do with time, and time was such a slippery thing.

"Okay," she said. Okay was always a good thing to say. It punctuated this English like a sigh.

But which home? The base home? Not her home, because once the letter she just wrote arrived in Kadoma, she knew that would not be a place she would visit again easily. And where she slept now was not so much a home as it was a cabinet for bodies.

Mineko thought of the place with the gate and the word COPE over the entrance in large metal letters.

If she ever owned her own place, she'd write her name over the gate, too, she thought, sleepily.

When *would* he leave? Mineko hoped it would be soon and that he would do so quietly; keeping Mae asleep for as long as possible between feedings was the nightly prize.

"You have it on?" James asked, and he picked up her hand.

He had given her a ring. He had bought it at a pawnshop after the ceremony. They walked in together, he looked, he chose. It was an older style, yellow gold and a dark black-green stone in the center, marquise cut. When she looked close, she saw tiny dots of red. She wondered who it had belonged to and why it had been sold. The pawnshop made her sad, just standing inside surrounded by the things people had loved and lost.

"Very nice choice, sir. You are very lucky to find this ring today." The pawnshop owner spoke slow, choppy English and looked only at James. Mineko knew that he was embarrassed to have her in his shop, a Japanese woman with a half-white baby in a pram. It felt unfair that she should have to carry the weight of shame alone, but Mineko stood straighter, just to irritate the man who was judging her with his inattention.

James had handed her the ring and she had slipped it on herself. It fit well.

"Tell her what it is, what the stone is," James said, repocketing his billfold.

The man fixed his eyes on James but spoke to Mineko.

"It is a very beautiful stone, it brings strength and energy to all who wear it."

"Not in English. Tell her in Japanese so she really knows."

The pawnbroker cleared his throat. He began again.

"This gentleman—"

"My husband, sir," Mineko said, tiredly.

"Your husband has bought you a bloodstone."

Mineko looked down. It did look like blood splattered across dark moss. With this, she said thank you to both James and the salesman and pushed Mae out of the store.

Finally, James stood to leave, finding his pants, his shirt. He was unusually quiet tonight. It was not the silence of anger or sadness. Mineko wondered what it meant. This man was a mystery to her. She hoped she would grow to know him better, but worried about what she would discover. Perhaps there would be fondness, a warm love in their future. Perhaps the few glimmers of kindness he had displayed would be more plentiful over time.

He did not kiss her goodbye, but this was not their way. Instead he put on his jacket, lay a few coins on the table next to the door for the morning market, and slipped outside, shutting the door a little too hard. When he did, the room and its contents shook, even the minogame that was hidden in the corner beneath some rags. Mineko sighed as Mae began to wake with a cry.

"Come now, baby dragon. I know what you need." And Mineko rose to feed Mae, shuffling into her slippers and removing the bloodstone ring, worried about its sharpness against Mae's tender body.

Chapter 13

Aunt Mae stands on a stepladder at the sliding glass window that leads to the "balconette," a senior-safe balcony that features no more than twenty-four inches of walking room and a wrought iron railing. She is chatting about the weather outside, that storm clouds will be gathering soon, as she hangs the curtains, beautiful polished cotton chintz with cherry blossoms that my mom and I ran up on her sewing machine during the last few days. Even Grandminnie admits they are nicely done, heavy and lined, weighted on the corners with washers sewn into the seam.

"Goodness, I better get home. Need to get dinner on," Aunt Mae says, checking the time with a snap of her neck, causing her heavy black ponytail to swish. "I don't think I'll be able to be back for a couple of days, Mom. I've got new inventory, and Sallie's coming in to look at reception locations, but she doesn't have much time, so I was going to—"

We don't hear what she says, because Aunt Mae is always moving, carrying her conversation with her. She is now in the bathroom, bringing a shower cap out in one hand (it has a hole and needs to be replaced) and Grandminnie's pill case in the other. She shakes it gently.

"I thought we were giving these to the nurse."

"What the Sam Hill—" Dad looks out of place, having come from a site. He's changed out of his work boots, but there's a remnant of cement on the hem of his jeans and a well-rubbed patch of dirt on his thigh. He pulls his cap off and rubs his head. "Mom, what's the use of you being here if you can't trust the nurses to do their job."

"It's blood pressure medicine, that's all," Grandminnie says. "And those fish oil things."

Grandminnie sits in a new wingback that reclines, going through the odds and ends that Dad scrounged from the old house, now placed in a nice, new plastic container with a snap-on lid. The lid matches the rusty-pink in the cherry blossoms, which blends with the recliner and the nice, muted rug beneath it. She doesn't have a chance to answer.

"Oh, crud! Minnie, I forgot to get coffee filters!" My mom is a few steps away, in the kitchenette, wiping the counter for the umpteenth time. She puts her hands on her hips and surveys the room. "I'll bring them by tomorrow—or, no, I'll get them now, and Mae, you leave, and Paulie, baby, you go back to work, and Lia, you stay and go through these last boxes and I'll have the front desk buzz you when I have the filters. Oh, and a shower cap, too! What do y'all think about that?"

No one thinks anything, because no one can keep up with her marching orders. Mom's perkiness over coffee filters and shower caps overwhelms the now beautifully decorated room. I can see the determination in the poodle puff of her blond bangs and the arch of her eyebrows. She is literally one Piggly Wiggly trip away from being free of her mother-in-law.

The way Grandminnie has acted toward her the last two weeks, I can't blame her. She has smoked openly in every room of my parents' house, leaving a small black wormhole on my mom's upstairs iris rug; she has complained about every meal my mother has cooked; she has called the socks my mother bought for her one of the worst words in the Minnie Cope dictionary—*cheap*—and during movie night, she did the unthinkable and plopped down next to my dad in Mom's spot on the couch. Finally, she has consistently taken up my father's time with nonstop financial questions, and nothing worries my father more than money. When my father is stressed, my mother takes it as a threat to her borders. Let it be noted that the country of my mother's wifehood is mostly borders.

Dad announces that he's going to get home, make a few work calls, get the dirt off of him, and come back to Autumn Leaves for dinner service.

Mom reminds him curtly that they have dinner plans.

Aunt Mae squeezes my mother's arm, pats Dad's back, kisses Grandminnie on the temple, and points a pretty finger at me.

"You are a *peach*, Lia. You've devoted yourself to helping us the last two weeks, and I can't thank you enough!"

The last two weeks I've done everything I can to stay away from my bedroom phone. I've either worked or shopped for Grandminnie's decor with Mom. When someone needed to drive into Plano for pillow shams, I gladly took the job. And when the manager at the store asked me to work on weekends to help unpack boxes of Easter supplies, I did that, too.

After some tense whispers out in the hall, my parents come back in and ask if I wouldn't mind staying for dinner. My mother, grabbing her purse and a sweating Styrofoam cup of sweet tea, whispers in my ear, *You're not a peach, baby, you're a saint.*

I, Saint Lia of the Elderly, sit with Grandminnie at a corner table. They are heavily draped with white and forest-green tablecloths, the remnants of our flounder almondine and green beans in front of us. Tonight, for a special dessert, there's a chocolate fountain set up on a long table in the dining room, and there's a line of residents waiting their turn. Grandminnie is excited about this, although she doesn't dare let on. My grandmother would eat a carpet tack if it were dipped in dark chocolate.

We make our way to the table but instead of walking to the back of the line, Grandminnie goes to the front and blatantly cuts. She fills a bowl with chocolate and orders me to grab the fruit and only *some* of the shortcake because she doesn't want to get all *fat* and *old*-looking like *some* people.

Mortified, I apologize to everyone around me and follow her out of the dining room.

Back in her apartment, Grandminnie puts the bowl of chocolate and the plate of fruit on the side table next to her recliner, and I lie across the bed, just close enough so I can snag a strawberry. Before sitting down, Grandminnie digs through my backpack for the tape recorder. She tosses it at me.

"What was that all about? I thought you were supposed to be making friends here, not pissing people off."

Grandminnie dips an orange slice into the chocolate.

"At least they have dessert. I was worried with all the diabetes people we would only be getting that sugar-free gelatin."

"Very funny. You know, they're not going to kick you out, if that's what you think. They have your money, you're paying *them*. They won't like you, but they won't make you leave."

"Maybe they will. Maybe they'll call Paulie and say, come get your old Jap mother!"

"No one says that anymore."

"Not to your face, Lia. People will always say what they always say."

I wonder what that even means and watch as she picks up a piece of pound cake, dips, and stuffs it into her mouth. Then a slice of banana. She pushes the plate an inch toward me, then pulls it two inches back.

"This stuff is not good for you, Lia. Bad for complexion. Bad for—" And she shifts forward and pats her butt.

"Don't be tacky, Grandminnie. You know I wish it weren't like this. I wish you could have your own place again."

"But your daddy was right. And I was tired of that old house. It was falling down around my elbows. I could only fix so much. So, no house. And your mother needs her space. And Mae needs her space."

"Did you even ask Mae to live with her?"

"Me and Mae don't talk about such things. Mothers and daughters—well, *you* know."

"In some ways you're closer to Daddy."

"Some ways, yes. Like you."

Grandminnie pushes the plate of fruit and cake back to me. Her smile is grim. She shrugs, then pops a strawberry into her mouth in faux cheerfulness.

My father and I have always been close. When I lived in Austin, I would call my mother about the little things of my day. She knew where I had gone to dinner the night before and if I had taken my allergy medicine by the sound of my sniffles during cedar season. But I called Dad and we could talk for a long time about the bigger things. Finances, questions about cars, and big career choices. A few times, I'd be sad about something or the other, and we'd talk and he'd cheer me with his unconditional belief in my abilities.

With Grandminnie moving out, Mom has a newfound focus on me. She wants me back in Austin. She tries to chat with me about job opportunities, about my apartment, about Stephie. It's like she's tapping, tapping, tapping on me, looking for a hollow space. But if she finds what she's looking for, what will my mother do? She acts like she wants to know what happened, but she really doesn't. She just wants it *fixed*.

But Dad. He's the one who has seemed so hurt that I haven't confided in him. He always said that when he was growing up, he watched his father do all the wrong things, swore he'd do things better. Right. *Perfect*. And that's the worst part of all, maybe.

After the happy hour at Dos Compadres, after he had offered me the board position, things actually changed with Darren—in fact, he wasn't around as much at all. The application showed up at my dorm at the main desk, a note paper-clipped to the front with a smiley face and his initials. He stopped coming to lab nights, leaving us with the grumpiest TA in teaching assistant history.

And while he didn't show up at our next desk crit, the result of his edits and his sway over the profs was evident. The memory of my "mullet" design had seemingly been erased, and the team was not only complimentary, they said it was the strongest in our group. My design had won. Antares and Rochelle accepted defeat with grace. Bradley mumbled and groaned, but eventually got on board. As we created models, all the groups turned toward themselves, barely living outside their pods of four. The conference room hallway was a hum of voices, working into the night, with the exception of Group 5, which fought constantly, now down to three members because Aimee had stopped showing up and the Group 5 guys said that she wasn't responding to any phone calls.

"I guess she doesn't have what it takes," Bradley had said, measuring a thin plank of balsa wood. "I do miss her skirts."

I felt bad for Aimee. In the past few weeks, I had gotten to know her a little better. She was friendly, always willing to chat. I had learned her mother managed a grocery store and her dad wasn't really involved in her life. I had learned that she had a notebook of Texas town squares and that she loved the look of those old courthouses. She wondered why architecture wasn't *pretty like that* anymore.

"It's weird—don't you think?" Antares had said.

"Very mysterious," Rochelle agreed. Somewhere between sketching and modeling, Rochelle had recently pierced her eyebrow, and now I couldn't stop glancing at that.

Darren was notably absent from our model unveiling, another professor covering for him.

Rumors flew that he had been tapped for a big museum project somewhere overseas, but that seemed flimsy to me. I felt a little abandoned. He was like a mentor to me, wasn't he? Or maybe I misconstrued things. Maybe his interest in me was just a silly blip. I was concerned about my future within the school, but came to the conclusion that Darren had given me a good chance with the board position, and that was enough. I looked forward to that meeting, certain he'd be there and we would catch up, but when the day came, Darren snuck in late, gave me a quick smile and a wave, and was gone again in twenty minutes.

Then, the semester was over. My group had scored the highest on our (my) shelter design. Overall, it was said that the structure exhibited "the dual qualities of protectiveness and beauty, a place for women to heal and blossom." It was both invigorating and eerie how well they had understood my design impulse, but I didn't have time to ponder their praise. My group had first dibs on studio space and because we had formed a weird family of sorts, we raced to nestle ourselves into the largest area in the corner of the floor with a view of the campus. Then it was time to worry about internships. I included the critique and photos of the design in my summer applications for places all over Dallas, planning to live in Curtain and commute. Meanwhile Bradley and Rochelle found themselves in San Francisco at the same firm, sharing a sublet. Antares went to Houston to intern and live with his cousin.

I returned to UT in the fall, excited to start Design V, the big show. I decorated the walls of my studio with images of my favorite buildings, pausing before hanging up a collection of rock-encrusted ranch homes that I had photographed over the years after a graduate student walked by and asked if I was planning on eventually going residential.

"No, commercial all the way," I had stammered.

"Yeah, thought so. That's what Darren had mentioned."

"You've seen him? He's around?" I asked. It had been a week of classes, and I hadn't run into him anywhere.

"Oh, he's around all right. Moved offices, though."

Darren's new digs were closer to the dean's. More rumors swirled, this time that he was the chosen one to take over because the current dean was disappointed with some of the politics regarding campus structures. Rochelle always joked that Big Buildings, Even Bigger Egos was the unofficial tagline of our department.

I feel a tug on my cardigan sleeve.

"Lia-chan? Did you not hear me? Get her out!"

I know what Grandminnie means. I go to the closet and slide open the mirrored door; there, in the corner, is the bowling bag right where I left it. I pull out the minogame and cradle it as I walk through the room.

"Do you want her someplace? Maybe on a shelf or next to your bed?"

"Oh no. I think she'll live in the bag and come out sometimes. I don't need nosy people asking what she is. And it's bad for your brain to think about the past all the time."

"But it's normal. Everyone thinks about the past."

"Like you? Always lost in la-la land?"

I have stepped right into Grandminnie's trap. I ignore her and go into the bathroom.

Curious about Darren's new location, I had walked up to the dean's floor that first week of classes. It was late and most of the offices were dark and I was hopeful that Darren's would be, too. I wanted to see him, wanted to find out where he had disappeared to last spring, but also didn't want to seem too forward. I paused when I saw the new nameplate on his door but turned to leave without knocking.

"What are you doing? Pranking me?"

Darren was coming down the skinny hall. He moved quickly toward me.

"I heard you moved up here. I just wanted to say hi."

"Well, hi!" Darren opened the door and motioned for me to come in. The bright white furniture had been replaced with heavy wooden mahogany and burnt-orange walls. He shook his head. "Don't judge me by the decor. It's not my doing."

"You got busy in the spring and my group was worried about you. Thought you might have changed your mind about Texas."

"Not at all. But I am disappointed."

"About what?"

"Your group was worried? I was hoping that *you* were wondering about me."

I felt a rush of unease.

"Sure, yes, me, of course," I said, my words choppy.

Darren rubbed his chin. "Let's go."

"Okay, yeah, I'm sure you have plans—"

"No, together. Let's go grab drinks. I want to hear about Dallas. Heard that you lit that place up."

I doubted that very much. I had mainly made copies and poured coffees, ran easy AutoCAD fixes and flitted around the edges of the teams, taking notes. My main contribution was moving the locations of sinks in a downtown high-rise bathroom. But I thanked him for his kind words and walked next to him down the hall and into the elevator.

"So, a fourth year. How does it feel? Are you excited about your project?"

"I'm less excited and more terrified. Have you heard about the brief?"

"A little. What is it again?"

"Designing a headquarters for a fake major corporation that inhabits that corporation's mission and values."

"You'll do well. I have a book you need to borrow that will help you a lot. Stop by and grab it next time. But I bet you already have a concept cooking."

The elevator door dinged open.

"Margaritas or wine or beer or . . ." Darren took his keys out of his pocket. "Moonshine? Do they have that here?"

"Wrong state."

As we were rounding the Architecture Building's corner, heading to the parking garage, we saw one of the new assistant deans coming our way, the first woman to serve in that position. Madeline Grant. She was tall and thin, with bright white hair that she wore in a French twist. She wore a black pantsuit, flats, and pearl earrings every day without fail. She rarely smiled, except for a pained expression on occasion. It was this tight-lipped greeting that she gave Darren.

"You're being summoned, Mr. Miles," she said, looking directly at me. "For drinks with us tonight. You got the note?"

"Yeah, I did. I wasn't aware that it was for tonight," Darren said. His voice had changed.

"Attention to detail, Mr. Miles. It really does help when one is teaching." She stood by, as if ready to escort him. "You can drive with me. I'm heading to the wine bar now."

Darren turned to me, flustered. It was strange seeing him this way.

"Rain check—and let me know if you need anything," he said. While walking away, I heard him call me a promising young student he was mentoring.

"Of course," Mrs. Grant had said.

The minogame sits between us now. My grandmother pretends to feed her a chunk of browning banana. The light is fading outside, and the storm clouds that were hypothetical earlier are building up in the distance, but the sun is setting a riotous pink. There's a chance of severe weather tonight. All the warm heat from the day and a cold front coming through. The opposing forces causing a ruckus in the atmosphere. I have a fondness for opposing forces in design, how it draws one's attention to the lines of a building or the use of shadow or texture. But with weather, it's dangerous. For now, though, it's pretty. I point this out to her, the colors, the light.

"Prettier on my own land. Prettier through my own windows."

"No, your windows didn't face the sunset."

"In my head, I think of a house with windows that face the sunset, Lia. One set of windows for morning, one set for evening. No, that old house didn't have anything in the right places, not in my right places. James's family, yes. Not me. When I got there, I remember pulling up in the truck and I . . ."

It's so stupidly simple and perfect I can't believe I hadn't thought of it yet.

"I have an idea."

"I thought the land was pretty in a funny way, but the house, oh, the house looked like trouble. We moved in, and I don't think any of us were ever happy there. Not James, not the kids, not me. Or, not happy, but what's the word, what's a good word that doesn't mean happy but doesn't mean sad, means the in-between feeling?"

"Peaceful. You never felt any peace."

"Yes, that's it. Peace."

Suddenly I'm antsy. It is such a good idea, such a beautiful, risky thought.

"Did you hear me, Grandminnie? I need to tell you something."

Chapter 14

Tachikawa Air Base, Tokyo
October 1952

At the end of the day, when the scent of frying Spam lingered in the air—
the P/X was *always* stocked with canned meat—the letter arrived by courier. Mineko stepped outside to sign for it and realized that the delivery
man was simply going door to door. She scribbled her initials in English
letters, MC, she had learned that much in class, and watched as he walked
down her two steps to the house next door, up the Greens' steps, and
rapped on that door, too.

Etsu stepped out, her youngest clinging to her leg, her oldest peeking
out behind her. Her daughter was a year behind Mae and would be going
to school next year as well.

Etsu bowed, signed, and looked over to Mineko. Her husband called
her Ettie.

"What is this, do you think?" she asked. Then a peculiar look crossed
her face. She took one step to the edge of the little patio and threw up
onto the yew planted there, a sickly plant now covered in vomit.

"I am so sorry, Mineko." Etsu blushed. She slipped the letter into the
front pocket of her apron and picked up the toddler boy before he began
to wander away.

"Don't worry, Etsu. I'll get a bucket of water and wash it off. You go
in and rest."

"You should, too. Rest, I mean."

"Oh no. Feeling much better. I'm more worried about you." The homes on base had been constructed using lightweight supplies brought from the United States. Every time Etsu emptied her stomach, Mineko could hear it. It was loud enough to make her gag.

Etsu patted her pocket. She frowned.

"Bad news, I know. They sent a courier. Always bad news when he comes."

Mineko clucked her tongue, and she realized how much she sounded like an old woman.

"Nancy, you help your mother with your brother. Etsu, just rest. Not all news is bad."

Mineko went inside and retrieved the bucket from under the sink, filled it with water, picked it up, muscles straining, and waddled to the front door again. Outside, some dribbled onto the rag welcome mat—she had made that herself—and then she did her best to toss the contents the five feet toward Etsu's yew. It splashed and the vomit fell from the leaves and into the pine mulch and Mineko sighed. It was the best she could do.

Now, the letter, she thought, and set water boiling for tea. James would be home after work, so she wouldn't know what the letter said until well after she fed him dinner. She might not know, depending on his mood and his needs, until morning. Her stomach knotted. Etsu would know sooner, her man, Timothy, was more open to her and if need be, Mineko could knock on their window after dinner. That's how she had learned other things in the past.

But no, they had plans tonight. Etsu had mentioned it earlier in the day. Timothy had a friend visiting from another base and they had planned to go into the entertainment district.

Mineko watched the steam rise from the kettle. She took the letter out and held the envelope up to the light. She could steam it open, read it carefully, and then return it. The gummy seal would surely dry before James returned, and if she put a heavy book on it, there wouldn't be any crinkles. If military envelope glue was as cheap as their houses, then it shouldn't be a problem at all.

If James found out, he would be mad, but he was the one who told her she should become more acquainted with American culture. At Bride

Class, there was a portable library. Cooking books, etiquette books, US history books. All translated into squished, unreliable, uneven Japanese. There were four mystery books that were immensely popular; the waiting list for those could be two months long. But Mineko had persevered. That Agatha Christie. She had taught her to do this.

Holding the letter with noodle tongs, Mineko counted to thirty as the steam penetrated the seal. Then, using a fish knife, Mineko carefully loosened the flap, starting from the corner and working straight across. It worked perfectly and she said a quick thank-you to the gods for letting this occur without mishap. She unfolded the letter, found her English-to-Japanese dictionary, a stubby little pencil, and dug through Mae's arts and crafts basket for paper.

It took a good hour for her to translate the letter. When she was done she looked at the clock. Mae would be walking back from the base school soon. She read through the notice.

Captain James L. Cope:

You are hereby notified that the wartime Occupation of Japan will be concluding in effect at the end of this year. Your service will be continued with full pension and rank, as requested, at JFW Air Base, Fort Worth, Texas. The US Air Force will be returning partial ownership of Tachikawa to the Japanese Government in July 1953, therefore you will be required to vacate Married Soldier Housing by June 15, 1953.

Mineko felt a flutter in her belly. She sipped her tea and carefully folded the letter and placed it back into the envelope, set the kettle to boiling again, resteamed it, and placed several magazines and the Christian Bible sent for Mae's birth on top. Then, worried, she moved the stack to a kitchen chair and sat on it, feeling the outline of the Bible in her rear. It was disrespectful so she apologized to Jesus, as if he were watching while leaning against the fridge.

Now what? Mineko looked around her. As much as she sometimes disliked base life, she had grown used to the schedule, the way things worked. *One can get used to most anything,* her father had told her when she had returned home for him to meet baby Mae. She had just shown up with Mae, surprising her father, desperate to be seen. Hiroshi, stooped and tired, soon softened and she followed him into the garden, where Mae was laid on a blanket between them. For a long time, she had thought he meant that *he* would get used to this new situation. That the family would relent and she would be back in their graces in due time. Now, she wondered if the comment had been meant for her, personally: you, Mineko-chan, you can get used to most anything. What had he seen clearly that she had not?

James had been reminiscing more and more with his Texas buddies living on base—chicken fried steak, the smell of the barn, Grammy's pie— and the talk had bored her more than anything. No, she thought, shifting on the Bible. It had angered her. She had not been able to speak of the past, not with James, not with anyone. She did not appreciate the effortless way James and his friends could pull up memories without any pain or remorse.

Mineko did the math. At least her next child would be born here, in Japan, although it would be born on base, which was officially American soil. American soil in Japan. American children with a Japanese face. When she walked through certain neighborhoods in Tokyo, she was glared at by old women and men. Perhaps she was a traitor to the empire, but no more so than the noblemen who had decided to go to war with half of the world and then stayed rooted in their walled palaces, letting boys fight and die. She did what many other young women had done. She had survived within the occupation. And even though her family no longer corresponded with her, they did accept the letters with money for food. When she paid dearly to send a three-pound bag of white rice at the New Year—white rice, so impossible to buy without going to a black market—they hadn't sent it back.

Mineko felt like she had lived a hundred years in just the six since moving into base housing. She preferred not to think of the past, but now she'd be leaving with James, now she'd be saying goodbye. She thought of Fumiko—*sweet, foolish friend, how I miss you!* After Mae arrived, Mineko had tried to heal the friendship between them. She had apologized to Fumiko for her anger and Fumiko had apologized for her outburst. But things had remained off-key, their meetings tainted. Fumiko now lived in Tokyo proper, married to a man who came home from war with one less eye and one less testicle, both removed at a Russian prison camp. But Mineko could tell from their brief visits that she loved him and they were happy: childless, hungry, and weary, but, at last meeting, happy.

Mineko was fertile, well fed, and rested. She attended Bride Class on Tuesdays and Thursdays, wore clean Western-style dresses and little shoes with funny heels. A few times a month, the Bride Class Girls on her housing row would gather together and give one another permanents, one holding the hair dryer for the other, until all their hairstyles matched— black, loose curls, most to the nape of the neck, pulled back with barrettes on the side. They learned English phrases together—well, they tried to learn English phrases together, it was not progressing well for some—and they learned recipes together. Mineko's Jell-O mold with canned mandarins wiggled with orange delight. The color reminded her of her coat, which reminded her of Akio. But she still made the Jell-O.

The Bride Class Girls were from all over Japan. The Bride Class Girls all hoarded food. The Bride Class Girls all had nightmares. They all flipped through movie star magazines. They all wrote letters home, some returned, unopened. They walked their children home through the base lanes from school. They tried to understand the Bible. Many Bride Class Girls had been baptized, sprinkled with water—*water!*—by a chaplain. The Church Girls were nice and gathered together, a group within a group. Their husbands seemed a little more loving, a little more lenient, maybe more understanding. Mineko had wondered if this Jesus really did help people out. That's why she kept Mae's Bible out on the table even if she had stopped spending time with the Church Girls, who tittered nervously at her questions. But still she kept Jesus around. Couldn't hurt. Might help.

There was a knock on the door. *Mae!* She had forgotten to stand outside and wait for her. The door creaked open. Mineko made a mental note to oil the hinges. They had such things at the P/X.

"Mama! Guess who won the arithmetic contest? I got through all my addition problems the fastest!" Mae took her shoes off at the front door and lined them nicely next to Mineko's. Mineko forced a smile, despite her upset. Mae often won contests, so it was hard to keep up enthusiasm for each new accomplishment. Eventually, she hoped, Mae would just feel proud of herself and not need this constant reinforcement.

"Mae, dear, can you pour me another cup of tea? Mama is tired. What else? Were you good?"

It was a question that she knew the answer to.

Mae nodded and poured the tea, carefully. She pursed her little lips in concentration.

"We learned a poem."

"Oh, really. Let me hear," Mineko said.

"It's in English," Mae said hesitantly.

"That's good, that's fine. You need to practice." She took a sip of tea and let it slide down her throat, feeling a bit shaky. "I need to practice, too."

Mae took a dramatic deep breath in preparation, but then let it out and looked at her mother, closely, cocking her head like a little canary in the market.

"Something is wrong, I know it."

Oh, here we are, Mineko thought, daughters will know the truth, there's no hiding things from them.

"How do you feel about a little trip into the city with me? Visit an old friend?"

"Yes. But why?" Mae was already walking over to slip her shoes back on. She loved getting off the base. "Can we visit the candy store?"

Mineko nodded and pointed to her shoes, which Mae dutifully delivered, along with her little drawstring purse. Mineko thought about writing a note, but James had been coming home increasingly late in the last few months—he had taken up bowling with a group of friends—and he didn't read kanji and her English writing was so rudimentary, it would have taken an hour to write half a sentence.

Before leaving, she propped the letter from the USAF against the chrome toaster, no worse for wear.

There was a short bus ride to the center of town, where Mineko and Mae boarded a little tram to get to Fumiko's. Construction abounded and the air had a powdery quality that coated the streets, dulling the colors, infuriating the capillaries in the eyes. Mineko had tied a scarf over her hair and wore sunglasses; when she caught a glimpse of herself in the window of the tram, she looked like an American woman, she thought.

Mae pointed to the missing buildings on the streets. Like a mouth without teeth, she whispered to her mother, and it was true. Mineko had never taken her near the places where, still, there was nothing but carefully scraped earth. Entire neighborhoods gone and picked clean. That would be a mouth without teeth or tongue or lips. A gaping hole in the face of Tokyo. And who can live without a mouth?

Mineko thought of home. Kadoma had been on the very edge of the firebombing of Osaka, some even wondering if they had been a planned target at all, or just a place to unload extra bombs. She had tried to carefully build a wall in her brain—a high wall with steel rebar, much like the buildings being reconstructed in Tokyo—so she could not think of Kadoma for very long, of her family, of her turtle house. Mineko tried and succeeded during the daylight. But at night, she saw fire and smelled charred bodies. At night, she dreamed of a dog, a beautiful white dog, its fur in flames, running through the desolate streets, looking for its owner, screaming as it ran. Not barking, not whining, not yelping. Screaming like a human baby.

At their stop, the tram screeched and everyone covered their ears. Mineko rose and Mae followed. They walked up the hill, so steep with her protruding stomach pulling her down. Fumiko's building was next to a park, a strange new apartment building with four floors and a kawara roof, its tiles ibushi, the color of storm clouds. In the little entry, she untied her green scarf and removed her sunglasses, tucked them into her drawstring bag—*Oh, Mineko-chan, why don't you have a pocketbook?* some of the Bride Class Girls would say. Mineko looked at Mae carefully.

"We are visiting a friend I knew when I was young. You've met her, but probably don't remember. Be polite. When it's time, we will walk in that park over there and you can play."

Mae nodded, eyes big, clearly intimidated by these new surroundings.

Fumiko's apartment was at the very end of a tight hallway facing the back of the building, two other doors perpendicular. From Mineko's perspective, she surmised that the shape of Fumiko's apartment would be a skinny box, just a slip of a room.

Mineko realized that she hadn't even called the building, not that the line would have worked. Phone lines were still being installed in some places, but fully functional in the wealthier neighborhoods. She hadn't sent a note. She rapped two times. There was a good chance that no one would answer, that Fumiko wouldn't be home.

The door slowly opened, a chain stretched across to create a space of only a knuckle's width. An eye peeked out, then a wide smile, the chain undone, and there was little Fumiko.

"Mineko-chan? What are you doing here?"

Fumiko's voice was the same: high-pitched, birdlike, the squeaking Hana had despised and covered her ears when she would hear. Her hair was pulled into a short ponytail; she wore a skirt and a white button-down with a faded quilted jacket on top. Mineko remembered the jacket—it had been Fumiko's mother's. Shadows from the darkened hallway and the electric-lit room shrouded her, but when Mineko stepped into the room and Fumiko stepped back into the light, she saw the scar, lightly concealed with makeup. If Mineko had turned to see Mae, she knew that the little girl's mouth would be covered by a gloved hand.

"It's been so long! I am so glad, but not prepared! Not a bit of food to serve my sweet friend!"

"Fumiko, it's fine, it's fine." From her bag, Mineko withdrew a can of mixed nuts, the kind that she set out for James and his friends on poker night. "You know me, the most prepared girl in all of Kadoma!"

Mineko felt Mae's hand on her skirt.

"Dear friend, we must catch up, but this daughter of mine has been cooped up in school all day and needs to get some fresh air—can we go to the park?"

Fumiko looked relieved, it seemed, at the prospect of leaving the stale little apartment. Mineko could see all of it from her place by the door: bed, kettle, sink, low table, one chair, hooks for clothing where no clothing hung, all the color of dirty dishwater.

With Mae racing across the grass away from them, Fumiko quietly watched. "She moves like you."

"She runs as fast as she thinks."

"Why didn't you call before coming?"

"I called last year, remember, and you said that you couldn't meet? I decided that this was the best way. I have news to share, and I need to tell someone. Someone whom I treasure."

"Please do not say such things about me, Mineko-chan."

Mineko bristled. "Let's not go back, Fumi. We have both apologized."

They stood side by side for a few quiet minutes, watching Mae. Mineko pointed toward a crane peeking up between the trees, a load of beams hanging from its metal neck.

"Have you ever imagined such a thing?" Mineko said.

"So much change in just a few short years. Do you remember how destroyed it all was?"

Mineko had traveled to Tokyo on Fumiko's request two months after Japan accepted defeat, the trip long and tedious because train lines had been melted by fire and twisted into a Western-style ringlet. And it was unseasonably cold for fall. She had gone from walking to a buggy to the back of a truck. She had half expected a mule over the next hill, but she was already there, Tokyo, what was left of it and what was being built back. What year was this again? Oh, years, they all get muddled together in chaos. November of 1945. Americans were everywhere in Tokyo, and Mineko had gone from neighborhood to neighborhood inquiring about Fumiko. A cousin of a cousin of a cousin had pointed her to Utsukushī House, slightly south of Tokyo.

A Recreation and Amusement Association house. A brothel.

There was a line of occupation troops: light blue, navy blue, olive drab.

It had been only a few months. If war life was as quick as a pulse, after-war life was a pulse racing. This was Fumiko's job. This was the opportunity of which had been spoken.

Mineko reached out to touch Fumiko's arm.

"We're leaving. At least, I think we're leaving. James got a letter. By early summer."

"Leaving? For where?" Fumiko looked at Mineko with wide eyes.

"Texas. He's been speaking more of it lately to his friends. Then the letter arrived. I see now what has been happening."

"And this is allowed? The American government will let you in? And Japan will let you go?"

"The US has said yes to others in our same position. And Japan doesn't care—one less mouth to feed. James gets what he wants. I pity the government that tries to stop him."

"And he wants you."

"Fumiko, he wants his home." Mineko looked quickly for Mae and, finding her picking tiny fall wildflowers, she took a deep breath and faced Fumiko. "And before you say anything, it is not your fault."

"I don't deserve your forgiveness. When I got to Tokyo, I wandered and was hungry and cold."

"I know, you've told me this before."

"A woman came to me and said she knew of government jobs. She seemed like a good woman. And there was a trolley leaving soon. All I needed was to give my name to the driver and he'd give me a piece of paper and there would be food and a clean room and work. Some of the girls were from different places. But many were Japanese, too."

"Fumi—"

But Fumi held her hand up for Mineko to stop. Her eyes bored into Mineko's.

"They needed more girls. Sometimes thirty men a day. They asked us, 'Who do you know from your hometowns?' They said that they would give us extra money and extra food if we could get more girls. And mostly, they said with more girls there would be less men for each of us each day. I met a boy from outside Osaka, he knew Kadoma, he had a friend there, they were meeting up somehow, I told him to get word to you, to tell you I'd been located, but not the location. I made him promise."

Fumiko put a hand on Mineko's arm.

Mineko could suddenly feel Mae's breath on her elbow. Mineko looked down at her daughter.

"They have ducks and turtles in the little pond. There's a woman selling crumbs. Do you have a coin? They look like they're hungry."

Mineko dug through her little bag and produced money and handed it, wordlessly. She felt like her insides had been excavated.

"You sent for me because they *asked* you to."

"I knew you would come. I didn't think they'd get to you, I thought . . .

I thought you wouldn't work for them. And that you'd come up with a way to help me leave."

Mineko hadn't become a comfort woman. Instead, those in charge, nameless, faceless men and women—all Japanese, all government-paid— had looked at her plainness, her muscular body, stocky even through hunger, and made her the downstairs girl. The girl who served drinks to those waiting. She would deliver little slips of paper with English numbers on them, brightly colored cuts of coral and mint, to different men, as pre- scribed by the oldest matron in charge, a sour-faced woman, and the men would take the slips to the corresponding rooms.

She was the deliverer of sweat and thrusting, of alcohol breath and animal-like noises. Mineko hated herself for this. She hated her weakness when shown the bags of rice she could buy, when she had told them no, my parents are far away in Kadoma, how would a bag of rice from the black market *here* help them *there*? There was no mail system, all had been destroyed or stopped by the Americans. Then they explained the couriers. Couriers were cheap, they were mostly trustworthy, they would deliver whatever she wanted to send. Yes, work for them, a girl from a good area with a good head for numbers, she could collect the Americans' money, count it out, deliver it to the matron. She could help run the down- stairs. It was good, after all, this work. Did she know how unsafe every woman and girl child would be in the country if these occupiers were allowed to just run like wild dogs?

Her sister sent word from Kadoma. Her father was sick. Stomach in pain all the time. Sent home from his job when the Americans took over the train system. Could barely move from his bed to outhouse. He was lonely in his room, but what could be done? Please send medicines. Bismuth subsalicylate. Can you find it? The food she sent and the money, it helped the family. They didn't know how she got it, how she had managed. I ride my bike in the black market, she lied. *Of course she did*, she knew her mother would say, that unusual daughter of hers, finally of some use.

Mineko and Fumiko watched as Mae paid for the crumbs and started to toss them into the murky pond. It was a new park, but had not been completed yet and wouldn't be until the housing was done. Weeds sprouted here and there, and the land had the distinct feeling that it was haunted by whatever had stood before in this spot. The little pagoda, which was a brilliant blue, was already chipped and soot-covered from nearby construction.

"Your father?"

"Alive," Mineko said. "And Mother is well. Hisako is still single. It's funny, the fire changed us both, we're closer now. But the man she was promised to passed after returning home finally."

She heard Fumiko murmur with surprise, Mineko's eyes still trained on Mae.

"He killed himself," Mineko said.

Fumiko grasped her wrist and squeezed it.

"Many have," she said.

Mineko let her touch her, she didn't shake her loose, although this emotion, this display was too much for her. But what did she expect? She had come to say goodbye, left the base with nothing but a longing for home and the only bit of home left was Fumiko. Home can disappoint, she thought.

"It has been hard for everyone. I had a choice to leave, but I felt duty to my family, so I stayed at Utsukushī until it was closed. I stayed because I had nothing waiting for me elsewhere." Mineko waved Mae back to her when the girl glanced up. "Now I have Mae, I have a baby to come. They are my family."

"You must wish," Fumiko began, but Mae was upon them. The sun was dipping lower. Mae's nose was the tiniest bit pink from the coolness that was settling into the shade where she had been.

"No. I do not wish anything," Mineko said. She said it quietly, as if Mae weren't listening, but she knew the little girl was, she was always listening. It was hard to hold the girl at arm's length, but she did so quite well and would try to do so with this next child, too. Mineko felt as if she were a gaping hole in the ground and that if they were to get too close, they would tumble in.

"America will be good. My children—they are fine on base with the other hāfu, but in Tokyo, it is not so. They will not have a life here off the base. There will be more opportunities in Texas, surely."

Mae looked at her mother with pleading eyes. Mineko instantly knew that Mae would remember, always, that she heard about their move across the ocean in a conversation. That she had heard this life-altering information after feeding turtles in a dirty park.

Chapter 15

Dennis, Texas
March 30, 1999

Waking up in Autumn Leaves is like waking up in a business-class hotel. There's the sound of trays and the soft-soled assistants delivering medicines; there's a whir of noises that I can only imagine are showers and toilets, coffee makers with automatic timers, and somewhere, the gentle ding and rumble of the elevator.

The sun is coming through the curtains because we forgot to close the blackout portion last night. My grandmother's glasses are on her stomach, moving up and down with each snore, and we are wearing what we wore yesterday. We have gone through an entire package of sandwich cookies, and I feel the tiny crumbs on the bedspread as I sit up. All around us is graph paper. I made a late run to the office supply store, getting there right before they closed for the night and before the sky opened up, dumping water troughs of rain, and bought whatever I felt was needed for the project at hand.

It was what she had wanted all along, but had never said it in the way we both understood. A house. Just for her retirement. But built to her specifications.

Grandminnie sits up with a groan and puts on her glasses. She looks at me blankly, brushes crumbs off my chest, and mutters that we are both slobs. But then she smiles, remembering our work, our plans from the night before.

On a twenty-four-inch-by-thirty-six-inch piece of graph paper is the turtle house, as it is in my grandmother's memory and the one blurry photo she has. She paced out how big the main rooms were last night. We had to go out into the long hallway at midnight, and she closed her eyes and walked from the genkan to the back wall. How many feet wide? How tall were the ceilings? We guessed, then did math. Each graph paper square is a foot, each foot a part of the past. She helped me sketch the front from her memory, the sides, the back of the house that faced the river. She dictated as I drew the grounds, the river below, the road leading to the bamboo forest. Pages and pages of paper are all over Grandminnie's studio apartment.

Then, at two in the morning, with pea-sized hail hitting the balconette window, we shrank the turtle house. One story became two, the rooms smaller. Again, we paced and, using the proportion method, we made it the right size for one woman, one cat, and an occasional overnight guest. We placed it on Cope land, near the creek, using our own memory-based aerial map.

Off and on, all night, I recorded her memories of the house, of the colors of the tiles and the thickness of the tatami. The types of flowers in the garden and the types of stones that paved the walkway. We used up two mini-cassettes last night. I label them with the date, and I store them in a purple Crown Royal velvet bag in my backpack, all in order from day to day, story to story.

"We're off by feet, you know," I say, pointing at the final incarnation of the house plans. "I need a computer with AutoCAD to really get this figured out."

My grandmother is up, making coffee. She finds pushpins in a shoebox of desk stuff and tacks the old turtle house and the new turtle house on the wall above the television set.

"Then find one."

"Not that easy."

"Your old job?"

"Impossible," I say, taking a cup of coffee from her.

"You know, this house will be very expensive to build. Many things will have to be shipped from Japan. A lot of money. How will I make all that money?"

"You have retirement funds. And I can pitch in."

My grandmother laughs and points her finger at me, a little cannon.

"Only if you go be an architect again. Bow money isn't going to help much."

"I'm not a real architect."

"Where is your—" Grandminnie balls her hands into fists and holds them out like a boxer. "You know the words! Your tough stuff!"

I think she's talking about confidence. Where was my tough stuff? I don't think I ever had a wealth of it. And my tough stuff took a hit that fourth year. That studio was led by a snarky professor who overcompensated for inexperience by talking a lot and offering very few answers. Even kind and eager Antares was peeved by the end of the first month of classes. Bradley was livid. Rochelle was murderous. But they all kept working on their steel-and-concrete masterpieces.

I, however, was stumped, spending far too much time researching. My fake client was a multinational oil and gas company, something I knew next to nothing about. I decided to research the history of oil and gas headquarters throughout the Southwest. Then the companies themselves. Then I began studying petroleum, the science of its creation. I told myself daily that it was time to turn my attention to *my* design, that I was, again, two weeks behind the rest of the group, an amount that would wreak havoc on my schedule. But I kept going back to the library, diving down rabbit holes, spending so many dimes at the copy machine that I had to go to the bank to pick up another twenty dollars' worth of dime rolls.

"Honey, we're gonna name this Xerox room after you if you keep this up," the librarian joked with me.

The pressure to succeed again, to be the ideal commercial architect, kept me up nights. Staring into my mini-fridge, hungry again after staying up so late, I tried to squelch the words in my head: I just didn't care about this corporation and their building. But it was my career to care. I settled on a piece of American cheese.

It was the prof, Mr. Snarky, who also had me shaken, calling my initial thoughts regarding my design "watered-down."

I couldn't move past it.

All of my insecurities melded into these words. I felt like he was describing me. I was too smart for my three-stoplight town (two if there had been a storm), but not bright enough for my major here. I was the girl who was the Almost Asian in Austin, but who still was taunted with chants of "Chinese, Japanese, dirty knees, look at these" when I was a kid in Curtain. I was watered-down Lia Cope. The girl who didn't fit anywhere.

"Go talk your concept out with Darren," Bradley suggested, all of us finally packing up our backpacks to go home well after midnight. This, sadly, was what we called an early night. "You've always been his favorite—he'll help you through this."

But I didn't want to, because he had helped me last time and I felt like I should be able to figure this out for myself. Besides, I didn't like being called his favorite. Rochelle told Bradley to mind his own business and Bradley responded, *It's not like she's an Aimee or anything*.

"What are you talking about?" I asked.

"Rumor mill shit," Rochelle said. But Bradley explained that one of Aimee's former group mates had run into her off campus and he swore that she looked *rough*.

"Can't a girl have an off day?" Rochelle had said. We were waiting in line at the snack machine, junk food glowing in front of us. Later, she had sidled up next to me. "Let's talk," she whispered, and we went to the fourth-floor bathroom.

"I feel like I need to say something, to someone," she said.

"What?" I asked, curious. I was picking at my cuticles.

"So, last semester, very end, I saw Aimee and Darren in the parking garage together."

"And—"

"She was really upset."

Aimee had never returned to class, and it was common knowledge that she had dropped out of the program.

"Well, she had chosen to quit and I'm sure that was a hard decision for her," I suggested.

"No, it wasn't like that. He was backing away from her like she had the plague. They were having an argument."

"What do you think happened?"

"I don't know. We both know that Aimee's *popular*. She even slept with Bradley last semester—"

"What?"

Rochelle rolled her eyes. "It was after that Cain & Abel's night. Not a big deal. But did you ever pick up on, I don't know, something off with Darren?"

I felt my stomach flip. I thought of that night with Mrs. Grant.

"What does this have to do with me?"

"I don't know. Just thought you should know."

I am back to sketching the front elevation of the turtle house. I open up the box of fresh colored pencils and hold a blue-gray up to my eye. Considering they're office supply quality, not fancy art store, they're pretty smooth.

Grandminnie is slurping hot coffee, watching me.

"Cut it out. Let me color in peace."

But she doesn't move and, instead, bends closer.

I think of the dean and Mr. Snarky, both leaning over my shoulder during a desk crit, discussing my work later that semester. It was no longer considered watered-down; instead they said it was too feminine for a petroleum company.

I wanted to slide to the floor and worm my way to the elevator. Then Darren, who had been in the back of the pack of roving profs, told me to meet him in his office later so we could *fix* this.

I sigh, then blow my bangs out of my face. Grandminnie squeezes the cartilage in my ear and tells me she is going to the dining room to procure a late breakfast for us. You need your strength to get your tough stuff back, she jokes.

Chapter 16

In the months leading up to the move, Mineko busied herself with preparation. She sent another letter to her family, letting them know what was happening. After many years of silence, she received a letter from both her father and mother. Her father urged her to use her money, any money she had, to invest in Japanese pearls, so inexpensive now; that way, if she found herself in need, she could sell them easily in Texas and have something of her own. Her mother asked about base life and the children, then concluded with the question surely on the family's mind: Would she continue to send money from Texas?

Out of the bit of allowance James gave her each week, Mineko had saved back a small amount, an amount that wouldn't be missed. On the last Friday of the month, she would travel into Tokyo, away from the base postal office, and mail her parents money wrapped in a letter. She had learned that since her father's forced retirement and illness, they had taken in a boarder. This, odd jobs for her sister, and her money kept her family safe.

She responded yes to both letters. On the advice of Etsuko, she asked for money from James for Japanese necessities for their new home, and he had begrudgingly said yes. She had asked in front of bowling buddies, who slapped the table and laughed. All the wives had been asking, all wanted to ship great packages to their future homes.

"It's like they don't think there are stores at home!" one friend had exclaimed.

"My wife bought a soaking tub, and it's sitting in the living room at Ma's," another announced to great laughter.

It was Timothy who said quietly, "Well, they're right about something; it won't be like here. Ettie is going to miss her family. And I've grown to like her old man." He snubbed out his cigarette. "But we'll be close enough to y'all, Minnie, just up in northern Oklahoma. You and Ettie will be able to see each other. Only four hours away."

There was uncomfortable silence, broken when someone thought it best to get to the lanes. Mineko found her chance to slip away to bed. She disliked asking for money. It made her feel lowly, but she had done this and many other things she could never have foreseen herself doing. Ironing his uniform. Curling her hair. Waiting up for him at night. Plucking her eyebrows. Awakening before him to fry sausage and make biscuits like she had learned. And she knew that if it had been Akio's expectations, she would have done all this and more. But he would have only expected her to be Mineko.

Sometimes, when Mae was in school and before she was so big and pregnant, she would sneak away to the Zanbori River. It was a lazy tributary of the Tama, and she would follow it until, at a small fork where a road had been cut, she would climb the tiny hill and then work her way down the rocks to where the two rivers met. There, she'd soak her feet for a while, always thinking that, no, she wouldn't swim today, but eventually she'd strip down to her Maidenform and underwear and work herself deeper into the water. No one ever came by. There she would float and look at the sky, letting the gentle water carry her, then flipping over and stroking back up to where her shoes sat perched on a rock like a lighthouse. Sometimes, for a moment, she felt better. Not happy, not even a pleasant feeling, but a few degrees better.

It was on a late-March afternoon when James came home early with boxes to be put together, labeled, taped, and then delivered to the post. There, they would be stored and loaded onto the boat for their departure in June. They would be home in time for the Fourth of July, James kept saying, the importance of which Mineko understood from their celebrations on base and the education from Bride School. It would be important, this arrival. The P/X had a sale on red-white-and-blue-printed fabric, and she had made Mae a festive skirt with red trim. For herself, she worried that baby weight might stick to her longer this time, so she just sewed a little scarf and attached a bit of red fringe. She was thirty-six weeks pregnant.

"Just put these boxes together. You can figure it out." James had been cheerful, pleasant to her, more even in his temperament. "Don't go crazy with stuff. A lot of this can be sold or left for the next family," he said, looking around.

"Yes, James," Mineko said while popping the cardboard tabs into place. The box she was putting together was square and deep and she knew exactly what would go in there.

"Keep that one for me," James said. "That's a good size for all my things. Should even fit my bowling ball, bag and all. Won't need it on the ship."

"Do we have others like this?" Mineko asked.

"No, we got what we got, that's it. Like I said, most of this crap can stay. Won't need it at home. Got an entire house of stuff there. Anything we don't have, we can get from Mama or buy."

As Mineko packed for the rest of the afternoon, she kept her eye on the deep box. She located the minogame, long since hidden behind a wardrobe in the corner of their bedroom. Mineko folded it in a quilt and placed it in the box, where it fit like the compressed Spam in a can. She wondered what she'd tell James. He would ask. He wasn't the type of man to forget.

After a Friday night dinner of pork chops and sweet potatoes, James went into their bedroom and came out with his bowling bag, ball still in its case.

"Why's this here? Thought it would be in there—that box is already packed and taped. You forgot? What's wrong with you?"

"Oh, Etsuko has another box. She will bring it in the morning time," she said, hoping that the strain in her voice wouldn't give her away.

"No, Minnie. I asked what's in the damn box?" James put his bag down with a thud that vibrated the floorboards and went to where the box was stacked with the others. Angrily, he picked up crates and slammed them down—their contents rattling despite the newsprint wrapping—until he reached the bottom of the stack. There, he took out a pocketknife and sliced through the red-and-white paper tape. James dumped out the contents and out rolled the minogame. He looked at it and then up at Mineko with a set jaw and piercing eyes.

He picked it up, shaking as if to weigh it with his hands, and held it out to Mineko, the turtle's face looking at her. When he had started visiting her room, Mineko had kept it hidden under a blanket. Since then, she had moved the minogame from place to place, until she finally settled it into the hard-to-reach bedroom corner. Mineko's mind struggled to come up with a story.

"What's this here?" James held it up to look on the underside. "What the hell is it?"

Mineko held out her arms for the turtle.

"Give to me. It's mine."

"Oh no. What's mine is yours and yours is mine. Now tell me where you got this and why you took such great care to hide it from me. God, you are sneaky."

Mineko had never mentioned Akio to James. She never would dishonor his name that way.

"It's from a friend. A family member. To remember Kadoma by."

"Well, what is it? A friend or family?"

Mineko stood straight. She had taken James's temper in a variety of ways. Indifference, cowering, cajoling. None of them had ever worked.

"You give it back and I'll pack it someplace else. You let me do this."

"I'm taking this piece of Japanese horseshit and I'm going to sell it to one of the boys here; he collects oriental stuff like this and ships it to New York. Sells real good there. Then I'm going to take the money and buy all my guys drinks all night long and whatever else we might want. That's what I'm going to do. I can't believe you, Minnie. Hiding things from me. You're gonna have to learn that I'm in charge. All the other girls, they listen to their husbands! What makes you so goddamn special?"

Mae poked her head out of her room.

"Git back in there, girl, this is between me and your mama!"

Mineko's heart raced. She pictured her minogame in some relic store in a busy city, far away. It was hers, it had to stay hers.

"I'm so sorry, James-san," she said, lowering her eyes. "I will repack the box now. You can take the turtle tomorrow, okay? You're going out tonight, right?" She moved slowly toward James, who stood angry in the middle of the room.

"I'll pack your bowling ball and your bowling shoes."

Mineko took the minogame from James's hands and put it on the kitchen table, fitting it between the dirty dishes she had yet to clear. She walked back over and picked up the bag and placed it carefully in the crate. She scuttled into the bedroom, found his embroidered jacket with his name on the front, a bomb and bowling pins on the back, his shoes. She raced back into the living room, kneeled, and put them carefully in the box. Her hands shook as her fingertips left the heavy satin fabric. As she rose, James grabbed her by the chin and kissed her, hard, right on the lips. His evening beard had started to sprout—and it was rough against her face. She didn't push away or move, accepting this kiss as a temporary act of surrender.

In bed, she propped Akio's small photo on James's pillow and lay next to the turtle, which made a deep depression in the mattress. She wanted to simply look at it one more time, memorize it before it was gone. It was only an ornament from a house that wasn't hers. But she thought of Akio freeing it from the sloping roof that summer night, the sky pulsing. So much was coming that they didn't know. Mineko rolled to her back and looked at the ceiling. She wished she could push out everything bad from her memory and keep only the good.

James had left that night for the Nagoya District with his bowling buddies, something they did regularly, trading their bowling jackets for slick suits and fedoras. The intensity of American men's appetites had surprised her. With James, everything was more: ingestion of food, of drink, of fun, of women. And yet, intensity, she understood—had she not practiced her strokes until she could outswim everyone, had she not sewed entire dresses all night long until they were perfectly complete? But some of the soldiers' desire, as she observed carefully in James, was insatiable. Yet her own people, they were still hungry, still exhausted, and forever ashamed. Everyone hungry for something.

It made her overwhelmed thinking of it all. But it was the fly that buzzed and the lone cricket that chirped. Add to it the drunken stories that she and the other Japanese wives on base overheard: atrocities committed by Japanese soldiers and recalled by men over poker games lasting far into the night. These same women overheard similar stories from their brothers and fathers, told much in the same way, to each other, in secret. Mineko saw that she and the other Japanese base wives were the meeting points of pain, bearing the sadness from both sides. And expected to do it willingly, smilingly.

For the wives who truly loved their husbands, this was a burden that they could carry on their backs along with a baby. They found a graceful balance beneath the weight. These women, like Etsu, had married against all the rules and wishes and had done so with great love inside them.

Mineko looked at the statue again. She couldn't stand the thought of it decorating some American's living room.

She breathed as deep as she could with the baby shoved into her lungs, and she went through the memories again: turtle heads protruding from the water for the old noodles, Akio's feet turning blue in the cold pond, the nubby material of the orange coat, the tart sweetness of citrus slices, the scent of Akio's hair smoke skin oil salt breath . . .

She found herself taking a sleepwalking Mae to Etsuko's house just a few minutes later; her little girl curled up on the Greens' sofa and fell quickly into dreaming again.

"I need to run an errand," she explained to Etsuko.

With her papers in hand, a scarf tied around her hair, and her drawstring purse in the front basket, she biked to the guard shack.

"A little late to be leaving?" the soldier commented, looking at the booklet where there was a photo of Mineko and her husband's name. The late-night guard posts rarely spoke Japanese. Much to her dismay, this one had a decent working knowledge of it.

"I have a gift for my friend. It came at the PO today from the United States. I want to hide it in her home to surprise her in the morning."

The soldier cocked his head and glanced at the parcel wrapped in a blanket and tied down with twine.

"Japanese tradition," she lied. "It's a stand mixer. The kind that you can plug in?"

The soldier said that he had never heard of this tradition before. And Mineko, her voice steady, told him that it was particular to her village and that the longer he lived here, the more he'd understand, though it might take two lifetimes.

"Well, that's a pity, because I'm heading home in June," he said and waved her through.

Mineko pedaled away leisurely to keep up the ruse and then, turning the corner, began her ascent up the street, pumping hard to keep the bike going, until she was breathless. By her calculations, it would take forty minutes to arrive in Fumiko's neighborhood. But only if she went full speed, an impossible thing to do. Slowly and steadily she pedaled, back on even ground. After hills, stopping to catch her breath, straddling the bike in shadows and breathing deep until the tightening in her belly stopped and relaxed.

When Mineko reached the final steep hill that led to Fumi's building, her bra was soaked and her back throbbed.

"I'm so sorry, baby," she said.

She walked the bike, the minogame in its basket making the enterprise heavier and unsteady. Mineko was tired, unbearably sleepy, and every centimeter of her ached. What had the doctor called them at her last visit? Practice contractions.

Mineko laughed out loud. *Practice contractions.* Like there was any true practice for splitting one's body open for a baby?

At the top, she took the path to Fumiko's apartment, parking the bicycle near the front and feeling overwhelmed with luck when she saw the entry door propped open.

She went into the building, up the tight stairs, and finally rapped on Fumiko's door. After a minute or so, a sleepy Fumiko answered and, seeing

Mineko, began to worry that something was wrong at home, let a sob escape.

"No, no one is dead," Mineko said. "I just need for you to take care of an old friend."

Mineko unwrapped the minogame and placed it on the low table near the center of the room. "I can't take it. James isn't going to let me. He said he's going to sell it, but if you just hold on to her for me, one day . . ."

Mineko couldn't finish. She didn't know what one day would look like or when it would even take place.

Fumiko lit a small bamboo lantern that she kept near the door. Carefully she shook out the match, releasing its sulfur smell. Then she ran her fingers over the minogame's rippled shell.

"I am happy to watch her for you, such a small thing to do. Is there nothing else? Can this be the only way I repay you?"

"This is everything to me, Fumiko. You are keeping my history safe."

"And James? What will you tell him?"

"That I sold it myself tonight. Then I'll give him some of my savings."

Fumiko clutched Mineko's arm.

"I'll keep her protected forever if I have to."

When her husband rustled in the bed, Fumiko looked over her shoulder at him and then back to Mineko.

"I wish you could meet formally, Mineko-chan."

"We will, when I come back."

"So you will come back? You must promise," Fumiko said.

"As soon as I can, I will come back."

"Very soon, then," Fumiko said, but Mineko simply squeezed her hand and left, unable to look at the minogame or her friend a moment more, wanting only the dark of Tokyo around her again, the oblivious yawn of night.

Paul Cooper Cope came the next morning, just an hour after they arrived at the airfield hospital. He had so much hair on his head that it nearly fell to his shoulders when the nurse washed him in the little sink. He was a voracious eater with a dark-eyed stare and a serious little mouth. Mineko loved him instantly, even faster than she had loved Mae, who had been a pleasant, observant newborn. Paulie, however, had eyes only for her. He had a strong neck for one so soon from the womb, and when the shift changed and the Japanese night nurse rounded, she had remarked that clearly this boy would be stubborn.

"Strong-necked babies always are," she said, and Mineko agreed.

James came to help her home with the baby, pushing the pram, and they walked the short distance across base, although she wished they could have driven, her parts still aching from that strong-necked baby's head.

"I need to tell you about the turtle statue."

James squinted as if trying to remember. Mineko regretting bringing it up. Maybe he had forgotten about it in the excitement of Paulie's birth? But then he grunted in recognition.

"I sold it. To save you time. After you left that night. I have money at home for you."

"Made a good deal?"

"Best that could be made for such an old thing. Wasn't worth much."

James walked in silence. He seemed to be thousands of miles away. Mineko wondered if he was thinking of Texas.

"I'll feed the baby first. Then I make you dinner," Mineko said to James as they reached home. She picked Paulie up out of the basket and went into the house, calling Mae to follow her. They went into the baby's room, also Mae's room, and Mineko settled onto the floor, crossing her legs and putting a pillow on her lap.

"Close the door, Mae. This we do together." And Mae shut her father out, slowly. The three of them on one side of the thin pressed-wood door, James on the other, the house quiet.

Chapter 17

Dennis, Texas
April 1, 1999

My grandmother meets me in front of Autumn Leaves, looking like she just robbed a bank. She has a large bag slung over her arm. It's seven a.m. on the dot, and she has signed herself out.

"Drive, drive," she tells me as she slams the car door.

"It's a trip to the library, not a trek into the Amazon. What do you have in there?"

She opens her large duffel and I peek inside. Snacks, water bottles, a magazine her friend Fumiko sent, a sandwich bag stuffed full of silver change, and the minogame.

"You sure about this?" I ask, but neither of us says another word. Austin is a nearly four-hour drive. If we work fast and get on the road again by two p.m., we'll be back at Autumn Leaves before they clean up Mexican Fiesta Night.

I am pretty certain that I have covered my tracks perfectly. I have concocted a story that hits both of my parents' soft spots. I had told them that I was taking my grandmother to the Japanese food store and, while in Dallas, I was going to North Park to buy a pastel-hued dress of appropriate length for myself for Easter. And white shoes. We would be gone the entire day. In actuality, I bought my dress last night at the ancient Bealls in Dennis, and I will be heading to the Japanese food store next week.

I go through the prep work again with Grandminnie in the car.

The University of Texas Architecture and Planning Library was my grandmother's idea. I had accidentally given her seed for the thought when I stated how I wished I had design journals and books to copy ideas from for her house. And where is the best place to get these? she had asked, innocently. Before I knew it, I was telling her about the beautiful reading room at the architecture library. Grandminnie then battered me with demands until I called the librarian, and, remembering me, she kindly held back ten different books about traditional Japanese architecture from the Tokugawa period to the present.

The thought of returning to campus makes me want to pick the small scabs at the base of my hairline, but I keep my hands on the steering wheel. This trip could make Grandminnie's house perfect, and, I keep telling myself, it's very unlikely I will run into Darren at the UT library.

My body emits a growling sigh, somewhere from under my rib cage, the sound of anxiety and disgust and fear. I fake a cough trying to mask my subconscious grumbling. Grandminnie just says hmph. I can't tell if it's a shut-up hmph or an oh-you're-thinking-about-your-secret-again hmph.

My grandmother gives me the side-eye and sips her coffee from the Thermos lid, holding it with both hands and slurping with petulance. When she's done, she rolls down the window a few inches and lights a cigarette. I have spoken to her about smoking in my car, and she doesn't respect this at all. Not shocking for a woman who has already dismantled the smoke alarm in her own assisted-living bathroom.

"You have asked some hard questions, you know? You ask hard things, but then I ask, oh sweet Lia-chan, why are you so sad, why are you so mopey and working at that horrible job . . ."

"Wow. Tell me how you really feel."

"And that is a stinker job for a smart young woman. All I wanted to do was go to college. But not allowed. Then the war."

I feel awful. Of course she's upset that I've thrown away my education. I reach out and try to hold her hand, and she slaps mine away.

"Nope! Nope! Not fixing this problem with hugs and stuff. Not me! You will tell me why you quit your big-time job. Maybe not today. But when you tell me, you will feel better and we will fix the problem and—"

"Like how you're going to tell Aunt Mae and Daddy about Akio and how you met my grandfather and how you really didn't want to leave and about—"

My grandmother blows smoke in my face and I dissolve into both coughing and laughter.

Our arrival in Austin surprises me, like it always does. The highway gets cramped, then divides like a magic trick. There's construction that's been going on since I did a college visit back in high school. Then, out from behind the gray half-built overpasses and orange reflective barrels, there's the capitol with its rosy pink granite.

I think for a moment, *home*.

I want to parallel park my teeny car and walk to get some enchiladas. I want to toss some coins into a hairy man's velvet-lined guitar case. I want to walk down by Lady Bird Lake, sunglasses perched on my head, an *Architecture* under my arm. I want to see bats fly out from under the bridge and then go drink a beer on my balcony. I want to slice through the water in the hot-pink kayak.

My grandmother mutters a triumphant *Aha!* I think of how she must see me: leaning forward in the driver's seat, a smile on my face.

We cut through downtown and find our way to Riverside Drive. Traffic is light, which is remarkable. White rock cliffs, the beloved Austin stone, prevent us from seeing down to the river. We curve around, an S shape, then I turn down a short road that accesses the backside of the parking lot for my apartment complex. I type in my code and the wrought iron gate bounces to life on its track. I guide us to the spots closest to the water.

"Very fancy."

"It's actually an older complex, but it was totally rehabbed. I don't want to freak Stephie out. She's not expecting me."

"Want to walk down to the river?" Grandminnie asks.

"That's the shack where the kayak is—and over there is where I usually put in."

"The water is very green."

"Yeah, it's pretty, isn't it?"

"Turtles?"

"Lots."

We keep our seat belts on. Grandminnie is suddenly gentle; she takes her hand off the door handle. She waits.

"I can't." I reach up to scratch my scalp, and she gently removes my hand and puts it back on the stick shift.

"Then we go to the library. Next time, Lia. Next time you'll take me."

We drive silently back toward campus and then pay to park near Guadalupe. I ask my grandmother if she thinks she can walk to the library, and she laughs at me. She pulls her large handbag out of the duffel, stuffs in the five-pound sandwich bag full of silver, and emerges from my car like a returning conqueror. She starts walking and I have to run to catch up.

The Architecture Library is a design icon. It is one of the early buildings that inspired the rest of the campus. The white limestone walls gleam in the sunlight, and the red-tile roof is just a shade off of burnt orange. It's shaped like a bread box, but a bread box with style.

I pull open the door, and a blast of icy air-conditioning hits us. Inside, the floors are glossy and clean, the upstairs reading room is proud with its carved wooden niches and long tables.

The librarian recognizes me and puts down her mug of tea. She scurries to a back room and returns pushing a cart.

"Hope you have some time today—my assistant found even more! Good to see you, honey."

My grandmother opens a thick book that is all about roof tiles. Her eyes get wide and then she laughs softly. We settle in with our twenty-two books. I hand Grandminnie a new block of sticky notes.

Soon the house I sketched transforms in my brain from the one I thought I understood to the one that Grandminnie really wants. I close my eyes and walk around the rooms. When I can't see what a certain wall looks like or a door, I flip through a book and ask questions.

Three hours pass and our stomachs start to growl the time before we look at a clock.

"Lunch?" I ask, and my grandmother looks worried about leaving our place. She's been peacefully flipping through pages, sometimes whispering to me in Japanese, and I have to tap her on the arm to remind her I have no idea what she's saying.

The librarian provides us with a table tent that says "In Use—Please Don't Touch."

Outside, it is a perfect spring day. It's warm, but not miserable, and everything worth blooming *is* blooming. Flowers that burst forth in late April in Curtain manage to wiggle out of their buds a few weeks earlier in Austin, that much closer to the equator, that much warmer. I cut by buildings, making my way to a sandwich place that has some nice outdoor seating. When we get to the main road and our destination, I am so filled with back-in-Austin glee, I barely notice a sleek, black BMW slowing as we walk.

My grandmother tugs my arm and says my name in a worried whisper.

The car is rolling down its window, and I see him. Darren. Another car, tired of his slow-driving shenanigans, gets on his tail and honks, so he speeds up, yelling out *Wait*, then something else that I can't make out. He turns away from where we're heading because of—bless it—one-way traffic and road construction.

As I stride back to the safety and the interior of campus, tugging Grandminnie along, I'm clumsy with nerves, turning the wrong way and then having to backtrack. We finally make it back to the library and sit down at our table. The librarian says, "That was a fast lunch!"

"Who was that man?" Grandminnie whispers fiercely to me.

"No one."

"That's very funny. I'm not eating lunch right now because of that no one."

"My old boss, that's all."

"Your old boss, huh?"

Grandminnie stiffens, clears her throat, and continues to flip through the pages of her book. I try to focus on the book in front of me, a collection of printed screens, but I can't stop thinking of a strange night my fourth year. I had finally decided on a design and felt confident enough to create a rendering. I had gone back to the beginning of petroleum, the real beginning, as in phytoplankton, the images of their fossilized bodies that looked almost like lace my inspiration. The model was going to be a beast to build, and I needed to start, but instead I spent the evening organizing my materials like my mom organized the pantry. I even made labels.

Finally, the floor phone buzzed. One of the few other students still around on a Friday night in the studio answered it and called out my name.

"Lia, Mr. Miles says he wants you to come up?"

I had seen him in the hallway earlier in the day and he had mouthed *Come visit*, but I hadn't felt like it.

Just the same, I gathered up my backpack and tied my flannel around my waist. I would tell him that I wasn't feeling well. That I had a headache and might be coming down with something. That we could talk about it next week. But the elevator slid open, and there was Darren.

"Come on, no more hiding."

He seemed genuinely upset. I followed him back to his office.

"Not hiding. I have a killer headache."

"You're floundering again."

"Listen, I've got to go."

"Please, sit down for a bit. Want something to eat? I have some pretzels." Darren reached into his desk drawer. "You haven't stopped by. You were clearly in need of some help on this project and you didn't reach out. I'm worried about you."

He handed me a bag of pretzels and I took them, opening up the snack bag that had clearly been given out on a plane, little double As and wings on either side. He then stood up and walked over to the windows, closing each blind. I felt him behind me, heard the twist of each plastic wand.

"It's Sandy, isn't it? My wife. That's why you've been keeping your distance? I know there's been rumors."

I choked on a dry bite of pretzel. What could he be talking about? I think of his alleged run-in with Aimee. As I coughed, tears sprang to my eyes. Darren was patting me on the back, and he handed me a glass of water from his desk. I took a huge gulp.

"It was so hard on both of us."

"I don't listen to rumors," I said, trying to slow my breathing.

"That's good of you. Thing is, it's true. She wants to keep trying, but I feel like enough is enough. She's clearly not over it. And I don't know if we are even meant for this next step. The loss was so hard. And to make it worse, it started—the miscarriage—in my old office. And after that, I didn't know if I wanted to be there anymore, you know?"

"Hold on a second. I'm sorry, but what are you talking about?"

"I'm talking about my wife, Sandy. How she was pregnant and she lost—we lost—the baby late last spring. The whole pregnancy was hard from the beginning. It was stupidly hot and she wasn't feeling well, but came up to the office to say hello, and, well, she was about five months along, so it wasn't a little thing, it was, you know, the whole process and . . ."

I felt horrible. Horrible for doubting him. It all started to make sense. How Darren had disappeared at the end of the semester, how he was barely around for class critiques and why he was moved to a different office. He wasn't climbing the administration ladder, I thought, he was mourning. And he wasn't at all interested in me in that way. How silly and self-centered we all were—Rochelle included! Stupid kids, all of us, trying to understand and misconstruing everything. Darren dug the heels of his hands into his eyes, rubbed, and gave me a sad smile.

"I'm so sorry, Darren. I hate that you and your wife went through that. Can I do anything to help?"

"Let me help you. That will get my mind off it. Your project—"

"The too-girly corporate headquarters? One semester it's the mullet, the next—"

"Take it easy on yourself. It's not that bad. It's all how you sell it. It's a retelling of the petroleum story. You're going with a Mother Nature vibe, right?"

"The base ingredients in petroleum, ancient marine life, namely phyto-plankton. Their unique shapes and colors."

Darren ran a hand through his hair.

"Here's my advice: maybe you keep going and work on the critique defense? Get ready for your rebuttal. I can help."

"Maybe. I don't know what else I could come up with."

"You doubt yourself. You have vision."

"But they don't *like* the vision."

"*Make* them like it."

He sat on the small sofa, closest to the guest chair where I perched, and leaned toward me. I noticed that the lines around his eyes appeared a little harsher than the previous semester. That his blond hair held a touch more gray.

Then.

He reached out and grabbed my hands, holding them tightly between his. I sat straight, uncertain as to what I should do. Should I lean in more, give this oddly grieving man more of my hand, my arm, but what happened next felt like one of those dreams that you can't quite remember but can't quite shake. Darren pulled my hands to his mouth and kissed the right one on the soft mound between my thumb and forefinger. It was slow and he kept his lips there for a breath. Then, it was over. I was standing, I was walking away, I was in the dark and moving across campus, I was tucked into my extra-long twin bed in the dorm.

I feel tears trying to push into my eyes and I fight them back, but my nose begins to leak instead. I walk over to a box of tissues, grab a few, and then blot my nose, hiding my face in a wad of white Kleenex. I then look at Grandminnie's face, clouded with concern, and I know whatever suspicions she had have been added onto and are taking further shape. She squeezes my hand, tells me she isn't that hungry, to forget about lunch, and quickly begins to flip through the remaining books, looking for pieces of the home she has lost.

Chapter 18

In all, a cargo ship would take forty-two families from the base to the United States, stopping in Hawaii to refuel. Mineko, Mae, and baby Paulie had received their immunizations, been fingerprinted, measured, and weighed. A man in a dark green suit with a brown tie, a young Japanese interpreter, and a woman with bright gold hair and bright pink lipstick, clacking on a little typewriter, had interviewed each "bride" just two weeks before leaving. Why they had not called the group "wives," Mineko and Etsuko could not figure. Individually, the ladies went into a Quonset hut, sat on a little backless stool, and answered questions, one after another. Questions regarding family name, birthplace, birth date, siblings, and father's employment turned sharply into questions of loyalty, political party, and reasons for leaving. Mineko answered each dutifully: Kamemoto, Kadoma in Osaka Prefecture, March 1, one sister, stationmaster, no loyalty to the emperor, no political affiliation. Mineko paused on the last question. The interpreter repeated it, although she had understood most of it in English.

"Why, Mrs. Cope, why do you want to leave this country?" the man repeated, then the woman typed something and looked up, expectant.

Why did she want to leave? Her husband was leaving, James was her husband, *for better or worse*, the chaplain had said, and she had children with James and she wanted them to have a better future. And James was that. A place for the children to run around. Clean earth, James had said. Good, hot sun. Good schools, cousins to play with, places to see, all these reasons he had said over and over again and that Mineko had soaked into her ears.

"A better life for my children. A home in the countryside. A new beginning," Mineko said, and she must have said it well, because after the translator was through speaking, the man in the dark green suit grunted and grinned and the woman typed away happily.

"See what I'm talking about, Betsy? Some of them are thankful."

The interpreter looked down at his feet and Mineko put a smile on her face, even though she thought she understood what the man had said.

On Friday night before the day they left, there was a party. The American Red Cross threw an official going-away celebration at the Tachikawa Community Center #2, complete with bright pink punch, balloons, and a cake that said "Good Bye and Good Luck, G.I.s and Brides." The women had planned ahead and kept their best dresses out of the packing boxes for the overseas trip. All the way to their new homes, they'd have to cart their fanciest frocks with yards of tulle petticoats.

Mineko and Etsuko, along with James and Timothy, arrived together. There was shrimp and a few platters of perky crustless sandwiches. Sushi rolls and deviled eggs. The men piled up their plates and, laughing and smiling, wandered outside together to a covered pavilion to roll dice and play cards. James, in a jovial mood, kissed the top of her head, Timothy leaned in close to kiss Etsuko on her temple. The ladies sipped punch, gathered with the group of Bride School graduates, and admired one another's dresses. Mineko thought they looked like a box of pretty candies. Rose and blush, lavender and light mint green. They seemed to all be wearing matching pearl earrings, and Mineko wondered if they, too, had bought extra pearls to sell in the United States, just in case they wanted to go home. She had sewn hers into an old pregnancy girdle.

After chatting for about thirty minutes, each woman shifting in her pumps, one of the soldiers came in and, unscrewing the lid from a bottle of Old Crow, spiked the strawberry punch. Watching, the women giggled.

"Oh no!" Etsuko said. "Alcohol! This is not what we need the night before we leave home!"

"Why not! It's going to be forever until we see each other again. Maybe a toast?" another said.

Mineko ran her words through her head again, gluing them into a new sentence. Leaving home forever.

"I suppose," Etsuko replied, and before long there was a line of fluffy dresses near the punch bowl.

Mineko still had the word *forever* circling around her, like a buzzard. She wandered to the bowl of shrimp, only a few left, the platter of sandwiches growing stale. The cake had been cut haphazardly by one of the officers' wives and only *bye* and *Brides* remained. Mineko hated the crooked lines and took a knife and cut a few slices to clean up the cake. The word *bye* was now separated and waiting for the next passerby on a little glass plate.

She was not a drinker. While others picked it up early during occupation, she never had. It seemed foolish, to dull one's senses in an already senseless place and time. But the frothy part of the punch was now gone, leaving a cheerful pink liquid at the bottom of the bowl. Mineko leaned forward for a sniff and her nostrils burned. She looked over at Etsuko, holding court with the Church Girls, and Mineko thought of forever, of never returning again, and took the ladle and filled a cup to the brim, sipping as she walked, choking a little as she went. She listened to Etsuko chatter about Bartlesville, the town in Oklahoma where she was set to live. The others threw the names of their new towns out as well, so many names that Mineko had never heard before. After a while, bored with the conversation and a bit dizzy, Mineko excused herself and went looking for the others.

Outside, she wandered to the playground, where the brides who had been drinking were gathered, singing.

"I'll be seeing you, in all the old familiar places . . ." They were off-key and sounded nothing like the Andrews Sisters, but there they were, singing to the moon, swinging on the swing set and sliding down the steep slide. A mound of petticoat slips and dye-to-match pumps lay near the picnic table.

"Mineeeeekkkoooo! Always so serious! Come sing with us!" one girl squealed before going down the slide, a little too quickly, and landing with a thump on her bottom, causing an explosion of giggles.

"We need to start calling each other our American names," another bride said bossily. "I'm Cindy, you're Mollie, you're Jean-Anne, you're Nicky, and she's Minnie."

"Like the mouse," Mineko said with a sigh. She hiccupped and again, giggles from the group.

"You're lucky! Minnie is at least close to your name. Jean-Anne is so hard to say! How can I be someone else when I can't even pronounce the name! I sound silly!" said the woman Mineko had known as Isumi.

"But we look beautiful," the woman who was now Mollie said, putting her arms around the two women closest to her, stumbling a bit. "We look like beautiful American women, and I know we'll have very good lives."

The women huddled together, Mineko's head buzzing. She imagined herself alone among a bunch of black cattle like in the sketches James had done so long ago. *Alone.* She suddenly missed Mae and Paulie, and the little base house with the humming fridge and the porch light that blinked on and off whenever she shut the door too hard. It wasn't home, but it was as much of a home as she'd had in years. Why, it wasn't all that bad! Now Mineko felt foolish for ever disliking it. The lanes that gathered water with every rainstorm, the kids splashing home in the puddles. The backfiring of the soldiers' jeeps and the way all the Japanese women ducked and covered each time, no matter how many times it happened. She liked doing the laundry in the sun next to Etsuko and hanging it on the lines together. James was often gone, but that was a blessing. Who knew what he did, who knew who he was with. There was always food and always someone to speak to, even if it was just about which shampoo was better for their daughters' hair.

Mineko said her goodbyes, and she walked quickly, blisters forming because of her new shoes, then she reached down and took them off, running in her pantyhose. A few old mamas had gathered all the children together at two houses, and Mineko stopped by to find Paulie asleep with all the other babies on a pallet on the floor. Mae was still awake, running wild with a few other girls in the backyard, high on sugary gumdrops and cookies.

At home, she washed their feet and hands, washed their faces and behind their ears. She tucked tiny Paulie into the basket next to her bed, then, thinking about a drunken James, coming in and stumbling over him, she moved him to her side of the bedroom. Mae wouldn't leave her, suddenly scared of the dark, so Mineko let her curl up close, and then dangled her arm over the edge of the bed so she could stroke Paulie's cheek.

"Are you scared, Mama?" Mae said. Mineko was thinking about the boat, the endless miles of waves.

"Do you know how many people I had to talk with to let us leave? If I said one wrong word, they would keep us here. So maybe that's a good thing, right? Must be a very wonderful place to be protected by so many questions."

Mineko could feel Mae nod her head next to her shoulder. Before long, she felt the little girl's body flinch, and then relax. Mineko leaned over and touched Paulie's nose again. Had her own mother loved her like she loved these two children? Had she touched her eyelids in the night, had she felt her downy head in the darkness? She felt as if a war of words and thoughts was battling inside her. *Was she scared? Was this forever? Will she be alone?*

"No," she told herself aloud, and Mae wiggled a bit in her sleep. No, no, no. And whatever was facing her, she would be fine, just fine.

Chapter 19

Dennis, Texas
April 1, 1999

We get back to Autumn Leaves in time for Fiesta Night. Brightly colored papel picado banners hang on the gas-log fireplace in the entry, and on each flat surface is a sombrero. There's one lone mariachi roaming, a white guy in full black-and-silver regalia, playing a twelve-string.

"You're going to *hate* Oriental Night," I say as I look around.

I am carrying Grandminnie's massive duffel, and she's toting the binder of photocopies. She spent the trip home three-hole punching and arranging as I drove. I had read that panic attacks are like waves, that they can last only so long and then they recede. If that's true, then between Round Rock and Burleson, I was in the middle of a hurricane. We stopped for gas and I raced into the stinky brown-tiled bathroom to throw up, but nothing was there. I just dry heaved over the porcelain sink.

My grandmother drops the flyer for Fiesta Night on my lap. There will be salsa and guacamole and watered-down elderly-appropriate margaritas served during happy hour. The dinner menu is enchiladas, rice, and beans. Dessert is flan. Exactly what I wanted in Austin, served here at Autumn Leaves. It's a sick joke.

Grandminnie shoves me her cordless and I call Mom to let her know I'll be staying.

My grandmother has applied a new coat of Shiseido red lipstick. She looks at me, opens the apartment door, and holds out her hand. We walk to get our fill of appetizers before the place becomes a sea of white hair.

After dinner, we open the balconette doors and Grandminnie squats close to the edge, smoking and dropping ash over the side into the cone-shaped Burford hollies below. We watch the sun disappear in silence. The three Autumn Leaves margaritas, equaling only one-half a normal margarita, have calmed me a bit, and I lie across Grandminnie's bed on my stomach. The minogame is out of her bowling bag and looking at me from the nightstand. I ask for my grandmother's photo of Akio, and she digs through her bra and hands it to me.

"We need to get this thing scanned and reprinted. Laminate a copy and then you can keep this original safe somewhere."

Akio stares back at me, wire-rimmed glasses, a lock of black hair falling across his forehead. I wonder if any other photos of him exist. He's handsome in a kind way, I think. I might go out with him, if he came up to me and started to chat.

At the beginning of college, I dated a nice guy who eventually transferred to a small private school somewhere in California. I received a couple of letters from him, but that's it. I went on a few dates the spring of my freshman year and a few more the first semester of my sophomore year. Nothing special. Then it was pretty quiet on the dating front as school took up more and more time. At BT&B, I went out for a couple months with a guy I met at a young professionals gathering, and Stephie and I double-dated with him and his roommate. It was fun until the roommate and Stephie broke up. Mom says my seriousness is intimidating. My friends say I'm a goody-goody, which is somewhat true, and any dude can smell that a mile away. Aunt Mae says I'm the marrying kind and that I'll be a top-notch mom one day. Dad stays pretty silent on the subject, probably picturing me in footie pajamas still, hair in pigtails.

That Design V fall, after revealing his wife's miscarriage, Darren was a regular visitor to my studio space. He brought snacks and silly jokes, strange factoids about famous architects, stayed for a few minutes, made an observation or suggestion, and then was gone again. He would some-times visit other students quickly as well, and I appreciated it when he did, because his attention, albeit kind, was something I couldn't explain easily to my friends. The rounds of critiques went far better than before, the team more open to my concept and appreciative of how a massive petroleum company could be portrayed through one of nature's smallest organisms. My presentation, practiced again and again in front of my dorm mirror, went smoothly, and I answered the jury's questions directly, meeting their eyes, as coached by Darren. Fake it until you make it, kid, he had said. Pretend you're better and you know more. His advice had worked like a magic incantation.

In the hallway, between presentations, Darren caught up with me and what began as a high five ended with a clasped hand. He moved close and whispered "See?" and I left the Arch Building giddy with success.

Before I drove home for Christmas, Darren had even dropped off a gift for me, clearly a book, wrapped in red-and-white peppermint paper. The note said not to open it in the studio, so I waited until I was at a gas station halfway down I-35, filling up my car and buying a Coke to keep me awake.

Inside was a heavy art-laden first edition of *The Architecture of I.M. Pei*. A note inside was written in Darren's block script.

"For your reading pleasure this holiday season. You'll need it in the spring (hint-hint) and I hope you enjoy it as much as I enjoy your pres-ence. You've made an unbearable fall far better than it deserved to be. Yours fondly, DM."

A rap on the door brought me back to Grandminnie's apartment. She yells out, gruffly, *No thank you, do not need them!*

"What was that all about?"

"Antacid cart, I think."

"No, really? I mean, that's thoughtful . . ."

"I hate this place. Don't you forget, I'm moving out into my own house. You can stay here if you want, but I'm leaving."

"Then maybe I'll live with you."

I sit up to see my grandmother point her hand straight at the horizon, dramatically. She juts out her chin. I can tell she's grinding her teeth. She rocks a little back and forth, thinking.

"You think you can leave problems. Everyone tries that when they're young. Oh, something awful has happened, I'll just go, I'll just run off like a rabbit! But some things follow. Maybe most problems follow, like smoke in your hair."

"Are we talking about me now?"

"I'm talking about us. I thought, maybe it will be better in Texas, yah? Maybe I can forget everything and make a new life, even if I know James was not too good always. And I did. New life, new language, new foods, new everything. You know the first food I bought at Dimple's store?"

I think about her favorites. Ice cream, candy bars, orange slices.

"A package of hot dogs. Mae and I loved hot dogs. We ate them for every lunch until we were both sick of them!"

My grandmother laughs at this memory. For a moment I figure she's back there, in the ranch house kitchen, staring down a hot dog.

"You can't hide from bad things, Lia. That's what I know. And when you go back to your problems—"

"You make things right again? Is that what this is all about? I need to face my—"

"Nah, Lia-chan! You never make things *right* again. Never! Things are *just wrong*."

Grandminnie collapses into her chair. She turns to me and makes her finger into a little cannon, pointing it at my chest. There's a hardness to her expression, one that is both familiar and new to me. She pushes her finger into my sternum, right at the center.

"But you can make things different and maybe, just maybe, part-of-the-way better."

Book 3

Chapter 20

Curtain, Texas
July 3, 1953

Ghost-white. Not a warm white, but a whiteness where the gray, weathered boards could be seen just below the surface. It was two hours past death, and that's what Mineko thought, staring at the farmhouse for the first time. They were parked at the end of the gravel drive. They had driven all night. Mae was asleep in the middle and slumped on her lap, Paulie asleep in her arms. She had been hot for hours, stifling in a cardigan, but since both were sleeping peacefully, she had not moved to take it off. So she sat there, James pointing out the landmarks of the ranch. Sweat in her hair and between her breasts and running down her stomach, her eyes taking in the white house and the flatness, a sickness in her throat.

It wasn't that the land was ugly, she decided, it had a starkness that was interesting. The lack of elevation was jarring; she had never seen any place so level for so far a distance before. The grasses grew tall and swayed in a slight breeze. There were trees along the fence line and up around the house. *Pecans, a whole grove of them,* James had kept saying, and she didn't know exactly what this meant, until he said it was a nut tree and she nodded with some understanding.

And where the land turned greener and small bushes and trees sprung up, that was the creek, Curtain Creek, and he said she could look at that later, but it had good fishing and a swimming hole. Mineko felt a wave of thankfulness wash over her. But there were snakes, water moccasins, so it was best to always bring a shotgun with you, just in case. Mineko's heart sank a little, yet to swim, maybe killing a snake wouldn't be too awful.

But the house. As they drove closer, Mineko could see that it was nothing more than a tall box of a place with two sides that jutted out. It was perfectly congruent other than that—windows, a long rectangular porch on the front. The brackets that held up the roof of the porch were barely decorative and, like everything else, the trim, the lattice that hid the underbelly of the home, the pillars—white.

"Needs repainting," James said, "you can help do that this fall."

"We choose the color?"

"*I* choose the color."

"Oh."

They parked under the shade of one of the pecans. James opened his truck door, bounded out, and left Mineko and the children in the cab. He walked up onto the porch, pushed against the posts to see if they shifted, stomped his feet to check for rot, looked up—what is he looking for? Mineko thought. It wasn't until later that week, when Mae was stung by a wasp, that she figured it out. James peeked into the windows. Mineko couldn't see his face, he didn't turn around nor did she expect him to. Maybe he was happy now, home at last. She hoped he was, but it was a thin want, the long wisp of a spider's web.

She buried her nose in the top of Paulie's head. They all smelled of their own flavor of sweat. Hers, like heavily pickled daikon, Mae's was peppery, and Paulie, with only milk in his belly still, was a sweet sourness. They all needed a long bath and clean clothes. She desired nothing more than quiet and a moment's peace to take in her new surroundings. If she could just be still—no boat tossing her, no truck bumping her—and have some silence to think. Yes, she could figure it out.

James went into the house, no key needed, closed the door behind him. Mineko looked at Mae, still asleep, her bangs stick-straight and stuck to her face. Paulie was hot in his sleep against her. Should she go in? Should she wait to be invited? As she was trying to figure out her next steps, another truck came down the drive in a cloud of white dust. This truck parked a good distance away. A man with the same thin shoulders as James, the same square jawline but with a smile, a true smile, got out. A woman with blond corkscrew curls tied up in a bandanna, short and curvy with a light bouncy step, was gesticulating to him. Mineko watched her climb up onto the porch—mint-green short pants and a sleeveless peach top. She turned and looked back at Mineko in the truck and, surprised to see someone, hit her companion with the back of her hand and pointed— Mineko could tell they were married. But then they, too, went inside.

Mineko opened the truck door, expecting to feel some sort of breeze, but it was equally hot and still outside. She carefully awoke Mae by shaking her lightly and then pushing her to sitting. Mae opened her eyes and blinked, mouth a little agape, dried saliva on her chin. Mineko retied the bows at the ends of her braids and slid out of the truck, holding Paulie. Clutching Mae's hand, and with Paulie now gurgling on her shoulder, she walked up to her new home.

"This is where we live now, Mae," she said in Japanese. Mae nodded.

"It's kinda funny. I don't know if I like it," Mae said, her voice still gravelly with sleep.

"You will always remember this day," Mineko said to Mae, but Mae didn't respond, just climbed the steps and, like her father, looked in the windows.

"Do we go in, Mama?" Mae looked up at Mineko. All Mineko had to do was open the door. She wished someone would take her hand and guide her gently in.

Mineko pushed open the door and walked into the darkened room, musty and old. Furniture still covered with white sheets. James had told her his sisters-in-law would come and air the place out. But no one had done any such thing.

In the kitchen, a square box of a room that Mineko hadn't seen from the front, an obvious add-on, she heard James and his family. She didn't understand everything that was being said, but she knew that Mae understood all of it, so she watched her daughter's face as she took it in. The grown-up talk passed over her, boring her, but still she stood close to Mineko, listening.

Mineko had realized upon arrival in California—San Francisco—that base English classes had not been as comprehensive as she had originally thought. But Mae, who had heard English and Japanese from birth, was fluent. So in the quiet, when James had left to wander the motel grounds each night of their four-day drive, or when it was just them, James asleep, and she was nestled next to Mae instead of her husband because James wanted his own bed to stretch out, she would ask Mae what was said. Mineko would lay out her gathered words. Mae would pick them up, one by one, explain mostly they were directions to a new highway or where a good hamburger could be found. A few times they were explanations; home from war with his Japanese wife, yes wife, and their two children. A man wearing overalls and carrying a tire iron had lost a younger brother in Bataan and he was still angry, yes very angry, about this loss. His brother's buddy had survived and told him all about it. Mae had relayed this solemnly, as if she had killed the brother, as if she had shot him in the back as he relieved himself. A girl who had not even been alive.

In Arizona, to yet another gas station attendant: *Yes, they're mine, funny how life is, never saw this happening, but Japanese women are good at things.* What things? Mae had asked. Just things, Mineko had said quietly.

In Oklahoma, to a pretty young woman at a fruit stand: *Think they'll be helpful on the farm, my woman is strong as a man.* Well, you are very strong, Mama. You can always open pickle jars. Mineko sighed.

And now, Mineko gathered words. Between James and his brother Calvin: *Party, yes, yes, ranch, fine, Minnie, clean, time, tonight.* Then the woman, who Mineko had realized was Delilah, Calvin's wife, and who everyone called Dimple, the sender of the pink booties: *No, help, no, food, home, kids, no, Japanese, no.*

"Minnie?" James called out. "What are you doing? Mae?"

"Daddy, can we see the creek now, the one you told us about?" Mae walked toward her father's voice in the kitchen, pulling Mineko along.

"Attagirl! Does she know how to fish yet, James?" Calvin asked. "Dang if I forgot my pole."

"You ain't got time to fish this morning. We gotta get down to the store, check in on things. That cousin of mine ain't worth a plug nickel and I got a shipment of frankfurters comin' in, day late, of course, but people'll be wanting them to grill for tomorrow." Dimple's words came out fast and loud. Some words seemed to stop midtravel, others bumping into them. This was definitely *not* the English she had tried to acquire on base. Yet Mineko understood three words of Dimple's diatribe: *fish*, *day*, and *tomorrow*. She squeezed Mae's hand and Mae squeezed back. She had to try.

"I like fish," Mineko said, and there was silence. Dimple rolled her eyes. Calvin grinned kindly. James cleared his throat.

"That's not what they were saying," Mae said quickly and under her breath. She realized that Mae was embarrassed and in the half second afterward, just enough time for a fly to buzz once around her head, she realized the source.

"James, y'all just got in. Don't be throwing a party tomorrow. Let us host—" Calvin said, gently. "You got young ones and Minnie there seems tired to me. That's a big trip for a little family."

"I ain't hosting the dang-blasted family," Dimple said quickly. "I'm not prepared myself. I'll make up some potato salad tonight and some baked beans. Have jars of okra put up. Your cousins will bring the cake, and those good-for-nothing sisters-in-law of mine will need to do something. I'll call them from the store." Dimple's words were like train cars on a track, always coming.

"Minnie'll make something."

"Oh, for heaven's sake. She can't do that." Dimple was agitated.

"She went to American Bride school on base. She can cook something."

"I'm sure she can, but you just dragged her across an ocean. And I think you're forgettin' about how folks are gonna feel about having her *here*."

Mineko listened as Dimple and James talked loudly back and forth, and Calvin, hands tucked into his pockets, rocked from his toes to his heels.

"C'mon, you two. Let's keep the peace." Calvin looked at Mae and winked. Mae timidly smiled back at him, and Mineko felt lost, the words a storm around her, and she held Paulie tighter as he drooled down the back of her blouse.

"This is gonna happen how I say, Dimple Cope. Minnie'll clean, and I'll take care of mowing around here so people will have a nice place to eat and watch fireworks. You call everybody up, tell them what's going on, even if they made other plans. Make your food, Minnie'll make hers.

There. Happy Fourth of July." He was gruff, his words loud and short, each sentence harder than the next. Whatever he said, Mineko thought, it surprised Dimple. Had James been kinder before leaving for war? Had Dimple known a different James?

She had only known him one way.

Mineko realized she was standing so straight, her knees were locked. She felt dizzy. She looked at Mae, held Paulie tight. James took Mineko's arm, his right hand wrapped around her bicep. Paulie burped and spit up.

James opened a small closet, and inside were a broom, a mop, and a bucket. On the shelf, something that looked like a bleach bottle, something else yellow in a bottle, something else blue.

"Here. You clean." James spoke in broken Japanese. Then, in English, "I'm heading out with Mae. You'll need to cook later, for the party, so get it done pretty fast." But she had figured out what he wanted before he said it. The ranch house was old. Mineko could tell that dust and dirt bubbled up from the wood floors. And it was large. Nothing like cleaning the tiny base house.

Dimple and Calvin left. Mae looked over her shoulder as her father guided her out. Mineko hated to see her go. Paulie pulled at her hair, and she knew it was time to feed him. Pulling back the sheet on one of the sofas—old-timey things with wooden legs and carved backs—she untucked and lifted her blouse and Paulie latched on. She was sleepy then, feeding always made her relax into a stupor. It was a good feeling. She had nursed Mae far longer than the American nurses had suggested; she nursed her into her first year in private, because it felt good to be close to someone and it especially felt good to rest.

It was still and warm, the air soft with heat, and Paulie continued to nurse, a coal against her. Paulie was now the best size of baby—not newborn fragile, but not moving around yet and able to get into trouble. He was a feisty baby, a hungry, loud, bright-eyed little thing, with black hair that stood on end, fuzzy as a duckling. He was hard not to adore. And it had been him that had gotten her through watching Japan slip away on the deck until it was nothing but a black smudge of ink on the horizon. Mae was her translator, her helper, but Paulie was her life force.

Mineko closed her eyes. Sleeping was a horrible idea, but resting, just a moment, how bad could that be? Then he would nap and she would clean. And it would be okay. She closed her eyes and almost immediately she felt herself fall and the gauziness of dreams took over. What she saw was the dappled light of trees, of ginkgos and live oaks, the mint-green of Dimple's pants, the edge of her mother's dressing gown shot through with sunlight, the jiggling lime-green of a Jell-O and pineapple salad; that's what she'd make, and didn't the recipe call for a nut of some sort? Was it this pecan nut? She heard a gentle laugh from Fumiko and the splash of a river rock and the hiss of a snake and somewhere, beyond it all, she knew Akio was there, in the trees, the light so bright it blinded her so she couldn't make him out.

"Git up!" A pain in her thigh.

How long had she slept? The light looked different, less intense, the shadows were deeper in the room. A mantel clock close by, it had a cape of gray. Mineko lifted her head and James was there, with Mae behind, muddy and wet, terrified. James had kicked her with his pointed-toe boot and then did it again. Mineko held Paulie as she sat up quickly and dodged his next kick.

"Tell your mother it's two p.m. Tell her that she's wasted over four hours. Tell her that we did our part—we went to the store—tell her that she's lazy."

Mineko stood.

"It's okay, Mae-chan. It's okay. Take your brother. Go upstairs and pick out a room. Get him comfortable and be my good girl and watch him. Go now. It's going to be okay."

Mineko handed Paulie to Mae and she took him carefully and found the staircase. Mineko listened to Mae's feet climb as she buttoned and tucked her shirt back in. She would not apologize, she decided, but walk back into the kitchen and start cleaning. James said things, he gesticulated, and it was clear that he was swearing at her. Those words she had not learned in class, but at the RAA house. Every few seconds, he'd sprinkle in a Japanese word—stupid, slow, and finally, whore.

I am not, I am not, I am not.

He hates me in two languages, Mineko mused, as she found the rags and the bleach and placed them on the counter.

"You're good for nothing," James said, but he seemed more calm, as if kicking her and yelling had removed some of the anger, like a boiling pot, stirred down. He turned and left from the kitchen door, slamming the screen behind.

The first night in the new house, her body aching with exhaustion, Mineko climbed the steep stairs to the bedrooms. She had put a sleeping Paulie in an ancient cradle that she had found in the corner of the room, under a sheet.

Mae was in a double bed in the same small room. Quilts from home made up her bed—they would need to buy sheets as the ones that they had in the base house belonged to the army and, strangely enough, were returned upon departure. It was a miracle that the quilts arrived at all and were waiting, a small kindness that Mineko held on to that night as she created a makeshift bedroom for her children.

On the base, James had people to drink with and only seemed to do so with them. He never had to drink even half a beer alone. But tonight, he did, on the porch, something from a brown bottle that he had brought back with the groceries from Dimple's store in town. So when he made it upstairs to their bedroom, and the mattress bare, he cussed and swore, pulled off his boots, called to her to bring him a blanket, but passed out in his underwear on top of a towel that he had found instead.

The house was quiet, except for the occasional croaking of a frog and large grasshoppers that flung their bodies against the windows and fell away, unhurt, only to try it again. It was clean. Top to bottom. In the old refrigerator that shimmied and coughed for the first few hours after being plugged in, gallons of sun tea waited for tomorrow. On the counter, sacks of Sunbeam white bread and onions, ready for slicing. Dimple had dropped off pickles and okra—ten jars in a box—on the front porch while Mineko was cleaning. James had been home when a truck and a tall trailer pulled up in the early evening—*it's for horses, Mama*, Mae had learned and explained—and a large black metal cooker of some sort was lifted out and placed among a stand of trees. In Tokyo, street vendors had something similar for yakitori, but this one had a domed lid that lifted on hinges like a clam.

Mineko turned off the small lamp next to the couch, said goodnight to the stupid grasshoppers, and climbed the stairs. She looked in at James, facedown, legs splayed, and sighed.

She went into her children's room, touched Paulie's fuzzy head. Mae was quiet in bed, so she listened for her breathing. It was not deep, so Mineko whispered her name.

"I'm awake, Mama. I can't sleep here."

"I will sleep with you. That will be better."

"I don't know if I like Texas," Mae whispered urgently. "I know I'm supposed to like it, I know Daddy wants me to like it; he kept telling me that I would and that it's the right place for me, but I just don't know."

"New things take time, Mae-chan. We will all learn to be happy here."

"Paulie's lucky. He won't remember home. So he'll always like it here."

They lay in the dark and Mae reached out her hand to Mineko's and squeezed.

When she awoke at four a.m., unable to toss and turn any longer, men were in the front yard with flashlights around the black grill. Its cavernous mouth was open, and they were laying large chunks of beef on it. Smoke poured out of the crevices. James was there. The ends of cigarettes lit up the dark edges. How many were there? Mineko put on her housecoat and went downstairs; she poured herself a cup of coffee and retreated to her room quickly. At sunup, a few people arrived with large bowls and containers of food. The refrigerator was soon full and the porch lined with ice chests. Six watermelons, fifteen cantaloupes. Vats of potato salad and something called coleslaw, but Mineko had understood as "cold saw" and continued to mispronounce it that afternoon and for the rest of her life.

As the women knocked and came into the house, put away their food, they didn't call out to meet her, so Mineko, for the most part, stayed upstairs and busied herself with what she could, unpacking the few cases that had arrived and feeding Paulie. Mae had escaped with her doll and a parasol, and Mineko watched her from the window, darting through the trees, spinning and twirling, a little girl who had been traveling for so long, happy to stretch her legs. Then Mae had gathered long limbs from all over the property for the men to burn in the smoker. Mineko watched her play and realized how miserable she must have been on the ship and how the ample amount of land and sunlight had seemed to revive her. Eventually someone new arrived and when he walked up, a girl about Mae's age was hiding behind his legs. Mae chatted with her and, slowly, she dropped her father's hand and followed Mae across the yard.

Mineko felt a strange mix of relief and panic. She put on a better dress, located the scarf she had made, and whispered to Paulie, "Let's go make some friends, too."

On the front porch were a few women, wives of the men gathered around the smoker, who all looked the same to Mineko, ash-blond and dishwater-blond, freckles peeking through makeup, light eyes. Mineko said, "Hello, how are you?" in English, and after waiting for their variety of responses she said, as clearly as possible, "Oh, I am fine, thank you for asking, very nice meeting you."

They smiled, and while she doubted that she handled the engagement successfully, they were kind enough to pretend. But Paulie had no problems communicating with these visitors. He smiled his best gummy smiles and made his best noises for the ladies. Within a few minutes, they seemed to look through Mineko, but were enchanted by Paulie, commenting on his duckling-down black hair and his pretty eyes. His mouth was a perfect bow and his cheeks smooth, round, and golden in the sun that poured onto the front porch. James came by once, during such an encounter, and stopped to chat.

"Oh, James, I don't know how you're gonna get a lick of work done with those cattle. He's just too precious," a woman said. She had just arrived with a lidded bowl, nestled it into the fridge, and had bestowed warm side hugs to the rest of the ladies. She had a different hair color than the others—a warm orange, the color of an autumn chrysanthemum—and bright blue eyes. Mineko at first decided that she was perhaps her favorite, based on her smile, her hair color, and the large bowl of rice salad she contributed. It was the first evidence of rice she had seen in the

United States, and she felt a flood of relief. For nearly a week, all she had eaten at roadside cafés were potatoes in all their various forms.

"Yes, I am going to make the long trek to visit y'all, because you're just too cute!" the orange-haired woman said.

"Yep, he's a charmer, I'll give him that. He's got his mother's coloring and my good looks!" James grinned at the pretty woman, reaching out to touch her on the shoulder, and she let him.

"Git on out there and tend to your brisket, Jimmy Cope," she said plainly, but not without tenderness.

Mineko watched as he left and the orange-haired woman walked across the grass to her car. Of the four women who had passed through the house, dropping off food, Mineko noticed that none seemed to connect the children to her. To these women, it was as if Paulie and Mae had appeared out of thin air, as if James had conjured them from nothing.

Before long it was noon and while a couple of men stayed on to drink and "keep an eye on the smoker," everyone else left to get out of the heat and ready themselves for later. The party wasn't to officially start for another five hours, and already Mineko felt worn and tired. Mae wandered back from playing, dirty and hungry, and Mineko found a piece of bread and a slice of cheese for her. She peeled a few small familiar fruits—*They're little peaches, Mama*—that Mae had picked somewhere on the property.

Afterward, Mineko wiped the dust and peach juice from Mae and laid her down for a nap, along with Paulie. Feeling safest next to her sleeping children, she also eventually dozed off. They all woke to a knock from Dimple, who stepped inside, put her hands on her hips, and uttered a long and winded diatribe that neither Mae nor Mineko could discern. She folded up the blanket, straightened the comforter on the bed, and pushed Mineko toward the bathroom across the hall to "freshen herself." When she returned, Dimple had already rebraided Mae's hair, located the red-white-and-blue skirt Mineko had made for her on base, and put it on her. She was changing Paulie.

"Good job on Mae's little outfit. You're good at this stuff," Dimple said while fastening the safety pins through Paulie's thick diaper. Dimple unceremoniously handed him to Mineko and shooed Mae out the door.

"And watch out for that fire-haired gal. Don't like to see any woman, Jap or not, be fooled by that ten-cent floozy. She'll be moving on soon. She left James for the city years ago, and she'll never come back permanently, not for nothing."

Mineko gathered Dimple's words like chicken eggs for later. It would take her a month to figure out what a floozy was, but once she did, she'd never forget it.

Dimple led her and Paulie down the stairs and into the loud living room, people everywhere, a party in full swing. Dimple parted the crowd with her arms.

"Found 'em! Now give 'em some room and don't be grabbing at that baby, she needs to feed him." And Mineko and Paulie emerged into the living room.

Chapter 21

YOU ARE SO LOVED is written on the front in a twirly brush-calligraphy font.

I shuffle this stack of cards into a "on the loss of your loved one" spot. No, I think, not the right place. I check the label that's affixed to the box. The cards are thick and creamy, with a beautiful watercolor river flowing across hilly terrain. A small house is tucked between trees, hiding. The label says nothing, just the SKU number.

I'm the manager on duty today and the only cashier. Choice is mine. I look back at the cards. *YOU ARE SO LOVED.* Maybe it should go in the "for someone special" spots. Or maybe in the "friendship" section. I open the card, the inside is blank. I really have nothing to go on.

I stifle a yawn. I was up late last night, my thoughts flip-flopping between Grandminnie's house and seeing Darren. The excitement of one and the disgust at the other are combining in my body and giving me some sort of trembling push. And Grandminnie slept deeply beside me, snoring like a diesel motor.

I think of her, poring over the books at the library yesterday, how her face lit up to see the insides of homes that simply looked *familiar* to her. How she marveled at the beautiful library, at the students quietly working, all friendly with an old Japanese woman flipping through international design journals. How the color photocopier was like magic to her.

I put the stack of cards down near the cash register and grab a past issue of *Architectural Review* from my purse. I. M. Pei stares back at me. It's a retrospective of his work, including the small collection of homes that he has designed, one in Fort Worth that is the middle of every local modern architecture junkie's bingo card. I go to the dog-eared page and trace the triangular facade of the entry.

I remember Mrs. Grant showing us a slide of this beautiful structure the first day in her Design VI class. I had never had a female architecture prof before, much less one so earnestly delighted with all aspects of architecture, residential included. The weather threatened an ice storm outside, but the warm hiss of the slide projector flipping through Mrs. Grant's favorite buildings made it cozy in the classroom. She was a Pei aficionado, and it made sense why Darren had gifted me that book at Christmas.

Mrs. Grant turned out to be sharp, funny, and very thoughtful in her teaching approach. She wanted to focus this semester's project on multi-use architecture. She explained that ever since ancient times, the ability to live where one works has been a natural impulse. We would look at this interplay, working with already-standing structures, remodeling them into something new and more usable.

"This is just a tricky way for us to design some houses," Bradley had complained as he picked a chicken strip from the twenty-piece box we were sharing.

Antares wiped his hands on a napkin and then wadded it up, clearly irritated with Bradley's negative talk.

I had been given the assignment of redesigning a dormitory on the UT campus, originally built in the 1920s and then added on to in the 1950s. Instead of my previous bouts of near-crippling doubt, I already had a plan forming in my head. I wanted to include modern amenities where students could study and be social, and the warmth of a traditional home, so students could feel comfortable and safe within their new environment.

"It's not residential, it's mixed use. It's a tweener," Rochelle said. She was tasked with redesigning an automotive assembly plant into an office building and apartment homes.

"I like her," Antares said. "She's sincere."

• • •

After staring at the magazine for a while, I force myself back to work. I look closer at the greeting cards. *YOU ARE SO LOVED.* On a rock, sunbathing in the middle of the watercolor river, is a tiny turtle. If you weren't looking closely, it wouldn't be visible.

I take the stack of cards and find what I feel is their proper location: "On your moving day." I nestle them into the cubby.

The bell chimes, and I turn to see the shiny, overly rouged moon face of Mrs. Whitehall, who was in Aunt Mae's high school graduating class and is the mom of one of the girls I went through school with. Her daughter, Krissie, went off to Tech, and married the pitcher, who is now playing in the majors in some midwestern town. I'm not a baseball fan, so I can't ever remember which one, except the rumor is that he could be the next Nolan Ryan.

We had all attended her wedding because most of the town had been invited. The event, from its gold and white flowers (team colors, I was informed) to her nine bridesmaids, irritated me somehow.

Mrs. Whitehall wiggles her fingers at me and asks how my mom and aunt Mae are doing. She asks about my cousins' weddings, wonders when they'll make it back to Texas. She says what she always does—that I'm the spitting image of my aunt at my age. I nod and thank her. Folks on my mom's side say I'm the spitting image of *her* at my age. I've asked Grand-minnie about this, and she says that people see what they want and do not listen to any of it. I look like me.

Mrs. Whitehall picks up a package of silver tissue paper and starts looking at cards. She asks about a gift she ordered a few weeks ago and I go into the storeroom to find the two-fake-wood-angels-holding-a-heart figurine and check the box to make sure it is in good condition. At the cash register, Mrs. Whitehall signs her name to a check with a giddy flourish.

"I'm so glad you're back, Lia. This town needs young blood like you to keep it going. And you're doing a great job here. But if you ever want to get back to what you were doing before"—she pushes her sunglasses back down from her head and onto her face—"I know someone. My cousin in Dennis. He's in architecture."

"Oh, really? That's very helpful. Thank you."

"Designs sheds. Nice ones, of course, for yard equipment, mowers, hay, that stuff."

She gathers up the sack I have just expertly prepared for her and throws me a little wave before leaving, the bells tinkling again.

I sit on the stool behind the cash register and open a bag of Reese's Pieces. At first, I just pick out a few of the orange ones to eat. Then, frustrated, I pour the whole bag into my mouth and chomp down.

I come in the back door, quiet. Sun has set and Dad's truck is in the drive. After work, I drove around, thinking about silly old Krissie Whitehall and her baseball-throwing hubby, thinking about how much infinitely cooler Austin is compared to wherever they live and how I miss it so much. Before I knew it, I was out at Grandminnie's land, where the house once stood. I had spent holidays there—July Fourth, especially, and we'd go early and stay until the last bottle rocket had been shot and my aunt Dimple no longer was muttering, "Well, there goes *his* eyebrows."

I expect to feel remorse or dislike for this spot, but I don't. It was a happy place for me. A place where I trailed behind Sallie and Sam and played hide-and-seek, a place where there were old toys to dig through—things my father played with as a boy—and a barn that smelled dark and damp. There were almost always cattle, but sometimes a goat, a few times chickens. My grandmother's house was where misfit farm stock went to spend their golden years.

Of course, I sprung up after the shadow of my grandfather had left the house. And maybe I could feel it, a tinge of coldness to the edges of rooms, a history that I didn't understand fully. Grandminnie was always too busy hosting us to spend much attention on me. But I see now that it wasn't intentional as much as the aftermath of something.

I layer the new knowledge with the old feelings. I see how memories and misunderstandings soak through life, like our days are as thin as coffee filters.

At home, I sneak upstairs just as my father comes out of my room. He has a look on his face, like he's smelled something foul and is investigating where it's coming from.

"Your phone was ringing off the hook."

My father's face is doing this thing where I know he's ping-ponging thoughts all over the place, but his forehead and lips are trying to remain calm and still.

"The library. You got an overdue book."

I nod, but Dad still doesn't move out of my way.

"So, no sooner than I hang up with the librarian, you got another call, some man this time. Darren. Said he really needed to speak to you about something important. Left his number. Are you applying for a new job or something?"

"Daddy, you don't have to grill me, I'm an adult."

"You're living at home and hanging out with your grandmother every spare moment. *Adult* is not the word I'm thinking describes this situation."

I let out a groan. My father cocks his head. *See?* his look says.

"Lia, honey, do you have something to tell me?"

I am stalling but trying to come up with a good reason for stalling.

"Corporate at Bags-N-Bows said that they are interested in developing my career path so that guy is with HR."

My father is both visibly relieved but also irritated that I'd even consider staying with a franchise gift-wrap store. I take a deep breath. *Here goes.*

"But you know, I'm not interested. I've been thinking about Stephie and moving back . . ."

Dad reaches out and squeezes my shoulders.

"Atta girl!" He breaks into a grin. "I knew you'd come to your senses!"

"Yeah, well, I'm going to call that Darren back and tell him I'm not interested. At all."

I say this with faux bravado.

"I won't keep you then! Mom's got dinner in the oven, staying warm for you. Just come down and eat when you're done. And she made sugar cookies."

Grandminnie is right, no matter what I decide, I've got to get out of this house.

The Design VI semester flew faster than any before it. I felt at ease within this project and Mrs. Grant was supportive of us all, overseeing the desk crits with a firm but gentle hand, introducing new members of the critique jury, including a couple local architects whom she knew personally and who framed their opinions carefully and constructively. Darren was noticeably absent from the jury, and when I saw him in the hallway one afternoon, I asked him why. It was an innocent enough question—he had been a major player on every other critique team.

"Why, what did you hear?" Darren said. And I didn't know how to respond. He was remarkably tan.

"Nothing. Nothing at all. I was just wondering. And you haven't been around much this semester."

"Miss me? I've been busy with some projects for administration. Paperwork is killing me."

Before I could say anything else, Darren pulled me around the corner and behind the false wall that hid the custodial closet door.

"Lia, I need to tell you something. Be careful with Madeline. She's not what you think. She's been saying some stuff and, well, she's a snake."

I must have frowned because Darren shook his head. I couldn't imagine Mrs. Grant misleading anyone.

"Lia, she's not going to help you like I have, no way. She doesn't have the chops. Please, trust me. And if you need any help, call me. I want to be there for you."

He turned and left quickly, leaving me confused.

I asked Bradley if he had heard anything, since he was usually at the pulse of all the architecture gossip. He said that he had heard that Darren and his wife were breaking up. That something had happened and he was looking for a bachelor pad near campus.

"I don't believe it," I said.

"It's true. Someone saw him walking out of the building with a Realtor, talking about locations."

"That could have been about anything!"

Bradley also said that someone had overheard him telling the dean that Sandy had been gone for two months and had no plans to come back from her family's place in Aspen, and he'd be happy to play tennis with the dean anytime, since he had no one at home anymore and that's what he was doing in his spare time.

"That would explain the tan," I said.

"And why I'm heading to the courts later," Bradley said.

Despite his best efforts, Bradley never got an invite to bat around a tennis ball with Darren. He also struggled with his mixed-use project and it was Antares, Rochelle, and me who stepped in to help him figure out what he was doing. The models were larger than anything we had worked on in the past, and we spent more time than ever in the studio. I wondered how many brain cells I was killing off with cyanoacrylate and the acetone used to remove the glue from my fingers. But my work was beautiful. My dormitory had large two-story windows that allowed light into the study lounge, and I even figured out how to get a gaming room into a former basement. For the first time in a long time, I was having *fun*.

Darren came by one night, or, more accurately, one morning, about two a.m. The room was still relatively busy, half of us working the night away, portable CD players and long cords, candy bar wrappers littering the flat surfaces. We all had the scent of humans away from a bar of soap for too long. I sniffed myself as Darren came closer and then removed my bright yellow headphones.

"You look awful," he said, laughing.

"I should. I've been here three days straight. But look—" and I stepped away from my model, a wall of glass made from plexi that I had hand-painted to reflect the campus.

But he had already turned away and was pulling something out of a Brooks Brothers shopper, a large white bakery box that was wrapped in layer after layer of plastic wrap.

"What the hell is that?" Bradley asked.

"This, my beloved students, is the remnant of a building destroyed."

He sliced open the plastic with my X-Acto knife and lifted the lid of the box. Out came a cake in the shape of a perfect cube, decorated with fondant that had been stamped with an intricate pattern. The fondant sweated a bit, as if having been frozen and thawed.

"I just came from a party," he said. "And it's my anniversary. Would have been."

I didn't know how to respond. His eyes were glassy. I realized that he was drunk.

"Is that your wedding cake?" Rochelle asked.

"That *was* my wedding cake. In the deep freeze for three years, now thawed and ready for you to enjoy. I found it, looking for vodka."

"Wait! Is that the top of the Cleary Building?" Bradley put his face a few inches from the frosting.

Classmates gathered near, squinting. It was. The intricate stamping was from the etched glass that gave the Cleary its one-of-a-kind look and put Darren Miles on the map.

Darren took the X-Acto and slowly sliced the cake into thirds, working to create perfect skinny slices.

"This is weird," Rochelle whispered to me. I nodded. But we both accepted a piece of cake that Bradley was helping to serve, using a stack of fast-food napkins. He gave me an I-told-you look, and I felt sad.

"So let me get this right," I said to Darren when he came closer again, wiping white fondant on his black tuxedo pants. "You went to a fancy party tonight, went home, looked for some vodka, found the top of your wedding cake from a marriage that I'm guessing is now over, and decided to bring it here, to the studio, to share."

"I didn't need it in the house anymore, and it had been a really good cake, really expensive, and very, very tall."

"I'm sorry. About Mrs. Miles."

Darren shrugged as if all of it was just one of those things that happened.

"Your model—it's nearly done, I see."

I took the last bite of very dry cake and watched as Darren squatted level with my updated version of the dormitory. In addition to the building, I had created a section of a dorm room, working with watercolor to paint the comforter of a miniature bed and constructing a small L-shaped workspace for a student. I was very proud of this part.

"The construction is well done, very clean. It's a fantastic model."

I waited. "And . . ." I prompted.

"It's functional. I can tell that you are listening intently to Mrs. Grant."

But Darren wasn't smiling. He shoved his hands into his pockets. He started to say something, but then stopped. I looked over at the plastic-wrapped cardboard that had held the cake and all that was left was crumbs.

"You need to decide who you are, Lia. As an architect. Do you want to go for the big jobs or do you want to do something more smaller scale? Residential, maybe. Only you can decide. You can't be both."

Then he left, leaving the sack and the white cake box on the shared table.

"What the fuck was that?" Bradley asked. But I couldn't respond. I instead straightened my space, putting the cap back on the X-Acto knife, stacking the odds and ends of my supplies. Slowly the volume turned up on the room again, and I slid my headphones back over my ears. I didn't know how to account for my feelings. I tried to strip his words from the event, run them over in my head, and tell myself that it was nothing, that it was okay, that I was still good at this, that I was still worthy.

The phone rings on my desk and I let it go, worried it is Darren again. I refuse to call him back. The downstairs phone immediately starts going off. I hear Dad answer, then his heavy footfalls climbing to the landing.

"It's your grandmother," he calls out.

I get up and stretch, make my way to the extension that's on the landing, and answer.

"You didn't come by today. We have a lot of work to do."

I don't know how to tell her I just couldn't. That I got stuck in my own thoughts and couldn't move forward.

"I'll be by tomorrow. Wait, I have to work. I'll be by after that."

"You don't sound so good. What's going on?"

I want to tell her. About how Darren's still finding a way closer. But I hear a click on the line, and I know that my mom or my dad has picked up and is listening in. "I'll see you tomorrow, Grandminnie."

"Lia-chan, you can always trust me. Maybe you will tell me tomorrow."

Chapter 22

Curtain, Texas
September 1961

Evangeline Thomas went by Evangeline, not Evie or Lena. The full name. Hard to say. Four syllables chock-full of vowel traps. By the time Mineko was invited to the book club at the Thomas ranch, she had long since given up saying "My name is Mineko, but you may call me Minnie." Now it was just Minnie from the start.

But on the day of the book club, Mineko was feeling grateful. Eight years in Curtain. Eight years struggling with a new place, a new language, her kids always the spark for improving her English. Paulie, the nearly nine-year-old prankster, tried to get her to say tongue twisters, *The old gray rat ran up the roof with a lump of raw liver.* When she had realized that he was teasing her, she had grabbed him by the arm and swatted his bottom with a wooden spoon, but then, as the tears came, she ran her hand through his hair and fished out a handful of gumdrops from the fat-pig cookie jar where she kept them and pressed them into his hands. *I'm so sorry.*

Now she could speak and understand the surface stuff with fluency. Seasons and weather, food, familial connections, favorite mayonnaise brand, and activities. Her list: fall, cool, hot dogs, wife and mother, Duke's and sewing. And this seemed enough to make a few casual friends and, somehow, get an invitation to the book club on the second Wednesday morning of the month at the Thomases'. When she told her sister-in-law,

Dimple, she seemed surprised, then annoyed. Even after this many years, they weren't close, but they were within reach of each other, their paths crossing while feeding cattle, shopping at Dimple's store, family dinners. It was a relationship that had warmed just enough to be comfortable, like a wool blanket washed until it was nearly soft, but not quite. This pleased Mineko as she had always secretly thought that they could somehow be friends. They had too much in common—a lack of frivolity and a blunt manner—not to be.

"I've been invited for years, and I'd rather slit my wrist than chitty-chat with *that* pack of scootie-pies, but if you're going, I suppose I'll be neighborly and go, too."

So on the day of book club, after the children were off at school, Mineko stared at the clothes in her closet, settled on her newest dress, a floral print of mauve and maroon roses on a white background. She styled her hair, which was newly permed, then chose a cardigan and a bouquet brooch that the kids had saved up to buy her for Christmas from the Sears catalog. She picked off a few stray cat hairs. She stared at herself in the mirror and, for a moment, couldn't recall the last time she had looked in the mirror. She noticed a few creases around her eyes. Mineko checked for gray hair and, finding none, felt relief. She checked her nose, checked her breath, checked her nails.

Details, details, details. Acceptance is in the details.

Book club was also a potluck luncheon, and she was bringing black cherry cake, her newest favorite. For fifty cents and eight Jell-O proofs of purchase, a collection of recipes had been sent to the house. It really was amazing what one could make from flavored gelatin.

Mineko parked the farm truck closest to the gate, even backing in to give herself a sure path to the road. She did this as a just-in-case maneuver, but she was pleased to be out of the house, even if she was a little nervous. She sat in the truck for a few minutes before going in, calming herself.

News from home was difficult to read. Her father was dying. He was not expected to live through the fall, but Mineko had been waiting for this letter for fifteen years, since his stomach problems began. He can barely eat, Hana wrote to Mineko; he has become so small that sometimes I don't see him in the garden, it is like he's shrinking away.

Mineko would have felt more comfort if Hisako were still living near home, but after Mineko had arrived in Texas, she received a letter from Osaka. Hisako had met an American soldier, on leave from service in Korea, and had fallen in love. They were married at home in Kadoma— their mother planned the wedding herself—and she was readying to move to Indianapolis. Of course, Mineko had thought, old resentment rising from her gut. *I send the money and she gets the blessing.* In a later letter, Hisako wrote to Mineko, *Dear sister, please forgive me my trespasses, as I have found the Lord and realize that the hurt that I inflicted will keep me from my heavenly savior.*

Mineko was not surprised to learn that Hisako was quite concerned about a savior, heavenly or otherwise.

James was James. He formally retired from the military in 1960, although ranching had long since been his primary activity. He had grown even more distant, moody at his best, cold and angry on the average day. She had decided that there was no changing him and that the best way to live within this marriage was with low expectations and distance. It didn't take long for her to realize that the woman who showed up at that first Fourth of July picnic was an old flame who never wanted to be a ranch wife and who had left for Houston. Soon after the picnic, she had married, which had put James into a jealous gloom. But every so often, he'd say he had business in Houston and disappear for a few days.

The first time Mineko felt sullen, lingering on the edge of jealousy herself. But only the first time. From then on, she made her favorite Japanese-inspired dishes that James didn't care for and let the kids stay up late, taking them into Dennis for a movie and to the five-and-dime for candy. James was an inconsistent father to Mae and Paulie. Sometimes he belittled them, pointing out every flaw. Other times he was dismissive, treating them as near strangers who happened to share his breakfast table. The one emotion he never seemed to hit in his pinball parenting was loving. That's where Mineko tried to make up for his deep lack.

But what made her feel most lonely was the growth of Mae and Paulie. The children had not only learned English and had forgotten all except the most rudimentary Japanese, they had learned *American.* Yes, Mineko thought, it was time to join some groups, try a little harder, be a little more open to change. Whether or not she was truly ready. Whether or not it would truly work.

Mineko straightened her dress as she held the cake in one arm, her handbag looped over the other. Pausing to breathe and practice her hellos in her head, she then rapped on the door to no answer. Silence, then the scuttle of feet. The door was flung wide, and Evangeline, tall and golden, beamed.

"Minnie! You're here!"

Behind her, a roomful of ladies holding skinny glasses of iced tea and cups of punch. They, too, smiled. Mineko stifled a bow, still an automatic reflex. She smiled, as Mae had reminded her. *Smile, Mama, people want you to smile.*

In the bright room of pinks and yellows, of ash-blond and oaky-hued brunettes, as Mineko stepped in, she felt dark. On the outside, black hair and dark eyes, skin deep bronze from working in her garden. On the inside, dark as a storm cloud, and she wondered what happened to her hope, her feeling of long-awaited acceptance.

"Minnie, darling, doesn't that look delicious? Let me take it, put it on the table." Evangeline gently took the glass cake pan, which Mineko realized she was clutching a little too tightly. But Evangeline didn't leave her side, instead handing off the cake to a waiting woman, who in turn disappeared into another room, as if on wheels.

Evangeline's hand was on her back, and Mineko realized that she was perspiring.

"I did not know what book we will read, so I did not"—Mineko paused, thinking—"*prepare.*"

"Oh, honey, not to worry. Usually it's the Bible, so that's an easy one . . ." Evangeline flittered her hand.

"But just the New Testament!" said a woman, whom Mineko recognized from school events. "Those crazy names in the Old Testament drive me batty!"

Dimple arrived, wearing a simple plaid dress and flat shoes. If Mineko was out of place, Dimple was as well. She was the only woman in the bunch who worked, the only woman who knew how to pull a calf *and* take a store's inventory. From the ink that smeared her right hand, along the tender side of her pinkie finger, inventory was exactly what she had been doing before arriving.

Dimple dropped off a large platter of fried chicken, waved off hellos like they were gnats, and cut across the room for Mineko.

"Well, hell froze over and I'm here." She took out a handkerchief and blew her nose. "Hay fever."

Mineko nodded. She was jealous of Dimple's flats. Had she been more brave, she would have worn hers, instead of the oxblood patent pumps.

"Gotta say, least I have some time away from Wayne. He's about to drive me bonkers. I'm worried about that boy. Kid doesn't have common sense." Dimple's youngest was in constant trouble at the elementary school and the one cousin Mineko told Paulie to stay away from.

"It's good to be invited to things," Mineko said in a whisper.

"It's good to get your stuff done and go to bed on time. But I couldn't let you wander into the coyote den by your lonesome."

As touched as Mineko was by the sentiment, her stomach vibrated at Dimple's words. A lemon-yellow punch was passed their way. The little linen napkin had the curled initials of the hostess. There was clapping, then a rapping of metal against wood. Voices hushed. Exuberant hands folded into laps.

"Ladies! Gracious, it's lovely to see you all today. It's been too long. I've been traveling some this summer—I have photos!—and now with school in session, I am just so pleased to be starting up our little tradition again."

Evangeline was standing, front and center. Mineko looked around to see if anyone wasn't in rapt attention. She caught Dimple's eyes, and Dimple raised her eyebrows and flared her nostrils.

"We have two new faces, of course. Minnie Cope and her sister-in-law, Dimple, have *finally* joined us!"

There were pleasant claps and a few whispers. Mineko felt herself on show, but smiled, clutching her napkin, which was damp with punch condensation and sweat from her palm.

"As many of you know, I earned my degree in English, so I've helped

Minnie with her reading and language skills." Evangeline paused for more polite clapping.

Mineko was stunned. She couldn't believe her own understanding. Surely Evangeline had said something else, so Mineko just nodded, yes, yes, she has done what she said, still replaying the words slowly through her head.

Dimple whispered, "The nerve!"

Perhaps Evangeline meant she *planned* to help her.

Mineko continued to ponder this, letting her posture drop, her legs, previously knees-together-angled-to-the-side, as taught at Bride School, began to gape a bit. She felt herself withering, and Dimple touched her arm slightly. Mineko sat up.

"We're prayin'."

Indeed all heads were bowed, except for hers and Evangeline's, who smiled beatifically at her and Dimple.

Mineko lowered her head, but didn't close her eyes, keeping them on her knees and the flowers of her dress. She thought of the truck. Pointed to home. But she was the farthest from the door. She couldn't leave, she wasn't even certain if she had good cause.

The ladies murmured amen.

Mineko drank the warm remains of her punch after the chatter began. Like so many things in this town, Mineko felt again the hidden rules that had tripped her up so many times before. They were invisible, lightly strung cobwebs, easy enough to walk through, but persistent, the filament stuck against the chest, always found later. Another moment of delayed embarrassment, another thought in the night as she stared out at the flat fields, the light in the barn. *I said it wrong. But how did I say it wrong?*

And James. His judgment. It was as if he realized his folly too late. Mineko would never dissolve into America like sugar, and he could not break her into true obedience. And whatever gratitude she felt for his help after the war would never be worshipful. He wasn't her savior and she wasn't his prize. James was punishing her for it. Punishing all of them.

She missed home.

She saw Akio's face. The turtles swimming. Could almost hear his laugh. She shuddered and tried to shut the door on this thought.

"Min, you don't look well. Everyone's lining up for the buffet. Let's sneak out for a breath?"

Dimple led Mineko through the living room, opposite to where the women were gathering in a knotted line, down a few stairs to another sunny room—this one with a large, empty birdcage in the corner—and through doors that led to a tiny private sunporch.

"Stupid woman. She used to have all these cute little birds, but she forgot to have someone put a heater in here and when it got so cold last winter they all froze to death. Careless, careless." Dimple shook her head, slipped her hand into her handbag and produced a pack of Chesterfields and a book of matches. "Not your brand, but it'll do in a pinch."

Mineko greedily sucked on the cigarette.

"This ain't no book club."

"I thought we'd be reading real books. That it would be hard, but that Mae could help. I hoped for poetry."

Dimple peered at her through smoke.

"The Japanese have good poetry, don't they?"

Mineko nodded. They had to memorize and recite in grade school.

"Many poets. Shiki was my favorite in school. There are others, too. Akiko. Sachio."

"You don't talk much about school in Japan."

"I was good at it. All the subjects. But I liked math and science best," Mineko said, and Dimple nodded.

"Poetry would be a good way to learn to read English, if someone were to help you. Maybe check out something at the library, even though I reckon we have a piss-poor poetry section."

Mineko smiled at this comment. Piss-poor. So many funny sayings.

"You look better, but you don't have to stay, you know, if you're not feeling up to it or something. I'll get your dish and bring it back to you."

Mineko thought about this.

"Evangeline did not teach me English."

"Course not! She's a piece of work, that one. Nothing is as it seems with her." Dimple began to reach for an ashtray that was perched nearby on a white wrought iron table, but then paused. With a sly smile, she tapped her cigarette and ash fell to the ground.

"And I just used an ashtray," Dimple said, stamping out her cigarette on the porch, her brown flats grinding the remains into the rug.

Mineko felt the glory of a laugh come upon her. It shook her body. Nothing was okay, but for a moment it was bearable. She had never been a quiet laugher. Dimple wasn't quiet either, sounding like a spooked goose, all sound exploding out at once.

"You know, I wasn't sure of you at first and I'm mighty regretful about that."

Then Mineko flicked her ash onto the rug and Dimple spurted into a laugh again, her shoulders shaking. She felt a friendship with her, a true friendship. It was powerful and Mineko felt stronger because of it, strong enough to go back into the home and fill her plate and eat. Then, when it was time to move on to the actual book study, a couple of pages of Revelation, she picked up her purse and left through the front door.

Chapter 23

Curtain, Texas
April 3, 1999

It's Saturday morning. Mom and Dad are yelling through the house. Mom is telling Dad that Autumn Leaves is on the phone and something's wrong with Grandminnie and my dad's boots are loud and fast against the floor and I'm awake and stumbling down the stairs.

She's dead. I just know it. She went to bed and didn't wake up.

"Mom, you say you started feeling funny after breakfast? Funny how?"

I'm so relieved I could cry. If she's talking, that's a good sign.

Dad screws up his face with her response. I can't hear her words exactly, but I can hear her voice through the line.

"I'm coming, Mom."

Brow furrowed, Dad leans in to kiss Mom on the cheek and says "Bye, sugar" to me. My mom offers to call Grandminnie's primary care doc and goes off to locate her little address book full of numbers, the one with so many business cards stapled onto pages, it doesn't even close.

I feel left out that he didn't ask me to come, but then I remember that I have work today, a full shift of smiling at frosted-haired ladies while they buy Easter basket toys and gift bags with bunnies printed on them.

"I feel like I should go to the hospital," I say to Mom, who has come back in and is flipping through her book.

"You can go after you get off work. The first few hours, they'll just be running tests, if that." My mom has already lost her parents. She has done hospital visits, both preplanned and in the middle of the night. "I know you're worried. She'll be okay."

The day before Easter promises to be a big one at Bags-N-Bows. We have a holiday section that carries hollow chocolate bunnies and stuffed animals plus those little plastic toys that jump and chirp when you turn the key. We have jelly beans sorted by color that I have to make sure are weighed correctly at the register. So much Easter grass. Ten different pastel colors.

I grab a cup of coffee and go upstairs to find my hot-pink polo for work. My khaki skirt needs ironing, so I plug in the iron and wait for it to heat up and make its clicking noises. I turn the steam on high and it spurts and hisses. I burn myself on a hot metal button. I realize I've been going over the wrinkles again and again until the khaki fabric almost shimmers. I scratch my scalp and a few flakes of skin float down to the ironing board.

Mom sticks her head in the room.

"Darlin', your work clicked through when I was on the line with the doctor. Good news—you're cut for the day. Your boss says they were swamped last night and all that's left is some basic green grass and black jelly beans. They won't need you."

She has caught me near panic attack, nerves about Grandminnie mixing with worry that Darren will call again, and my face must look like it, because Mom stares at me for a moment.

"What's up?"

"Nothing. Just ironing. That's great. I'll go see Grandminnie. Meet Daddy there."

"Take your time, I'm gonna make Grandminnie something good to eat for lunch—she loves my egg salad and she hates hospital food."

I tell Mom that's sweet of her.

"Oh, I love your grandmother. She drives me batty, but she's the one who raised your daddy. To bring up two good kids with that mess of a husband of hers, that's something."

I set down the iron and hug my mom tightly.

On the way to Dennis General, I drive by Curtain Pharmacy. Aunt Mae's car is gone, so I know that she's already at the hospital with Dad. I worked at the pharmacy between my fourth and fifth years. That summer, I kept myself busy, dividing my time between a drafting job in Fort Worth and Aunt Mae's pharmacy. I thought of that night in the studio often. A few days following what we all now dubbed "the cake night," Darren had written me a note and put it on my desk, apologizing for making things weird. He explained that he was broken up about his divorce and appreciated my discretion. But it was all of our discretion, because as far as I know, none of us told any of the architecture school leadership about the wedding cake.

I didn't see him for the rest of the semester, and the sign on his door read that he was taking a brief leave of absence to attend to a family matter. But what he said that night, and what he didn't say, stayed with me.

I meet Dad in the hallway outside a treatment room in the ER. The beeping and bright lights make me feel small.

"Good. Glad you're here. She's okay—they're checking her heart. Keep an eye on her. She's driving the nurses nuts. Mae and I gotta go make a call. Forgot about a meeting we had today."

Mae is already down the hall, her long broomstick skirt swishing.

I wonder what could be so important that both of them have to take off like this. I'm irritated. Am I the only one who really cares about Grandminnie around here?

Grandminnie is reigning in her adjustable bed, a nurse taking her pulse.

"You're just fine, Mrs. Cope. Steady as a metronome."

My grandmother looks up at the young woman and scowls.

"I asked for apple juice and some crackers," Grandminnie says. "Where are they?"

"What's with you? They're trying to help," I say, putting the egg salad on the counter that Mom had shoved into my hands before I left the house. The nurse winks at me as she leaves the room, closing the sliding glass door softly behind her.

My grandmother sits up and tells me that she thinks my dad and aunt Mae are up to something, but then she leans back and looks up at the ceiling, shuts her eyes for a moment. I can tell she doesn't feel like herself.

She's in a hospital gown that bags around her neck because it's untied in the back.

"Are you sleepy? Want me to dim these lights?"

Eyes still closed, she shakes her head no.

I pull a heavy guest chair closer, sit down on the vinyl cushion that releases a shush of air. It's cold in the ER. I pull out my sweatshirt and put it on.

"So what do you think is wrong? Dad thinks you're having a heart attack and Mom thinks it's just gas. What does Aunt Mae think?"

"Oh, she thinks the worst thing."

"And what's that?"

"She thinks I'm just old."

Another nurse walks in, she goes to one of Grandminnie's machines, pushes a button on the top, writes down a number on the clipboard in her hand, and leaves again. Outside, a voice through the speaker, asking for a doctor to pick up a phone and dial 474. A wheeled cart rattles by.

"I'm going to sleep for a while. But don't leave me, Lia. You stay here, okay? These places will kill you."

I don't feel like arguing with her logic so I agree and settle into the chair, realizing that it reclines a bit. I try not to think of how many people have lain in this thing, waiting for a doctor or a test result or for the steady, safe beeping to stop.

Fall of my fifth year meant two things. My final year in architecture school and the end of my dorm living. Between my paid internship and Aunt Mae's overly generous hourly wage at the pharmacy, I was now able to move off campus and into an apartment with Antares. My parents were against it until meeting him on move-in day. Antares is impossible not to like.

Antares and I had spent the first week eating all the worst fried foods imaginable and decorating our shared space. Our aesthetic was called *whatever is free and easy to spray paint*. It was fun hunting down furniture and hauling it back to the parking lot outside our place. We had used far too many cans of primary colors, and it now looked like we lived in a Mondrian painting.

"We are nine months away from being *done*," I had said, the realization hitting me as I looked around. We were sharing a bag of seasoned fries. Paint fumes had made us giddy.

"It's architecture. You're really never *done*," Antares said. "This is a lifelong mistake."

He was correct. From all that we had experienced, we were embarking on a career that thoroughly monopolized one's life and we were doing so willingly. The path through internship was long and the licensure would be challenging and expensive.

Back in the Arch Building, the day before the new semester, I had just finished cleaning up my studio space, getting ready for the next project, when a voice called out to me as I crossed the atrium. It was familiar with a twang stronger than even my mom's.

I turned to see Aimee.

Her hair was chopped into a jagged chin-length bob. She was wearing a long floral dress and a denim jacket. She waved excitedly and made her way closer. On her left hand I noticed the flash of an engagement ring nestled next to a wedding band.

My grandmother is awake again and she snaps her fingers at me. Her machine emits a loud, long beep. I see that she's taken something off her arm and whatever it is dangles from the bed. The nurse races in with a plastered-on smile that I figure she uses with her most difficult patients.

"Mrs. Cope, we really need you to keep your monitors on, please."

She slips the cuff back on Grandminnie, recalibrates the machine, asks if she could get me anything while I waited.

"I'm going to sneak out into the hallway to look for my dad and aunt. I'll be right back." As I leave, I hear Grandminnie ask about the juice and graham crackers again. And maybe an ashtray. The nurse laughs loudly.

I look for Dad and Mae in the waiting room and, finding it empty, take the elevator down to the lobby. They're there, having some sort of meeting with a man in a charcoal-gray suit. They're talking intently, and Dad is writing down some stuff in a notebook. Aunt Mae is twisting her hands and I slink away unseen.

I go back upstairs to report to Grandminnie, but find her asleep again, all hooked up to happily monitoring monitors.

Aimee seemed more mature, more *married*, I supposed. We hugged and then she nervously looked around her.

"I feel like I need to apologize that I just, well, disappeared—"

"Looks like you've been busy, though." I pointed at her finger.

"Yes, I guess I have! I got married a few months ago. My boyfriend from high school, Jason. After I left the program, I went back home and we met up again . . ." Aimee shrugged. "When you know, you know."

"I'm so happy for you! What are you doing here?"

"I need to pick up some of my early sketches and other things from my group. I spoke to a few of the guys, and they said my part of the project is still in the studio space. I'm transferring my hours to the University of Houston. My husband is working on a rig, always back and forth, so it's a good time for me to finish up."

"I'm glad you're getting back into it!"

"I've got a lot of catching up to do. But I think I can do it." She looked around. "Where is everyone?"

I paused. Aimee didn't look like she was struggling with anything like the guys had suggested. I wondered if they had made it all up.

"All over the place. But we'll be getting together for a meeting this afternoon that Darren arranged."

I hadn't meant to say his name. Aimee's face fell.

"I really didn't want to see *him*. I was told that he was off campus, actually." She twisted her wedding band. "Something about a family issue. I can only imagine."

Now Aimee was nervously swaying. I realized I was rocking along with her, subtle movements like we were on a boat trying to regain balance.

"What's wrong?" I asked, quietly.

"You can't tell anyone, Lia. But Darren. Remember when he asked me to come to his office after class one day because of that really shitty grade on my concept and sketches? I mean, I worked on it, but I was also trying to pick up some hours at Cain & Abel's—"

"Wait. You *worked* there?" I thought of how Rochelle and I had thought she was just a pretty girl with a partying habit and felt a stab of shame.

"Yeah. I needed to. I was trying to pay for sorority dues and keep up in school. It was too much. Anyway, something happened."

She looked around again, and we walked over to the corner of the atrium and sat down on the couches. She said she'd been practicing this, saying what happened, with her old high school guidance counselor, who'd been helping her through *it*.

"I end up in his office late in the day, everyone had taken a break from the studio for dinner. He tells me to come in and sit down on this sofa in his office, so I do. Then he comes to sit next to me with a notebook and I'm like, okay, cool, he's going to walk me through what I did wrong, and he does, he gives me this great information, but each time he tells me something, he's scooting closer and closer. Then he has his hand on my back, like, comforting me, and I just sit there, because . . ."

She dug through her purse and pulled out a package of gum. Her hands were shaking.

"Sorry, I just need something."

I waited until she took the silver wrapper off the stick of gum, stuffed it into her mouth, and wadded up the wrapper.

"Want to go somewhere else to talk? Maybe one of the student conference rooms, those should be pretty quiet."

We made our way to the last room in the hallway, the one Group 5 used to use. She settled into a chair, one leg folded beneath her body, clutching her purse.

"So, yeah, he's all close to me and, you know, he's not, like, an ogre. He's handsome and I thought, maybe he likes me, or maybe he *thinks* I'm more upset than I really am. And it's not the first time some professor has gotten a little handsy, no biggie. I can manage."

Aimee looked down at her lap.

"Then, just like it's normal, he puts his hand down the top of my skirt in the back where there's a gap and . . . I was wearing this stupid thong, so it's like he's playing with a rubber band, and he keeps talking about my *process*."

Aimee was starting to cry now, tears sliding down her cheeks. She dug through her purse again and took out a package of tissues. I felt like the room was tilting.

"I tell him to stop and he does. Moves away and apologizes. He asks if I want a bottle of water and so he goes over and opens this little fridge and hands it to me. I'm nervous and sweating like crazy."

I waited. I wanted to know what happened next, but I was scared to know what happened next. Mostly, I felt awful for Aimee, who had clearly suffered.

"He tells me that he had some work from his own portfolio that could help me. I could have it, use it, copy parts of it even, if that would help me get my legs under me. And I said, sure, that would be great, because—"

"You needed the help."

"I needed the help and I was getting it from the best, right? So we talk for a few more minutes, but then he's on me again. His pants are off, I don't even know how he managed to do that so fast. I kinda remember him jerking away the notepad I was using for notes and he took off my jacket and pushed down my stupid tank top and it was that shelf kind, you know, so you don't have to wear a bra, and he was like, *Thought so*—"

Aimee buried her head in her hands.

"I'm so embarrassed. I didn't say no. I wish I could say that I said no, but I didn't. I felt like I had marbles in my mouth. Maybe I was in shock. And then, then he's up and he digs through his file cabinet—bare-ass naked, Lia—and hands me a brief on this library his old firm built. And I fixed my clothes and I stuck the brief and my notes in my backpack, and as I was leaving, he said, *This was fun*."

I felt nauseous. I reached out for Aimee's hand.

"Did he do it to you, too?" Aimee was calmer now. "Did it happen to you?" I could hear it in her voice. Hope.

I quietly said no.

We sat in silence.

"A few people saw you out at lunch later that semester. They said you looked like you were in trouble."

"I couldn't sleep after it happened and I got some sleeping pills from a guy I worked with, something to help me settle down. They were too strong or I was taking them wrong, whatever. And I couldn't eat. It was awful. Then, one weekend, I thought, fuck it, I'm going to tell my mom what happened, and I went home for the weekend and my high school boyfriend was in town. The rest is history. But right after I quit the program, I wanted to tell him off. I had been drinking and I was taking those sleeping pills. I came over and waited for him in the garage like a crazy person, told him I was going to tell the dean that he traded old sketches for sex."

I thought of Rochelle, of what she had seen. "What did he say?"

"That everyone knew I wasn't a good fit for the program. That I took that file from his office with the plan to copy it as my own work."

Aimee ran her hand through her hair. She gave me a sad smile. "I believed him. I still kinda believe him. About not being a good fit."

"I liked your work, Aimee. I'm glad that you're starting over again in Houston."

Then she grabbed my arm. "Thank you for listening."

"Anything I can do?"

Aimee's story seemed too terrifying to be real. I thought through the timeline of that semester. How Darren disappeared at the end but said it was because of his wife's miscarriage. That they were both happening at the same time.

"Want to wrangle my work from my old group? They said they were too busy to mail it so if I wanted it, I would have to come and get it. Jerks. But now, all I want to do is get on the road and go back home."

"Sure. I can do that. And Antares is heading toward Houston in a few days, I'll ask him to drop it off."

She hugged me tightly. Aimee wiped the mascara from beneath her eyes. I told her that she was welcome to any notes or anything I had to get back up to speed. I watched her walk down the corridor, back to the elevator. Then I went to find Rochelle.

"Lia, honey, has the doctor stopped by for rounds yet?" Aunt Mae pokes her head into the room. Grandminnie is snoring.

I shake my head no. It's only been me, me and all my ghosts that I've been carting around.

"Just talked to Sallie, she wants to drop in and see you after we look at

reception places next week. I think she wants to ask you to be a bridesmaid."

I smile. Sallie is a photocopy of Aunt Mae. During my most awkward
years, of which there were many, she'd visit and help me with my makeup,
talk to me about relationships. She had struggled as well in Curtain
schools, so much so Aunt Mae eventually put her in private, my aunt
and uncle taking turns driving her to and from Dallas daily. There, Sallie
found her stride, and when it was time to apply for colleges, it was Ivy or
nothing. That's where she met her husband-to-be.

"I know that will be a bridesmaid dress worth keeping," I say, and
Aunt Mae rolls her eyes. Sallie has remarkable, yet expensive, taste.

"I don't think anything major is going on with Grandminnie, honey, if
you want to get on home," Aunt Mae says. But I don't believe her. Something *is* amiss.

Aunt Mae perches on the arm of my chair next to Grandminnie's bed
and wraps her arm around me. "Sweet Lia-Bird," she says.

"What do you know?" I ask.

"Nothing, besides that she's getting older and all this stress with moving has probably been too much. I hope she can find some peace at this
new place, some rest, maybe some new friends. It's all any of us can ask
for, isn't it?"

"I don't know. Maybe she doesn't want that. Maybe she wants a different option."

"I'm sure she does. Mom has always wanted something that she can't
have. That's her way. But what she might want and what she needs are
two different things, I think."

Aunt Mae hands me a bag of barbecue potato chips from the vending
machine, and I open them up, quietly. She reaches in for one and we sit
there like that for a few minutes, our fingers turning red, watching Grandminnie, who slowly begins to wake up and stares at us, confused for a
moment. Rubbing her eyes, she sits up.

"Those have so much cholesterol. Why you eating those things?"

Aunt Mae looks at me, twisting her mouth into a tired grin.

The nurse comes in, followed by a young doctor who looks like he
hasn't slept in days.

He's wearing running shoes with his scrubs, and Grandminnie is fast to notice his casual attire. She starts to say something, but then thinks better of it, for once, and lets the nurse check her pulse again while the doctor flips through a clipboard.

"Mrs. Cope, we think you've been overdoing it. Seems like you need to up your protein intake and stop smoking. Everything seems to be in fine working order, but based on what we hear from Autumn Leaves, you've been staying up very late."

Grandminnie sits up, her spine long. Her chin lifted. "Who told you these things?"

"Mom, c'mon, they're just trying to help." Dad has come in with his hands shoved into his pockets. He looks like a kid who has gotten into some trouble. I know from his look that he's the one who's been talking to Autumn Leaves.

"Their job is to keep an eye on you. The staff there says that you've had your granddaughter staying with you quite a bit and that you two have been doing some walking and *counting* in the hallways?"

All eyes are on me. Grandminnie clears her throat with a large, fake cough, causing a ripple of real coughs. The attention on me wavers for a moment. My grandmother waves off the nurse and the doctor, who have taken a step closer to her.

"Yes, Lia has been staying with me because she's been very upset."

"Oh, really?" The doctor seems amused and unbelieving.

"She's very, very anxious. And she is trying to figure out what to do in her future, you know. She has these panic attacks and so we walk in the middle of the night to help *her*."

"Grandminnie!"

Grandminnie reaches her hand out to me and grabs my wrist. She squeezes hard.

"We count because it's calming."

"Oh, sweetheart," Aunt Mae says. My father walks over and puts his arm around my shoulders. Even the doctor and nurse look sympathetic. She has them eating out of her hand.

"But good news, I think she's doing better," Grandminnie says. "So she'll stay at home and I'll sleep well at Autumn Leaves. I'll eat more protein. I'll do the other things, too."

"The smoking," the doctor says.

"Whatever," Grandminnie says. "I just want to get out of here."

Aunt Mae leans in for another tight squeeze, then leaves with Daddy to sign release papers. He turns and looks at me as he leaves the room with so much sadness that I feel sick.

"You sold me out," I immediately hiss when they're out of the room.

"I told the truth. You *have* been upset."

"Yes, because you're stuck in assisted living and deserve your own place!"

"Oh, bull wash! You don't say a thing to me."

"Fine, Grandminnie!"

I pick up my backpack and sling it over my shoulder.

I stomp out of the room, without a goodbye. Downstairs, I pull away from Dennis General and start to sob, loud choking scream-like cries that scare me. *What should I do?* Cutting off onto the gravel road that leads to Cope land, I slow, small rocks popping around me. I'm trying to keep everything in my head, all of my thoughts in rows. I again drive to the blank space where the ranch house once stood. The dirt is turned over, as if awaiting seed. I park and I pick at my scalp, and in the waning light of the afternoon, I wait for answers to questions I don't even know how to ask.

Chapter 24

Curtain, Texas
1965

According to a flyer on the corkboard at Dimple's Grocery & Gas, the Dennis State Home for Mental Impairment needed nursing aides. Mineko looked at it a few times before writing down the phone number. The manager lived in town, a man with thick glasses and ugly ties—Mineko had seen him before, even though he went to church in Dennis. James had been ill all fall, tired and weak, his back aching from the time his feet hit the floor in the morning to the time he was horizontal in the evening. He had thrown up after dinner many times, had even accused Mineko of poisoning him. *If I wanted to poison you*, she thought, *it would actually work*. Then he began to lose weight. Mineko had called the doctor out to the house, but James refused to be seen and instead climbed gingerly into the truck and left Mineko and the doctor on the porch, the man clutching his black leather satchel.

James was unable to work the ranch, although he couldn't admit it, and started keeping Paulie from school to help.

"If there aren't any cattle being cared for and sold, there won't be any money," he said. "That's why I have a son," he told her when she brought up how often Paulie was absent.

Mineko hated this for Paulie. He was small for his age, serious, kind-hearted to a fault. He had just started playing in the Curtain Consolidated

Marching Band and was good at his cornet, borrowed from the band director.

"He's good at most everything," Mineko bragged to Fumiko in letters, and Fumiko would write back and in her sweet way, remark how happy Mineko must be to have two such remarkable children and how she wished she could see Mae and Paulie again. Although they had tried, Fumiko and her husband had never been able to conceive.

Mae had aced all of her classes in high school, was president of the science club and Future Homemakers of America, had entered the Miss Flame pageant, and had, with her admirable piano playing and bright smile, come in as the runner-up. The winner was the Thomas girl, but with the Thomas Ranch as sponsors, Mineko figured that Mae was the real winner. The world was just opening up to her and she had been accepted to the University of Texas with a partial scholarship when James announced that he didn't think she was quite ready for a real university, and besides, he needed her to work on the ranch a couple more years.

"But if we had money, would you let her go?" Mineko had asked as James had shuffled off to bed, stopping to lean against the doorjamb before climbing the stairs. He didn't answer.

She snuck away for the interview under the guise of needing new fabric for some shirts for Mae and Paulie. Sweaty, her stomach grumbling, she sat in the truck in the parking lot of the home and wondered if she should just go back to the ranch. But she knew she would see Mae and Paulie on their horses or Mae and Paulie in the fields or Mae and Paulie fixing fences, and she just couldn't face them.

She sat primly as possible in the sloping chair opposite the manager's metal desk, waiting for his arrival.

"You don't have any experience with those with mental impairment." Mr. Lewis didn't mince words as his shoes squeaked across the peach linoleum tile, waxed to a high gleam. He was wearing a brown tie with lighter brown swirls. Mineko wondered if Mrs. Lewis hated her husband and that's why she picked out such a horrid thing.

"Yes, but I am a very hard worker and good with children. I have patience. And have an excellent memory."

"Hmmm. Your English. Your accent is thick, you know that?"

Of course I know that, cow-patty-tie man.

"Yes, but after a while, people get used to it. And maybe it will improve by talking with the children."

"They aren't all children, just childlike. Some of them are strong as an ox, violent at times, too."

"I am very strong from years of ranch work. I have much experience with people with uneven temperament."

"And your citizenship, I can't keep you on long if you don't get it."

Mineko sighed. She had been worried about her citizenship, except for different reasons. She feared that James would die and she wouldn't be able to receive any of his military benefits. Every five years, she had to refile paperwork to stay in the United States, something that James eventually signed off on, although he hemmed and hawed about it each time, as if she were not worthy of his signature. But true US citizenship would mean giving up her Japanese one. There would be classes, a test, a swearing in.

She would never be able to claim Japanese citizenship again. She thought of the lonely desperate nights soon after arriving in Curtain. How she had tried to tell the kids stories about Japan and James would shut the conversation down. How she would daydream about leaving, going home, fading into the throngs of travelers at Shinjuku with Paulie strapped to her back and Mae's hand firmly in her right. Her passport in her pocket. Nothing with them but what they had on. Starting over, at home.

But she had never left and would not leave anytime soon, not while she was still needed by the kids.

The state home tryout week turned into two, then three, all at half pay. Finally, after a month, Mr. Lewis assigned her to nights, nine p.m. to six a.m. She thanked him with a cake she and Mae baked, a lovely lemon bundt, the color of the walls in the home's television room where everyone gathered around the console for *Mr. Ed.*

The night shift was grueling. Like being both a nurse and a mother to humans who were bigger than her, stronger than her, and who had needs that were far greater than she could have imagined. Most of the residents were lonely for family, having been transitioned to the home when their age had grown past their abilities or they had lived longer than their parents. But Mineko took it all in stride, learning their likes and needs, their moods and quirks. She sang Japanese lullabies, and no one asked her to speak English. They didn't call her Nurse Cope, as expected. They called her Minnie and some even called her Mommy.

James hated having his wife work outside the home and sometimes yelled at her all the way out to the truck at night and greeted her with just as many jabs and barbs the next morning. But they had now been married for eighteen years, and Mineko knew that aside from his piercing words and rough touch, James was a known demon. He could go only so far to hurt her before he began to damage the person who kept his life together.

The state home pay, while low, added up. By early summer, when the temperature reached 105 for three days in a row and a cow had keeled over from heatstroke, Mineko announced to the kids that she had saved up just enough to help send Mae to the University of Texas in September and hire a part-time helper on the ranch, leaving Paulie free to go to school as long as he came right home after band practice.

Mae, tears in her eyes, hugged her mother and then ran off to tell her boyfriend, Hollis, who had just pulled his truck up to the gate. She paused at the door before leaving and broke into a huge grin.

When James came downstairs from his nap, Mineko shooed Paulie out to the barn and readied herself to tell James.

"What did you go and do now?" James opened the fridge and stared at the contents, finally choosing a pitcher of lemonade. "Pour this up for me, will ya? I need lots of ice cubes, I'm dying of heat. Dizzy."

Mineko handed him the glass of lemonade and told him calmly as she'd rehearsed. James looked as if she had announced that she herself had been named Miss Flame of Dennis County. When the shock wore off in a few seconds, he threw the glass at her head but, practiced, she ducked to the side and it hit the bulky white Frigidaire, shattering. He jumped up and started to come at her, but then midstrike, he went down, hard. Pale and trembling, then shaking, contorting his face and staring up at her. For a moment, Mineko froze, his body heavy on her feet. She moved one step away and he rolled onto his back.

Mineko picked him up under his arms and, half stumbling, dragged him to the living room rug. He looked to be asleep and Mineko could still feel the breath in his body, the warmth. His pants were wet from urine. Ambulances didn't come out as far as the ranch, so Mineko knew she needed to get him to the hospital on her own.

She called in Paulie, who blanched at the sight of his father, and Mineko thought of how unworthy of his son's love James was, and then they both carried him out to the truck, leaned him into the passenger seat, where he awoke. He threw up and then was gone again. Paulie climbed in and held his father against his chest. Mineko stepped heavy on the gas and rocks hit the truck.

As they reached the highway, she turned left, toward Mae's boyfriend's house.

"You get out, tell Mae, have Hollis take you back home. Wait for me. You don't need to be there."

"Please, Mom, let me help."

Mineko had to lean and push Paulie out the truck door, then sped off, watching him turn and run toward the house in the rearview.

Mineko sat at the kitchen table in the early morning, one light on above the sink, the room heavy with shadows. The Frigidaire was rattling along, ice trapped near the fan, the clock on the wall keeping time. After telling Paulie and Mae that their father had passed, she had tucked them both into her bed like they were little again and told them to sleep in.

Now Mineko squinted again at the clock, 5:12 a.m. local meant it was 7:12 p.m. in Tokyo. Fumiko would be home, surely, feeding her cat, putting together dinner for her husband. She pictured her friend in an apartment like the one she had visited the last time, although Fumiko had moved since then. They hadn't spoken in at least three years, the last call when Mineko had been hurt badly by James—a cut on her lip, a bruised rib—and she had called Fumiko from Dimple's store after it closed one night.

After the international operator said *Go ahead, please*, Fumiko answered cautiously.

"Mineko-chan?"

"How did you know it was me?"

"How many people do you think I know calling from the States? Oh, friend. How are you?"

"I am . . ." Mineko paused. "He's dead. James died tonight. Last night, I mean."

Fumiko gasped and Mineko could hear the television click off on her end.

"His heart. They think he had cancer and it spread everywhere, then it got his heart."

"So quickly! Did you say goodbye?"

"He woke up for a few seconds before he went and he said, 'I guess we'll all be going home now.'"

"And . . ." Fumiko prompted.

"That's it. 'I guess we'll all be going home now.' Then he was dead."

"Strange, no? Now what do you do?"

Mineko didn't know if her friend meant immediately or for the rest of her life.

"Burial. It will be a big funeral. Big family, you know. Then Mae will go to university. I'll keep working. I don't know what to do about the ranch—that was always his business. It seems it takes more to run than we actually make. Paulie knows more than me."

Fumiko was quiet for a moment. Mineko could hear her husband come into the room, talking, and she must have shooed him away.

"Maybe he meant for you to come home. Here."

"No, not that man. He never wanted me to even talk about home."

"Oh. But you could."

"You mean come to Tokyo? To visit?" Mineko tightened her grip on the curly phone cord.

"Or to live. Osaka is rebuilt, all that damage is gone, it is very pretty again."

"But Paulie and Mae! I couldn't leave them. And what would I do for money? I'm nearly an American citizen now."

"After Paulie graduates and Mae is on her own! You could get a little job, doing something and get paid in cash. You know. Under the table."

"Like what?"

"Teach swimming?"

A laugh caught in Mineko's throat; she took the cord and stretched it across the kitchen, out the back door onto the porch, and laughed so hard she could no longer stand upright. She couldn't breathe and she could hear Fumiko on the other end of the line, her familiar titter turning louder. Mineko leaned against the wall and slid down to the porch decking, letting the screen door creak closed on the nearly straight cord. She was in her pajamas and her legs stuck out straight in front of her, rag-doll-like. She pointed and flexed her feet. The sky was getting lighter.

"But," Fumiko said, still breathless, "you could, you know."

Chapter 25

I'm in my bed, flipped onto my stomach, toes hooked over the end of the mattress. After getting home from Grandminnie's old place, I ate my dinner in my room and said I had a headache when my mom wanted to chat. It's clear that Dad has filled Mom in about what Grandminnie had told everyone. I can almost feel my parents' concern floating up through the floorboards. And as awful as I feel for up and leaving Grandminnie so quickly, I'm still pissed that she threw me under the bus like that.

Maybe I didn't need a sister growing up, after all.

I try my version of counting sheep: remembering architectural time periods in order with dates. I find myself in the neo-Georgian period, known in certain circles as the Wrenaissance (proving that architects can be funny if a pun is readily available), but can't continue. I think back to that day when Aimee told me her story, how as soon as she had left the Arch Building I had taken the stairs by twos and found Rochelle at the snack machine in the break room. We sat down on the long bench that lined the wall. Most everyone was out grabbing lunch, so the floor was quiet for once. I told her what Aimee had told me. Rochelle slowly ate her package of cupcakes.

"What do you think? It couldn't have happened that way, could it have?"

"You tell me. You're the one he pays attention to. Has he ever tried anything?"

I thought of our past interactions. Of the water fountain, of him outside my old dorm and of the kiss on my hand. Strange, yes. And given what I had been told, creepy. But he had never done anything like what Aimee said he did. And of course, I was nothing like Aimee, I told myself.

"Listen, I know what I saw that morning in the garage and that, that rings true. She was out-of-her-mind mad and he had this weird-as-shit look on his face."

"But pushing himself on her like that!" I couldn't croak out the word. "Maybe there's a missing piece. Maybe she drank too much with him and is really embarrassed about what happened and she's—"

"Maybe. But even if she did, it doesn't make what happened right. He was her prof! We've been unfair to her. *I've* been unfair to her. When I used to make fun of her outfits and the stuff she'd say."

"We don't know what really happened, Rochelle." I pulled my hair up into a scrunchie, suddenly finding the weight of it on my neck unbearable. "Darren can be weird, but he's not a bad guy."

I thought of all the times he had helped me over the past year and a half. *I owe him.*

But then I recalled how Aimee shook while telling me her story, how she seemed to have a broken motor inside her body that vibrated with terror.

Rochelle fell back against the bench's dirty cushion. She eyed me curiously.

"Just watch yourself, Cope. Even *if* she's stretching the truth a little, the elements are all still disgusting and point the finger at Darren. I'd hate for anything to happen to you."

Later, I remember seeing Rochelle in the studio, telling something to Antares, who looked down, shaking his head. I knew what she had said. I felt a wave of anger at Rochelle, revealing something that I wasn't even sure I should have told. I wondered if she'd also tell Bradley.

Antares didn't keep Aimee's story to himself. A few days later, he confronted me in our kitchenette while I was toasting a waffle. He said, very plainly, that even though I was close to Darren, he felt he needed to tell someone in administration because it was a serious claim. Even if it happened to be mutual, it was wrong. He'd keep Aimee's name anonymous, but he couldn't go on like this, not saying anything.

I worried that if Aimee was lying, it would ruin Darren's career. But Antares shook his head at me and handed me the maple syrup.

"You don't need him, you know."

"He's helped me so much. I don't know what I would have done without him."

"You should be confident. You have everything. You belong. Everywhere."

I squeezed too much syrup on my waffle. I shook my head as tears began to fall.

"You do, Lia. Try being me."

I wanted to tell him that he belonged, too, but I was aware of what he had experienced; I had seen how some classmates had treated him, even Bradley and Rochelle. There was a distance. Antares was brilliant and the best of us all. And the most generous, the most gracious. But I don't know if he actually was his full self with us. Once, I had seen him hanging out with his Chinese friends, a group of guys from across majors, and I thought how different Antares was around them, he was more relaxed, less careful. I felt simultaneously happy that Antares had these friends and jealous that I didn't have the same understanding.

My waffle was now a dark, soggy mess. I looked up at Antares and he smiled.

"He's too big to go down. His career and legacy will be fine. Guys like that are always fine," Antares said, tossing my waffle in the trash can and popping another in the toaster for me. "And you'll be fine, too. You just have some figuring out to do."

Antares told Mrs. Grant, who very calmly took notes and told him that she'd relay what she had been told to the dean. She told Antares that she'd keep all of our names out of it, just to protect us from any negative consequences.

But a week later, it was announced that Mrs. Grant was retiring, even though she hadn't been within the UT system for very long. There was no party for her, no sheet cake in the conference room.

Then, we waited. Our last studio was thoroughly devoted to residential. I was designing a river house. Bradley a brownstone. Antares an entire apartment block. Rochelle a loft space with retail beneath, still inspired by Grant's mixed-use project. We arrived together, we worked together, we left together. Darren saw us at a distance. The first couple of times, he waved and smiled. Bradley and I waved back. Rochelle and Antares ignored him. Then, slowly, nothing. He stayed away from studios, he kept to his Design IV class and his office.

"Well, that's suspicious," Bradley had said once, after Darren had changed course and gone back into his office when we walked by.

I couldn't deny it. It was.

Nothing else happened. Nothing at all. It was as if Aimee and Mrs. Grant had never existed. We were busy with internship applications. Despite everything, our group continued working together, helping one another.

At winter break, we all went home but called each other every few days. Rochelle asked me if I was worried about my internship opportunities, where I'd end up. She and Bradley had received acceptance letters in late December. Antares had decided that he would apply for graduate school. I hadn't heard anything yet. Every afternoon I darted to our mailbox and peered inside, only to be disappointed.

"Don't worry, a lot of people find out where they're landing in late January, even February." Rochelle was supportive, but something had changed between us since the Aimee event. I knew I disappointed her with my reluctance to implicate Darren, even though he hadn't been much of a mentor in a while. Part of me wondered why I even believed in him still.

The spring semester started, and I dove into portfolio prep. Instead of designing models, we were now designing report covers. A few of the students with more money actually hired graphic artists from the art school to do theirs. I designed my own because I knew what I wanted to see. Something had finally clicked into place during Mrs. Grant's class last semester. I had become more confident in my own procedures, my own conceptualizing of problems and creation of design solutions.

Then the rumor circulated that Darren would be leaving for Seattle during the summer. There was a boom, and he would be working with a large firm to create a museum near the sound. The campus architecture magazine ran a piece on him in which he thanked the UT system for such a perfect experience and would always consider Austin home.

It was mid-February before I received the call from BT&B. I raced up to the studio and ran across the floor to my group, squealing my good news. We hugged and danced around. It was one of the best firms in Texas and, even better, I wouldn't have to leave Austin, something I had been dreading. When I got to my work space, I saw a little envelope thumbtacked to my corkboard. I recognized the handwriting immediately and figured it had been placed there after we had left the studio the night before. In the card, Darren apologized for being so distant lately, that there had been some lies floating around the department and that he would be glad to be leaving, but sorry to part ways from me, and that he hoped I knew that he would always be someone I could lean on.

In the postscript, written on the back, was the sentence: *Enjoy working at BT&B.*

It's an hour later and my tossing in bed has built up a hunger. I quietly tiptoe past my parents' room and down the stairs, careful to avoid the one that always squeaks. In the kitchen I toast a bagel and coat it with peanut butter. As I'm walking back to the staircase, I hear a familiar noise, the heavy sound of fingers on a large calculator. My father is up, working. The paper receipt tape rolls and whizzes as he prints. It's a comforting sound. I open the door, gently.

"Hey, Daddy."

"Why you up, baby girl?" Dad rubs his eyes. He has an empty glass of milk next to him, a bowl of M&M'S, mostly gone.

"Taxes?"

"Nah, but something like that."

"You have to do it tonight?"

"Tonight just turns into tomorrow, bug. You need to get to sleep, though. It's getting late."

It isn't getting late for a twenty-five-year-old, I want to say, but I look at his soft gaze and think of how I used to curl up in his lap when he did taxes, content to listen to the whirr of the adding machine.

He's punching the keys and writing something down again.

"Daddy?"

"Yep, sugar."

I thought about Grandminnie and all of her hidden stories. I'm angry with her, I feel used and exposed.

"Do you feel like you're very close to Grandminnie?"

"Close? What do you mean, honey? I just got her off my back." My dad puts down his pencil and yawns and stretches, then laughs at his little joke.

"You know what I mean."

He's quiet for a moment. "No, not always. We went through a lot together. I mean, I always felt like I was loved. She wasn't all touchy-feely when I was a kid, but she was always there, had my back with Dad. She's helped me out when I needed it."

"But do you feel like you *know* her?"

My father pauses again, as if about to say something hard.

"I kinda wonder who I know these days. Mae and me, we see things different, she remembers a lot of stuff about growing up that I don't."

"About Japan?"

My dad nods. "And your mama—she's relieved to have her gone, but I kinda think, damn, I only have one mother."

"With Grandminnie, one mom is enough," I say, trying to cheer him up.

"And there's you."

"Me?" I look down at my feet.

"Yeah, you. What Grandminnie said today—baby, that's worrisome. I know that you're on your own path, but you can talk to me, you know."

"I'm getting it figured out, Dad."

"I do like how you two've gotten close. She was so distant from you when you were a kid. I think you wore her out."

"What? I was an easy kid!"

Daddy laughs and shakes his head, remembering something. "That time she kept you out too long, trying to wear you out for a nap and you nearly got a heatstroke! God, your mom was so mad. Your grandmother felt awful about it. Makes me feel good that you have each other, even if she's a hard one."

"She's not as hard as you think. Or maybe I'm learning from her."

My father looks at me, like he's seeing me for the first time in a while.

"Yeah," he says, rubbing his stubbled chin, "maybe that's it. But tell you something, I sure do love you. And I'd do anything for you. I hate that you're struggling."

"I know, Daddy."

I wish Darren was a problem my dad could fix for me, like a balding tire or strange rattle in the engine. I remember the times I'd break a toy and he'd glue it together, using clamps while it dried. Once it was my favorite Barbie, and I was terrified that she'd be out on the workbench all night as the glue set. Dad had grabbed a handkerchief from his truck and spread it out over her, with a pack of tissues for a pillow. *Look, it's like she's camping.*

I give my father a hug and tell him not to stay up too late. He tells me the same. And for a moment, I linger with my arms around his shoulders, knowing that while we might be mirrors of each other, when one is a reflection, it's hard to stand side by side, touching, connecting.

Chapter 26

The Silver Belles was a fifty-five-plus line- and square-dancing team that had sprung up from the Curtain First United Methodist's senior citizen group. They did their best moves to country, specifically anything by the Oak Ridge Boys, sliding, stepping, and turning. Much to Mineko's surprise, Dimple had joined up on a lark during deer season, tired of being left by Calvin for the lease, where he'd sit in a stand for days, eating nothing but bologna and drinking nothing but Lone Star. She had slyly asked Mineko for help on a few circle skirts, plying her with compliments until Mineko gave in and ran them up one Saturday morning, adding rickrack and eyelet to the bottom. Dimple stood over and watched, sipping an iced tea.

Mineko had always thought that as her children aged and moved out of the house, her life would slow down to a reasonable pace. She'd no longer be juggling their schedules and hers, no longer making meals for three, cleaning for three, worrying for three. True, she could make do with a sandwich for lunch and some rice for dinner, and it was nice to wash only one load on the weekends, not four or five. But as for worrying for three, that continued. And it grew, because with each new calendar hung on the back of the pantry door, her family grew.

As Mineko suspected, Hollis couldn't be away from Mae, so when she left for college in Austin, it was a matter of months before he found a job there, too. Within a year they were married. Mineko begged Mae to not become pregnant before she graduated, but less than a year later, at Christmas, Mae and Hollis made the announcement. While Mae was in pharmacy school, Mineko drove down to their little rented place in Cedar Park on her off days to help with Sallie or allow Mae to study. One baby became two before long—Sam was born just two years later. After a few years of working at a big pharmacy in Austin, Mae and Hollis returned to Curtain, taking over some land that had been in Hollis's family. Mineko chipped in to help buy the Curtain Pharmacy with some of her savings, happy to know that her daughter would only be a few minutes away.

Paulie graduated from Curtain High and began community college, but his high energy and love of the outdoors ended his college career soon after it started. He began working construction and before long was leading crews. He met Tammy on a blind date, and the two were inseparable and married quickly. Mineko was hesitant to like Tammy; Paulie's absolute devotion to someone who wasn't herself made her feel forgotten, but she did admire this woman, who was as organized and hardworking as any Mineko had met. And she took good care of Paulie, so Mineko begrudgingly accepted her as her own.

Tammy and Paulie endured two unsuccessful pregnancies, the second one lost a few weeks shy of term. Finally, Lia Renee was born, and Paulie, now desperate to ease Tammy's sadness and prove himself an adequate father, despite little education in that area, vacillated between overworked provider and overcompensating parent. He even read books about being a good father, dog-earing pages, highlighting passages— Mineko had seen these next to his bed when visiting one afternoon and was smacked with a sense of intense guilt followed by overwhelming love. And as Lia grew, he adapted, often following Tammy's lead. When he didn't know how to respond to a tantrum or some little-kid drama, he wouldn't snap as James had, but turn inward, become quiet, until he had some inclination about how to proceed. His mind was methodical and Mineko saw herself within him.

Mineko helped with Lia when she could, but didn't want to step on Tammy's toes and, to be honest, was working overtime in order to eventually retire. This was her next goal, and in letters to Fumiko, she made promises to visit: as soon as Mae's family no longer needed her, as soon as she sold off all the animals and no longer had to worry about their feedings, as soon as she left Dennis State Home. She had been there for more than twenty years now. Twenty years that had flown by.

"You gotta do something other than work and think about retirement! Good God Almighty, Minnie, you're getting to be as much fun as old Calvin."

Minnie handed her sister-in-law the denim circle skirt and Dimple admired the lace.

"Better'n store bought," she said.

Dimple dropped her polyester shorts and slipped up the skirt, giving it a twirl. Then she put on her Capezios, bright silver, like the rest of the Belles. She explained that while some ladies wore those short cowboy boots, the Belles thought that they made their ankles look thick, to which Mineko just shrugged.

Dimple joining a dancing group was just about the silliest thing Mineko could have imagined her sister-in-law doing and resented the amount of time it took up. Before the Belles, they'd get together every other Saturday night to potluck their dinner and watch television, maybe play cards if Calvin was so inclined. But now the Belles would take the Curtain UMC van into the city and line dance on Saturdays.

"It'd take you an hour to make one of these for yourself, Min. I have some practice shoes you could borrow. Could get you all fixed up in time for the van to leave at five!"

"I told you, Dimple. I'm no dancer. Especially this kind in a line!"

"Oh, anyone can do it. I bet you'd be good at it. You have great balance."

Mineko raised an eyebrow. She knew when she was being played. Mostly.

"The dancing's fun. You don't need some man to ask you, although if you wanted to dance with one of the gentlemen, there are a few widowers and divorced men. Not bad-looking, no drinkers, no slouches."

"You know I don't want any of *that*."

Dimple had tried to set her up a few years after James's death with an old friend of hers who had come into town for a high school reunion and had taken a shine to Mineko when he met her at Dimple's store. She had made a big dinner, invited her over, and attempted a surprise double date, which irritated Mineko and she left before dessert, although she did show up the next morning around breakfast to take a big piece of cake back home with her. In the kitchen, over coffee, Dimple apologized for interfering, and Mineko did the same, feeling ridiculous for getting her feathers so ruffled. Dimple admitted she couldn't understand, really, why Mineko was so dead set against dating. It was clear that there was no love lost between Minnie and James, and here she was, heading into the sunset of her life, alone. Calvin was a stick in the mud, but he was her stick in the mud, at the very least. Mineko hadn't responded, instead slurping her coffee in silence.

Dimple twirled again in her new skirt, and Mineko saw a stray thread that needed trimming and went off in search of her scissors.

"Well, it's just as good that you aren't coming. Old Evangeline decided that she might want to come and try us out. I dread it and kinda hope she twists an ankle, but . . ."

Dimple waited, quiet for her friend.

"Oh, is that so? She's not even Methodist," Mineko replied, thoughtfully.

Mineko emerged from the spare bedroom with her scissors. She had a pencil behind her ear and her glasses had slid down her nose. Her hair was still as dark, somehow only four or five grays had sprouted near her crown. Dimple put her hands on her hips and pursed her lips.

"Having her there will kill the joy in the group," Dimple said. "She'll make us pray before we eat our ribs, and don't even get me started on what she'll do when she sees the margarita machine."

"Tonight? At five?" Mineko asked.

"On the money. Can't be late."

Mineko grunted. She was never late.

Tumbleweeds was a long, low building off the interstate, right on the edge of the Fort Worth Stockyards. The parking lot was as big as a football field and, glancing around the van, Mineko wondered how a few of her dancing companions would be able to make it to the front door.

The Belles were a far older group than she had anticipated, some getting into their eighties. When the van looped around to the entrance, where a crowd of ladies in dresses and men in starched Wranglers filed in slowly, she felt both thankful and embarrassed. She looked at Dimple with a sneer, to which Dimple burped out a cackle.

"Oh, it'll be fun. Don't be such a snob."

A snob? Her? Mineko was out of the van and in the crisp early-December air and then under a blast of heat combined with fiddle music before she could formulate a response.

The walls appeared to be covered with black tightly looped carpet and framed and signed photos of singers in rhinestones hung everywhere. A long ramp led down into a dance hall, wooden floors scuffed, a couple of disco balls turning, and a few saddles hanging from the ceiling for good measure. The bar was closed, but a neon sign reading PICKEN'S BBQ hung over a snack bar area, where perky teens were serving up sandwiches and plates of ribs, heaps of yellow potato salad and white slaw on the side.

"First we eat, then we dance." Dimple hooked her hand around Mineko's elbow and pulled her into the line. "Church pays for our dinner—but we have to buy the margs and beers once the bar opens."

The women settled at a round table, and from there Mineko could see that Curtain was not the only church represented. Dimple pointed out different towns' "fum-sees," which it took Mineko a bit to understand stood for FUMC, or First United Methodist Church. Also in the mix were many senior citizen center groups, one from nearby Dennis, and a couple of Presbyterian groups as well.

She didn't see Evangeline and when she asked Dimple about this, her sister-in-law looked at her dumbly.

"She was never coming, was she!"

"Honey, she's *Baptist*. They don't dance!"

"Oh, you liar!"

Dimple laughed and reached up to grab a couple slices of cake from a tray being passed and stuck the Styrofoam plate in front of Mineko.

"Eat up, and none of your bellyaching. I can't watch you get old in that damn house, waiting for whatever you're waiting for."

Mineko thought about her words for a minute. Was she waiting for something? She hadn't thought about it. In those past years, she had been ticking through her checklist of daily, monthly, and yearly items. Repairs were made to the tractor, trim was repainted on the house. She did manage to finally repaint the entire place, a cool barely blue, almost gray, that reminded Mineko of the low fog that sometimes gathered at the base of the mountains near Kadoma, thin and wispy like it had been placed gently with a giant hand.

But she hadn't been waiting on anything. Except retirement. And then she would have the freedom to travel back to Japan. The thought of seeing Tokyo again, of seeing Osaka again, of seeing Kadoma—it made her stomach clench. Like she was about to get on a big stage and sing or jump from a plane with a parachute.

Mineko jumped up and started for the floor, her hands in fists. Dimple had to walk fast to catch up, clearly pleased that she had lit a fire under her friend.

"All right now, you just follow the crowd . . ."

The speaker flipped on, the music got louder, and within a few seconds "Louisiana Saturday Night" was blaring, Mineko bending her leg and kicking, then bouncing a few steps back, arm in arm with Dimple, her other arm hooked through that of a tall man who had quickly joined in, just as the movement started.

As they began to gallop around as a line, it was clear that theirs was the fastest, and soon they came nose to neck with the line in front, which was moving slower. The man on Mineko's left tugged her and away the line whipped like a snake, cutting in front of the slowpokes and stretching out again as if planned. The fact that this maneuver was completed as she heard the lyrics "single-shot rifle and a one-eyed dog" made Mineko laugh.

"See, I told you!" Dimple yelled.

The dance steps came quickly to Mineko, and she especially liked the trickier turns. Even when Dimple's hip started to ache and she wanted to get a glass of lemonade, Mineko waved her off, ready to learn the next dance. It was surprising how much she enjoyed this music, even though she'd lived in Texas for years and never once sought it out. Her original line mate, the tall man, who Mineko learned was named Ewell, would show up next to her every few songs and grin, singing loudly.

"You're good! Why haven't I seen you before out here?" Ewell was sweaty, and he took a handkerchief from his back pocket to wipe his head, removing his felt hat in the process and revealing a scalp as bald and as freckled as a bird's egg. Mineko realized that he must be at least ten years older than her.

The line dancing had paused and a waltz had begun, with half the dancers moving off to the sides and the married couples latching their hands and beginning their slow one-two-three, one-two-three steps around the circle. Ewell pointed to the floor, and Mineko shook her head no.

Instead they found Dimple and a few of the other Belles and sat, watching. Ewell had sold cars for most of his career, recently retired, his oldest son taking over the family business, which was now two lots of shiny Buicks. He had a lake house that he shared with the family, but was selling the "big house," where he had raised his kids, because he was tired of using so few of the rooms. Dimple took the bait and asked what had happened to his wife, to which Ewell had said cancer, five years now she's been gone.

Ewell liked music and travel, he loved going to his grandson's T-ball games and enjoyed hunting, on occasion, but just dove, because deer took up too much time and he kinda felt sorry for the things, after all.

"Amen," Dimple said. She elbowed Mineko. Mineko felt lost in this conversation, wanting instead for the slow dancing to end and the lines to form up again.

"How much longer do we have?" she asked. A line had formed at the beer bar and a few ladies milled around with short plastic glasses of frozen neon-green drinks.

"We'll be doing the Chicken Dance before too terribly long," Ewell said.

"That's the last one," Dimple explained to Mineko.

"Oh," Mineko said, suddenly feeling glum. She checked her wristwatch. It wasn't even eight p.m.!

"They gotta get us out of here before the younguns arrive. They get here around ten or so and keep it hopping until last call."

A squeaky song started up and everyone made a whoop, some sounding sad and others pleased. Dimple excused herself to the restroom before the drive back. Mineko watched as the dancers began to get in their pattern again, this time with hands tucked under armpits and flapping like a bird.

"I don't know about this one," Mineko said to Ewell, who laughed.

"It's dumb, I'll give you that. But want to go out and try, once more? Best to end on a high note."

His cheerfulness was endearing, and Mineko nodded and followed him to the floor where they, too, began to dance like chickens.

Ewell followed the Belles out into the parking lot, the sky winter dark. Mineko asked him point-blank where his ride was, and he pointed to a shiny new GMC truck under a parking light.

"One of the perks of the business," Ewell said kindly, as Mineko eyed the truck. She was still driving James's old farm truck, and despite Paulie and Mae's begging, she had yet to go buy something new, instead continually tinkering with the engine and the brakes, the suspension and the condenser.

"Of course, the ladies always have an eye for the Riviera convertible. Good-looking car, that one."

Mineko couldn't tell if he was trying to sell her a car or make small talk, so she stayed quiet and kept her arms folded around her belly, mainly to keep warm, but also because she felt that Ewell was a step too close to her.

At the church van, the driver had the doors spread wide and everyone was carefully pulling themselves up and in. The driver—the young assistant pastor who everyone thought was just biding his time until he got a bigger congregation—bounced into the front seat to start up the van. Mineko wished that the elder Belles could move a little faster, as she was tired of chatting with Ewell under Dimple's arched gaze.

The van made a sputtering noise and the engine refused to turn over, despite the pastor's effort. He twisted the key again and again, to which Mineko shot over to his side to get him to stop.

"You'll flood the engine," she said, tapping the steering wheel. "Pop the hood."

While the rest of the Belles sat primly in the van, Mineko, Ewell, Dimple, and the pastor stared into the hull of the Econoline's engine bay.

"The starter," Dimple said.

"Could be the alternator," Ewell said. "And I wish we had a flashlight." Mineko dug through her purse and produced a penlight. She held it out.

"Nah. Nearly dead battery. Go get your truck. You can give us a jump."

"Well, we'll see," he said, walking over to his truck.

"Mineko Cope! I think he likes you," Dimple whispered after the pastor walked over to inform the Belles it would be a few more minutes.

Mineko sighed. He was a nice enough man, but he was dead wrong about the alternator.

"I'm not—"

"Oh, I know, I know. You're not interested. But what's the worst that could happen? A double date with me and Cal? A good deal on a new Buick?"

"I like Chevy." Mineko wondered if Dimple had long thought of her as a third wheel, and the idea started to dim the shine of the night.

Ewell's headlights flooded across the women, blinding them for a moment. He had the cables in his hands before Mineko could search through the van.

"I got this, ladies, if you want to warm up in the van or in my truck." Ewell smiled again at Mineko.

"Oh, I'm fine out here, aren't you, Dimple?" But Dimple was already moving toward the passenger seat of the van, leaving the two of them alone.

Mineko watched as Ewell looked down at the clamps in his hands.

"Red first," Mineko said.

"Wouldn't dream of doing it any other way."

Mineko stared at him, the skin of his jaw a little saggy, his nose a little hooked. Older, but not a horrible-looking man, she decided.

Ewell attached the clamp to the van, then his truck, then the black, ending with squeezing the final clamp onto the side of the engine block. He climbed back into his truck and started the engine, letting it idle. Rolling down his window, he called out to Mineko and asked her to come sit with him.

Mineko shivered. She was cold and it was only for a few minutes. And she was tired of Dimple staring at her through the windshield. She

climbed in next to Ewell, whose truck was warm and clean, smelling of
the little dangling pine tree around the rearview. The instruments on the
panel glowed a pretty orange.

"It's no Chevy," he said.

"Oh, you heard that."

"I still have good hearing."

"You in the war?"

"Belgium."

Mineko nodded. So many men of his age were near deaf from the ar-
tillery.

"What did you do?"

"I was an intelligence officer. Didn't see too much combat, but some.
And you? Where were you?"

Mineko paused. She wondered if he was joking, perhaps.

"Japan. I'm Japanese."

"Well, I can *see* that. Where? Big city? Little town?"

Mineko tried to recall the last time someone asked her about where she
was during the war. Most everyone here had moved on, of course. But
even after arriving, no one asked, no one pried. And if they had, it usually
was because they were holding a grudge. She tried not to appreciate Ewell
for this interest.

"I bet it's charged," she said instead.

Mineko opened the door and slid out of the truck and began removing
the clamps in the opposite way they had been placed, working quickly. She
rolled up the cords and handed them back to Ewell, then pointed to the
pastor to start up the van.

"Moment of truth. Still could be the alternator, Mineko."

Mineko paused. He had called her by her real name, not even butch-
ering it.

"How did you know?"

"Asked Dimple. You don't seem like a Minnie."

She was trying so hard not to have a kindness for this man because she
had decided, after James was gone, that she preferred being alone. She had
her great love and her horrible marriage. Where some women might try
for something in the middle, Mineko didn't have the patience for it. Yet she

had to admit he was a nice person, maybe a good friend. Someone to play cards with. Someone to go to dinner with. She even liked his tidy GMC.

The church van roared to life and the headlights clicked on. A few cheers could be heard from the Belles inside.

Mineko uncrossed her arms and let the cool air wrap around them through her sweater. She suddenly felt very silly in her circle skirt and dance shoes. Silly for dancing like a chicken. Silly for standing under the neon of Tumbleweeds.

Ewell handed her a business card, which she squinted at. Raised letters gave his first, middle initial, and last name, something French maybe. Brussard Buick, Honesty and Integrity.

"I'm tired of being alone, Mineko," he said quietly. "Don't you think we all deserve a second chance sometime?"

Mineko placed his card in her sweater pocket. She extended her hand for a shake, and he gathered her fingers firmly.

"Thank you for the help. And the dancing."

Feeling the attention of everyone in the van upon her, she quickly made it to the sliding door, jerked it open, and got in. The van pulled away as Ewell waved, and Mineko watched him walk to his truck, put down the hood. She watched as he opened his door and climbed in, the interior lights warming up for a moment as he took off his hat and placed it on the seat beside him.

A nice enough man, but he isn't—

Mineko patted the business card. Maybe she'd call one day. Maybe. Or maybe she'd leave the card in that pocket. Maybe she'd make some green tea tonight after driving back to the ranch. Maybe she'd wrap up in a blanket and look at the stars, wait outside until she spotted a falling one, then go inside and dream of Akio swimming with turtles.

Chapter 27

On Easter Sunday, after church, my dad goes to Autumn Leaves to fetch my grandmother for lunch, even though she has made it quite clear she doesn't feel like coming today. When Grandminnie arrives, she starts small-talking apologetically. She complains about her loud neighbor, who needs to have her hearing aids refitted. She tells me about how the young lady at the Autumn Leaves front desk—the one who replaces Sadie some nights—has a man coming to pick her up after work and that man has many, many tattoos. Too many, she feels, to be a good fit for her.

She tells me that my skin looks good, well moisturized.

She tells me, leaning in and whispering, that she loves me.

I try to remember her saying this before and cannot.

"Fine!" I say. "Fine, you're forgiven. And I love you, too."

My grandmother huffs her relief.

Today it is just the four of us, with Aunt Mae and Uncle Hollis visiting his side of the family. My mom has the table set with pastel pink napkins and salt and pepper shakers in the shapes of bunnies. There's a ham with apricot glaze in the oven, and the house smells savory and sweet.

"Oh, the flowers!" Mom yells from the kitchen. "Go cut some irises, will you?"

"Your daddy was very, very quiet on the drive over," Grandminnie says as we walk over to the patch of yellow irises growing by the fence.

"Well, he was up late figuring out some financial stuff, maybe he's tired."
She sets her jaw, and I can't tell what she's thinking.

When we get back to the house, Dad is in the kitchen taking the ham out of the oven and trying to pinch off a pretty, caramelized piece, burning himself. Grandminnie takes off her sweater and drapes it on the back of a chair. She is dressed in a Creamsicle-orange top and white slacks and some sort of comfort sandal with pantyhose. It's a new outfit that my mom dropped off earlier in the week. Rebuilding my grandmother's wardrobe, bit by bit, has been one of her pet projects since the fire. And for a woman who seems to barely stand her mother-in-law some days, she knows exactly what will fit her body, what shoes will work with my grandmother's flat feet.

I put the flowers in the vase, ready on the table, and my mother is telling my grandmother that she missed a good sermon this morning, to which my grandmother nods. Grandminnie isn't a regular churchgoer, although whenever there's a potluck or a piano concert, she'll attend. She has gladly driven her truck (back when she had one) to get it washed in the church parking lot to help the youth pay for their mission trip. We pass plates around and fill up Mom's china to the edges. There's enough scalloped potatoes, gooey cheese still bubbling, for six more people. After saying grace, my father's job, although he dislikes it and usually tosses the duty to my mom, he clears his throat and my grandmother looks up at him and locks eyes.

"Well, I wanted Mae to be here to tell you this, Mom, but I've got some news to share."

I put down my fork.

"Now, honey?" my mom says. "This should wait. Mae said she'd come by for dessert and coffee."

"Ugh, Mom, let him talk." My mom's eyes dart to me with a you-have-no-idea-what's-going-on look.

"Yesterday, I wanted to tell you, but so much was happening. Mae and I have been meeting with this developer. He is planning on buying up some land in Curtain and putting in a little subdivision. Thinks there's a market for it and that the next ten years are gonna be changing for Curtain—big cities are spreading out. He wants to buy our land. We went out and drove it. Nice guy, really. And we've settled on a number. Mom, it's enough for you to live well for a long time, not worry about a dime—"

"Dame dayo!" My grandmother is on her feet; the heavy dining room chair falls back behind her and crashes into the china cabinet. My mom gasps and jumps up to steady the cabinet. One of her champagne flutes— never used, I don't think, not in my lifetime—sways and falls, creating a domino effect.

"Dame dayo!" she yells again.

"Daddy, this isn't fair!"

"It's for the best!" Dad says sternly.

"Lia, I could use some help here," my mother snaps, opening up the cabinet and gingerly picking up two broken flutes.

I push my chair back to help my mom. She hands me a shard of crystal glass, and even though I'm careful, the splintered stem slices the pad of my index finger, deep enough for blood to immediately form and a drop to fall onto Mom's white Battenberg lace tablecloth.

My dad is up, getting a wet towel, my grandmother is taking the broken glass from me.

"For heaven's sake, don't cut yourself, too. That's all we need!" And my grandmother flares her nostrils, puffs out her chest.

"I loved those glasses. They were a wedding gift! From my aunt La-verne!"

"Mom, meet the guy and take a look at the numbers. You need this—" Dad says, coming in with the handheld vac.

My grandmother is speaking rushed, relentless Japanese. She picks up the phone and dials Aunt Mae's number, then, remembering that she's not at home, turns off the cordless and slams it down into the charger.

Grandminnie pokes me in the ribs. "Get it," she whispers, and I know just what she means. Clutching my finger, where I swear I can feel my heartbeat, I go upstairs and, without bleeding anywhere, manage to get the plans out from beneath my bed where I had hidden them. I bring them downstairs, unroll them on the table. My mom is unsure whether we should sit down and eat or clean up the food, then remembers my finger and heads to her bathroom for a bandage. My dad is leaning on the counter, staring at us, and Grandminnie, hands on her hips, is staring back.

"What's this all about, Lia?" my dad says. I hear his teeth grind and the sound makes my jaw tingle.

"Grandminnie doesn't like Autumn Leaves."

"She's been there a week!" my mom says, handing me two Band-Aids.

"She wants to rebuild. Don't you, Grandminnie?"

"What? Mom?"

My grandmother continues staring him down. It's like a shoot-out in an old Western.

"Just look at this, Dad, it's a house. One story. Like the one she loved in Japan. We drew it together. It's small. You could build it *easy*. And we have the land. I can build a model—"

"No! No. Absolutely not," Dad yells. I haven't seen him this mad in years.

Mom has given up on Easter and begins clearing the table. She carries the ham in, then the deviled eggs, she puts her apron back on and gets out the Tupperware, banging around and shaking her head as my grandmother stomps outside with her cigarette case. I follow her out.

"I don't know what to say."

Yoshi comes up close and rubs Grandminnie's leg. I put my hand on top of my grandmother's hand and she looks up at me, but her eyes don't meet mine. Instead, her gaze is fixed on my chin, her mouth downturned, her shoulders slumped forward. I have seen this before. When we picked her up from the airport after her abbreviated trip to Japan, the same downtrodden look. Dad carried her suitcase into the house, and when he asked if she wanted some company, maybe we could come in and have some coffee with her, she had said that she was tired and that, no, she just really wanted to be alone.

Inside, grabbing her purse and my backpack, I can hear my parents arguing quietly in their bedroom, the door closed. I take advantage of the empty kitchen and dig into the leftovers, creating two full plates for my grandmother and me and cutting a ridiculously large piece of coconut cake out of spite. I wrap it all in plastic and put forks and knives and a wad of napkins into my backpack. I carry all of this out to my car. The cut on my finger smarts.

"Let's have a picnic," I suggest in the car. My grandmother gives me a tired, straight-lipped smile, and we head to our part of Curtain creek on Cope land. When we get there, it appears someone hasn't re-covered the metal furniture, the tarp thrown to the side and weighted down with a big rock.

"Who the hell has been out here?" But I know it's probably the man who has been looking at the property.

"Some Easter," I say, carrying our food to the chairs.

We uncover our plates and start eating, chewing quietly. We're halfway through when my grandmother speaks.

"You suffer for your children."

"But it isn't fair."

"Nothing is fair. You suffer for them. Your parents are suffering for you. I am suffering for them."

My grandmother takes a bite of a yeast roll and I don't know what to say. Are my parents that worried about me? She chews and thinks. Ducks land on the small swimming hole and, seeing us, take off again.

"You said you wanted better for your kids. What did you want for Daddy and Aunt Mae?"

"To get away. But not too far away. I worried that when they left, I'd be so alone. And I have been alone, even though they've been close."

"But you stayed here for so long, Grandminnie, after Grandfather died. Don't you think you had a choice—"

My grandmother finally meets my gaze. She's been eating a piece of coconut cake, bite by bite. All she has left is the white, frothy frosting top, sprinkled with toasted coconut. She takes a big pinch and puts it into her mouth like it's a wad of tobacco and then licks her fingers with defiance. The mockingbirds and blue jays, mortal enemies and equally matched in their bird pettiness, squawk and titter at each other. I look behind us where the house would have gone. We had drawn in a front flower garden, monchu, and gate. We had daydreamed of flying to Japan together to go shopping for traditional furnishings, shipping them back.

"It's not just me who doesn't like Autumn Leaves. You don't want me to live there, either. Because you need to build this house. You need to do what you are trained to do. But won't. Because of Darren-on-the-coaster. Darren-in-the-black-car. And Darren-on-the-phone."

I feel a blitz of electricity go through my body, panic move through like a missile. I let my head flop backward and look up at the trees, their little baby leaves fluttering.

"You want to go back. And this person is stopping you. That much I figure out."

In bits and chunks, I tell her everything, feeling the whole time like I'm coughing up something bitter and awful. I think about how hard it is to tell a story like this. At how easy Grandminnie has made it seem, as she has spoken her stories into my silly recorder. Then I realize that she has practiced, maybe, all these years. Maybe she's told herself her own story over and over again to make sense of it. I wonder if I'll have to do that, too.

I think of Aimee, practicing with her guidance counselor. I am gutted.

"But then there's something else," I finally say, catching my breath.

"What else? He's a bad man, Lia-chan."

Oh no, Grandminnie, I think. It gets worse.

I remember the worst part like this. I hadn't seen Darren since graduation, and only at a distance then. He had waved and then disappeared into the crowd. After that, nothing. Not until he showed up at work as my new boss. And I did meet him up like he suggested at Dos Compadres. We had dinner and it was fun. He filled me in on all that he had been working on and doing. He ordered a pitcher of more margaritas than we could possibly drink and, as a lightweight, I stopped after one.

"You know what the most exciting thing is?" Darren was a little slurry, and I pushed the basket of flour tortillas toward him and suggested he eat one. I had walked from the office, but Darren had driven and I wondered how he would manage to get back home.

"The most exciting thing is a top secret project that I think has your name written all over it. The city wants to develop part of the lake into an outdoor music venue. Cities are doing this all over at some really cool locations. And it's just the beginning. There will be hotels, restaurants, an entire entertainment district."

I couldn't imagine it. So much of the land around both Travis and Lady Bird was protected wildlife areas.

"And this is a done deal?"

"Which part—the district or your involvement?" Darren then stood and came to sit next to me on my side of the booth. He grabbed a napkin and pulled out a pen from his blazer. He sketched what he'd been thinking of, and I was amazed, once again, at his sheer talent and vision.

"But, you didn't answer me."

"Both are in flux. Birkit is working with some key leaders to get this thing pushed through, then we will be able to bid on it."

"And we'll get it?"

"We have friends within city hall. In the meantime, we'll be working on some ideas, quietly, you and me. When it's time to sign, we're already ahead of the game."

"You and me? I'm not even licensed yet."

"I'll sign off on the plans. As soon as you get your license, you can join as a full member of this team. Hell, you could even run it."

Then, his hand was on my leg. Not an accidental brush, not a patronizing pat, but a full hand running up from my knee to my thigh, disappearing under my skirt.

"Darren!" I pulled away.

He laughed. "Oh, shit, what is it, Lia? C'mon!"

"I'm not— This isn't—"

Darren threw his head back and moaned his displeasure. I looked around, hoping no one was watching.

He moved his hand but wrapped his arm around my shoulders, putting his lips close to my ear. He told me he was sorry, three times, took out his wallet, tossed a fifty on the table, and tugged me up.

"Let's go, let's get out of here."

I followed him to his car, still rattled but blaming it on the tequila. At his SUV—the same beefy Defender as before—I said that he was too drunk to drive and my car was still at the BT&B garage.

"Fine, I'll walk you there and sober up along the way. Then you can drive me back here."

"I don't think you can sober up that fast," I said.

"Then take me home with you."

"Nope, that's not—"

"You can't let me drive like this, think of what could happen to me."

I stomped off, shivering in the wind. But Darren caught up and again wrapped his arm around me. I tried to walk faster, but he stayed close. I thought of Aimee. Over and over again, her words and her big blue eyes; her trembling hands, unwrapping that stick of gum.

We climbed the stairs in the parking garage, which was empty. Every cautionary tale of strange men lurking in dark places echoed in my head. And yet, here I was, with Darren. I pulled my keys out of my coat pocket, holding them like Dad had told me to, like a little knife.

"Oh God, Lia. Look at you. I think you've got the wrong idea about me."

"I have no ideas. I just feel like I need to get home."

I put my key in the lock. Before I could open the door, Darren's hip was leaning against it, wedging me between the driver's-side mirror and himself. He had stubble growing in, some of it gray. I couldn't believe I ever thought him handsome.

"Please move, Darren."

"You're the kind of girl that I wish I had ended up with before Sandy. You're smart and sexy"—he bit his bottom lip—"and you play so hard to get . . ."

"That's enough."

He moved closer and with one turn of his body, I was now sandwiched between him and my door, his hands placed on top of my car, his head blocking out the buzzing, flickering garage lights.

"I saw the way you looked at me, I felt it, I know I'm not alone."

"Aimee," I said.

He took a deep breath. Then he laughed.

"A mistake. Nice girl, total mistake. She was in over her head. And you saw me then, I was lonely and stressed—and what can I say? I'm just a *man*."

I was looking around for someone to help me, but the BT&B parking garage was completely deserted. I felt a million miles away from anyone. I thought of how *happy* I had been that afternoon before the rooftop announcement and that even on the other side of this, whatever and wherever that was, BT&B was ruined. *Austin* was ruined. A twitch of anger squeezed my fist into a ball, scrunched my toes in my shoes.

"I'm drunk, I don't know what I'm doing," he said. He laughed again. "I'm so gone."

The keys were in the lock, which were shoved up against my butt. When I looked at him to say no, he put his mouth against mine so hard I was talking into him, my words lost and muffled.

"Just relax," he said, grabbing a breath.

I moved my rear away from the door, closer to his body, feeling behind me for the keys.

"See?" he said. "You want this."

Quickly, I jerked my keys out of the lock and into his ribs, as hard as I could. He fell back in surprise, stumbling a few feet away. I kicked what I thought was his shin, and I jerked open my door, jumped in, and started my car.

I heard him yelling behind me and I looked in my rearview, but he was still there, arms in the air, where my car had once been. He was yelling something. I slammed on my brakes to hear, I don't know why.

"You wouldn't have gotten through school without me!" Darren was shouting through the hatchback, then my window.

"You owe me, Lia!" I gunned the engine again and felt the tiniest of bumps under my left back tire. I looked in the driver's-side mirror and saw Darren was crumpled on the ground, writhing, but I drove down the ramp and into the night.

I realize I'm shaking, telling the story.

"He deserved that," Grandminnie says.

"I drove over his foot, Grandminnie. I crushed it."

"Good Japanese car. But how did you find this out? You didn't go back to help?"

"No! I'm not stupid. Stephie told me. I never went back into work. I didn't tell her anything, I was too— I don't know."

"You feel bad about not believing the other girl."

"Yeah."

"So you quit."

"So I quit."

"And he threatened you."

"I think so, but I don't know if anyone else would see it the same."

Darren is too smart to threaten me over an answering machine. It was what was under his words that frightened me. That control, that ability to work things in his favor, that he was trusted by so many, that it was clear there wasn't much anyone could ever do to stop him.

"So he threatened you in the way that *they* do."

"Yes."

"I understand." My grandmother puts her hands on her thighs and leans forward, as if she's about to bounce up out of her chair, but she stays put. When a breeze blows through the opening in the trees, she closes her eyes to it, letting it ruffle her hair. We both smell rain. It's coming.

I feel lighter. I reach for her hand. She takes mine and squeezes. Grandminnie then stands up and walks a few feet away, turns due north, and paces, one foot in front of the other. After twenty steps, she looks over at me and motions for me to come.

"Don't be a lazybones. Get your big feet over here. My feet are too short. The measurements will be off. Let's walk the house. Let's see what could have been."

Chapter 28

When it finally happened, her retirement party, Mineko could hardly believe it. Thirty-three years is nothing, she thought. It's like a short nap. It's like two sneezes. It's like a pinch of salt.

Her grandkids had all graduated from colleges—good ones, at that—and had started important jobs around the country. She had coaxed a kitten in from the barn, a pretty one that reminded her of a cat she had growing up in Kadoma, and after a few years, it was finally letting her pet it with regularity. And she had promised Dimple that she would drive with her and Calvin into the Colorado mountains in the late summer, feel some cool air, learn to fly-fish. She was still the third wheel: she had tried to start over with Ewell so many years ago, but after dating for a while, they both figured they would work better as friends. In the end, she was not his beloved lost wife and he was not Akio.

Then, in the fall, she was going to finally redo the main ranch house bathroom, install a decent soaking tub. She had sketched out her plans and had given them to Paulie to take a look at, make sure she wasn't missing anything. She and Paulie would do most of the renovation, subbing out some of the plumbing, but she wouldn't have minded Lia's eyes on things. The three of them together, working on one project, filled Mineko's soul with a trembling happiness. Retirement was going to be just fine.

Mineko's farewell was much bigger than she had anticipated. She had hugged her favorite residents goodbye and told them that she'd be back to visit when a few began to cry. Mineko didn't get teary herself, but did remind her replacement, one more time, of who needed extra servings of macaroni, who needed two pillows in their bed, who could be comforted by reciting the Dallas Cowboys' starting lineup roster.

Mineko was sent off with leftovers of a sheet cake decorated with coral-colored roses, and once she got home, she carried it into the kitchen, swiped a rose off the top, and licked it from her finger. Then, out of habit, she tied on her apron that hung on the mudroom wall and walked down the long drive to check the mail at the road, where the bright white mailbox stood crooked from one of Paulie's friends' cars. As she walked, she noticed the mowing that needed to be done, her favorite dark burgundy irises that were tucked into their fat buds and getting ready for blooming. She thought for a moment, about what to make for dinner, if she was even hungry. She contemplated what her days and nights would look like. She supposed she'd have to switch to a normal sleep schedule and wondered if she could even do it, after all these years.

The door to the box always stuck this time of year—something about spring heat—and Mineko made a mental note that maybe it was time to get a new one. One that wasn't ghost white, perhaps. She shuffled the envelopes in her hands. In between the bills, a thick, tape-sealed letter from Japan. She knew it before she flipped it over to see the return address— letters from home came in envelopes that were not as brightly white, a shade or two darker, the same with the writing paper. Mineko always liked to think it was from the trees still peeking through. *We're still in here.*

The letter had an address in Osaka she did not recognize. Mail from Japan was increasingly rare. Maybe three letters a year. Her mother had passed only five years after her father, a stroke. Hisako had taken care of her burial, and Mineko had written her sister a check and a letter of thanks.

Mineko cut through the front pasture, walking carefully through the grasses as she didn't have her boots on. While she walked, she sliced through the envelope with the folding knife she kept in her apron pocket. At Curtain Creek, she crossed the rock bridge, and on the other side was a live oak tree with a trunk that curved into a perfect hammock-like seat, then shot back up into the sky. How it remained standing was a testament to its massive roots that grew up and out of the ground and then into the creek itself, hiding schools of fish in their shade. She settled into the crook of the tree and, with nervous hands, pulled out a folded piece of mono-grammed paper and a smaller something, wrapped like a package in thin brown paper. She felt queasy unfolding the letter, and it took a moment for her eyes to adjust to the handwriting, all in Japanese. Realizing her glasses were in the house, she squinted, held out her arm, and read.

Mineko,

I am certain you remember us, even though you have traveled far. You loved our son and because of this, we have never forgotten you, although we have not written out of respect for your life in the United States.

I am doing well, although age has made it difficult to see. I am nearing ninety-two years old and I live with my youngest child in Osaka. My husband passed many years ago and my eldest grandson is writing this letter for me today. He is a very talented young man studying science at the best school in Osaka, although he wants to attend graduate school in the United States at Massachusetts Institute of Technology. Perhaps you have heard of this place. I know he is embarrassed to write such things about himself. But I must gloat. We are so very proud.

The reason I write is because of our long-since-departed Akio, whose memory resides still in my old heart. Do you still have the photo I gave you? I know it must have caused great confusion with your American husband. Perhaps you left it with your parents? I only hope it is safe.

A few months ago, we received word that as an effort between governments, remains from the house where Akio perished were found. They are demolishing the mansion to put up an apartment block, and the contractor, who must be a very good man, gathered all of the fragments of bone and teeth.

I know it is very shocking—this is Akio's nephew—my grandmother has begun to cry and can't seem to finish this letter, so I will do so here. The words following are my own.

Let me try to explain. After my uncle was poisoned, his body, along with the other officers', was burned within an interior garden. The home, due to damage from our soldiers' later retaliation that night, was unlived in for many, many years, then purchased and refurbished. The rooms I believe my uncle called "the annex" were forgotten for an even longer time. But when it was time to knock it down, it was there that construction workers found his delivery bag and all of its contents and sent it back to my grandmother. It is a miraculous thing, and the kindness of this stranger has touched all of our hearts.

There was a letter to you, sealed and addressed, in the bag. We have wrapped it (as the paper is very fragile) and enclosed it. My grandmother says that we do not want to interfere in your current life. She also says that she has not opened it, although she was very curious as to what the letter said.

We hope that this correspondence finds you living a good life. My grandmother has spoken fondly of your devotion to my uncle. You will notice that my family has not forgotten this young man—my name is the same as his.

Sincerely,

Mrs. Naomi Sato and Akio Sato

Mineko read the letter from the Satos several times. She ran her finger over the young Akio Sato's signature, wondering if he perhaps resembled her Akio. Her hands shook as she peeled back the tape on the package. She tried to calm herself by taking a few deep breaths, but there was no peace to come. The envelope, the handwriting, her name, her old address. Using the same pocketknife, she slit open the envelope.

The paper was so yellowed it was the color of toasted yeast bread. *All those years, the weather changing every season, it had lived alone in that pack,* Mineko thought. A photo was inside, the back to her, the lightest of characters stamped there. She flipped it over and there she was, hands in front of her, clasped below her waist. She was wearing the orange coat, she could tell by the shape of it, but no hat. And there, behind her younger self, was the turtle house, the roofline sharp against the sky, missing the minogame on the corner. She glanced next to her young feet. There it was. Like a waiting pet. Mineko stared at her happy face and wondered how she ever thought she was unworthy.

Oh, Dear Empress of Turtles,

I write to you from a new year's celebration in name only. The year is changing but being so far away from you and from home, there is no feeling of jubilation, although I am happy to serve the empire . . .

Mineko ached; she knew that he had to write that last line to keep his letter from being delayed. He always put such lines in his letters—she wondered how many soldiers had done this, stretching the truth so their words could stretch home.

I have ridden a thousand miles and I'm hungry like a turtle in a pond, waiting for old noodles. But I decided to write this first, in the hope that after dinner, I can escape to the mail house and sneak this letter in the evening bag. We messengers are to be fed first, just because some of the leaders are still traveling to the party, and this is a treat, as usually we underlings are the very last and thus the portions meager. Although I am happy to do this for the empire and our most noble emperor, who is divine in his ruling.

Mineko gulped. So if the messengers ate first, but did so in their own quarters, no one would have known about their deaths. Mineko felt sick, she wished she could yell into the letter—don't go to the dining room! Don't leave your desk. Oh, how soon after writing this did Akio go to dinner? How long after writing this letter, sealing it, placing it in his messenger bag did he take a bite, then another, and then start to feel ill.

As you have noticed, I included a very special photo. I took two that night, but didn't have a chance to get them developed until this month. The one I have is of you with your arms out—the silly one—because I like looking at how big your smile is in it. You have the photo with the more serious side of you. I didn't want you to forget our future home. Please visit regularly and let me know, immediately, if any ruffians move in. We'll need to move them out somehow. I'll leave that, my love, to you. You're good with ruffians.

But this photo is the small gift I have for you. The BIGGEST surprise is something that has taken months and months to procure. Before I left, I had one of my father's assistants look into who really owns our turtle house! A bank, surely, but with so much time and chaos, which one was the question. Master Hayato has figured out the mystery, and I then moved on to the second phase of my surprise: buying the turtle house. The price was surprisingly inexpensive, and between the monies earned from working in my father's patent office and what I would have spent in school this year . . . and a little extra from future inheritance . . . I have just enough. I have entrusted the funds to Master Hayato with the blessing of my parents, and the turtle house will soon be ours. Feel free to jump around in happiness, my love. Just don't hit your hard head.

I close with this: I am wishing I were with you or you with me. I am wishing we could be nibbling on gyoza together from the food stall, close to the temple where the cymbal is being hit and monks are starting their ascent to pray. I am wishing I could hear your laugh—such a good laugh—and listen to all of your ideas that are more fair, more right, more sustainable than any other words I have ever heard. Please wait for a letter from me before you move into the house and begin your refurbishing. And say hello to the turtle children for me.

With love, forever, Akio

Mineko, still in the crook of the tree, made her way to the ground, needing something firm to sit upon, something steady. She pulled up her knees and rested her head on them, as if the world were forming her into a ball. She squeezed her eyes shut so hard that behind her eyelids there was not darkness but bright bursts of purple and fuchsia and white, stars created by the pressure.

The turtle house had been hers, really, all these years. All these hard-scrabble years, all these lonely years, all these stranded years. She could have been home, maybe, in her house with her children. Mineko wept. And then she stood, eager to get back, ready to begin packing.

Book 4

Chapter 29

Curtain, Texas
April 5, 1999

There's a downpour outside, the kind that turns the bar ditches into rapids. Dad is home because of it, and Mom can't work in the flower beds. I happen to have the day off, and there's nowhere for me to be. We are together in a house that feels too small. Mom and Dad are irritated with each other over Easter yesterday, each thinking the other could have handled something better. Mom is fit to be tied with me because she thinks I'm siding with Grandminnie, and Daddy is just pissed about everything.

He keeps circling the kitchen table where my turtle house plans lie unrolled, secured at the corners with paperweights. The photocopies of the Japanese homes are splayed next to the plans. I left it all out on purpose.

I've called Grandminnie at Autumn Leaves and she's not answering. I can see her, sitting by the phone, dismayed and disgruntled, thinking that it's one of her kids trying to reach her. I can't imagine she's anywhere but there, not like she's suddenly taken an interest in the Monday afternoon Board Game Club. I leave several messages. I think of telling Grandminnie everything about Darren last night, and for a split second, I wonder if she's disappointed in me. I go through the evidence again, like I've done so many times, to prove my innocence to myself. Then I replay Darren's messages in my memory, the ones he left and I erased.

Listen, I don't know what happened a couple of days ago. I was really drunk. I hadn't had a margarita in forever. Tequila, man. I do know that you ran over my toes. And maybe you're embarrassed by that. But that doesn't mean I'm holding it against you. We can still be together, Lia.

Went by your place. It's cute. I think I saw you from the bridge. Pink kayak? I didn't know you kayaked.

I heard from your roommate that you are going to quit. I don't get it. You are going to submarine your career. BT&B will never have you back if you do that.

You'll never get another job because of the way you bailed, you know? Your career is over unless you call me back.

After that last message, I finally broke down and called the one person who understood what I was going through. Even though a few years had passed and I had no hope that she was still living with her mom in Sealy, after five rings, I heard her cautious hello. I babbled on about how sorry I was to be calling so late and how I was surprised she was there, and how I regretted that I hadn't reached out sooner when she calmly, kindly interrupted me.

"Lia, it's about Darren, isn't it?"

Aimee had kept up with him through rumors and trade journal blurbs about who was working where and on what. She had run into one of her former professors at U of H, and he had just happened to mention Darren leaving Seattle and settling again in Austin.

"I think I knew it was just a matter of time. Tell me what happened."

Aimee's warmth made me feel safe for the first time in weeks. I climbed into my bathtub with my jeans on, sliding the curtain closed and leaning back against the tile wall.

"So, he forced himself on you."

I told her step by step what had happened, every detail I could remember.

"It was luck that I got away from him."

"It wasn't luck. You made a decision and acted on it. That takes guts, Lia."

"I ran over his foot and ruined my career."

"He would have ruined your career had you *not* done that."

"I thought it wouldn't happen to me. I thought . . ." I didn't say how I thought that I was better. That I thought I was smarter. I thought I wasn't a target because I was a more serious student, how I thought I wasn't a target because he respected me more. And then I realized what that meant I thought about Aimee. "I'm sorry."

Aimee sighed. Then she told me something that gutted me.

After the night in his office, after she had gotten back to her apartment and had taken a shower, there was a message waiting for her from Darren. He said that he had been thinking about it and because she was such a promising student, he wanted to recommend her for the Student Advisory Board.

I did the math. Just two days later, after not hearing back from Aimee, he had offered it to me.

"I heard from the group guys that you had been announced as the board rep. That's when I knew you were on his list. I should have done a better job of warning you. I could tell that you didn't get it after we talked, and I've felt bad about not making it more clear. *I'm* sorry."

After we hung up, promising each other to check in soon, I started packing. With each shirt I shoved into my duffel, I wondered how much of my career I had earned and how much had been slipped toward me because of Darren's attention. When I thought about each block that had built me into an architect on BT&B's premier team, I couldn't ignore those blocks that had Darren's fingerprints. My commercial architecture career was a giant game of Jenga. Removing the Darren-related moments made everything topple over in a heap.

I call Grandminnie again but hang up before I leave a message. After we had paced the house out last night, we sat and watched the sun dip low beyond the horizon, slipping until it was nothing but an orange line. Then we gathered up our stuff, covered the furniture properly, tossed some chunks of bread to the turtles, and I took her home.

When I asked her if she wanted me to walk her in, she said no, but then she did ask for something interesting; she asked if she could borrow the tape recorder and tapes. She said she wanted to hear her own story for herself.

At dinnertime, we get a call. Mom lets it go. She has picked up a pizza—something she rarely does, which demonstrates her anger at all of us in a very typical Mom way. She's too angry to cook. The phone rings again, and Daddy, on the fourth ring, picks it up.

"What? No, she's not here. Yes, I'm sure. And she's not at my sister's? Never signed out? So she's somewhere there!"

My dad hangs up the phone and gets his truck keys. Yelling out from the living room where we hear him pulling on his boots, he tells us that Grandminnie hasn't been seen today. All day. That her room was left unlocked and she didn't come down for after-lunch cookies and how she missed dinner at five.

Mom and I simultaneously look at the digital clock on the microwave: 7:32. We race to find our shoes and then out the front door to where Daddy is pulling out of the drive.

"We're coming, too!" Mom blurts out, letting me climb in first and onto the skinny bench seat in the second row.

Autumn Leaves is all abuzz. Sadie, the front desk lady, asks us straightaway if we want to call the police.

My dad looks like the thought of Grandminnie being in real trouble hasn't truly crossed his mind, that she has just misplaced herself, and that Sadie's question has brought the image of body bags and swirling red and blue lights into his mind.

"Not yet, let's just look."

We split up and scour Autumn Leaves, knocking on each door, even though the staff says they have already done this. Mae decides to walk around the building with a flashlight, now that night has fallen.

"She's not a cat, Mae," my mother mutters, instead digging through Grandminnie's drawers.

"Looks like she's missing some underwear, maybe some of the clothes that I bought her. Lia, go check the bathroom. She's not going to go anywhere without her Shiseido!"

Mom's right. Her face creams are gone. The tube of red lipstick is missing.

"How about her walking shoes?" Dad asks.

Gone as well. Along with her purse, her Japanese crackers, and her carton of cigarettes that we aren't supposed to know about.

I open her closet again and push back a few things to reveal the corner where the bowling bag had been kept. Gone.

"What's this?" My dad has the bag of tapes and the tape recorder in his hands. "They were sitting on top of the microwave."

I wonder if she intended to leave them.

"A project we've been working on," I say, letting each word inch out of me slowly.

"Does it have to do with that silly house?" my mom asks, arms crossed. No. Yes? *Silly!* I stay quiet.

"I think she's run away! But where?" Aunt Mae says, looking through another drawer. She's still in her pharmacist coat, having raced over from work. Her hair is in a high bun, twisted just so. "Who else could she have gone to besides us?"

Aunt Mae's lips are in a tight line, and I know that Dad has called her and told her about Easter.

"I'm going to tell Sadie that we want to call the police," Dad finally says.

Everyone is moving around me, like a bunch of bumper cars. They don't get it. I feel like my skin doesn't fit me anymore, as if I'm wearing a too-small shirt. I start to sweat. *Don't be a scarediddy-cat*, I hear in my head.

"Jesus, what is wrong with you people?" I yell. I touch my throat. I can still feel my vocal cords quivering, so yes, that came from me.

"You don't get it! You don't even try! If you love her like you say you do, then—"

"Lia Renee Cope! What has gotten into you?" My mom slams the bedside drawer she's been going through. My father's jaw is set. Aunt Mae's eyebrows are so lifted, a ripple of wrinkles has taken over her usually smooth forehead.

I hold out the bag of tapes. "If y'all would just listen, I think you'd figure out why I've helped her with this house thing. Not because I wanted to hurt you or anything, but because Grandminnie . . ."

I don't know how to say it. They are waiting for me. My dad has his hand on the door handle.

"You all have been really unfair with her. She never wanted to live here; she just wants another chance at a life that's her own!"

"Okay, Lia. We'll listen to these tapes. Let's not argue." Aunt Mae puts both hands on my shoulders and looks deep into my eyes. "Please, we talk about everything once she's found."

Someone calls the corporate office of Autumn Leaves first. Then the Dennis County Sheriff's office. They say that they'll send someone out, but she's an adult and there's been no obvious foul play.

Before we meet them, we climb into Dad's truck, Aunt Mae and I squeeze into the back, and we cruise Dennis looking for any sign of Grandminnie. I'm terrified she's hurt somewhere.

I push Play on the first tape and as we drive, we listen. My father's face softens when he hears my grandmother's voice. My aunt Mae puts her forehead against the back of the passenger's seat. My grandmother is talking about her own mother, her sister, the home she slept in, and the other home—the turtle house—where she played. It is quiet in the truck; we listen and we drive slowly around and around Dennis town square.

At the end of tape one, Mae looks at me. "I knew about the house; she mentioned it when I was a child. But I had no idea she loved it so much."

"She never said anything to me," Dad says.

We take the familiar roads to the assisted living and the sheriff deputy is there. His car is parked out front, lights going, and it's the same small, muscular man from the night of the fire, the new hire. The one whom Grandminnie had scoffed at.

It is decided that he'd send out word to the surrounding counties, fax her photo around, and do a little search himself, drive by Dimple's store, her home, too. But us—we should go home, rest, she'll probably come back tonight. Hell, she's probably at our house already.

We all get in the truck and head back to our house, where the cold pizza awaits. What they don't say, what they can't say, is that they want to hear more of their mother's voice. I ready myself for their questions. I never intended for them to listen like this, though I guess I don't know what my intentions were back when Grandminnie and I started recording. But in the truck, I push Play.

Chapter 30

Kadoma, Osaka Prefecture
June 27, 1998

It was a dark, bottomless feeling, loving a country so changed that nearly nothing remained the same.

After landing in Osaka, Mineko had linked arms with Fumiko as if they were young girls again and explored Osaka for a few days before taking the short ride to Kadoma. It was as if one of her favorite soap operas was being rewound, but instead of the characters moving backward through familiar settings, everything was altered. Concrete everywhere. Neon everywhere. Newness everywhere. Osaka was incredibly different. Kadoma unrecognizable.

And the characters—she and Fumiko—they pointed out their age spots and wrinkles; Fumiko lifted her shirt to show her sagging belly. This made them both laugh, but Mineko felt as old as she ever had before.

In Kadoma, nothing was left. True, the bombs had destroyed most of the village, but it was being rebuilt in the same manner at her last visit, taking Mae to see her father for the first and only time. Yellow wood had simply replaced gray. New screens had replaced older ones. Even baby plants had been lovingly replanted, same roses, same ferns.

But now, now, now—Mineko couldn't stop repeating those words—streets cut through where houses used to stand, and the shopping district had been razed and then rebuilt bigger. Stucco covered the outsides of buildings. Red bricks. Strange cement walls. Awnings in bright crayon colors. Telephone lines and streetcar lines and poles with even more lines that connected to buildings here and there without any semblance of organization. More signs than she could count, more signs than were necessary. More corner stores. *How many damn snacks in a plastic bag do these people need?* And they were her people, she stopped to think, dumbfounded. Her people, who had changed over time.

And everything was paved. Big squares and rectangles of pavement, connecting to other squares and rectangles of pavement. Gray, darker gray, black.

"It's not so bad, Mineko-chan! It's different, yes, but isn't it nice to be back?" Fumiko clasped her hands under her chin. They were sharing a room in the hotel, and Mineko was staring out the window—eleven stories up!—overlooking a sea of flat roofs.

The hotel's breakfast, at least, was decent, and because it was a hotel that locals favored—Kadoma was clearly not a tourist must-see—eggs and bacon were not featured. Although she did have a soft spot for well-crisped bacon, Mineko was happy to see a spread of miso soup, tsukemono, and the fermented soybeans that, even though she could buy them in the fancy Japanese food store in Dallas, were made like Fumiko's own mother had done, so many years ago.

Today was the day. The day to visit the turtle house. They had procured maps of the area from the library and charted their journey. Now that Kadoma was so much bigger and they were staying farther from where she would have started her walk as a young woman, they would take a bus. Bus number 29. *Which means there's a reason for twenty-eight other buses!* Then, Mineko hoped, things would begin to look more familiar.

Mineko dressed for a hike. Sensible shoes, a hat, a backpack. Fumiko, now so much of a city dweller, giggled at her friend's attire. She was wearing palazzo pants and a light sweater and Dr. Scholl's sandals. They sat close together on the bus in the seats reserved for the elderly. To everyone getting on and off, boys with tight black T-shirts and earrings, girls with bright lipstick and miniskirts, they were little old ladies.

"But Mineko-chan, do you think that the payment went through? Do you need to contact the Satos? Did Akio own the house or did—"

"I told you, I don't know!" Mineko was edgy about this topic. Fumiko had brought it up a few times since Mineko had landed at Kansai. She had struggled over reaching out to Mrs. Sato—worried about seeming opportunistic, caring for the house only for the value of the land, when it was worth so much more. So instead she had done nothing.

The bus bumped over intersections. Turned sharply down streets, then up hills. Fumiko pointed out to Mineko what had been there, and together they sketched the past on top of the present. Finally, they turned onto the road that would have led out of town and on to the next village, but no longer was it unpaved and skinny, it was six lanes wide and stores, businesses, and apartments lined either side.

To be looking for the bamboo stand was pointless.

"Here we are!" Fumiko said brightly.

"This? No, surely it is too soon!"

"No, this is it, I'm certain of it. The map says."

They took the big steps off the bus and were on a street corner. It was more suburban than downtown Kadoma, a little quieter, and Mineko could make out birdsong. There were, indeed, more trees, but not the grassy expanse she had hoped for. And instead of tall, waving bamboo, which she would have to walk through sideways, there was a church. White brick, a combination of rectangular prisms stacked on top of each other, a red cross over the door.

"Very modern," Fumiko said.

"It's ugly," Mineko replied.

"Follow me," Fumiko said, and Mineko did. They held hands like little girls. They went to the right of the church, following the sidewalk.

What they passed: a small dental office, a tiny park space for dogs, and then they came to another street, perpendicular to them.

On the corner. One monchu. It was the same shape, but the rough ridges had developed a dark patina. Mineko licked her finger and tried to rub it off. What could it be?

"Dirty air," Fumiko said. Her voice was quiet, as if she were conversing with a spooked deer.

Air pollution, yes, Mineko thought. That makes sense. She squeezed her eyes shut and opened them again, thinking that by doing so, the other monchu, the one that stood like a sister and led the way to the house, would reappear. But no. Next to it, a telephone booth. From there, where the path would have been to the main steps, was a monstrosity.

She couldn't breathe.

Mineko stood in front of a pharmacy, a Sundrug, the neon bright even in daylight. She looked behind her at the lone monchu, the cement reaching its base, a few weeds sprouting between the rock and the sidewalk where it had appeared to have been planted after the fact. Yes, just fifty paces beyond would have been the steps.

Mineko dropped Fumiko's hand and walked to the edge of the pharmacy, where there was an alley. Surely beyond this there was the pond? The river? Where was the river?

The gazebo, the water lilies, the ancient turtles' grandturtles!

"Oh, my friend. I knew this, in my heart. Your excitement made me hope, but I knew."

Mineko opened a high gate in a wooden fence, but it led only to another alley, which she then went down. Just beyond, she was sure it would still be there. At least the turtles. The house was gone, but maybe where she swam. Mineko ran, leaving Fumiko clopping behind her in her sandals. She passed a dumpster and an air-conditioning unit and a large electric box and then another gate, which she pried open.

There was a drainage ditch. Yellow lines painted along the edges with the words DO NOT PASS THROUGH. The ditch was flowing slowly, the water cloudy.

Fumiko, shaken and breathing hard from trying to keep up, handed her friend the map. Mineko unfolded it, dropping her sunglasses. She pushed her sun hat back on her head, as if a ray of direct sunlight would prove that all of this was wrong and the turtle house still existed, just two stops away. *How does Fumiko know directions anyway?* Mineko thought. Then Tammy's funny phrase that she always used: that girl couldn't find her way out of a paper bag with a pair of scissors.

But on the map was a squiggly blue line that flowed back toward downtown. Kadoma River, it said in tiny print. Darkness edged in on Mineko's vision; she felt like a horse with blinders, able to see only the cement in front of her, but nothing beyond.

"Let's go back," Fumiko urged. "Let's rest before lunch."

But Mineko walked closer to the water, her toes over the yellow lines.
"You'll fall!"

Mineko took a centimeter step closer. She raised her arms to the sky.

"Akio!" Mineko's voice was not the yell like she wanted, but a croaking
noise. "Oh, Akio. Look what they've done."

Fumiko put her hand gently on Mineko's wrist and tugged her away
from the ditch. Mineko felt as if everything in her was loose, out of joint.
Her knees knocked as she turned.

For the next few days, Mineko faked enjoyment to the best of her limited
ability. Anger boiled inside her stomach, every food that settled into her
gut churned and growled. When Fumiko offered to go to the pharmacy
for antacids, Mineko thought of the pharmacy where the turtle house
stood and firmly said no, not necessary.

Her family home, the one she had helped to rebuild after the bombing,
was gone, another house in its place. They visited her family haka at the
temple, where she dutifully washed the tombstone, placed her father's
favorite flowers, lit incense, and prayed. They visited shrines, parks, a few
old ladies whom Mineko barely recalled from school. Then they took the
train to Kobe, and briefly, Mineko was comforted to see a town that had
been spared. The old part was a historic district, and strict rules existed
to keep it such. But just the fact that what she desired was considered
historic irritated Mineko greatly. In the end, she bought most of her sou-
venirs here, and when Fumiko mentioned that she still had two months
in the country and didn't need to buy everything at once, Mineko gaped.

"Two months?" And it was then that she knew she wouldn't last. Not
here. Not this visit.

They made their way to Tokyo, where Mineko immediately took the
train alone to Tachikawa, fully in Japanese hands since 1977. It was now
home to a portion of the Japanese Coast Guard, along with other government groups. She stepped off the bus at the main gate and walked up to
the guard shack to ask if American Village Phase I still existed. The young
Japanese soldier had to ask his superior what she was talking about, and
the older man shook his head no, saying that it had been torn down many
years ago. But, he said, some of the other buildings remained, including

the airfield, but she'd have to have a special pass to visit it. Maybe the officer clubs? she wondered. The P/X? No, he said, although he pointed her in the direction of a brand-new 7-Eleven if she happened to be thirsty. Mineko thanked him and walked away.

She made her way around the perimeter, noticing that the base was slowly being dissolved into green space. She paced up and back, trying to make sense of this new place, using the landing strip as her compass. But each time she thought she was perhaps in the right location, doubt crept in. Why am I even trying to find a phantom of a base house! She had lived there, hadn't she? Even if they hadn't been knocked down for new construction, the homes would have fallen apart by now anyway.

Finally a teenage girl pointed her toward a park where she had heard that the United States once had housing, and Mineko entered it, looking at the map that was posted at the front. SHŌWA PARK the map stated proudly, named after Hirohito, the Emperor Shōwa. A kid flew by on a skateboard. Mineko wondered if he had any idea that the park he skated through was named after the emperor who had changed the country forever, a man to whom boys no older than he had pledged allegiance before going to war.

On the bus and train back to Fumi's, Mineko watched the city slip by her window. She comforted herself with the knowledge that now, at least, she would see the minogame again, and that, she was hopeful, had not changed. Fumiko had promised her she had kept it wrapped and out of the sun. When it came time to move, her friend had transported the roof statue personally, never placing it in a box that could have been dropped or lost.

"Look who I have here!" Fumiko said cheerfully. The table was decorated with food and flowers, tiny candles and photos of the old days. Mineko realized that Fumi had known that Tachikawa would be a disappointment and had planned this to cheer her upon entry into the apartment.

In the center of the table was a piece of red satin covering something, and Mineko knew what was beneath it. With a little smile, Fumiko removed the cloth and there she was, the minogame, having not aged a year.

"I guess this is the good thing about stone. It's already old," Mineko said, letting herself breathe again. She didn't know that she had been holding her breath since arriving in Osaka. While she believed her friend would take care of the turtle, she still somehow felt that perhaps something had happened to it. When it was there, laughing among the gyoza and blossoms, Mineko thanked every god she could think of for allowing Fumiko to take such good care of her. She put the heavy thing in her lap, letting it dig into her thighs, and held it like it was a baby. Fumiko came over and placed her cheek into Mineko's hair, her hands on her shoulders.

"At least you still have this," she said.

"Yes, at least," Mineko said. But there was no doubt in her mind that she had seen enough for one trip.

Mineko stayed with Fumiko for a few more days, out of obligation. She met Fumi's friends, polite women who inquired if Texas was anything like the soap opera *Dallas*. Mineko ate the foods Fumiko prepared, using the recipes passed down from her own mother, long since departed. She listened to Fumiko's dear husband talk about the factory he still worked at, forty years on the job. And Mineko slept fitfully on the nicest futon that Fumiko had lovingly set up—probably spending too much of her meager savings to do so, Mineko thought, guiltily. But even these feelings couldn't stop her from calling American Airlines one morning and changing her flight to the next day. The one blessing of it all was she would at least be returning after the annual Fourth of July celebration, moved to Mae's home this year. There was only so much that one could take.

On the twelfth day of her big retirement trip, Mineko said goodbye to Fumiko, this time at massive Narita airport, and hauled the minogame turtle and her carry-on down the long corridor toward the plane, bound for the United States.

Fumiko cried a little, as did Mineko.

A flight attendant directed her to her seat. Mineko managed to fit her statue below the seat in front of her.

Another young flight attendant, blond and smiling, helped her push her duffel back into the overhead bin.

"May I get you anything, ma'am, before takeoff?"

"Some green tea, please?"

"We only serve black on the way back to the United States, I'm so sorry. Would that be okay?"

Mineko nodded.

The flight attendant returned, dodging new passengers finding their way back to the rear of the plane. Mineko was so thankful that Mae had chipped in and helped her purchase a business-class seat.

The flight attendant carefully handed her a Styrofoam cup. "Be careful, it's quite hot. And I found these."

A tiny bag of rice crackers. Mineko thanked her.

"Happy to be going home?"

And Mineko wondered if that's what she was indeed doing. Going home. She again nodded yes and, pleased that she had done her job, the flight attendant smiled, pointed to the call button, and told her to push it if she needed anything at all.

Mineko clicked her seat belt and closed the little window blind. This time she didn't want to watch her home country slipping away.

Chapter 31

Curtain, Texas
April 6, 1999

We listen to the tapes in my parents' living room until the sky begins to lighten. Aunt Mae, puffy-eyed, blows her nose savagely into a tissue. My father paces from the upright piano to the living room couch and back again.

My mom brings in mugs of hot coffee and half-and-half. She sits on the couch next to Mae and hands her another tissue. "I get it—how do you even start to tell your children any of this?"

"We haven't been kids in a long time, Tam," my dad says. "And I wonder why I didn't *wonder* more about her."

"You two had a weird childhood." My mother isn't going to let them take any blame.

And maybe they shouldn't. Maybe it is what my grandmother always says, shikata ga ni. I finally looked it up, because I couldn't quite figure out the exact translation. Like so many other Japanese words and phrases, it means different things at different times. Sometimes it means something akin to "what can be done" and other times, and this is where Japanese is a trickster, it means, "it must be done."

"It *was* hard," Aunt Mae concedes. "Looking different."

"Being different."

"And Dad."

"And Dad." My father sighs, long and hard. "She put up with him all those years." He cracks his knuckles. My mom hates that noise and winces.

Dad turns to me, wraps an arm around my shoulders, and pulls me to his chest, the other arm closing around me, too. He smells like soap and coffee and, even though he hasn't been out in his workshop, wood shavings.

"You" is all he says, but I know what he means.

"I love you, Daddy."

Like Grandminnie, Dad's stingy with his hugs. But it was all I wanted the night I decided to leave Austin. I had quit my job that afternoon and had thrown all my clothes and belongings in my car, barely getting the trunk to close, knowing I'd be using side mirrors all the way home because all I would be able to see in the rearview was a wad of colors. I went for one last paddle into the mouth of Lady Bird Lake and turned around reluctantly. The wind was fierce and cold; it was an awful day to be on the water and I was alone. It took all I had to fight the waves back to my place, and my arms were shaking by the time I hung up my paddle.

This is what I had wanted when I drove home that day, a complete hug.

My mom hugs Dad hugging me. Mae stands and wraps herself around us, too. *We'll find her*, she says. We're like a tight bud, their bodies around me like petals. I was in the right place at the right time, I want to say. Or maybe she was. Or maybe we both were. Or maybe . . .

Aunt Mae yawns, causing all of us to do the same, jaws cracking.

We're all so tired, the coffee is barely working.

"Just one more tape," Aunt Mae says, pulling away from our embrace and reaching into the little bag.

"No, that's all of it," I say, knowing the tape I'd just recorded.

"There's one more, though." Aunt Mae holds it up.

No sooner do I hit Play than the phone rings. Dad yells to Mom, *Grab it!* and Mom picks it up on the second ring. I check the time: 6:03 a.m.

"Y'all, it's your cousin Wayne."

"Wayne's found Mom?" Aunt Mae asks, eyebrows up.

"Hell, no. Needs something," my mom says.

Cousin Wayne, Dimple's youngest son, has grown from the troublemaker kid to the one that the entire family can't stand. I don't even think Great-Aunt Dimple likes him; she must love him, but at every family gathering, she is always shaking her head at him. My dad thinks it's because he's always borrowing money for random car-related stuff—he's a mechanic, although a shoddy one—and never pays it back. Mom says it's because he makes stupid into an Olympic sport.

My dad takes the phone and pushes the speaker button.

"Hey, Wayne. What's going on?" Daddy has his grumpy voice dialed up to an eleven. He has very little patience with Wayne.

"Hey, cuz. Listen, is Mae there? Called her house and Hollis says she's done stayed at your place."

"I'm here," Aunt Mae says, much more kindly.

"Mae, I got myself into a world of hurt here. I sliced my hand open putting a new ball hitch on Mama's old Diplomat on Easter night, and I think I got this thing infected!"

My dad hangs his head and shakes it. "Wayne, we're kind of in the middle of something here. And why the heck did Aunt Dimple want a hitch put on that old station wagon? She's got one on her truck. What she haulin'?"

"Oh, you know my mom. Just told me to get my lazy ass outside after Easter supper and said, *Don't ask me any questions.* She did have the pasture mowed around that old Forester trailer. Maybe she's plannin' on selling that thing. Can't imagine. Gotta have fifty generations of critters in there."

The old trailer. And a ball hitch. And Aunt Dimple.

"Holy shit!" I yell.

We squeeze into Dad's truck and again speed down the road, this time toward Cope land. When we're on the smoother FM and we can't hear gravel crunching anymore, I push Play.

Chapter 32

The day had been rainy, and Mineko had been soaked visiting the Curtain post office, but she had an excellent reason. Fumiko had sent her the final season of *Unmei No Musume*, which was finally on videocassette. She had received a little yellow notice in her mailbox and had planned her entire weekend around watching it.

Tammy had been kind enough to drop by some leftovers, all packed nicely in fresh Tupperware. Some sort of brown steak in brown sauce with mushrooms and onions. It had appeared with a container of egg noodles, but Mineko was planning on making it with rice. Onions always made her stomach hurt, but she loved them, and she had even purchased a new tub of ice cream for the weekend.

She'd just pop a few Tums. She'd be fine, just fine.

At home, she sliced off the plastic on the boxed set of tapes. Oh, as much as she wanted to know what would happen to the beautiful heroine and her on-again, off-again love, she dreaded the ending. Then what? She'd call Fumiko and ask what she should watch next.

The eight months since returning had been quiet. Her family, at first concerned that her trip had been cut short, accepted her kites and kimonos and bags of candy, and then, thankfully, left her alone. Paulie had visited the ranch and had mowed the front part, weeded all of it, too, and replaced some siding on the house. Mae had dropped by for lunch and had accompanied Mineko to the Japanese store in Dallas and to Wal-Mart in Dennis a couple of times. Lia, now home for some reason she wasn't sharing, had driven out, too, and had asked her to make her favorite foods since she had missed the family New Year lunch. So Mineko had re-created it all for Lia, making extra inarizushi, something that Lia and the other grandkids had always called "sweet pockets."

"Lia," Mineko said to Yoshi, flipping on her rice cooker. "That girl has found some trouble, I think. She's too smart to be home. Her parents say she was lonely, but I say, nah, man trouble. They mess stuff up."

Yoshi meowed, and Mineko shook some food into her bowl.

Mineko wondered if she should intercede in any way, but each time she thought about how she would do this, she shook it off. Remembered the time that Mae had called her too nosy. She didn't need to be getting into anybody's business, especially a young person's. But it was Lia, and while she was close to Sallie and Sam, she always felt an odd distance with this one, although she was the most like her. Mineko had been so proud to watch her go through architecture school, learn so many things that she had wanted to learn as a younger woman. Sallie's law was fine for her but Mineko thought it horribly boring. And Sam was in finance and Mineko couldn't think of a more soulless enterprise. *Oh, Lia, I'll figure you out.* Mineko ate her bowl of rice and Salisbury steak (that's what the sticky note said, she thought) and finished off with an extra-large bowl of chocolate ice cream.

Then she popped the tape into the VCR, which accepted it into its rectangular mouth.

"Good boy," Mineko said to the machine.

On came the blue screen and then the black screen with red warning words in Japanese. Then a pause. Mineko settled into her recliner just in time. Yoshi hopped on the arm. The music began, and Mineko was transported back to so long ago. The theme song was an old one and the scenery of snow-capped mountains and fluttering cherry blossoms. Mineko felt her body get all toasty inside, like a heater had been flipped on in her chest. Yoshi yawned.

Up went the leg support on the recliner. Down hopped the cat.

Three hours later, it was dark. A limb that needed to be trimmed—Mineko made a mental note to climb up the next morning—scratched the roof. It was a rather windy night, but it was only February, and soon that naked limb would be heavy with leaves and pecans.

"Coffee?" she asked Yoshi, who was now curled up on top of the television, her head resting between the rabbit ear antennas.

Mineko had gotten smart with her coffee needs. Now she owned two Mr. Coffees. One purchased with a gift certificate from her retirement party and the other one, coffee-stained with age, now sat on the old hi-fi, one of James's most prized possessions. It was plugged into a splitter that was plugged into the outlet with the hi-fi, the television, two lamps, and a large handheld neck massager, a gift from Mae.

She had given up on the idea of sleeping at night a month after her return and had since been making a pot of coffee and sipping on it from ten p.m. until three a.m., just as she had when she was working. When she wasn't watching her tapes, she was being sucked into nighttime infomercials. She now owned a baked-pie maker and an ashtray that made a coughing noise and complained, "You smoke too much!" when touched with a cigarette. It hadn't curbed her smoking, but it did make her laugh.

Mineko measured out the coffee and poured in water from the plastic jug. She flipped the switch, which glowed bright orange, and she waited for it to sputter to life, hissing and steaming. Paulie had warned her, the month before, to unplug some of the cords when not in use. *This house is ancient, and I need to get someone out here to redo the electrical. I doubt it's even up to nowadays code.*

Nowadays! Mineko hated that word, especially since returning from *nowadays* Japan, and thus did not unplug a thing.

She popped in the third and final VCR tape.

She poured herself a full cup of stout black coffee.

She eased herself into the recliner and again propped up her Dear-foamed feet.

The television exploded into color, and Mineko watched episodes ten through fifteen. Afterward, she had a woozy feeling, almost as if she had drunk too much, which sometimes happened when she did this sort of thing. Maybe it was being wrapped up in the past too long? She pondered the last episode: number sixteen. Mineko rubbed her eyes and peered at the clock. The digitized green read 3:35 a.m. Had she the energy to watch the ending?

"Nothing to do tomorrow. Or the next day. Or the one after that." Mineko looked at Yoshi, still on top of the television. "What do you say about that?" she whispered at Yoshi. "I've turned into a slob."

Mineko pushed Play on the remote control and the same song tingled from the speaker and the same visions of Japanese beauty. Her heroine— the brave Princess Yamanobe—was to get her man, finally, from prison, and although his foot had been amputated in retaliation against his noble family and she had been tossed by her horse and fallen into a coma but had woken up with only a broken leg, they would walk (well, limp) off together into the sunset.

She knew it was what her kids called cheesy, but she couldn't help it. It made her happy. And *so what* if she did nothing but watch it again and again, drinking coffee and talking to her cat. *So what* if she was alone and this house was slowly falling apart around her. *So what* if Kadoma was the same as any other place and that she was getting old and ulcerated. *So what* if—

In the beautiful castle-like home of the brave princess came her handsome warrior. They walked toward each other, slowly across the tatami, he had a crutch under one arm. Mineko gripped the edge of the recliner. Princess Yamanobe was dressed in a scandalous nightgown, untied at the top, and finally, finally, they would be together, but out of the shadow came a face, painted white with cruel black lines and red around his mouth, a black-robed arm, and a knife.

"What? Oh no, no, no!"

Princess Yamanobe fought the evil man away. Her lover, clearly dead, had blood pouring from his mouth. She laid her body over his, ready to die on top of him, but when the evil man came back to attack again, he tripped and fell on his own knife—

Mineko pushed the off button and jerked the recliner upright.

"Chikushō!"

Yoshi jumped off the television and ran to the bedroom.

Mineko had not realized, as her heart thudded in her chest, how badly she needed that happy ending. How she needed the princess to dissolve into her lover's arms, how she needed to watch her shoulders emerge from her gown and how she needed the screen to melt into a peaceful mist.

Mineko was crying. Sobbing. Like a baby, she thought to herself. She couldn't control her noises. She sounded like a dying animal, and for a moment she wondered if she *was* dying. *Old and stupid and lazy and alone.* Mineko wandered around the empty house, finding herself in her bedroom with the closet door wide open.

Suddenly she was back in the turtle house, the afternoon Akio had met her there when everything changed and he was being sent to war. They stood in the main room and kissed and kissed. Why, she could feel his hands around her waist. She took off her dress to Akio's surprise and rolled off her stockings and unhooked her own underpinnings and let them all fall to the floor. Her small breasts cold in the room, her body goose-pimpled, waiting. And Akio was on her, asking if she was certain, and that's when she cried, Yes, you are mine.

Afterward they lay on the floor, wrapped in the quilt that Fumiko had stolen. Dear, loyal Fumiko! And that's when Akio jumped up and pulled on his trousers. *I have a gift for you.* And Mineko had put her orange coat on her naked body and had followed him outside where she found Akio clumsily climbing up to the roof, scrambling on top of the pitched overhang that shielded the front steps from rain.

One of the minogame turtles was loose and sliding down. Mineko, upon entering the house that evening, had worried about it, quietly. Watching Akio reach for it and wiggle it free with a little force filled her heart with joy. He had seen it, too, and he loved this house as much as she!

He climbed down, the turtle under his arm.

But she had not taken it home, and instead kept it in the main room, next to the sunken firepit, and talked to it when she visited. And because she hadn't removed it from its home, it had survived the bombing. When Fumiko went missing and Mineko became worried that she would never see her friend again, she visited the house and packed her turtle in a carpetbag that she had found in a trash heap, sewing up the burned-out spot with fabric ripped from a discarded chair. Then she carried the turtle to Tokyo, and then into her marriage and her house on base, and then to Fumiko, and then on a plane, and then into the home she lived in now.

When she got home with the minogame, she found James's old bowling ball bag, stuck the ball in the back of a closet, and carefully placed the turtle into the bag for safekeeping, laughing softly at what James would say. In the inside pocket, she kept the letter from the Satos and the last letter from Akio.

All these things, she thought, all these years.

She picked up the bag and headed back to the living room to look at it under the brighter lights. But in the hallway, she smelled a burning. Yoshi glued herself to Mineko's ankles. She walked down the short flight of steep stairs, and above her head was smoke.

Mineko gasped, and she picked up Yoshi and made it to the living room, where she saw it—the hi-fi was on fire, the fire beginning to lick the sides of the wall and reaching its tongues out to the television set. It was not a huge fire yet and she thought, quickly, she could pull the garden hose in from the outside and if she worked steadily, she could put it out herself. Hell, she thought, this is nothing compared to the Kadoma fires.

"Go, go!" she yelled to herself, but her legs, she found, wouldn't move, and she was rooted to the bottom step of the staircase, just watching. The smoke billowed up, up. The smell of old lacquer melting.

"The Cope Ranch has been in my family for generations, and there ain't no better feeling than leaving this godforsaken country and going home," James had said to his buddies.

"You love this place, this turtle house," Akio had said. "This is your true home."

"I don't want to leave Japan, Mommy. I don't want to live in a state with just one star," Mae had said.

"Mommy, when I'm big, I'm going to make this place a mansion for you," Paulie had said.

"You can't stop progress," Fumiko had said.

"Sometimes God takes messes and blesses, Min," Dimple had said.

And Mineko, with Yoshi under one arm and the bowling bag gripped tightly in her hand, walked out the front door of the Cope ranch house, stood under the trees, and watched it all burn.

Chapter 33

Curtain, Texas
April 6, 1999

The sun is coming up, but we barely notice because we are concentrating on Grandminnie's words. There's a strange silence that has settled thick around us. Maybe it's shock. Maybe it's peace. It's definitely not anger.

We are bumping along the long Cope drive, then Dad takes a sharp left toward the creek. Before he gets there, he swerves around some cedars, fat, shapeless trees, and then along a well-beaten path. I know where we're going.

The tree stand has one way in, on the other side. You have to enter from a break in the fence that's protected by an always-locked gate and a cattle guard. I don't think anyone's used that entrance since my grandfather died.

It's strange seeing a stand of oaks and cedars in the middle of a pasture. It just doesn't happen on grazing land. Native trees flourish at fence lines, the weed-like cedars are cut down as soon as they shoot up. But this one has stayed intact for generations. It's big enough inside for a cabin, which is what family historians (well, Aunt Dimple and Uncle Calvin) think was there: the original Cope homestead. A tiny house of logs and a stone chimney. Evidence of the chimney—a few oddly placed rocks—is all that remains.

"My fairy fort," Mae says.

Just big enough for a seventeen-foot bumper-pull trailer.

The trees are thick on our side, and we can barely see it, but Dad sniffs the air like a bird dog.

"Someone made sardines and rice for breakfast," he says, and he breaks into a grin. Then he sprints away, Mae close behind him.

"Mom?" they call, pushing their way into the trees. Then, I hear my dad's biggest laugh. "Hell, you got this thing tight in here, Mom! How were you planning on getting it out?"

My mother and I push our way through, too, cedars scraping my arms. In a room of dark green is the Forester. It's wedged in there like a foot in a shoe, with the rusty old station wagon pushed into the trees. It's still hitched up, because it was clear she had no room to maneuver once she pulled in. I'm surprised she didn't back it in, but the mud is thick around my feet and I know she managed this in a torrent.

My grandmother is on the pull-down metal stairs of the trailer, the door flung open. She has a cup of coffee in her hand and is wearing my old red hoodie. She's surprised to see us.

"That Dimple! She told!"

"Nope, not Aunt Dimple. But Wayne . . ."

My grandmother stomps her foot and the whole trailer shakes. "I knew she should have had someone else install the hitch."

She steps onto the ground and reaches out for me, wrapping her arm around my waist.

"You okay?" she asks.

"Me? Are *you* okay?"

"I'm fine, just fine. But I won't go back. I live here now."

"In a tree stand. In a trailer?" my mom asks. She stands on her tiptoes and tries to look in. "In squalor?"

"Oh, not that bad. Dimple cleaned it for me. Trapped all the rats."

"Mom. No. You can't do this. I won't let you." Aunt Mae reaches out for her arm.

My grandmother sticks her finger in the air and takes a step back.

"No more of this! No more bossing your mother around. I am a healthy woman. I have all my rocks—"

"Marbles?" my mom offers.

"Yes! Marbles. I know what's going on. I'm not crazy, and I have things to tell you. Many things . . ."

My dad places his arm around Aunt Mae's shoulders, and they look at each other.

In the tree stand, in the green trailer, we crowd around the little table, sitting on the benches that my grandmother has covered with old beach towels. Don't look under there, she tells my mom. My mom stands.

Grandminnie puts a bag of wasabi peas on the table and a candy jar filled with orange slices. She puts cans of Coca-Cola out.

"Little early," my dad says.

"I'm camping," Grandminnie replies.

On the floor, next to the bed, is a wad of dirt-encrusted clothes. Aunt Mae notices it first and points.

"Oh, yeah, got dirty yesterday."

"Doing what, Mom? Plowing the back forty?"

Grandminnie looks at Daddy like she's seriously considering this question.

"No. I'm starting to build my house!"

I worry they're going to say something. I wait for Mae to plead with her, for my mom to tell her that she needs the safety of Autumn Leaves, for my dad's exhausted sigh. I wait. Dad stands and puts his cap back on, pushing it down over his wavy black hair. He grabs a handful of peas and a can of cola.

"Well, let's go see what nutty thing you've been up to."

We go to the nice clearing near the swimming hole. There, my grandmother has begun to break up the land. She has wooden stakes on the corners of what we walked off on Easter night. A large rock in the center.

My dad walks around, measuring and multiplying square footage and cost in his head. He calls out to us.

"One-story, right?"

"Hai."

Hands on his hips, Dad looks around, surveying.

"It'll never work." And his words hang in the air around us. My grandmother tilts her chin toward him. Her eyes squint. She's about to pounce.

"Nah, nah, not that. I'll build it for you. But we gotta go up about a hundred feet. This is too close to the creek. If they ever change up how this thing is dammed and mess up the flow, this is likely to flood. Not gonna build you something that's gonna wash away."

I walk closer to Dad and survey the land.

"What do you think, Lia?" Dad winks at me.

"You're right, Daddy. We'll need a good soil survey."

"We will indeed."

And then I feel it. It's like I've left a cave for the first time and I can see the sky and straighten up. I feel lighter. It can't be helped and it must be done. And I come from tough stock, I am more me and more her than ever before. My grandmother knows the way she somehow knows things. She points a finger to her own chest and says something in Japanese, but I don't know what she means.

She stands tall. The wind ruffles her hair, and she puts her hands on her hips. We hear a cow low in the distance. We're all ankle-deep in black gumbo muck, and the world feels hopeful.

"Fine" is all she says. "Very fine."

Acknowledgments

The historical aspect of this novel was inspired by the life of my grand-mother, Mieko Kyosaki Gann, whom I interviewed during 2009. Her memories were told between snacks, smokes, and soap operas. Like Lia, I had to research in order to fill in the cultural and historical gaps in my knowledge. I am so thankful for these sources: *Embracing Defeat* by John W. Dower, *Memories of Silk and Straw* by Dr. Junichi Saga, *Japan at War: An Oral History* by Haruko Taya Cook and Theodore F. Cook and *Quiet Passages: The Japanese-American War Bride Experience* (Teacher's Study Guide from the University of Kansas) by Chico Herbison and Jerry Schultz. I also watched (and cried during) *Fall Seven Times, Get Up Eight: The Japanese War Brides*, a documentary directed by the talented Lucy Craft, Karen Kasmauski, and Kathryn Tolbert. Finally, photos and details posted on the Tachikawa Air Base Japan 1945–1977 private group on Facebook gave me visuals of the place where my own father was born and spent his early years. What a generous gift!

Sometimes, a snippet that my grandmother relayed to me was difficult to research, specifically the various ways Japanese women and American soldiers married and received U.S. recognition of marriage. My grand-mother explained that the rules regarding marriage to soldiers changed through the years and that many loopholes existed. The manner in which James and Mineko marry was not how my grandmother entered mar-riage, but a story she told to me about a friend from Tachikawa AB. An-other detail that was surprisingly difficult to ascertain was how often my grandmother had to renew her permanent residency status. Like Mineko, she did not get her U.S. citizenship as soon as it was available through the

McCarran-Walter Act and, as a result, did so later than many of the Japanese war brides. I am choosing to use her recollection of this procedure in the novel.

This all being said, please know that this is a work of fiction based on stories and research and I have tried to honor both the historical and emotional truths of my grandmother's lived experience.

The Turtle House would not have been built in this world without the Kyoasaki/Gann family: my one-of-a-kind Grandmommy, Aunt June, my amazing cousins, my Aunt Amy, and, finally, darling Aunt Mickey, who left us too soon. Mickey gave me my first ever book of Japanese folklore, something she loved, and she encouraged me during my creative writing program. Aunt June: thank you for reading with such an open heart. I always wanted to be an artist like you when I grew up. That's still my goal.

My mother was my first reading and writing supporter. My father made me believe that I could do anything if I gave it my all, words that have never steered me wrong. Thank you, Momma and Daddy. And my sister, Courtney, has told many strangers about "her sister, the writer." There has never been a feistier, fearless, nor more loving little sister.

Speaking of fearless: Sarah Bowlin, my agent, believed in this story and helped me make it so much better. There are a lot of intelligent people in this industry, but there are few who are as trustworthy, thoughtful, and loyal. Deep appreciation to you and to the Aevitas team.

Sarah Stein's brilliant editorial vision and steadfast faith in me has helped me become a better writer. She's also just a lovely person to know and I feel so grateful that we ended up together. The entire Harper Books team has been extraordinary, and I am forever thankful for your love and care of this novel. Thank you, David Howe, for your diligence and kindness.

I have attended many "summer writing camps" through the years, as my children called them when they were young, and my camp counselors and bunkmates were the best of the best. Endless gratitude to "camps" Lighthouse Lit Fest, Tin House (summer and winter), One Story, Community of Writers, and Story Studio Chicago's Story Board. Rebecca Makkai, Jennifer Haigh, Lisa Ko, Leni Zumas, Lidia Yuknavich, Vanessa Hua, Laura Warrell: thank you for your insight and encouragement.

And from all my various cabins over the years and in no particular order (we're going to keep this metaphor going, friends): Nay, Z, Katherine, Rebecca, Jumi, Amber, Emily, Rona, Sveta, Ariana, Scott, Lorina, Neil, Elizabeth, Carla, Cherilyn, Hayward, Tara, Maura. . . . I know I'm missing so many names here, but know you are deeply appreciated.

I would not have been able to finish nor revise this novel without the support of Dairy Hollow and the generous Tasajillo Residency.

My writing group is called "The Sisterhood" and we are *not* kidding about that. My darlings: Sara Cutia, Christie Tate, Carrin Jade, Grace McNamee . . . I look forward to every Zoom and every email, I love you all fiercely. And, dear Grace: We have texted novels of words between us and I hope this never ends. You are a part of my heart.

This book would be just a bunch of words in a document if I hadn't sat next to Janika Oza in workshop at One Story. Thank you for cheering me on and for reading early versions. And thank you for being the *best* agent sibling ever.

The University of North Texas graduate creative writing department is where I became brave enough to call myself a writer. Thank you to Dr. Barbara Rodman, Dr. Ann McCutchan, and Dr. Haj Ross. Also, Ruby and Tim, thank you for those early years of encouragement.

The Writers League of Texas is the greatest and my fellow Fellows are the sweetest group of humans: Stephanie, Jean, Jamira, and Amanda. Becka Oliver: Thank you for being the heartbeat of this organization.

To the members of Rebecca Johns Trissler's Guilt-O-Rama accountability group, especially the incomparable Elizabeth Wetmore, thank you for sharing your daily numbers with me and the cheers of support for mine!

I would be remiss to not mention the loving care these young ladies gave to my children while I was off at a coffee shop or conference, trying to figure out this novel: Mackensie C., Rebecca W., Ana J., Paige R., Zoe C. I am so thankful for y'all.

Dr. Nora and Dr. Sandy: oceans of gratitude for your guidance all these years.

For all the friends who I do life with, every day, in the car lines and the bus stops and the workrooms, at the church and at the meetings and in the grocery aisles, at the barre class or on the text chain with *all* the emojis: thank you for supporting this big dream of mine and always encouraging me. Especially Carrie S., Kristina R., Laura S., Heather R., Brendy C., Lindsey Q., Sarah T., Jaye L. Thank you, Mackenzie H., for letting me bounce architecture school questions off you at Girl Scout events! For those who were there for my family in January 2020: this doesn't seem like it's related, but it definitely is. This book was eventually finished because you gathered together and held us up. A special thank you to the Grooms.

Finally, my reason for everything: John, Megan, and Jack. I love you with all that I am. Thank you for loving me, too.

About the Author

AMANDA CHURCHILL is a writer living in Texas. Her work has been featured in *Hobart Pulp*, *Witness*, and *River Styx*, among other publications. She was a Writers League of Texas 2021 fellow and holds a master of arts in creative writing from the University of North Texas. *The Turtle House* is her first novel.